D1210610

BRIGHT SIDE

KIM HOLDEN

Published by Do Epic, LLC

This book is a work of fiction. Names, characters, places, and incidents are either a product of the author's imagination or are used fictitiously, and any resemblance to actual persons, living or dead, business establishments, events, or locale is entirely coincidental.

Bright Side Copyright © 2014 by Kim Holden

ISBN (Paperback): 978-0-9911402-3-7

All rights reserved. No part of this publication may be reproduced or transmitted in any form or by any means, electronic or mechanical, including photocopying, recording, or any information storage and retrieval system, without permission in writing from the publisher, except by a reviewer who wishes to quote brief passages for review purposes only.

Cover design by Murphy Rae, www.murphyrae.com

Editing by Monica Parpal

Proofreading by Christine Estevez

❀ Created with Vellum

BOOKS BY KIM HOLDEN:

THE BRIGHT SIDE SERIES

Bright Side

Gus

Franco

STANDALONE NOVELS

So Much More

The Other Side

All of It

DEDICATION

B., Debbie, and Robin
Thank you for loving these characters as much as I do.

MONDAY, AUGUST 22

KATE

"What's up, turkey butt?"

"Ah, you know, just drove thirty hours straight or something like that, I honestly lost track. I haven't slept in what, two, three days? I downed like two dozen Red Bulls and fifteen gallons of coffee. So, the usual, I guess."

He laughs. "Dude, I think you might have a little trucker blood in you."

"That's Mother Trucker to you."

He laughs again. "That's awesome! I may have to retire Bright Side and start using Mother Trucker instead."

The conversation is good so far, natural, which is what I was hoping for. After the way Gus and I parted ways in San Diego a few days ago, I didn't know what to expect from this call.

Then comes the awkward silence.

We've never had awkward silence. Not in the nineteen years I've known him.

"So. Minnesota, huh?"

"Yup."

"You at Maddie's then?"

"Yeah."

"How's that going?" Gus asks.

"It's going." God, this isn't getting any better. He sounds almost bored, but I can hear that he's nervous as hell. I wonder why I haven't heard him light up a cigarette yet. And just like that, I hear his lighter click and the familiar sound of that first long drag. "You should—"

He cuts me off. "I probably better let you go, Bright Side. I just got to Robbie's, and it looks like everyone's already here for a band meeting, and I'm late as usual. They're waiting on me."

I'm disappointed, but I know other people's lives can't stop or be put on hold just because Kate wants it to be so. So, I put on my best smile, and I answer, "Yeah. Sure. Will you be around tomorrow night? I'll call you then."

"I'm planning on going surfing tomorrow after work, but I'll be around." His breathing has evened out, but I know it's because he's concentrating so damn hard on that cigarette, sucking the calm back into his body with the smoke and nicotine.

"Okay. I love you, Gus." We always tell each other *I love you*. Always have. He grew up hearing it from his mom every five minutes because she meant it. It was natural. I grew up never hearing it from my mother. Never, just the way she meant it. It was natural for her. She *meant* the indifference. I felt it every day. In my bones. I guess that's why I've always loved hearing it from Gus and his mom, Audrey. It would be weird to end a conversation with them and not say it.

"Love you, too, Bright Side. Bye."

"Bye."

I'm staying at Maddie's. Maddie is my aunt, my mother's much younger half-sister. Her much younger half-sister who she never knew existed until they met at my grandfather's (their mutual father's) funeral three years ago. My grandfather was out of the picture for most of my mother's life. He left when she was ten or something. Just disappeared and apparently had another family and everything, then came back into her life a few years before he died. I met him a few times, and I liked him. I couldn't judge him for what he'd done. I didn't know what his life had been like. Anyway, Maddie shows up at the funeral, and my mother has a conniption fit when Maddie announces she's her half-sister. I mean my mother waited a long time to have my sister, Grace, and me. Maybe waited isn't the correct word choice. Grace was an accident, and I was a weak attempt to hold onto a man that didn't want her or us. She was thirty-nine when Grace was born and forty when I came along. Maddie is only twenty-seven now, eight years older than me, which means my mother was thirty-two years older than Maddie. Yeah, you do the math; my grandpa was a horny old man. But again, it's not for me to judge.

So anyway, I have this aunt I never knew existed and barely knew except for the one visit she made to stay with us at my mother's house in San Diego for a week. That was two years ago. So, when I heard that I was accepted (and awarded a scholarship) to Grant, a small college in a tiny town by the same name just outside of Minneapolis, I called Maddie and asked her if I could crash at her place for a week before I moved into the dorms and school started. She hesitated like I was asking her for a goddamn kidney but finally agreed. And now I'm here in her spare bedroom, and it's only been an hour, but I already feel like a guest who's overstayed her welcome.

I unpack my suitcase and put my toothbrush, toothpaste, shampoo, conditioner, and razor in the enormous guest bathroom. Maddie has a really nice apartment. I'm not sure about the cost of living here in Minneapolis, but it looks expensive. It's way fancy. I know some people love fancy—whatever floats your boat—but to me, it's overrated. It makes me long for simple. Fancy hides a lot, while simple unapologetically puts it out there for everyone to see. It makes me think about the apartment I had in San Diego and how much I miss it. It was a converted one-stall garage that I rented from my mother's old gardener, Mr. Yamashita. Mr. Yamashita outfitted a small bathroom inside so he could rent the space out. The kitchen amounted to a mini-refrigerator, a microwave, and a hot plate, but no sink. You washed your dishes in the bathroom. It was small and cramped and dark unless you had the garage door up, but I loved it. It was simple. It was *home*. My sister, Grace, and I moved in about a year ago. We were looking for a place to stay, and Mr. Yamashita, being the sweet old man he was, made us a ridiculously cheap rent offer that I couldn't turn down. Grace and I shared a double bed and had a card table and two chairs that served as a dining room, desk, and game table. We didn't have much actual space, but it was cozy. It was one block from the ocean but on a corner lot that had a clear view of the water. Every night after we ate dinner and Grace had her bath, we would put the garage door up and sit on the edge of our bed and watch the sun go down over the ocean. And just as the sun would begin to dip in the water and the orange spread across the horizon, Grace would take my hand and raise our interlocked fingers in the air and shout, "It's showtime!" I would shout in agreement, "It's show-time!" She would hold my hand tightly in both of hers resting in her lap until it was pitch dark. The darkness coaxed a joyous round of applause out of her. I'd join in. She'd tell me, "That was the best one, don't you think?" I would agree, and somehow I always meant it. Then I'd shut the door, swing Grace's legs up onto the bed, and she'd lie down. I'd cover her up and kiss her on the forehead and tell her, "Night night, Gracie. I love you. Sleep tight." To which she would answer, "Don't let the bedbugs bite. Love you, too, Kate." And she'd kiss me on the forehead. I miss that so much.

After everything's put away for my very temporary stay, I wander out and try to talk to Maddie, but she's on the phone, so I motion to the kitchen as if to get permission to eat something. She nods absently as she giggles coyly into the phone. It must be a guy on the other end. Women only giggle like that when they're talking to someone they're having sex with. Or *trying* to have sex with.

Her little dog, Princess, follows me wherever I go. I don't know what breed she is, but if you blink, you'll miss her, she's so tiny. She's friendly, and I like her, but I have to keep reminding myself to watch where I walk so I don't misstep and crush her like an ant.

I trudge into the kitchen, my feet sliding across the tile at this point because lifting them is just too much damn work. I open Maddie's pantry and scavenge a box of mac and cheese, which is accompanied only by a can of vegetable beef soup and a protein bar that feels so hard I'm certain it expired before the turn of the last century.

I find a pot and start some water boiling to cook the mac and cheese, trying to drown out Maddie's conversation in the adjoining room. I hum to myself, wishing I had my iPod, but it's in the bedroom, which is like twenty steps away, and I'm afraid if I commit to that kind of effort, the sight of that splendid, beckoning bed will lure me in. And I really do need to eat. The last time I ate was several states ago, Nebraska, I think.

Maddie's off the phone just as I stir in the noodles and tear open the cheese packet. She wanders into the kitchen. "You hungry, Maddie?" I ask.

She shrugs. "I guess."

We eat in silence except for her complaining about the amount of fat that's in the mac and cheese and how awful it tastes. Though I notice she polishes off her half of the box and practically licks the plate clean. I thought it was pretty amazing, myself; you can't go wrong with mac and cheese.

I've waited until the end of the meal for her to do the hostess-y thing and engage in some real conversation, or even small talk, so when she doesn't, I take that as my cue. "So Maddie, have you lived here long? It's a great apartment."

"I've been here for a little over a year now. It's all right." She sounds bored, like talking is just too much work.

"*All right?* Christ, it's great. High-rise on the outskirts of the city. The neighborhood looked pretty hip driving in, lots of restaurants and shops. Your building's got underground parking and security and a gym and a pool. You've got it made, Maddie."

She shrugs. "It'll do for now. I'm looking at another place. Nicer neighborhood. More amenities. More square footage. But I just signed a six-month lease that I don't think I can get out of." She's pouting.

I nod. *This will do for now?* Jesus, I'm trying to reserve judgment here, but the longer I'm around her, the more something feels off. I mean, it's human nature to fill voids, and the list of filler is long, some good, some bad. I get the feeling that Maddie medicates herself with stuff, money, material things. She's to the point where she's always looking for more and missing the part where you're just grateful for what you have. It's sad. Greed's like that children's story about the spider and the fly. Greed, money, excess, that's the spider. And Maddie seems to be one helluva fly. I try to steer her away from the negative. "So, how's work? Lawyer, right?" It's been so long since the one visit I had two years ago with her that I'm digging through my exhausted mind trying to turn up any memories.

"Yeah. Rosenstein & Barclay. Downtown Minneapolis."

"Nice." I guess it's on me to carry this. "So, you must be super busy with work, but any hobbies? What do you like to do in your spare time?"

At this, she brightens up like I've finally touched upon something that interests her. "I like to shop, get my nails done, hair done, I tan a few times a week." She eyes me up and down as she rattles off her list. Clearly she's figured out we have nothing in common as she takes in my hair arranged in a messy knot on top of head, nails bitten down to the quick, and my sweat pants and Manchester Orchestra T-shirt that's worn thin from frequent wear and washings. I am tan, but that's not from a tanning booth, it's just from being outside, and I'm sure she knows it. "Oh, and I *have to* work out every morning." The emphasis she puts on *have to* is a little disturbing.

"So, do you work out in the gym downstairs off the lobby? I peeked in on my way up. It looks nice. I might go for a run myself on one of the treadmills tomorrow."

She gasps as if I've just asked her to take a bite of a shit sandwich. "Oh, God no. That place is vile. I work out at a private gym near the office: The Minneapolis Club."

Of course you do, I want to say, but I nod until the urge passes. "Well, that sounds awesome, Maddie." I push back my chair and grab my dishes. "I guess that's me off to bed then. Thanks for the mac and cheese. I'll buy some groceries tomorrow; I'm just beat right now."

"Can you pick me up some nonfat blueberry yogurt?" she asks as I put my dishes and the pot in the dishwasher.

A *real live* dishwasher. I'm so enamored by the machine that I almost don't hear her. I fight the urge to kneel down and kiss it, worship it. "Sure thing. Hey, do you have a coffee pot? Mine didn't survive the move, and I'm kind of addicted."

I can hear the "Humph!" from the other room, and I get the distinct impression that I've somehow insulted her. As I pass her on my way to the bedroom, where I plan to get comatose for a good seventeen to eighteen hours, she's shaking her head and looking at me like I have a third eye. "Why would I have a coffee pot? There's a Starbucks right next door."

"Oh, right, of course." I guess that's how lawyers roll. I nod my head and make a mental note to pick up a coffee pot tomorrow when I get the groceries. "Good night, Maddie."

"Good night? You're not *really* going to bed, are you? It's five o'clock." Her hands are on her hips. "I thought we could go out for drinks tonight."

"I'll have to take a rain check on that, my dear. Tomorrow night would be great, though. Because you see, in my world, good night should have happened last night, but I skipped it because I was all hopped up on caffeine, so I'm going to have to exercise that good night *and* tonight's good night simultaneously. Right now. See you tomorrow."

TUESDAY, AUGUST 23

KATE

I WAKE up at 10:37 am, and goddamn if I don't feel continental this morning. Getting caught up on sleep is something I've only recently had the luxury of enjoying. The concept has been foreign to me for the past, oh I don't know, all my life.

Maddie must be at work, so I get out my laptop and search for a nearby grocery. There's one within walking distance. I take the elevator down to the gym and run for thirty minutes, and then I shower and grab my wallet and phone and head out for the grocery store. When I exit the building, I find myself drawn to the Starbucks next door, like a moth to a flame. I don't like fancy-schmancy coffee shops. I like mom-and-pop, small local joints. But I'm already through the door and my veins are practically humming. I order a large black coffee, which I know pisses them off because I'm supposed to order in pretentious coffee-speak, but it's been ages since I've been in a commercial coffee shop and I'm desperate for my coffee. I don't have time to peruse the gigantic menu of froufrou drinks to get the jargon just the way they like it.

I get the standard litany of questions. "Milk, soy, non-dairy creamer?"

"No, thanks."

"Flavor shot?"

"Nope, black's good." I'm bouncing on the balls of my feet in anticipation. And when she hands it to me, what I want to say is, *Come to mama*, but what I really say is, "Thank you *so* much," with extra emphasis on the *so*.

I find the grocery store and pick up what I can carry back to the apartment. As fate would have it, they also have a small two-cup coffee pot that I score for fifteen dollars on sale. On the walk back, I hold the grocery sack in one hand, clutching the coffee pot in the other like it's the fucking Holy Grail.

Back at Maddie's apartment, I decide to do some cleaning. I assume she probably works a lot because it's dirty as hell in here. It's not like I'm Mrs. Clean, but I figure it's the least I can do to help her out. I vacuum and clean the kitchen and the bathrooms until around five o'clock when she's due home.

At 5:15 pm, she announces she's starving and hasn't eaten all day and that I just *have to* try the sushi place down the street. I'm not really a big sushi fan—which I know is sacrilegious in certain crowds —and I'm also a vegetarian. That alone reduces my options, and when you factor in my distaste for rice, I'm not left with much to choose from. Of course, I don't want to be rude because I'm the guest, so I tell her, "Sounds good, let's go."

The restaurant is packed, but she knows the maître d' by name, and we quickly get a table.

"Do you come here often?" I ask, impressed by the quick service.

"No, only about twice a week."

I nod. I'm getting used to just nodding now to get past the shock of her lifestyle. I guess I shouldn't be shocked since my mother lived it her whole life, and after all, they were sisters. Maybe being high maintenance is genetic or something. It definitely skipped me and Grace if that's the case.

As I start to scan the menu looking for something edible, I realize that Maddie's ordering a round of martinis. My eyes widen, but hers are already glued to the menu. "What do you like?"

I lean across the table and whisper, "Maddie, I'm only nineteen. I can't drink, dude." It's not that I don't drink, but I'm not into it tonight. And I don't have a fake ID if our server decides to card me when he comes back.

She dismisses me with a wave of her hand. "I come in here all the time."

That's some sort of explanation? I shrug and raise my eyebrows. "Okay." I'll offer the drink to her when it comes. Something tells me she won't turn it down.

"So, back to the food. What sounds good?" She looks almost food drunk just taking in the menu. Like it's making her high.

"Um, yeah, so I'm vegetarian. What kind of options do I have to work with?" My eyes are racing furiously across the menu looking for anything that says vegetables.

Again, she dismisses me with a wave of her hand as the waiter returns with our drinks. "I'll order for both of us."

The food comes out, and by the time the waiter is done setting it all on the table, I'm stunned. Several long plates crowded with colorful rolls, bright pink and white fish, and mounds of wasabi fill the entire table. "Maddie, I think there's some mistake. This is a lot of food."

"No, this is all ours."

I frown. "But there are like six plates here, and there are only two of us."

She shrugs and looks at me like I'm speaking Japanese. "Sushi's not very filling. Besides, you want to have some variety. Try a little bit of everything."

I nod for what must be the hundredth time. "Um, okay. So, point me toward the meat-free items here, Maddie, because it all looks the same to me."

She laughs as though I've just said something childish. "I think you're safe with these two plates."

"You *think*, or you *know*? Because my bowels are on the line here." I feel like I have to cut to the chase to get my point across.

She wrinkles her nose. "Kate, that is *disgusting.*"

"Sorry. I'm just telling it like it is. This body knows, and it's a fairly swift rejection once it hits the point of no return."

Her nose is still wrinkled. "Just eat off these two plates and you'll be fine."

I'm about thirty percent confident in her advice, and unfortunately, everything on the table smells fishy because there are shitloads of it in front of me. I decide to trust her. I take a bite and it tastes funny, but I can't tell what might be rice and what might be fish. Either way, I have to fight my gag reflex with each bite. I eat three pieces, alternately downing water between each bite.

Maddie polishes off both martinis and an impressive amount of food and then denies a take-out box when it's offered for the rest of the food still sitting on the table. I'm not kidding, if this stuff didn't taste like ass, I would've been able to eat off what she threw out for a couple of days.

When the check comes, she reaches for her purse and delicately hits her forehead. She's got a flair for the dramatic. "Oh my gosh, I must have forgotten my wallet at the apartment." She turns fawning eyes up at me, and it becomes obvious that we will not be splitting this bill. "No problem, I'll get it," I say. I mean, I *am* her guest. It's the least I can do for her letting me crash at her place for a few days.

She pushes the receipt across the table, and I almost piss myself, because the bill is one hundred seventy-three dollars! I only have fifty bucks in my wallet, so I put it on my credit card. The one I reserve only for emergencies, which means I try never to use it. It feels a little bit like I'm turning over my firstborn as I relinquish my card to the waiter. I'm pretty thrifty with my money, not because I'm some sort of miser, but because I have bills to pay every month. And I'm responsible about it. I always allocate a little bit of money to have fun with or to help someone out, but I just blew that whole wad in one dinner. *It's okay,* I tell myself, and by the time the waiter returns, I'm resigned to the fact that this was a learning experience and something I'll probably laugh about later.

Maddie excuses herself to the restroom while I'm signing the credit card receipt. By the time she returns, my lower belly starts gurgling. It's a low, foreboding rumble, speaking to a time in the near future in which it will make me pay for whatever it was I just fed it.

We race back to the apartment, and I make it to the bathroom with about half a second to spare before I shit my pants. The culmination of my sushi experience is angry and explosive.

After I've been thoroughly chastised by my colon, I decide to just chill in my bedroom and read for a while. Around 9:30 pm, I start looking at the clock every five minutes. At ten o'clock, I'm pacing the floor. And by 10:30 pm, I've nearly worn a path through the carpet and my hand's sweaty from the death grip I've got on my cell phone. I've been staring at it for a good fifteen minutes now. It's still early in California. I tell myself that he's probably at the beach. But what if he's home and just avoiding me because last night's conversation was so uncomfortable? Ah shit, just call him and get this over with or it will eat you up. I scroll through the contacts on my phone and tap his name. His face appears on the screen with his long, million shades of blond, sun-bleached hair hanging over one eye. He's laughing, but the one eye that's visible looks like it's twinkling right at me. I look at this photo every time I dial his number for a few seconds before I put the phone to my ear because it's like he's greeting me in his goofy way before I even hear him answer. I smile, which relaxes me. The phone rings four times, and I'm waiting for the voicemail greeting after the fifth ring. But then he answers.

He's panting like he's out of breath. "Gus's fire department, you light em', we fight em'."

"Hey, where *is* the fire, dude?"

He takes a few deep breaths. "Sorry, I was just loading up my board, and I could hear the phone ringing, but the damn door of my truck was locked and—"

"I thought the locks were broken."

"They were. Now they aren't, I guess. I don't know what the fuck's going on. The electrical system is jacked."

"Maybe you should get a new truck?" I offer, but only because I know it will spur a debate.

"Why would I want to do that?" He's mock-offended. We do this at least once a week.

"Oh, I don't know, maybe because your truck is from 1989. Or because it has over three hundred thousand miles on it. Or because something's always broken." I'd be devastated if he got rid of it. I love his truck, mostly *because* it's a piece of shit. But he's so protective of it that it's fun to tease him.

"Dude, it's just getting broken in. It's got character." His defense is spectacular.

I laugh. "I know. I love your truck and all its broken character." Then I drop the act. "How were the waves today?"

"Sucked. It was crowded as all hell, and I think every tourist and his brother picked tonight to rent a board and try to conquer the waves. It was full-blown chaos. Why do people think because they watch a surfing movie once or twice they're somehow qualified to rent a board and try to fucking kill us out there? I mean, bull riding looked fun as hell when I saw a guy do it at the rodeo when I was six, but I wouldn't jump on one myself. There's etiquette, you know? There are rules."

"Yeah."

"Anyway. How's Minnesota day two?"

"Well, I had sushi with Maddie tonight."

"Sushi? You hate sushi," he says knowingly. I love it that there's someone out there who knows everything about me.

"Yeah, well it's not too fond of me either. I think Maddie was a little confused as to what was fish-free and what wasn't."

"Dude, not the meat shits?" He sounds concerned, but there's amusement in his voice, too. Gus hasn't eaten meat for years either, and he knows how even a bite can mess with your digestive system in a very violent way.

"Yup. It was hostile."

"Aw, that sucks. I'm sorry." But he's laughing that deep belly laugh that I love.

"It's only funny because you weren't the one who almost shit her pants in front of an aunt she barely knows." I'm laughing too, relieved this is a normal conversation tonight and not like last night's.

He laughs even harder and then takes a deep breath trying to rein it in. "Sorry, Bright Side. Oh, I needed that today."

It's quiet after a few residual chuckles escape him. And with it, the nervousness creeps up on me again. "Gus?" I try to mask it, but my voice betrays me.

"Yeah." It's long and drawn out when he says it like he knows what's coming.

"Can we just be honest for a minute? It...happened. We can't treat it like the elephant in the room anymore. We have to talk about it."

He exhales loudly. "Agreed."

There's a pause that neither one of us seems to want to address until Gus speaks up. "Listen, I know we were drunk, and it's like this big cliché, but it just happened. I mean, I didn't have this grandiose plan to get you wasted and have my way with you."

Is he being cavalier about this? Because we need to talk this through. "I wasn't drunk. I had two glasses of wine in like four hours. And I know you didn't have much more than I did. Are you mad at me? I don't want things to be weird between us. It's not something I planned either, you know."

"Yeah, I know." His voice sounds sincere again.

It's quiet for several moments. "You still there?" I ask.

"Yeah."

"So, what happens now? Because I don't think there's a handbook to navigate this one." My voice is calm, but my insides are churning, which I hate. I usually don't let things bother me. I can't. I haven't felt this way for a few months now.

And then he asks quietly, "Do you regret it?" He sounds almost timid.

I release the air I've been holding in my lungs, and a little of the nervousness goes with it. "Are you seriously asking *me* that? Gus. You know me. That's practically my motto: *no regrets*. Regret just leads to second-guessing and anger and sadness, and I sure as hell can't afford any of those."

"Yeah."

It's quiet for several more moments, and I wait for him to offer up more, but Gus is always quiet when he's thinking about something, so I give him time.

When I can't stand it any longer, I ask, "Do *you* regret it?"

He huffs and I can't tell if it's an exasperated huff or something else. But when the words come, I know he's amused. "Bright Side, I'm a twenty-one-year-old *fucking guy*. It was sex. What do you think?"

He does have a point, but I want answers from him. Not more questions. "But it was sex with *me*."

"Hold on a sec." I hear the click of his lighter and a deep inhale of breath as he takes the first drag from his cigarette.

"You should quit," I nag softly. It's habit to scold him about smoking, and even though I can't see him or smell the tobacco in the air, I have to tell him.

He takes another deep drag, and I hear him blow the smoke out. "I know, don't start with me right now." His voice suddenly sounds sad. So I stop and let him finish his cigarette because smoking always calms him down, kind of like playing the violin used to do for me. So I allow him his vice.

"Sorry," he apologizes. "I don't know, it was you, but it was... I mean, what happened a few days ago was... I don't know..."

I don't say anything because I know he's working through this. Choosing the right words is important to him. He's a songwriter, and he's emotional, and he wants to get it right. That's just how it's always been with Gus. He's a communicator. He doesn't talk just to talk. So I wait. I've always been pretty patient.

"Can I just talk to you for a second like a guy? I mean like you weren't there, involved, you know, in what went down?" It's calm, rational, honest Gus on the other end of the line now. My Gus.

"You can always talk to me, but okay if that helps, whatever."

"That night was, I don't know, it was fucking incredible." His voice is animated now, the way it is when he's just played me a new song he's written for the first time, or the way it is when he's just rode out a big wave and it carried him all the way into shore. "I know this sounds cheesy as hell, but you rocked my world." He's right, it does sound cheesy as hell. But it's Gus, and I know it came from the most honest, pure part of him because he's not embarrassed to talk like this in front of me. His voice comes down a few notches, and he continues. "I've been with a lot of girls, *a lot of girls*, but that night was different. It wasn't random. There was this...I don't know...this connection. I've never had that before. I couldn't get enough." He sighs and his voice drops. "And then it was over, and you left town."

"Gus," I say, trying to comfort him. To comfort both of us. Because everything he just said, I felt right along with him.

I hear him light up another cigarette. "I know, I know," he says. I wait, because at this point I'm not sure where this conversation is going. All I know is the person on the other end of this phone, his friendship, means the world to me. He's my best friend. Always has been. He's all I have.

"Bright Side, I'm not gonna lie. This is kinda fuckin' with my mind. I mean, I know we can't be together. Hell, I don't even know if that's what I would want anyway. You know I don't do relationships. No offense. I don't mean that as an insult. At all. It's just that...*dude*, you've been my best friend for like...forever. We've done everything together. We've been through some *serious, serious* shit together. And then, wham! You're moving a thousand miles away, and I'm headed for God knows what with this recording deal, and then we have sex... and it's the best sex I've ever had. And it's with *you*, my best friend. And I just feel like there's this...I don't know, that there's this...finality to it. Almost like a goodbye. But I can't lose you. I *need* my best friend."

Little does he know how dead-on he is. Sometimes I think he reads my mind. "Damn Gus, when did you get all philosophical on me?"

I mean it as a compliment, a confirmation, but he takes it wrong. I hate phones. I need physical interaction when I talk. I need to see the other person and for them to see me. I need body language and non-verbal cues.

And so does Gus obviously. He sounds irritated, even though he's just poured his heart out. "Bright Side, don't make light. *Fuck*, I'm trying to be honest here."

"I'm not, I'm completely serious." I must sound desperate. I hate being on the wrong side of a misunderstanding. "Damn, I wish I could see you right now. We seriously need to check into Skype or something, because this cell phone bullshit isn't going to cut it." Now I huff, which is just fine because we know each other so well that we can communicate through huffs and sighs and grunts, and convey messages and emotions that most people can't get across with words. I love that about our friendship. "Everything you just said, that's *exactly* how I feel. I meant what I said before; I don't want things to get weird between us. I love you. You know that. I'll always love you. I can't lose you either. I need a best friend more than anyone else on the planet right now, so you're preaching to the choir on that one. I mean, you are talking to Kate Sedgwick, God's chosen loner."

"Don't say that," he interrupts.

He's right. "I know, sorry. It's just that even though our lives are going in opposite directions, I want to know, I *need* to know, that you're just a phone call away. If I need to complain about a test—"

He interrupts. "You never complain, Bright Side. And even if you did, you've never needed to complain about tests because you've always been a straight A student, you freak."

I laugh because he's always teased me about my grades, especially after I graduated from high school with honors. But, he's always been proud of me for it too, because that's what best friends do. What he doesn't know is that I wasn't referring to school tests. But I let it go and continue. "And what about when I need you to search for a vegetarian restaurant for me because I have an ancient cell phone without internet, and I don't know how to get around Minnesota, and I *do not* want to get the meat shits again—"

He interrupts again. "Jesus, that's kinda putting the cart before the horse, don't you think? Do they even have vegetarian restaurants in Minnesota? Isn't there some sort of mandate or law or something against it? I mean, it is the Midwest after all. I expect it's meat for breakfast, lunch, and dinner, right?"

"Or because I just need to hear your voice, because you're my friend, and my family, and my past...and me."

He's calm Gus again. "I'm always here. You're going to do amazing things, Bright Side. You're going to be the best damn teacher the world has ever seen."

I don't thrive on compliments or encouragement, but my heart swells when he says that. I've always wanted to be a special education teacher. "I'd settle for just a teacher, how's that? And you're going to be the biggest rock star the world has ever seen."

Gus doesn't thrive on compliments or encouragement either. "And I'll settle for gigs that pay the bills, how's that? I don't think I can work in that fucking mailroom for another six months."

But I love giving out compliments, not kiss-ass, brown nose, I-just-want-to-make-you-feel-good compliments, but genuine, no bullshit, I-mean-it-because-I-feel-it-in-my-heart compliments. "You're *so* talented; you're going to be *huge*, Gustov Hawthorne. Just don't let your ego get out of control, okay?"

I was joking about his ego, but he answers sincerely, "That's what you're for, Bright Side. To keep reminding me I'm just Gus and I'm not as great as all the lying bastards tell me I am."

"Deal." But because I can't help it I add, "But you are great." He needs to know. He's the most gifted musician I've ever seen, and I've seen a lot of musicians. Before now, music was my life. Gus and I attended a private music-focused middle and high school in San Diego called The Academy. (It was just down the street from where we both lived, so I was blessed by proximity and a little talent. Gus didn't need proximity.) Gus played guitar, piano, *and* he could sing. I played the violin. People came from all over the country to attend The Academy. There were some crazy-talented kids, but Gus was always in a league of his own. He blew me away. And he's been performing with his band Rook for the past two years. He writes all their music and lyrics. They play almost every weekend locally around southern California, but a few months ago, an executive from a successful indie label was at one of their shows in L.A. and signed them on the spot. They just finished recording their first album two weeks ago. Gus doesn't like to be pigeonholed into a genre, but they're guitar-driven alt rock. They're amazing, and Gus is their core, their leader. He's going places.

For now, he's done being serious, and he's back to his joking, self-deprecating self. "Dude, you're supposed to be the antidote to my out-of-control ego. Stop stroking."

I laugh. I sense that the conversation is about to run out, and I'm glad it's ending on a good note. I feel like myself again, like just Kate and Gus again.

But then his voice turns serious again, almost nervous. "Bright Side?"

Which makes me nervous. "Yeah?"

"Can I ask you one last thing? And then I won't bring it up again."

"Sure." It comes out halfway between a question and a statement. Sure? Sure. Apprehensive.

He lets out one of his nervous laughs. "I'm not asking for any more ego-stroking," he says calmly. "But I just have to know, to bring closure to this whole, you know, to this whole thing." I cringe because I thought this was behind us. "How was it for you? I mean, I know you've been with other guys and everything...but was it, you know, was it different with me?"

I pause and smile because this isn't going down the road I thought it was going to. Gus *is* a guy, and he *does* need his ego stroked. And like I said, I don't just hand out compliments freely. They're heartfelt and real, so I answer honestly, "You rocked my world."

"Dude, don't patronize me." He thinks I'm twisting his cheesy but sincere phrase into something mocking.

"I'm not! That's it; I'm downloading Skype the minute I get off this phone. Listen to me Gus; it was probably the best night of my life."

"Hmm." I can hear the smile in his voice. His ego has been sufficiently stroked.

"Don't let it go to your head," I tease.

"Too late. I love you, Bright Side."

"Love you, too, Gus."

"Good night."

"Good night."

With renewed peace of mind, I fire up my laptop and do a Google-search for Skype. I'm going to find out exactly how it works, down to the very last detail. After that, I'll sleep.

WEDNESDAY, AUGUST 24

KATE

I SLEEP until nine o'clock and Maddie is already at work when I emerge from my hibernation chamber. Damn, do lawyers pump pure oxygen into their homes? Because I sleep like the dead here. I feel like such a lazy ass. I know that Dr. Ridley said I need to get more sleep, but I've had more sleep these past two days than I usually get in a week. I decide to take Princess for a walk and then go downstairs to the gym and pound out a few miles on the treadmill before I quit. I can't surf, so I run. I remind myself the pain in my exhausted muscles isn't pain, it's life. And life feels divine. Every day, every minute, every second.

I shower and run a comb through my wet hair and brush my teeth. I'm dressed and ready to go in ten minutes. Gus has never been able to figure how a girl can shower and be out-the-door ready in that short amount of time. It takes his primping ass forty-five minutes to get ready to go anywhere. I guess society does dictate certain expectations where women are concerned, I've just never bothered with them. Time is precious. And I don't waste it. Growing up, mornings were always rushed and I had to learn to fine-tune my routine. I've never worn makeup, and I don't own a blow dryer or straightening iron. Truth be told, I wouldn't even know what to do with any of it even if I did. Junior year in high school a friend decided I needed a makeover and put makeup on me and straightened my hair. It felt like I was wearing a mask with that shit all over my face. I don't like looking in the mirror and seeing someone else. I like looking in the mirror and seeing plain old Kate. The only thing I'm picky about is my clothes. I hate anything unoriginal. I mean, I wear jeans most of the time, but as far as tops go, I don't wear anything straight off the rack. I scour thrift shops, always looking for shirts with interesting patterns. I cut them up and salvage the best parts to combine with T-shirts Gus is always buying me. Gus calls it "rocker-bohemian." Whatever. I like it. As I zip up my duffle bag, I unfold the *I heart San Diego* T-shirt Gus gave me before I left. My fingers are itching to make something unique out of it.

I grab my sunglasses and head out to my car wearing my *Surf or Die* modified tank top. It's warm and humid today. It reminds me of home, so I dress for it. I'm happy as hell. And I need to check out my future home, so I'm ready to make the fifteen-mile drive to Grant and the college campus. I have no idea what to expect. I've only seen the campus in pamphlet photos and online.

Maddie's apartment is on the western edge of the Minneapolis city limits, just off the highway. Grant is due west of her place. I find the on-ramp and pull onto the highway, and within seconds, I've passed every car in sight. Ten of them. I counted. With that few cars on the highway, it feels eerie. Is the apocalypse coming and no one told me? Where is everyone? I'm used to traffic jams and honking horns or people driving ninety miles an hour on the highway. What the hell? People actually drive the speed limit here? I feel like some sort of criminal as I blaze past them, speeding through fifteen miles and rolling into Grant in only ten minutes. I slow down along the residential streets, and soon Grant College comes into view.

Grant is pretty, picturesque even. The campus is small, and the buildings are old, but not old like shitty and rundown, they're old like grand and well cared for. The dorms are old too. Four stories of brick, mortar, and ivy, but they've got character and look inviting. I sigh in relief. In a few days, that building will be home, and it looks like a home. It hits me that this is happening. I'm a college student in Minnesota. I'm also alone for the first time in my life. And even though alone is going to take some getting used to, at this moment it isn't as scary as I thought it would be.

Just beyond the dorms is Main Street in the actual town of Grant. I pull up to the stoplight and look around. It's a cute street lined with a flower shop, a liquor store, a deli, a small grocery/pharmacy, and a hair salon. Then I see it—a coffee shop. And not some obnoxious chain coffee shop, but a real-live, down-to-earth, unassuming coffee shop nestled at the end of the block in a brick building with big windows facing the street. And even though I've already had three cups of coffee this morning that I brewed in the Holy Grail at Maddie's, I can't resist checking it out. I tell myself I'll just stop in and introduce myself, but as I pull to the curb out front, I'm already debating whether I need a small or my usual large. Coffee is crack, I swear. I can't resist it. I can't say no. I begin to rationalize the visit by telling myself that they may be hiring. And I need a job, like yesterday.

The door is huge and intricately carved and looks like it must weigh a ton, so I grip the handle and push with all my might. I practically fall on my ass when the damn thing flies open, light as a feather. A bell clangs against the door. And it's *thunderous*. Wide-eyed, I look around the shop. There's a guy with his nose in a book sitting on the loveseat on one side of the room, a couple sitting at a small table on the other side of the room, and a guy behind the counter and they all look up at the ruckus I've created. It's instinct to try to quiet the bell and take the attention away from myself, but when I stretch my hand high above my head, I can't reach it. I'm five feet tall, and the bell is suspended at least a foot out of my reach. I smile sheepishly, and when the bell dies itself out, I announce, "I'm here," in little more than a whisper.

The dark, smiling man behind the counter confirms it. "Yes, you certainly are." He speaks with an accent, but I can't place it yet. He's probably around forty, with hair as black as coal, deep, toffee-colored skin, and huge, dark, smiling eyes. And his tone isn't mocking, it's kind and welcoming. I like him already. "You are new here, no?" He motions for me to come closer. "I'm Romero. Welcome to Grounds on Main, my friend." He salutes at me and instead of being silly, it's endearing.

I awkwardly salute back. "Um, yeah, and I'm Kate." When did I transform into a bumbling, socially inept fool? I clear my throat and extend my hand to Romero. "I'm Kate Sedgwick, and you're right, I am new here." I laugh. "Is it that obvious? Well hell, I've completely blown my cover. I was kind of trying to keep a low profile, but then I went and woke the dead with your bell."

He laughs warmly. "No worries. This is a small community. I know everyone. But you, you I have never seen, Kate Sedgwick. You are from California?" When he says California, it's like five separate words: CALL EE FOR NEE UH.

My eyebrows pinch together as I try to figure out how in the hell he knew that. "Yeah, that's right."

He sees my confusion and points out the front window at my car. "Your license plate. Where in California?"

The crease in my forehead relaxes. "Oh right, of course. I'm from San Diego, born and raised."

His face looks truly pained. "Oh, Kate, my dear, I wish you luck this winter. I am from El Salvador, and I can assure you that Minnesota winters are not for the faint of heart." Minnesota sounds like four separate words: MINN EE SO TAH.

I huff; he's touched on my one true fear about moving here, the cold. "Yeah, I hear they're a bitch."

He chuckles and his eyes sparkle.

The guy sitting on the loveseat reading a book chimes in. "They *are* a bitch." I look over, and his nose is still in his book, but he's smiling. He has red hair and a thick beard. I can't help but think he must be suffocating in this humid heat. His smile is innocent, youthful even. He has hipster written all over him. He doesn't say any more, so I return to Romero.

"So, Kate, what can I make for you?" Romero asks.

I glance up at the menu board behind him. I know I'll be a regular here, and I don't want to insult him right out of the gate by not following protocol. I'm relieved when all the items are arranged by price according to small, medium, and large sizes.

"Maybe I can recommend something? Do you like light, medium, dark roast? Espresso? Cappuccino? Perhaps a frozen drink to cool you off?"

I've never been a coffee snob. Coffee is coffee. I don't concern myself with the semantics. "Um, all I really want is a large cup of strong coffee."

Apparently, that was the right answer because he raps on the counter twice with his knuckles, a light tap. It's a happy gesture that says, *I agree with you one hundred percent and I know just what you need.* "Ah, you must try the house blend then."

Yes, I must. Right now. "Sounds perfect."

Romero tilts his head inquisitively. "Anything in the large cup of house blend aside from coffee?"

"No, thanks, just black."

His smile widens and he looks to the bearded guy on the loveseat again while pointing at me. "You hear that, Duncan? Just black coffee."

Duncan smiles and raises the ceramic mug in his hand toward me like a toast. "I heard that, Rome. Welcome to the club, new girl."

Romero's wide smile is still shining, but he lowers his voice. "No one ever wants just the coffee black." His accent is thick and I have to concentrate on every word to make sure I don't miss anything. "They ruin it with extras." He winks at me. "Very few of us know to enjoy the coffee black."

As Romero is pouring my coffee, I feel like I've broken the ice and we're friends, after all, I'm apparently in the club, so I gather my courage and ask, "You wouldn't happen to be hiring, would you? I just got into town, I start school on Monday, and I kind of need to generate some cash flow pronto."

Romero sighs as he hands me a giant paper cup. "Ah, Kate, sadly we are not. I own the shop with my partner, Dan. We only have one employee who helps out most mornings." He taps his chin with his pointer finger and his smile lights up again. "But, you can try the flower shop, Three Petunias, down on the corner. Mary told me yesterday she needs someone."

I slide two bills across the counter to cover the coffee and tip. "Awesome, you're the best. Thanks." I blow on the coffee and take a sip as I turn and walk toward the door. The coffee tastes rich and bold, just the way I like it. With my hand on the doorknob, I turn and raise my cup to Romero. "Coffee's epic, Romero. Have a great Tuesday."

He salutes. "You too, Kate Sedgwick."

The heat is stifling as I cross the street to head down toward Three Petunias. And then I realize that it's like ninety-five degrees with one- hundred-and-ten percent humidity, and I'm the dumbass drinking a large cup of steaming coffee. But then I smile at the cup in my hand because I can feel the caffeine kicking in, and I've got a job prospect two blocks away.

I push open the door to Three Petunias gently and damn it if it doesn't have a bell on it too. I involuntarily let out an exasperated, "Dude," in disbelief. What is it with small-town Minnesotans and their obsession with bells? This one is just a small tinkling variety, though. I get the distinct impression that I will become a connoisseur of bells while I'm living here.

The woman behind the counter is a dominating presence. She looks a little older than me, tall and curvy in all the right places. Some girls are cute, some are beautiful, and some are sexy. This girl is sexy. Her black hair is cut into a severe shoulder-length bob with bangs, and her dark eyes are accentuated with black, smoky liner. Her appearance is dark, but not in a gothic, depressing way. More like, in a take-no-prisoners way. I'm not easily intimidated by anyone or anything, but she's *intimidating*.

"And hello to you," she says, in answer to my outburst. Her voice is gruff like she's smoked ten packs of cigarettes a day since birth *and* she's been getting over a cold for the past year. I have a feeling her voice could single-handedly kick my ass. It's like her superpower.

Don't let her smell the fear, I tell myself. "Oh, hey," I say nonchalantly. "Sorry, that was rude. But what is it with the bells in this town?"

She takes in my appearance, but she's not looking down her nose at me the way Maddie does, she's curious, or amused. I can't tell which. "Bells?"

"Yeah, on the doors." I point to the door behind me.

She's still got that look on her face, but she answers matter-of-factly. "They let us know when someone's here."

"Well, no shit, Sherlock." I realize too late that my comment may have been inappropriate. Things aren't as casual here as they are back home, and I've only just met this woman—this intense, intimidating woman.

She lets out a stunned bark. I don't know if she's humored or insulted. "Yup, no shit," she confirms. "And I'm Shelly, not Sherlock."

I think I like this girl, even though she kind of scares me. She's direct, and I like direct; it takes out the guesswork. I approach her and offer my hand, though after glancing at her hands I realize that they're weaved intricately amongst the flowers in the vase in front of her. Instead, I say simply, "I'm Kate."

"Well Kate, what brings you in?" She looks back down at the arrangement in front of her again, like she's lost interest.

"I was just down at Grounds," I hold up my cup of coffee like some sort of proof," and Romero said that Mary might be looking to hire some help."

Shelly blows her bangs out of her eyes and looks back up at me, almost like she's trying to decide if I'm worthy of consideration. "Mary's my mother; she owns the place."

"So, are you hiring?" I ask hopefully, my cheeks suddenly feeling hot.

"You ever worked in a flower shop before?"

I shake my head. "Nope." That probably kills my chances, but I'm sure as hell not going to lie to her.

"You have any experience with gardening?" I feel like I'm being interrogated on some sort of crime show, and surely her partner is watching from the other side of a one-way mirror.

I shrug. "My last landlord, Mr. Yamashita, was a gardener. I suppose that doesn't count? Too many degrees of separation?"

She huffs. Yes. She's a huffer. I love her now. "Can you tell a carnation from a rose?"

"Sure."

The hard-ass façade remains, but to my surprise she says, "Get your butt behind this counter and help me out. I'm buried this afternoon. We'll see how you do."

I put on the apron she hands me. "Dude, that was one hell of an interview. You had me sweating."

She rolls her eyes at my sarcasm. "Whatever. *Dude.*"

The shop is small and old-fashioned. And by old-fashioned I don't mean outdated, I mean charming. There are several antique tables on the customer side of the counter that display plant and flower arrangements. It's cute. And the smell...*oh, the smell, it's heaven in here.*

Behind the counter, I notice that everything has its place. It's organized, obsessively orderly. Shelly works like a tornado. She's all over the room working on four arrangements simultaneously. I watch and listen, trying to pitch in where I can. Mostly, I fake it.

We work in silence for an hour, which is hurting my ears. "Don't you have a radio or something?" I ask.

She points to the shelf on the other side of the room without looking at me.

I feel like I should ask because I don't know if she just gave me permission or not, "Do you mind if I turn it on? This place could use some background noise. The silence is deafening."

She shakes her head.

I march over and turn it on because I need music when I work. Hell, I need music all the time, but especially when I work. Music grounds me. It's pure emotion, and I need that extension.

I fiddle with the tuner for a minute until I find a station. Shelly perks up at the sound. "This is a good song. They just started playing it last week. The guitar is fierce. Have you heard it?"

I nod my head as I return to our workstation. I know the song, and she's right about the guitar. I heard this song for the first time four or five months ago when this album was released, but I don't want to come off as some sort of know-it-all asshole, so I don't let on. "Yeah. It's good. Is this a local station?"

Shelly grunts out her response bitterly. "Yeah, this is the college station. It's all we have. All the other local stations are shit."

I elbow Shelly in the side. "Don't tell me you're one of those music snobs, Shelly?"

She raises an eyebrow like she knows she's been caught. "Guilty. I love music, and it's so hard to find the good stuff." Her face softens a little. "I sound like a damn junkie, don't I?"

I know how she feels. Gus and I scour the internet all the time in search of the newest musical diversion, like a couple of addicts looking for their next fix. We've shared our music collection for years, and it's beyond extensive. My iPod is maxed out, and the rest fills the hard drive on my laptop. "Maybe you just haven't found the right dealer. I'll bring in my iPod sometime. Do you have a dock or a speaker I can hook up to?" I love connecting with people about music, especially when I can turn someone on to new music they haven't heard before. Discovering something new is like magic. Music is out there to be heard, and I am of the opinion that as many people as possible should hear it. All of it. Because music is powerful. It connects people.

She hesitates, then nods. "Okay, yeah, I have a dock I can bring in. What do you listen to?"

"Oh, I'm all over the board. I listen to just about everything, though I can't bring myself to get on board with country. It sounds artificial. I don't know how to explain it, but it makes my teeth hurt it's so sweet. And it's kind of depressing, even the happy stuff."

She nods in agreement.

"Generally, I tend to gravitate toward lesser-known bands. I like to see the little guys make it, you know. And I have to support California bands. It's like this guilty, loyalty thing. Good thing they can bring it."

Her eyes widen infinitesimally like she's just figured out some sort of puzzle. "Of course. You're from California. I've been trying to figure it out all afternoon. I figured somewhere sunny since you're so tan, but I thought the *Surf or Die* T-shirt was too obvious. So are you a poser or do you really surf?"

I laugh at the blunt accusation. "I surf, sure."

"Really?" She doubts me.

"Yeah."

She nods. "That shirt is pretty sick by the way. Where'd you get it?"

I shrug. "I made it."

Again, the doubt. "Really?"

The scrutiny doesn't bother me. "Yeah. I make all my shirts."

"Huh," is all she says, and although she looks mildly impressed, I have a feeling it would kill her to admit it. She doesn't hide her emotions very well. They peek through the stern mask if you're paying attention.

We continue listening to the college station, and it turns out to be pretty good. Almost all indie and alt rock, it makes me think of Gus. He would love this station. I half expect to hear a Rook song start blasting through the speakers.

Shelly slaps me on the back when we're done. "You did all right for someone who has no idea what she's doing."

I frown. "Thanks... I think." And then I smile so she knows I'm teasing.

Her eyes allude to a smile, but they never fully commit. "Whatever. Can you work afternoons on Mondays, Tuesdays, Wednesdays, and the occasional Saturday?"

"Absolutely."

"You're hired."

I'm doing cartwheels inside, but I'm outwardly calm. "Thanks."

"I assume you're a student, too, though I never asked. I'm a senior this year at Grant. Music major, classical piano."

"No shit? Classical piano? Righteous, Shelly." I know I sound a little surprised, but I am. She's hard as nails, and I never would've pegged her for classical piano. "I'm a few credits short of a sophomore, so yeah, I'm a freshman." I cringe, thinking about my unusual path to college.

I graduated a year and a half ago with a full-ride music scholarship to play violin here, but then life happened...so I stayed in San Diego. I worked in the mailroom with Gus at his mom's advertising firm part-time and took classes at the local community college. I was happy. Everything was looking up. And then three months ago, in June, another bomb dropped. This one turned my fucking world upside down. I needed to get out of San Diego. So, even though the fall semester was quickly approaching, I applied to Grant again, minus the violin. I figured I didn't have anything to lose. I sweated it until mid-July when the letter arrived announcing that not only did they accept me, but that they were awarding me an academic scholarship that pays my tuition and room and board. You could have knocked me over with a feather. I gave notice to Mr. Yamashita and moved out of his garage the last day of July and moved into Audrey Hawthorne's spare bedroom, where I stayed until I moved here a few days ago. Gus's mom is one of my favorite people on the planet. I've known her my whole life. When I think of the word "mother," I think of Janice Sedgwick, but when I think of the word "mom," I think of Audrey. Gus still lives with her too. He's such a mama's boy.

Shelly gives me this sad look. "So, you're in the dorms?"

"Yeah, all freshmen have to live in the dorms, right?"

The sad look remains. "Right," she confirms.

"I drove past them today. They look great. I'm kind of stoked about it." I really am.

She pats me on the shoulder. "You just stay *stoked*." She's having fun mocking my vocabulary. "But a word of warning, this is a small school and very cliquish, if you know what I mean. There are a lot of entitled, trust-fund, spoiled brats here. Don't let them bust your balls is all I'm sayin'."

I nod, thankful for her concern. "Point taken. Good thing my balls are virtually bust-proof."

I swear she almost smiles.

We part ways, and I poke my head in at Grounds to thank Romero for the job lead before I head back to Maddie's. I make the trip in nine minutes this time and can't help but feel optimistic about my first day in Grant. I knew it was the right choice.

It's still early in Cali and Gus is at work, so I text him my good news.

Me: *Got a job at a flower shop today.*

Gus: *Sweet! Gotta jet to a band meeting after work. Talk to you tomorrow? Love you.*

Me: *OK. Good luck. Tell everyone hi. Love you.*

THURSDAY, AUGUST 25

KATE

THE HIGHLIGHT OF THE DAY: Gus and I try out Skype and decide that the person who invented it deserves to win the Nobel Prize, and/or a congressional medal of honor, and/or some other outrageously huge commendation, even if it's not technologically applicable, because Skype is *genius*.

The not-so-highlight of the day: I had my first appointment with Dr. Connell at Methodist Hospital in Minneapolis. It was pretty much what I expected. Just like Dr. Ridley in San Diego, Dr. Connell approached my situation with realism, which I appreciate, and respect. He gave me a rundown of treatment options and a treatment schedule. He's a more-is-more doctor; he wants to go all in. I'm a less-is-more girl; I don't. He wasn't happy about that. I left with his business card, an appointment date for a month from now, and his worried face etched in my memory.

Doctors usually have a better poker face. One thing's for sure. If I ever go to Vegas, I'm not inviting Dr. Connell to play the tables with me.

FRIDAY, AUGUST 26

KATE

I'M RUNNING LATE as usual, so as I enter the cafeteria, I scan the room quickly for any and all open seats. There are a few at every table, but I stop when my eyes land on a smallish guy sitting alone. He's wearing a vintage, pinstriped mailman's shirt, a plaid bowtie, intentionally short, red dress pants, blue argyle socks, and a pair of black and white wingtips. Somehow, I know that's where I'm supposed to be. He's got *great* style, and to wear something so bold, you need some pretty bold character to match. I decide that I need to meet him. As I approach I can tell he's trying to be stoic, but his shoulders look hunched, and he must be nervous as hell. I want to pat him on the back to relieve a little of the tension. But I don't. I'm a little touchy-feely, and I've learned through trial and error that it freaks some people out. Introductions first.

"Is this seat taken?" I ask politely.

He starts at the close proximity of my voice but turns to face me.

I smile. That bowtie is too damn cute. I ask again, "Is this seat taken?" gesturing specifically to the seat right next to him, even though every chair at the large table is empty.

As his smile widens, his shoulders start to relax. "No. No one's sitting here. Go right ahead." I know that the term *pixie* isn't exactly a widely used description, but it's the first word that comes to mind when I see his smile. He's a well-groomed, well-dressed little pixie.

"Dude, that shirt is the shit," I say, motioning as I take a seat. It even has a vintage nametag—Frank. He didn't miss a thing. "I'm Kate." I extend my hand, which he grips lightly and shakes once. His hands are soft.

"Thank you... I think. Is Kate short for Katherine? I'm Clayton." He's formal, but not in a stuffy, snooty way. Formal in a subtle, sophisticated way. Still, this guy needs to relax. "And your shirt is fabulous, too," he adds. I'm wearing a tank top that reads *Tijuana is muy bueno*. The text was taken from three different donor shirts, with straps made of thick black ribbon.

"Aww, thanks, Clay." He seems genuine. "And it's just Kate. Katherine is something not even my mother would've named me."

"You're welcome, Katherine." He smiles coyly. "And it's just Clayton. Clay is something not even my mother would have named me."

I laugh. "So, that's how it's gonna be?" I like this guy. He's witty. And he's not backing down, even though he looks scared shitless to be here.

Just then some campus officials file through the door and begin their hour-long spiel about the *Grant College Experience*. A small chuckle escapes me when the Dean actually says the words *Grant College Experience* as he welcomes us. Clayton stifles a laugh too and motions for me to be quiet with his pointer finger to his lips. I stop when I realize we're the only ones in the room laughing. The Dean isn't being funny or ironic, he means it. And everyone else is eating it up. *The Experience*. It takes about twenty seconds for me to realize that not only does the guy mean it, he's *really* pumped to tell us all about it. He lives *The Experience*. Now that I know this day has a name, I can't help but feel like I've just walked into some sort of a traveling tent church revival or a motivational seminar. The fucking enthusiasm that's pouring out of this guy is unbelievable. So, I give in and surrender to it for the sheer entertainment factor, and even though I'm not necessarily buying what he's selling the way everyone else in the room seems to be, it's still entertaining as hell to watch. Some of the lines he's throwing at us, even though he's serious as a heart attack when he says them, they're some of the funniest things I've heard in a while. Except for the stifled laugh during the introduction and the occasional glance in my direction when the Dean's said something particularly hilarious, at least to the two of us, Clayton is laser-focused as if he's being instructed on brain surgery and will be expected to perform an operation later today. His notes are so extensive that I start to feel like a slacker as I realize I haven't put pen to paper. In retrospect, there were a few classic lines that I wish I would've written down because Gus would've laughed his ass off. All that sticks in my head now are the overused clichés. The Dean is a *big* fan of clichés.

After we're bid farewell with a collective, "Live the Grant College Experience!" from the faculty, I offer up an unbridled, "Yee-haw!" It blends in nicely with all the clapping and hoopla from the other freshman. Clayton rolls his eyes at me like my enthusiasm has just embarrassed him. "What, dude?" I retort. "I'm just so excited. That was some inspirational shit." I point at him and impersonate the Dean's voice with a straight face. "'Your destiny is in your hands.' 'The future is bright.' 'We're all one big, happy family here at Grant.' 'Your life starts now.'"

He shakes his head solemnly, but there's a smile playing at the corner of his mouth. He doesn't do stern very well. "Katherine, that was an hour of my life I'll never be able to get back," he says dryly.

I laugh. "Aww, Clayton, I wouldn't take back that hour for all the coffee in Columbia."

"I think the phrase is 'for all the tea in China.'"

I shake my head. "I hate tea."

He shakes his head like he's not sure what to do with me.

I suppress a giggle and continue. "My eyes have been opened like a newborn babe to the Grant College Experience. It's going to be fucking magnificent."

He cracks a smile and throws his pencil at me. "Katherine, hush."

I point to his notebook still on the table in front of him. "You get any of the Dean's little nuggets of wisdom? Jesus, were you taking dictation, Clayton? Those are some extensive notes."

He blushes. "I'm thorough."

And now I feel bad for making him blush. I pat his shoulder as I stand. "I'm just kidding, Clayton. I'm a slacker. You're an over-achiever. We'll get it sorted out. Let's go find our dorm rooms."

I'm a little surprised that after he stands and slings his leather messenger bag over his shoulder, he loops his arm through mine. I'm all for touchy-feely, but he's not leading, he wants to be led. I'm beginning to wonder if I emit the scent of sour milk like a nursing mother, because certain people gravitate to me for one reason, and one reason only—they need to be taken care of. I have a new mission: to shelter Clayton from the storm, or at least to gently introduce him to it. I get the feeling life hasn't always been a picnic for Clayton. He's chosen the right friend. I make a *fantastic* buffer, believe me.

I cover his hand looped through my arm with my own. "Let's get this goddamn Grant College Experience started."

Our dorm rooms turn out to be right across the hall from each other. *Goddamn destiny.* Our names along with our roommates' are posted on each door. Clayton's is Peter Samuel Longstreet III. I say a silent prayer, *Please God,* please *don't let Pete be a homophobic bastard.* Because although I've only known Clayton for an hour, I'm 99.9% sure that sweet, lovely Clayton likes boys as much as I do.

My roommate seems to have been saddled from birth with the name—I'm not kidding you—Sugar Starr LaRue. Did her parents even think that one through? I'm trying so damn hard not to let my imagination run away with me, but the first thought that pops into my head is...stripper. I know, I know. She could be a lovely, chaste, prudish young maiden, but with a name like Sugar Starr LaRue you almost have to live up to the stage name, don't you? And once the stripper profile implants itself in my head, I find myself thinking I'll be disappointed if this girl turns out to be normal.

I help Clayton carry his belongings from his car to his room, and then he helps me. Peter Samuel Longstreet III shows up somewhere in the middle, so we help him carry his stuff, too. He's tall and a little heavy around the middle. He has light brown hair that's cut in a military-style crew cut, a mild case of acne, and he's wearing pleated khaki pants and a forest green polo shirt with slip-on brown loafers. The dude looks like a middle-aged insurance agent trapped in an eighteen-year-old's body. He's just your average-looking guy I guess, except that he looks insanely innocent. I mean, like, *insanely* innocent. After spending five minutes around him, I learn I'm not far off. He's really shy and really, really tense. I take a minute to give God a silent shout-out, *Thank you, God. Pete seems way uptight, but he doesn't seem like a hateful ass clown. Many thanks. Over and out.*

I know it's weird, but I like to think of God as my homeboy. I'm not religious; I just talk to him a lot. I ask for a lot of favors. Sometimes things go my way, sometimes they don't. That's life. You just have to make the most of it.

Of course, now that my interest is piqued, and I'm wondering if Sugar will set up her stripper pole in the north corner of our room or right in the center, she's a no-show. The mystery will have to wait another day. I unpack all by my lonesome, accompanied by my trusty iPod. I claim the bed farthest from the door, right next to the window.

Clayton comes over to borrow some toothpaste, and I follow him back to his room. *Jesus. H. Christ.* It's the tidiest, most organized room I've ever seen in my life. They're both unpacked, and everything's put away. Damn, it's kismet. Clay and Pete were destined to be roommates. What are the chances of two obsessively neat guys randomly getting assigned to the same room? I mean, the odds have to be like a million to one, right? I hope Sugar's not OCD like this, or she's going to be monumentally disappointed. I don't make my bed, ever. I don't put my dirty clothes in a hamper, ever. It's not that I'm unclean, I'm just messy.

It's late when I finish settling into my new home. The last thing I do is place two picture frames side-by-side on the desk near my bed. Before I turn off the light, I look to the framed photos. "Night night, Gracie. Good night, Gus. Love you both."

SATURDAY, AUGUST 27

KATE

I WAKE to my cell phone buzzing on my desk, and it's *way* too demanding for this early in the morning. I squint my eyes and through the sleep, my clock reads 6:47 am. My first thought is Gus. It's always Gus. But it's not even five o'clock in California. It can't be him. Unless he's been out all night, which is entirely possible. I strip the covers back and shuffle over to see what's so important.

It's a text from Maddie: *U left stuff here. B here b4 12 2day.*

"And good morning to you," I yawn at the phone. It's way too early for that many abbreviations.

I stretch and decide now's as good a time as any to check out the showers down the hall. I wear my beach flip-flops in the shower because Gus told me I could pick up some nasty foot fungus if I don't.

By 7:10 am, I'm out the door and headed for Maddie's. If she's going to summon me at the butt crack of dawn, she'd better be prepared to receive me.

She answers after my third round of knocking wrapped in a fluffy white robe and one of those sleeping eye cover things pushed up on her forehead. "Kate? It's seven twenty-five in the morning."

"Um, yeah?" *Duh.* "Were you sleeping?"

"Yes." She's pissed.

"Sorry. I thought your courtesy wake-up text was permission to come over." I'm in a great mood and trying to joke my way through this. It's the only way to deal with her shit this early in the morning.

"I woke up early because Princess needed to go outside and I texted you before I went back to bed." She barks a condescending laugh. "Really, Kate, don't you know anything about dorm life?" I can see that she enjoys the hell out of talking down to me, but to be honest, it's pretty damn entertaining, funny even. "It's common courtesy to silence your cell phone at night, or your roommate is going to grow to hate you. It's one of the first rules in dorm life. If it was silenced, *like it should have been,* my text wouldn't have woken you."

And because Maddie's one of those people who thinks everyone hangs on her every word, I indulge her. "Thanks, Maddie. I'll keep that in mind." *For crying out loud, I slept in the same room with Grace for nineteen years, so I probably know a thing or two about common courtesy and space sharing,* I want to add. But I bite my lip.

And because Maddie's also one of those people who clearly can't see when they're being a jackoff, she grins. "You're welcome." Then shakes her head and gives me a pitiful look. "What am I going to do with you?"

You could throw my shit out the front door so I can leave because you still haven't had the common courtesy to invite me in, runs through my head. But then I remember to put myself in Maddie's shoes. What would I think of me? She doesn't really know me, just what's happened to me. Maybe she thinks I need to be looked after, and this is her version of good intention. Whatever.

"So, I'll just grab my stuff and get out of your hair." I'm kind of done screwing with her. She's not funny anymore.

"Oh, right." She steps aside and gestures to a pile of clothes on the sofa.

"Awesome," I say as I scoop them up. "Thanks for not throwing them out on the curb or, you know, setting them on fire."

She screws up her face in confusion. "I wouldn't do that."

She doesn't know my sense of humor yet. "Kidding. I'm kidding, Maddie. Lighten up."

Her face smooths out, but she still looks hurt. I feel kinda bad. "Since you're already awake, you wanna grab something to eat?" Guilt's prodding me. I feel it like a sharp poke in the ribs.

She's super eager, and that surprises me. "Sure, just give me a few minutes to get ready."

"No problem, take your time."

If I'd known she'd take the *take your time* comment so literally, I would've said, *no problem, you have fifteen minutes*. An hour and thirteen minutes later, she sashays her ass out of the bathroom dressed like she's ready for a night out on the town. That's another thing about Maddie; she doesn't know how to dress down. I'm in sweats, a Sleigh Bells T-shirt, and running shoes and she's in a strapless minidress and embellished platform sandals.

"Wow, nice dress. But dude, it's just breakfast."

"Oh, Kate." She shakes her head as if to say, *Oh silly, silly, immature Kate.* "You never know when you're going to meet Prince Charming. You always have to look your best." She takes in my ensemble. "This is something you'll learn in time."

Pretty sure I won't. I guess everyone has different definitions of Prince Charming. My definition might be based a little more on substance and character—call me crazy.

The dress she's wearing shows a lot of skin, and it's the first time I notice how startling thin she is. Like *bone* thin. I can't help but blink my eyes away. It's like some sort of internal coping mechanism's been triggered to protect me from scary shit.

Suddenly, Maddie is bubbly and happy. She talks nonstop all the way to the café about her visit to the gym yesterday and the hot, rich guy who got her number.

I nod in all the right places. Somebody's on a manhunt. And she's accepting all applicants with a big wallet, a penis, and a beating heart. Good luck with that.

The scene at the café plays out in much the same way as the sushi joint: Maddie orders a lot of food. But unlike the sushi place, nothing here goes to waste. She inhales a plate of eggs, hash browns, sausage, bacon, *and* ham, as well as three pancakes the size of dinner plates, all dripping in syrup. When I don't eat the sausage links that came with my eggs and toast, she eats those too. This chick could compete in eating competitions. She must have a lightning-fast metabolism.

When we return to the apartment, I grab my clothes off the sofa. "Thanks again for putting up with me for a few days, Maddie."

She holds up a finger and begins walking away. "Just a minute, I'll be right back."

I stand there less than a minute before I remember that I didn't have my razor in the shower this morning. I must have left it in Maddie's shower. While I'm waiting for her, I may as well grab it. The guest bathroom door is shut, but she keeps Princess in there when she's not home. I slowly open the door, but as I do, I hear the contents of Maddie's belly empty into the toilet with a disgusting splash. The smell is overwhelming. My own stomach heaves. "Maddie, are you all right?"

I expect her to look sweaty or stricken, like the victim of some sort of freakishly violent food poisoning. She's sitting on the edge of the tub holding her long blonde curls back delicately hovering above the toilet, careful not to touch anything. It's the oddest thing. She looks purposeful and poised. I don't know about anyone else, but when I pray to the porcelain god, I huddle on the floor in front of it slumped over in submission. I'm a damn mess.

"What the hell, Kate?" She wipes her mouth with the back of her hand before quickly flushing. Her face flushes red, and I can't tell if she's pissed because she's embarrassed or pissed because she's, well, just pissed.

"Sorry, Maddie. I didn't know you were in here. I thought I forgot my razor, and I was—"

"You could have knocked!"

I'm speechless as I watch her scrub her hands, rinse her mouth with mouthwash, and then fix her hair in the mirror. If I didn't just witness her deposit fifteen dollars' worth of brekky into the john, I wouldn't believe it looking at her now. She's completely unaffected, and it creeps me the hell out. The alarm starts blaring in my head like an air raid siren. All the pieces fit together now: the binging at meals, the obsession with working out, using the bathroom immediately after eating, her frighteningly thin body—she's bulimic.

"Maddie, we seriously need to talk about this." I gesture to the toilet because I don't want to put her on the defensive by putting a name on her issue.

She shrugs with one shoulder, which tells me she's not into this conversation at all. "There's nothing to talk about." The irritation is gone from her voice. And I think I liked the anger better because now she's impassive. You can't talk to impassive people. They put up walls that deflect everything.

I follow her out to the living room. "Maddie, listen, no judgment. Honestly. Please just let me help you with this."

She lets out the most emotionless laugh I've ever heard. "You're going to help me? That's rich. What are you, eighteen?"

"Maddie, you're my aunt, my family. I care, okay, that's all I'm saying. How long has this been going on?"

"Little Kate, you're so naïve." It's the patronizing, I'll-talk-to-you-like-a-five-year-old tone again. But I don't care, because at this moment all I want is to get through to her.

"*Naïve?* Maddie, you just threw up your goddamn breakfast in the toilet...*on purpose.*"

"Kate, dear, it's *nothing.*" Her face is cool and nonchalant.

I shake my head, but I don't take my eyes off hers. This can't be real. "Dude." It's pleading and sad.

She shakes her head back at me. "Kate, I only binge and purge every now and then. It's not like it's a habit. Sometimes I just get really hungry. This way I can eat a lot, but I don't gain any weight. It's a win-win." She's trying to convince me with her dazzlingly white smile.

"Dude, it is not a win-win. You're screwing with your body.

Bodies don't like to be screwed with. At some point, they rebel." A person knowingly doing harm to his or her body is a pet peeve of mine. A lot of people would give anything for a healthy body. Your body is a temple. You don't shit on the temple.

She dismisses me with a wave of her hand like she's done so many other times this week. I'm losing her. She won't listen. And I don't have any frame of reference, no inside knowledge on the topic. I don't know what to say, so without thinking, I say the same thing I always say to Gus about his smoking, "You should quit." I feel stupid when I say it.

Her eyes are burning with anger now. I've pushed her too far. She takes a deep breath and says, "Kate, I think you should leave."

Yup, definitely overstepped my bounds. I've outed her secret, and she's furious, rightfully so. I need to give her some space. I gather my clothes and head for the door. "Thanks again for not burning my clothes."

I wait for her response, but there's nothing. Not even *you're welcome* or *kiss my ass*. It's the oppressive silent treatment. It sends a shiver through me. I look back, and suddenly I'm not in the room with Maddie anymore; I'm in the room with Janice Sedgwick. Maddie has taken on the image of my mother; even the way she's carrying her weight on her left foot and has her arms crossed. They could be the same person. My mother wasn't a monster. She just couldn't always help it. When she didn't take her meds, she wasn't herself, and when she did take her meds, she wasn't herself. Mental illness is no joke. There were times she was loving and kind. The rest of the time she was angry or indifferent. Anger and indifference are completely different, but when you're a kid on the receiving end of either, they'll break your heart. I learned early on not to take it personally, but when she did it to Grace, it shattered me. I tried to make sure that never happened. On the rare occasion that I failed, *I hated myself for it.*

I need to get out of here.

I walk out the door, and just before it shuts behind me, I say,

"Please get help." I don't think she's heard me until I see her shoulders slump a little through the crack.

Back in my dorm room, I research bulimia on my laptop for an hour. I stop after that, because it's depressing. My head is full of questions.

It's lunchtime, and even though eating is the last thing I feel like doing after the past hour's reading, I've got to get out of this room. I need to think about something else. I'm fairly good at compartmentalizing my life. If something bad is going down, I can focus on it for a while and then put it on the back burner when I need to. Managing a childhood like mine taught me that helpful lesson. I can't let the bad consume me, or it would eat me whole. The bad stays in the bad corner of my mind, I don't let it through the door to mingle with the good, because the bad is a goddamn party pooper.

So, I go across the hall and pound on Clay's door. Peter answers. "What's up, Pete?"

He nods his head stiffly. "Kate."

I reach out, take Pete by the arms, and shake him good-naturedly. "Relax, Pete. Hey, is Clayton around?"

Peter opens the door wide, and I see Clayton lounging on his bed reading a magazine.

"Hey, Clayton. What's up? I'm just headed down to the cafeteria to grab some lunch. You wanna come?"

"Good day, Katherine. Sure. This article is dreadful. It's putting me to sleep." He stretches and sets the magazine on his desk. Sometimes I wonder if Clayton was British in another life. Who else but the Brits say dreadful?

I look to Peter, still holding the door. "You wanna come, too, Pete?"

"I don't want to intrude." He's so formal.

"Pete, dude, it's just lunch. Besides, Clayton and I aren't even dating yet. He's totally ignoring my advances." I throw my best seductive smile and wink at Clayton.

He shakes his head. "Oh, Katherine," he says. I love that he gets my sense of humor.

"See Pete, it's going to take a lot of creative scheming and some seriously old-school courting. Clayton's a tough nut to crack. You are *so* not intruding."

Pete knows we're messing around because Clayton told him last night that he's gay. He said he didn't want things to be weird between them or to leave Peter wondering. Pete was cool about it. Somehow I knew he would be.

LUNCH WITH CLAYTON AND PETER WAS AWESOME. WE JUST SAT together, making jokes and telling stories. Turns out once Pete relaxes a little, he's actually funny. And Clayton, well Clayton is dry and sarcastic. We laughed our asses off. And considering laughter is like oxygen to me, I really needed it. I medicate with it. I found two people who make me laugh, like tears-in-my-eyes, almost-wet-my-pants laugh. Those are the kind of people I like to be around. And now I have two. Lucky me.

I return to my dorm room to find the place taken over like France during WWII. There's shit everywhere, hers and mine.

I wave to the girl standing, hands on hips, in the middle of the room. "Hey, I'm Kate."

She looks over at me, blows a stray hair out of her face, and tugs the band out of her ponytail. Looking at me coolly, she smooths all the stray hairs back before she fastens it tight again. "I'm Sugar."

She's pretty, like model-pretty. Long, blonde hair, big dark eyes, full pouty lips, and Jesus, is she tall. Her legs are practically as long as my whole body. She's thin, but fit. And she's got ginormous boobs. I can make a fail-safe judgment on her body because, well, she's not hiding a thing. She's wearing a bikini top and the smallest pair of denim shorts I've ever seen. When did they start making denim underwear? Yeah, this really doesn't help me with the stripper image.

"I had to move a few things. It just wasn't going to work for me,"

Sugar says, shaking her head and looking around at the mess. "No, it wasn't going to work at all."

"That's cool, we can figure this out."

Sugar gives orders like a Marine corporal. After rearranging the entire room three times, she's finally satisfied. I'm sweating like a pig. It seems suspicious that even though we each have the same amount of furniture, she's taken up two-thirds of the room. But, whatever. I have enough space for all my things, so I'm not going to complain. It's obvious Sugar always gets her way. Me? I pick my battles.

There's not a lot of small talk outside of interior decorating and furniture placement, but I ask questions. I learn that Sugar is eighteen years old and originally from Minneapolis. Her parents are divorced, and she has a three-year-old half-brother and a cocker spaniel named Mercedes. She knows "a lot" of people who go to Grant. She learns nothing about me. When people are interested in you, they ask questions. I asked. She didn't.

Oh, and she says nothing about stripping. And there's no pole.

Damn. I feel cheated.

SUNDAY, AUGUST 28

KATE

"Who's the guy? Boyfriend?" Sugar throws these questions at me the moment my foot crosses the threshold into our room as I return from the shower. She's pointing at one of the framed photos on my desk. Guess she's going to make up for not asking any questions yesterday.

"Nah. Best friend."

She smacks her gum. "Hmm. He's a hottie. Pretty eyes."

It's the same photo I have on my phone, though that one's cropped to show just his face. It shows up every time he calls. The one in the frame includes both of us. We're laughing. I'm standing up straight with my head thrown back, and he's doubled over, his long hair hanging over one eye. His other eye is looking into the camera with an expression of joy and mischief, calm and wild abandon. It's classic Gus. Our friend, Franco, took this photo a year ago when we were all at the beach. "Yeah, he's got great eyes." They're so dark brown, they're almost black. They sparkle.

She glances at the photo of Grace like an afterthought. "Who's she?"

"My sister." I linger on Grace's face. I took this photo one evening this past April when we went down to the beach to watch the sunset. Grace is posed in front of a blazing orange sunset. It's washed across the horizon and dancing on the water like fire. But it pales in comparison to the smile on her face. It lights up the photo. It's the same smile she wore every day. It's the same smile that made everything better. It's the same smile that was tangible proof I was surrounded by goodness. It's the same smile that made me feel like the luckiest person in the world to have her as a sister. That smile, this photo, it's everything that's pure and honest in this world.

"Well, I'm outta here. I've got people to see and places to go." She grabs her bag.

She's wearing very tiny white shorts and a white tank top with no bra. I'm all for letting the girls run free every now and then, but you can clearly see her darkened nipples through the thin white material. What if she just forgot her bra? I can't let her go out without saying something. "Um, Sugar." I gesture to my chest trying to be subtle.

She looks down at her gigantic and unbelievably perky boobs. Those can't be real, can they? "What?"

"Not sure what you're going for, but you do know that the twins are on full display, right?"

She shrugs. "Yeah."

I throw her a thumbs up. "Okay, you're all good then, sister. See ya."

I DECIDE TODAY IS THE DAY THAT CLAYTON MUST BE introduced to Grounds. I open the door gently this time and damn if the bell isn't thunderous again. The laws of physics have been proven false; the amount of force exerted on the door cannot be equal to the volume forced from that fucking bell. The beast cannot be tamed. Romero is here again and remembers my name, first and last. I introduce him to Clayton and Clayton orders a mocha macchiato with soy and light whipped cream. He looks on the verge of ecstasy the entire time he's drinking it. Can you climax from drinking a cup of coffee?

You'd think I'd know the answer to that. Clayton's rendered speechless. My black coffee is epic again too, but obviously not climactic. Maybe that's what's so great about putting all the extra shit in it.

Clayton and I spend the afternoon listening to music in his room. Clayton's strictly into electronica, dubstep, and house, which I'm all about. We dance our asses off like two thirteen-year-old girls. I love to dance. Gus and I went dancing a lot. There were always bonfires at the beach that turned into dance parties. Grace always loved the music, so I would bring her along. Or sometimes Audrey would take Grace for the night, and Gus and I would go to a club where he knew the bouncer who'd let us in even though we were both underage at the time. Gus is amazing on the dance floor. After having sex with him, one pretty much explains the other. Let's just say he's *very* comfortable with his body and knows it *damn well.*

Pete walked in on the dance party, turned beet red, did a one-eighty, and left again. Guess he didn't have any moves to bring to the floor. We'll have to work on that. Clay is good, though. You know when you go to a club, and there's one person who everyone watches? They make it look easy? That's Clayton. I'm impressed.

I'm sweaty when I leave to head back to my room around six o'clock. "Clayton, you can tear up the dance floor, my friend. We need to find a club that has a twenty-one and under night sometime."

His smile is pure elation, and he claps his hands so fast they look like hummingbird wings. "Oh Katherine, that would be fabulous. I've never been to a real club before."

That surprises me. "Really? Where'd you learn those moves, boy?"

He blushes, then asks, "Do you think there are any gay clubs in Minneapolis?"

I shrug. "Sure."

His blush deepens. "Katherine, would you, I mean if I can find one that we can get into, would you go with me? I don't have anyone else to ask."

I give Clay's shoulder a little squeeze. "Absolutely. Just let me know when."

He smiles so wide it almost takes over his entire face and throws his arms around my neck. "Thank you."

I pat his back, gently trying to prompt some release from his death grip. "No problem."

After I hit the shower, I arrive back to an empty dorm room and decide it's time to try out Skype again. I text him and by some stroke of luck, Gus is available. Rook is back in L.A. again. They recorded the entire month of July, and they've been summoned back to approve album artwork and prepare for their tour, which is tentatively scheduled to kick off at the end of September. After the release of the album, the label is hoping to get some immediate radio play to hype them up and encourage a successful tour. Sounds easy, right? It's going to be a stressful month, and if there's one thing that makes Gus crazy, it's stress. I'm already worried about him.

A warm rush of crazy happiness floods through my veins when I see his goofy smile light up my laptop screen. "Long time no talk, Bright Side. What up?"

"Hey, Gus. You first, how's it going in L.A.?" Even though we text each other a few times every day, I always want to catch up on details.

"Dude, it's been fucking exhausting." Looking closer, I can see dark shadows under his eyes.

"Yeah, you look like hell. When's the last time you slept?"

He yawns and thinks for a moment. "Thursday night was the last full night's sleep I got." The band got the call early Friday morning that they needed to be in L.A. by noon. So they packed up their cars and Gus's pickup and headed out. They've been in the studio since Friday afternoon working with their producer, going over the final cuts of all the songs. (Well, at least what used to be the final cuts.) This is the first they've seen daylight since.

"Dude, you need to get some rest, like ASAP."

"This from Mother Trucker who drives halfway across the US of

A without sleep?" He raises an eyebrow. "I'm a big boy, Bright Side, I'll manage. I do feel spent, though."

"I bet. So is everything wrapped up with MFDM?" The first time they met their producer in July, he introduced himself as the Dream Maker. Gus ran with it and after calling him DM for about a week, he christened him the Motherfucking Dream Maker. The dude was thrilled; Gus has had him wrapped around his little finger ever since.

"Yeah. We finally finished about a half hour ago. I mean I'm proud of it, but damn, these past few days have been brutal. Choosing the songs is like lining up your kids in front of a fucking firing squad. We all have a say, but MFDM makes the final call." He runs his fingers through his hair and pulls it back into a ponytail. He's frustrated. Five, four, three, two, one. "I need a smoke. Hold on." He picks up his laptop and starts walking, making the image on the screen jump and jiggle like a bad home movie.

"Dude, you're making me seasick."

"Sorry, Bright Side, I need to go out on the balcony to smoke."

The laptop comes to rest on a solid surface, and he's fishing through his pocket for his lighter, cigarette already between his lips.

"You should quit."

He smiles, cigarette held firmly between his teeth. "This is not the week I quit, or the month, or probably even the year with the way things are going, so don't start." He cups his left hand around the end of his cigarette and lights it. It flares to life, and he inhales like it's his last breath. After all the smoke is exhaled, he closes his eyes and slumps back against his chair.

"Better?"

He nods, eyes still closed, and takes another long drag.

"So, are you happy with the way the songs turned out?" I ask nervously.

He smiles sleepily, eyes still closed. "I'm happy." He means it.

I still don't know what songs made the cut and are going to be on the album. They recorded fifteen, but only eleven survived to thrive. Gus has insisted on secrecy up to this point. I think he's afraid he'll jinx it if he talks about it too much. Like he'll wake up and find out it was all a dream. "So, what made the cut? Can you tell me now?"

His eyes open and he smiles the smile that means he's really happy, like deep down in the pit of his stomach happy. "'Missing You.'"

I'm floored. "No shit?"

He's still smiling. "No shit. I didn't want to say anything earlier in case the song didn't work out, but when you were in the studio with us in July, MFDM went fucking bananas over you. He thought the violin was genius, *because it is*."

"Wow, that's...I don't know what to say...that's...amazing." I think back to July, recalling the experience in the studio. "He didn't act too jacked up about it while we were playing. I thought he was just yanking my chain when he said he liked it." I'm shocked. Gus wrote the song and told me it was a gift from me to Grace. It's one of the only ballads he's ever written. He wrote a part for violin and insisted I play on the song. I came out of retirement only for Grace. I went into the studio with the band and played, expecting it to end up on the cutting room floor somewhere. Which would have been fine, because simply playing in a studio was something I'll never forget. Another night, after everyone else had gone home, Gus coaxed me into singing with him just for fun on another song "Killing the Sun." This song is kind of their anthem at shows. Everyone sings along. It gives me chills every time I watch them perform it live. We sang it together, and once I even sang it alone. I'm not trained like Gus, but I like to sing, and I can carry a tune. We sing two-part harmonies pretty well. It was fun. He recorded and downloaded both songs for me, so I can say I had my rock star moment.

"Yeah, he was trying to play it cool in front of you, but the next day when we all listened to it again, he went apeshit. So thanks, you know, for being some kind of virtuoso." He winks as he stubs out his cigarette in an ashtray that's already overflowing. "Enough about the album, I don't want to talk about it right now. I want to hear the dish

on what's happening in the mighty metropolis of Grant. Fill me in."
He scoots his chair closer to the table.

"Okay, let's see, I'll make this short and sweet. I made two new friends, Clay and Pete. They live across the hall. My roommate Sugar—"

Gus interrupts. "Wait, hold up, your roommate's name is Sugar? As in nature's delicious sweetener?"

I nod. "Sugar Starr LaRue."

He throws his head back in laughter. "Oh shit, that's classic. What the fuck were her parents smoking?" He leans forward toward the screen. "Bright Side, tell me she's a stripper or...or an escort or something?" His eyes look bright and curious.

I clap my hands together and laugh. "That's what I said!" I shake my head, serious again. "She's not."

"Dude, that would've been fucking righteous. You know you just got robbed of some killer stories?"

"I know. I'm kind of sad about it myself. I still may end up with some good stories, though, because she is built for the profession and this morning she left for the day wearing a see-through white tank top sans bra."

He raises his eyebrows. "Damn, what's your address again? I may have to come for a visit sooner than later."

"Perv."

He shrugs. "Guilty. I'm a guy, it's embedded. So, what else? What about these two guys across the hall?"

"Clayton and Peter?"

"Yeah. What are they like? Do I need to be worried about your virtue?"

I roll my eyes. "Dude, you know that ship sailed years ago. But, um yeah, there's a better chance of hell freezing over than me getting it on with either of them."

"Why do you say that?" he says, looking almost hopeful.

"Well, Clay and I play for the same team, and I think Pete is one of those people who will either be a forty-year-old virgin or he's kinky as hell and into some weird shit but uses his super uptight persona as a front, so no one suspects it. Any way you slice it, I'm out."

Gus nods and smiles. "If I were a betting man, and you know I am, I'm gonna say Pete's a role-playing sex addict that gets off on S&M. Possibly bondage. Do you think he's the dom or the sub?"

I cover my ears and shake my head. "Eww, you know I'm going to picture Pete wearing only leather chaps and holding a riding crop every time I eat lunch with him now, right?"

He smiles wide. "You're welcome."

I stick out my tongue at him. "Bastard."

"Yup. So, your roommate's a clandestine stripper in training, and you've been hanging out with gay men and gimps. I had no idea Minnesota was so progressive. That's an impressive mix. Maybe I should've gone to school. What else? Tell me. Tell me." He's motioning his hands like bring it on.

I think for a moment. "I saw Maddie yesterday."

"Dude, don't tell me she got her food groups mixed up again, and you found yourself on the wrong end of the food pyramid. Second round of meat shits this week?"

"No, but food was involved. To tell you the truth, I'm a little freaked out."

"Freaked out? What happened?"

"Dude, she's bulimic."

His voice softens. "What?"

"Yeah. We went to breakfast. She ate like a champion and then ten minutes later, she's tossing it."

"Dude."

"I know. So, I walk in on her yodeling her breakfast. I confront her. She brushes me off. I appeal. She gets pissed. It was awful. I don't know what to do."

"Wow. She's pissed, huh?"

"Yeah, she totally deflected the intervention and asked me to leave."

"Shit."

"Yeah."

"What are you gonna do?"

"She's pissed. I'm going to let her cool off and then I'm going to try to talk to her again."

"Good luck."

"Thanks, I need it."

It's quiet for a few moments before Gus changes the subject. "Bright Side, do you have enough money, you know, for everything you need with school and food and—"

I interrupt. "I have a job."

"That's not what I asked."

"I'll be fine. Don't worry about me," I insist, even though I'm not sure it's true. I don't know what I'm in for during these next few months. My small savings may not last. I'll cross that bridge when I get there.

He huffs. "It's my job to worry about you. Do you need money? We got an advance on the album. I can send you whatever you need."

I smile. "Damn, what did I do to deserve you? Thanks, but no, I don't need any money."

"Would you tell me if you did?"

I shrug. "Probably not. I can handle it."

"Damn it, Bright Side. If you need anything, you call me, okay? I can afford it now. I know you and Grace had it pretty rough... God, I wished I'd known at the time. I guess I always thought your mom was loaded. I still feel bad about that. So, let me make up for it now. Let me help."

"You know how you can help me?"

His pained expression relaxes. "How?"

"You can wake up tomorrow morning, and the morning after that, and the morning after that, and work your ass off to make sure this album and tour are epic."

He smiles.

"Your new motto is this: *do epic*."

He laughs. "I can't *do* epic. It's an adjective. I can *be* epic."

"Look at you, Mr. Smarty Pants. You, my friend, can both *be* and *do*."

He grins and looks down with an embarrassed huff. "If you say so. That's a lot of pressure."

"I'm serious; you'd better blow my fucking mind."

"You're pushy tonight." He raises an eyebrow. "I like it. It's kinda hot."

I roll my eyes. "Whatever. That's the sleep deprivation talking. Go get some sleep, Rock God."

"Yeah, I should probably do that." He yawns. "Good luck with your first day of school tomorrow."

I throw my fist in the air. "I'm gonna live the motherfucking Grant College Experience!"

"That's the spirit." He laughs, but he looks a little confused like he's missed something.

I shrug. "I guess you had to be there."

"Apparently." He chuckles sleepily.

"Do epic."

"Do epic," he repeats.

"I love you, Gus."

"Love you, too, Bright Side."

"Good night."

"Good night."

MONDAY, AUGUST 29

KATE

THE FIRST DAY of classes is outstanding. I know I made fun of *The Grant College Experience*, but I had goose bumps all day. *I was living it.* I walked around campus with the dopiest smile pasted across my face. For so long I've dreamed about going to college, a real college. I never thought it would happen, but here I am. I literally crossed it off my bucket list this afternoon. My list isn't in any particular order, but "Go to college" was number five. I figure now is a good time to remind God that I'm happy with the way things are going. *Happy Monday, God. So, I just wanted to say thanks, you know, for Grant. It's a gift. Peace out.*

Shelly is in full-blown flower-arranging mode when I arrive at Three Petunias at 2:30 pm, but she stops long enough to ask, "Where's your iPod? I brought my dock today. Let's see if you've got anything good."

"Is that a challenge?"

"Take it however you want." It's a challenge all right. And suddenly I feel the need to defend my music's honor. I fish my iPod out of my bag, hook it up, and put it on shuffle.

The first song that plays is Mozart. Shelly pushes the button to advance to the next song and looks at me almost apologetically. "I play that stuff all day long. I love it, but I need to listen to something else when I'm at work."

"No worries."

The next song rips through the speaker. I start dancing right there behind the counter, and Shelly watches me, nonplussed. "Come on, Shelly. Shake what your mama gave ya."

She shakes her head. It's adamant.

My feet stop moving, but the rest of my body cannot stop. "What? Don't tell me you don't dance?"

She shakes her head again, and she's blushing. Damn, that's something I never thought I'd see.

"Well, we have to do something about that," I smile playfully. "You know I'm gonna get you out dancing before the end of the semester, don't you?" This girl needs to do something she's never done before, something out of character. Suddenly that becomes my new goal.

The blush is fading, and she shakes her head again to add conviction to her declaration. "I *do not* dance, Kate."

"And I think your inner dancing queen wants to be set free. She's screaming, Shelly. I can hear her, and she's pissed. Next time Clayton throws a rave in his room, I'm inviting you."

"A rave?"

"Okay, well, so it's minus the hordes of people and the drugs and the glow sticks, but it's still fun."

"And who's Clayton?"

"He's my neighbor. He lives across the hall."

She nods as I continue to sway my hips to the beat. She's demonstrating terrific restraint in the this-girl-is-entertaining-the-hell-out-of-me-but-I-can't-let-on department. "So, what you're saying is it's really just you and your friend, Clayton, dancing to your iPod in his dorm room."

I correct her. "*His* iPod, he's got some good shit. But, yeah, that's pretty much how it goes down."

She shakes her head, and a small but genuine smile emerges. It's the kind of smile that you give someone you like, someone who makes you happy. I have a feeling that Shelly doesn't hand these out too often. I feel honored. "Kate, you're too much."

Smiling, I dance back over to my station and get to work, toning down the dancing to mere head-bobbing; my body cannot be still when I'm listening to good music. It's like it runs through my veins and I physically can't disconnect from it.

Every few songs, when she thinks I'm not watching, Shelly leans over and glances at my iPod to read the screen. I smile discreetly. I have quite a bit of European music, and some of it isn't in English. I don't speak any of the languages: French, German, Dutch, so I have no clue what the lyrics mean. But it doesn't matter; the music is phenomenal even if I have no idea what they're singing about. One of those songs has just started.

She intentionally looks at the screen and then looks at me. "What the hell is this?"

"It's French hip-hop. You like?" I know she does, or she wouldn't be interested.

"It's all right." She grabs a piece of paper and a pencil and writes down the artist and song. I notice that she jots down six or seven other songs from memory. "Where do you find all this?"

"My best friend and I have been collecting music for a long time. It's kind of our hobby." I couldn't live without it.

When the next song begins, I ask, "So, Shelly, do you have a boyfriend?"

She nods, smiling a sweet, vulnerable smile. I think I just discovered the chink in her armor. She's whipped. "Yeah."

"Yeah? You're gonna want to write this one down. If an album was ever made specifically to fool around to, it's this one." Because it is. This band has a dark '80s vibe, and the frontwoman's voice is super sexy.

She writes it down. "The Boyfriend thanks you."

I smile and affirm, "Yeah, he does."

As the afternoon ambles on, Shelly randomly fires questions at me while we work. I guess she's decided my taste in music doesn't suck. This must be part two of the music challenge.

"Name your top three favorite female singers." Her eyes are narrow and twinkling. "And so help me God, if you say one damn pop princess, you're fired."

I laugh at the threat. I could answer this question in my sleep. "Top three? Number one: Romy Madley Croft from the xx. Number two: Alison Moyet from Yaz. And number three: Johnette Napolitano from Concrete Blonde. Honorable mention, because I've been listening to them a lot this week, goes to the chick from Royal Thunder. She can wail."

"How about best guitar player?"

"My best friend."

She looks doubtful. "All the great guitar players out there and you're going to say your best friend?"

I smile back. "Absolutely."

"Okay. Best bass player?"

"Easy. Silversun Pickups' Nikki Monninger. Her bass lines are wicked. Plus, she wears pretty dresses when she performs—so she's badass and classy at the same time. I like that."

"Best punk band?"

"Teenage Bottlerocket. Their live shows kick ass. So much fun to watch and the mosh pit is always raging."

"Most underrated band?"

"Hands down, Dredg."

"Who?"

"Exactly. It's a travesty. Dredg should be a household name."

"If you could meet any band or musician, who would it be?"

"I think it would be cool as shit to hang out with Dave Grohl. He seems so nice, humble. You know, just a normal dude. Except that he's crazy talented." Shelly smiles at this, and I smile back.

It's seven o'clock when she unplugs her dock and hands me my iPod. "Well Kate, I do believe I've found the ultimate dealer." Her list is in hand. "I've got to pick some of this up."

I appreciate the compliment. "I'm glad you liked it." I bow. "My job here is done."

She rolls her eyes. "You wanna grab some pizza tonight? The Boyfriend and his roommate and I are going over to Red Lion Road later for beer and pizza. We can pick you up." And just like that, Shelly's no longer intimidating. She doesn't take shit from anyone, but for some reason, she's warmed up to me. And the truth is, I like her, too.

"Dude, I'm sorry, but I can't. I've got homework, and I promised Clayton I'd eat with him tonight."

She smirks. "A date with the raver?"

"Nope. Just an evening of platonic fine dining at the cafeteria."

She pulls her apron over her head. "Well, you're no fun."

"I really am sorry, dude, thanks for asking. Another time, okay?" The truth is I don't have any extra money. I've got five dollars that needs to last until Friday when I get paid. That probably wouldn't even buy me a slice of pizza and the beer I'm not old enough to purchase. But I can't tell her that. I won't become the charity case. And the cafeteria is free. Besides, I can already taste the $1.57 cup of coffee from Grounds, the one I'll grab on my way to Literature tomorrow morning. Since the dorms don't allow coffee makers (even the Holy Grail), and the cafeteria coffee tastes like mud, my heart's set on that cup. I need those five dollars.

TUESDAY, AUGUST 30

KELLER

THE BELL on the door rings, and it's instinct to look. It's not so much a trained reaction as it is involuntary curiosity. Since Romero had an appointment early this morning, I'm working the coffee bar solo until he returns.

The first thing I notice about her is how utterly tiny she is. Then I notice her clothes, her whole look; she's not from around here. The third is the scowl on her face, pointed at the bell hanging from the door. I get the feeling she has history with this bell. She's the cutest thing I've seen in a long time. The kind of cute that makes you smile, even if you don't want to. As she approaches the counter, the scowl vanishes, replaced by the most genuine, sincere smile. Smiles aren't always happy, but hers is. It's open, content, and confident. She looks friendly in the most literal sense of the word, like you'd swear you've known her for years, and she knows all your secrets. And still likes you in spite of them.

After what I realize is an exaggerated pause on my part, I smile and offer my standard greeting, "Welcome to Grounds. What can I get for ya?" I realize that I sound much more excited than usual, and I clear my throat.

Her smile deepens, like she knows this is out-of-character for me, and when it hits her eyes, they smile, too. They're the palest shade of jade and tell a story all their own. Then it hits me how beautiful this woman is. Like a freight train it hits me; from her eyes to her smile, to her wavy sunshine blonde hair, to her petite but exceptionally well-proportioned body. Everything about her is beautiful.

Her magical eyes and mouth are still smiling at me. "Good morning."

Her voice is so sexy. I can't explain the sound, but it lands somewhere deep inside me and takes root. It's the kind of voice you don't hear as much as you feel. And as soon as I feel it, I want to feel it again...and again. I find myself trying to match her smile. The right corner of my mouth pulls up. "Good morning to you." I may be losing my mind, but I don't want this time with her to end too fast. So I flirt. Which I haven't done in such a long time. "Let me guess, caramel cappuccino, soy, no whip?"

Her brows crease a little and her head delicately tilts slightly to one side, but her smile doesn't fade. "So, are you pretty good at this? Guessing people's orders, I mean?"

I can't help this feeling. I want to be closer to this woman standing four feet from me on the other side of the counter. So I lean forward, lace my fingers together, and rest my elbows on the counter. Mission accomplished: I'm another foot closer. She has a faint dusting of freckles on her nose. They're beautiful, too. "Usually." Which is a lie. I've never done this.

She scratches her head like she's thinking over what I've said. When she pulls her hand away from her hair, it's even messier than before. That's not a bad thing. *At all.* She challenges me. "So, I'm a caramel whatcha-ma-call-it kind of girl? Damn, I don't know how to take that."

I keep my elbows and hands resting on the counter. I'd worry I just offended her if her smile wasn't back in place. But she seems feisty. "That's my best guess."

"Wow," she replies. "To tell you the truth, I feel a little slighted by your presumptuous assessment, but I'm gonna let it slide. I always thought I wore my passion for coffee on my sleeve, kind of like a badge of honor. Large cup of coffee, house blend. Black, please."

Black? She can't mean it, no one ever does. They mean black *until you put everything else in it.* I narrow my eyes. "Flavor shot?"

Her eyebrows lift. "Nope."

I press on. "Creamer? Milk? Soy?"

She shakes her head. "No, thanks."

"Sugar?"

"Nah, I'm sweet enough already."

Out of anyone else's mouth, that would've sounded cheesy and over-the-top flirtatious, but she says it so matter-of-factly I don't think she's even trying to be suggestive. *Damn,* she's got me falling all over myself here. I laugh and shake my head. "I bet you are." I pour the coffee, then offer her the warm cup. I almost jump out of my skin when she takes it and her finger slides over mine. It was clearly unintentional on her part, but I have to suppress a vocal reaction. I clear my throat again and attempt to sound normal. "Guess I had you pegged wrong. Welcome to the club."

As she hands me two dollar bills, she winks. "I get that a lot."

She winked at me. I'm grateful at this moment that I'm standing concealed from the waist down behind this counter, because I'm way too close to embarrassing myself on such a middle school level. I drop the change in her tiny open palm, because I can't risk physical contact again.

She immediately drops it in the tip jar and hoists her coffee in the air. "Thanks. Have a stupendous Tuesday."

Who says stupendous? She does. It may be my new favorite word. "Stupendous," I repeat. I can't stop smiling at her. It's like she's turned on this switch inside me. "You do the same." I offer a lazy salute. It's a habit I've picked up from working with Romero so long.

I glance at the clock. It's only 6:55 am, and this has already been a *stupendous* day.

What in the hell just happened? I feel like I've been asleep for years and I've only just woken up.

WEDNESDAY, AUGUST 31

KATE

I'VE BEEN in Clayton and Pete's room for the past two hours. We all talked the first hour and then Clayton suggested, "Let's play *Fatally Harm, Screw, Civil Union.*"

I look at Pete to see if he has any clue what Clayton's talking about, but he looks as confused as I am, and then it hits me. "Dude, I am *not* playing *Kill, Fuck, Marry.*"

Clayton looks astonished I'd deny him. "It sounds so obnoxious when you say it like that. Why not?"

I roll my eyes. "I haven't played that since I was like fifteen."

Pete's still confused. "What's *Kill, Fu—*" He can't even say the word. He's definitely never played this game.

Now I'm smiling because Pete's innocence is too damn adorable. "Clayton," I shift my gaze to meet his eager eyes, "John, our dorm RA; Hector, the dude who works in the cafeteria; and Sugar, my roommate."

His smile fades. "For God's sake, Katherine, those options are horrific."

I smile and taunt, "You're the one who wanted to play. And Hector's not horrific. He's super nice."

"How do you even know he's nice?"

"I talk to him every night when I drop my dirty dishes off in the cafeteria washroom."

"What you two do isn't talking. It's a sad combination of Spanglish and charades."

"He's teaching me Spanish. I'm teaching him English," I defend.

He smirks. "What has he taught you?"

I laugh because I know I'm caught. Hector's English is extremely limited and what we do *is* closer to charades than a verbal conversation, but we give it our best effort. I puff up my chest. "I know 'Mi nombre es Kate' and 'Como estas' and 'gato.' And 'Ami no me gustan las zanahorias,' which means 'Carrots taste like shit.'"

Pete looks skeptical. "He taught you how to say, 'Carrots taste like crap?'"

I wave my hand dismissively. "It probably means 'I don't like carrots,' but I prefer 'Carrots taste like shit.' Because they do." I eyeball Clayton, who's now squirming. "Back to the game Clay: John, mi amigo Hector, and Sugar. Break it down."

Pete still hasn't caught on.

Clayton sighs. "Fatally harm has to be Sugar, because I can't work with her any other way." He pauses. "The other two are making me nauseous."

"Play your cards, dude."

He covers his eyes, and I glance and see the recognition registering in Pete's eyes. His cheeks are the distinct shade of utterly embarrassed. Clayton sputters, "Screw John because he's just too mean to spend the rest of my life with and Civil Union Hector, even though I don't speak a word of Spanish, and his hairnet, baggy, acid-wash jeans, and white, clunky, old-man sneakers are atrocious." He can't get the words out quickly enough and crosses his arms over his chest in a pouty gesture. "I'm done playing."

I clap and laugh at the disgusted look on his face. "That was classic, Clayton." Pete looks uncomfortable as hell like he's afraid he's up next, so I switch gears. "Okay, new game."

I proceeded to make up a new game where one person comes up with a question and then we all have to go around the circle and answer it. I learned that Pete was born in Texas, but grew up in Omaha, Nebraska. His favorite food is rare steak with sautéed garlic and mushrooms, his favorite childhood toy was a microscope (is that a toy?), and he'd rather have his little toe cut off with hedge clippers than walk across campus naked. And Clayton's favorite book is *Lord of the Rings*, and he despises dogs—especially small ones. He competed in figure skating as a kid (I would have paid money to have seen that), and he would have no problem walking naked across campus as opposed to losing a toe, as long as he could wear thigh-high red socks and his black patent knee-high combat boots (I have to admit that's a statement I'd like to see).

After Pete went to sleep an hour ago, Clayton and I worked on homework. But now my eyes don't want to stay open anymore.

I close my European history book and whisper, "Clayton, you really know how to show a girl a good time, but I think I'd better retire. I'm beat."

"Okay, honey. I better get a little beauty sleep, too."

I throw my bag over my shoulder. "Night, Clayton."

"Good night, Katherine." He blows me a kiss from where he's sitting crisscross applesauce on the floor.

I blow a kiss back and shuffle across the hall. I notice the red ribbon tied to the doorknob, but unfortunately, it doesn't signal a warning in my sleepy head until it's too late. It all happens so quickly. All I see are a tangle of legs and bare butt cheeks. And then the moans are interrupted by aggressive cursing.

"What the fuck?" Sugar yells. She's trying to scream at me, but she's breathless, clearly in the middle of a fairly aerobic session here. "Get the hell out of here, you bitch!"

The scene, *and the red ribbon*, finally registers. "Oh shit. Sorry, dude." I pull the door behind me quickly. My heart is racing. I'm wide awake now. I head down the hall and use the bathroom, where I splash some water on face and weigh my options. Should I wait her out, or should I sleep somewhere else? I head back down to Clayton's room and knock softly. The adrenaline rush has worn off, and I feel sleepy again. Clayton answers the door, already in his pajamas. They're burgundy silk.

"Did you forget something, Katherine?"

"No. Dude, first things first, when did you turn into Hugh Hefner? Those pajamas are fantastic."

He smiles and curtsies. "Thank you."

I motion with my thumb over my shoulder to my door. "Um, yeah, so Sugar's riding the baloney pony and I totally just walked in on them. Do you mind if I room with you tonight?"

He throws the door open. "Of course not, Katherine." He glances across the hall at my door. "Didn't you see the ribbon tied to the doorknob?"

I shake my head and whisper because I don't want to wake Pete. "I know, I know. I guess I was tired. I wasn't thinking. Besides, we never discussed the signal for *don't interrupt me, I'm having wild monkey sex.*"

Clayton climbs into his twin bed and pulls the covers back. "Come on, Katherine. We're small, there's plenty of room."

"Oh no, Clayton, I'll just crash here on the floor."

He motions for me. "Nonsense, come on." He winks. "You're absolutely lovely, but you're not my type."

I smile and crawl in. "Thanks, Clayton. You're the best. Good night."

He kisses me on the cheek. "Good night, Katherine."

I've shared a bed with someone almost my entire life. I didn't realize until now, but I've kind of missed it. This is nice.

THURSDAY, SEPTEMBER 1

KATE

WHAT IS IT ABOUT COFFEE? It's the perfect beverage. It warms me, body and soul. And it makes me insanely happy. Even the thunderous bell doesn't faze me this morning. I've decided to make peace with it since I know it cannot be outsmarted or reasoned with. I tried a medium push on the door just to be sure. Still loud as hell.

It's early, and Romero offers me his usual salute. "Good morning, Kate," he says while I take my place at the end of the short line.

While I'm waiting, the guy who was working Tuesday walks out from the back room. And yeah, he's still *astounding* to look at. He doesn't see me yet, but I watch as he draws an apron over his head and haphazardly ties it in the back.

He looks older than I am, but I'm guessing he's a student since he works here. He's average height, lean, and wiry but looks strong as hell—I can see the contours of the muscles in his triceps and shoulders—and unassumingly confident. It's confidence that I'm guessing is rooted deep down, but that fails him on a fairly regular basis. I would also wager that no one notices when it wavers because he's so good at covering up his vulnerability with his likable personality. And it's not over-the-top, in-your-face likable. It's subtle. The kind of likable that lures you in and before you know it, you've bought the ticket, boarded the bus, and are miles into the pleasant journey before you question where you're even going in the first place.

And luckily, this journey comes with spectacular scenery. His hair is messy like he's just rolled out of bed and so dark brown it's almost black—just like the stubble on his face. And oh my God, his face. He has this baby face that you just know lets him get away with murder. Not that it's innocent, it's just a face that I'm positive no one could say no to. All that aside, the most striking thing about him are his eyes. They're light blue, aquamarine even. The fact that they're rimmed by these thick, long, black lashes makes them look so intense and deep you feel like you could fall right into them. Overall, he's just ridiculously good-looking.

He greets Romero with a deep, friendly, "Morning, Rome," and turns to help the next person in line, which—as dumb luck would have it—is me.

Silently, I throw out a *Thank you, God. The man standing before me is a staggering specimen. Excellent work. Later,* before looking up at those blue, blue eyes.

One side of his mouth turns up into a crooked smile. "Ahh, the expatriate returns." Up close his eyes are even brighter than I remember, and they twinkle. He could be all kinds of trouble for me. Good thing I'm just looking.

I smile in return, because I can't help it. "Expatriate?"

"Yeah, you're definitely not from around here."

Romero glances at us while he steams milk at the espresso machine. "Kate is from California." It comes out as five words again: CALL EE FOR NEE UH.

"Ahh, California. I was right; not from around here." Coffee God looks from me to Romero and back again before his eyes land on Romero. "Kate? You two are on a first-name basis? Throw me a bone here Rome, how about an introduction, man?"

Romero laughs, and his shoulders bounce. "Keller Banks, this is Kate Sedgwick. Kate Sedgwick, this is Keller Banks." He looks to Keller. "And she likes the coffee *black*."

Keller smiles. "I recall that, Rome. She's in the club." He turns his attention to me and extends his hand. "It's nice to officially meet you, Katie."

I accept his hand. It's warm, and his fingertips are calloused where they meet the back of my hand. His grip is strong but oddly gentle, inviting even. I don't want to let go, but I do. "Likewise, Keller. And it's just Kate."

He smiles his crooked smile and nods. "Large, black house blend?"

"Yup. Today's not the day to go breaking tradition—" My mind drifts to Clayton's ecstasy-inducing mocha macchiato. "—or testing theories." I'm hot enough just standing here looking at Keller Banks.

His eyebrows rise in question as he presses the lid on my coffee cup and hands it to me. "Testing theories?"

I shake my head as I hand him my money. "It's nothing." I bite my bottom lip trying to subdue the smile that wants badly to erupt.

The smile returns to his face as if he can read my mind. "Let me know if I can assist you with testing any theories." He places his elbows on the counter and leans down so we're eye to eye and drops his voice. "I can be *extremely* helpful." He slides my change across the counter.

My heart rate increases to a mad pounding in my chest. I hope it doesn't show as I drop the coins in the tip jar. God, it's like he knows there's some sort of hidden sexual reference, or maybe he's just this flirtatious with all girls. I raise my cup to him and smile. "I bet you can, Keller Banks. *I bet you can.* Have an outstanding day."

He doesn't take his eyes off me. He doesn't even blink. "Outstanding indeed. You too, Katie."

My insides are still buzzing as I walk outside. Holy hell, is it bad that I innocently walk in for a cup of coffee and walk out wondering what the guy behind the counter looks like naked? And how he is in bed? I take a deep breath. I even let him call me Katie.

Goddamn.

FRIDAY, SEPTEMBER 2

KATE

Gus and I have been getting by for several days on just daily texts or two-minute phone calls while he's on smoke breaks. His schedule has been brutal. They've only been back to the apartment for a few hours every night to grab some sleep and then back at it all over again. So I'm shocked when I get a text while I'm at the cafeteria dining with Clayton and Pete. It says, *Wanna Skype?*

I text back, *HELL YES! Give me 15.*

I excuse myself and run back to the dorms to boot up my laptop.

That familiar rush of happiness stirs when I see his face on the screen. He looks exhausted, but content. "Hola, señorita bonita."

"Como esta, dude?"

"I'm good, Bright Side, I'm good. You?"

"Fantastic. What's happening in the world of rock and roll these days? You gonna tell me which other songs made the album or what? How long do I have to wait? My patience has reached its limit."

Gus is out on the balcony, and he already has a lit cigarette in his hand. No wonder he looks so calm. He smiles. "You ready?"

I'm bouncing in my chair. "Yeah, I'm ready! You're killing me here. Dude, I've been waiting, like, my whole life, forever, to hear this news. Spill it." And because I haven't said it yet, I point to the cigarette on my laptop screen. "Oh, and you should quit." I'm so excited about everything else that it doesn't sound convincing at all.

He just smiles. And then he runs through the list.

I'm mentally ticking them off in my mind as he names them. I'm so stoked. "Dude, I have to tell you something."

He looks worried. "What?"

"This *is* going to be the greatest album of all time. I hope you're prepared to get crazy rich and famous, move to your own private island when you're not touring, marry a new supermodel every couple of years, own a pet lion, and live on whiskey and heroin."

He laughs. "Bright Side, you make it sound so glamorous. You promise that's how it's gonna be?" I love it when he's sarcastic.

"Definitely, though if you want a monkey instead of a lion, or vodka instead of whiskey, hey, knock yourself out. You're the master of your rock and roll universe."

He laughs even harder. "I knew I wasn't in this for the music, not when there's this whole world of debauchery out there."

"I think debauchery and day to day are synonymous in the Rock God world. You say poh-tay-toh; I say poh-tah-toh."

"Oh, you know me, Bright Side, even if by some stroke of luck we have some degree of success with this, I'll still probably live with Ma, surf every minute I can, and live on veggie tacos and cigarettes."

I smile because he's right, even if he were a multi-billionaire, that's probably exactly how he'd live. He's grounded and down to earth. Money means nothing to him. That's probably why we get along so well. People are our priority. I love that about him. "Seriously, I am *so* fucking proud of you. When do I get to hear it?"

"I'm hoping I can get my hands on something next week to send to you, but you have to promise not to bullshit me. I need honest criticism."

I raise my right hand. "I solemnly swear not to bullshit you."

He smiles. "That's my girl." Followed by a pause. "Dude, I was listening to 'Missing You' today, and I was wondering if, you know, if you've given any thought to playing your violin again?"

I shake my head. "Nope, honestly I don't really miss it. That's kind of sad, huh? Maybe someday I will. Who knows? I just can't right now." It reminds me of Grace too much. It hurts too much.

"Okay." His voice is sad. "It's just that the world's a more beautiful place when you play. That's all I'm saying." He pauses and when I don't speak, he continues. "What's happening in your world? How's school, work, the stripper, the gimp?"

I'm relieved by the topic change, and I laugh. "School's great—I still can't believe I'm actually here. And work's rad. You'd love the girl I work with, Shelly. She's kind of angry on the outside and sweet on the inside."

"Right on. Sounds like my kind of girl."

"The stripper is, well, the stripper is, how shall I put this politely?"

"Politely? Shit, that's never stopped you before. Give it to me."

"The stripper has a fairly active sex life. In our dorm room. I witnessed it firsthand."

"Firsthand? Minnesota is turning you into some sort of sexual deviant. You watched? Next, you're gonna tell me you're making pornos with the gimp across the hall."

"Dude, I walked in on her. I was fucking mortified. She swears like a champion, even mid-thrust."

He tips his chair back he's laughing so hard. "No way! That's too funny."

"Yeah, well, not so funny when I'm the jackass marching in on her. And another thing, correct me if I'm wrong, but when you go to some chick's place for a horizontal workout, you don't stick around to snuggle it out the rest of the night, right?"

He's still laughing. "Dude, that's One-Night Stand 101. You get your ass out of there as soon as the deed is done." He stops laughing. "Wait. Back the bus up. Where did you spend the night while she was playing sleepover?"

"Oh, Clayton let me sleep with him."

His face is suddenly deadly serious. "Whoa, is Clayton the gay neighbor or the leather-clad perv?"

"Clayton is definitely one hundred percent attracted to men."

He's taken on this fatherly tone, "Bright Side, you can't just crash in a room with two dudes you just met."

"Gus, they're completely harmless. Baby kittens are scarier than these two."

He runs his fingers through his hair and pulls it back into a pony-tail; he's getting frustrated with me. He always plays with his hair when he's frustrated. "Bright Side, listen to me, you have no idea how fucking gorgeous you are or the effect you have on guys. They want to get in your panties the instant they see you. And then they fucking fall in love with you after they spend five minutes with you." He huffs. I know another cigarette is coming any second now. "All I'm saying is you have to be careful, all right?"

I roll my eyes. "Exaggerate much? Gus, you're talking to Kate Sedgwick, remember? I don't date. And I know how to ward off unwanted advances."

He shakes his head. "You couldn't ward off a rape, Bright Side. You weigh a hundred pounds soaking wet. Just please promise me that you'll be safe and watch out for yourself. If some son of a bitch forced himself on you...*fuck*. I'd have to come to Minnesota and commit murder, and I'm pretty sure prison isn't in MFDM's game plan."

"Gus—"

He interrupts. "You're going to get a lot of attention up there. Guys are going to be throwing themselves at you. Be selective, because you deserve so much more than some random dude fucking you in the back of a van or your best friend in his mom's guest room."

That about sums up my sexual past. There have only been a few guys and I *was* selective. I'm not a slut, I was opportunistic. Once and done, no strings attached, no apologies. I enjoyed all of them. But Gus was different. He wasn't planned, but he's also far from random.

And this is somehow now about him. "Gus." I wish he wouldn't do this. He's vilifying himself.

"No, Bright Side, listen, you are *so* special. You deserve someone who takes you out on real dates. Someone who buys you flowers and shit. Because if there's anyone in this world who's capable of insane amounts of love and who deserves to be loved that way in return, it's you."

I shake my head. "I don't do hearts and flowers, Gus."

"When you find the right guy, you will. You just haven't found him yet." His voice sounds sad.

Life has never afforded me time or opportunity to date. Friends and family have always been my priorities, and I've loved them with my whole heart. Guys, sex, they were just a physical attraction, a physical act. With Gus it was more, it was love, but it wasn't *love*. *Love* is an elusive, unrealistic, foreign concept. I know some people feel it, and it's not that I'm hardened. I'm an optimist, but first and foremost, I'm a realist. My life will not follow a fairy tale, and that's okay. My life is reality. And in my reality, people don't fall in love and get married and live happily ever after, because life is complicated. And messy. I'm happy knowing that fairy tales exist out there for people, like Shelly. (Shelly would probably kick my ass if she knew I put her name and fairy tale in the same sentence.)

This time, I hold my finger up to interrupt the moment. "Hold on a sec." I stand and walk across the hall and knock on Clayton and Pete's door, because right now I need to make Gus feel better.

Pete answers. "Hi, Kate."

"Hey, Pete. Can you and Clay come over to my room? It'll only take a sec."

Pete looks at Clayton who's concealed behind the door. Clayton's voice chimes in. "Sure thing, honey."

They follow me across the hall. Gus's head is resting against the back of his chair, and his eyes are closed. He's halfway through a cigarette. He's concentrating so hard on the calm that's filtering through him that he doesn't hear me re-enter the room.

"Wakey, wakey, sleeping beauty."

He smiles before he opens his eyes.

"I want to introduce you to two friends of mine." I step aside so Gus can see Clayton and Peter.

Gus smiles as he takes them in. He's clearly not as concerned for my safety anymore. They are the two least threatening guys you'll ever meet, and I'm fairly sure that resonates loud and clear, even across a computer screen. "What's up, dudes?"

Clayton waves and his cheeks flush. "Hello." Oh shit, I may have just witnessed love at first sight. Gus isn't wearing a shirt, and he does look really good. Clayton's practically hyperventilating. I feel like I should get him a paper bag or administer CPR. Does our dorm have a defibrillator?

Peter raises his left hand but looks confused and terrified at the same time. "Hi."

I intercede and point to the screen. "This is my best friend, Gus Hawthorne. Gus, these are my Minnesota friends, Clayton and Peter."

Clayton and Peter look panicked. I guess Gus is kind of intimidating. He's tall and broad and muscular. And has this presence that's intimidating, even on a computer screen. And when guys are as good-looking as Gus is, people seem either to want to challenge them, flirt with them, or cower in fear. Clay and Pete are definitely cowering, even though Clay still looks smitten. I guess Clayton and Peter don't know it yet, but Gus is a big teddy bear.

Clayton and Pete suddenly trip over their words and talk over one another, saying, "It's nice to meet you," and, "It's a pleasure to meet you." They're both so formal.

Gus smiles, and I know he's about to laugh, but he's trying so hard to be polite. "Nice to meet you two as well."

I clap my hands. "Okay, awesome, everyone knows each other. We're all one big happy family." I look at Gus. "Are you happy now?"

He's wearing the biggest shit-eating grin. "You have no idea."

I look back at Clayton and Pete. "Thanks for coming to meet Gus. I'll be over as soon as I'm off this call."

They both nod, speechless.

Gus is loving this. "You guys have a stellar evening and take care of my girl, okay?"

They nod in unison again, mouths slightly open, and follow each other back to their room, one looking just as confused as the other. Pete's in awe and Clayton probably has a raging hard-on. Gus has this effect on people.

Gus claps his hands and bursts out laughing when he hears the door click shut. "Oh Christ, Bright Side, not that you don't need to be on your guard, but you're safe as houses with those two. I'm telling you, Pete is definitely not into role-playing or S&M, but goddamn if I couldn't stop myself from picturing the dude in leather chaps like you said. That's some funny shit."

I try not to laugh, but I can't help myself. Gus's laugh is infectious. "I told you."

"Seriously, though, they did seem decent."

"That's because they are. They're good dudes."

He smiles and nods. Then we're quiet for several seconds.

"Thanks for worrying about me, though," I muster. "It's kinda nice to know there's someone out there who gives a shit. So thanks."

"Anytime. It's my mission in life, to give a shit."

I smile.

He smiles.

"Well, Bright Side, I'm gonna let you go for tonight. It's been awesome, possum."

"Always. And likewise."

"I love you, Bright Side."

"Love you, too, Gus."

"Good night."

"Good night."

I shut down my laptop and head across the hall. The door's been left open for me, so I walk right in.

"Sorry if that was weird, but thanks. Gus was a little freaked out about me sleeping in your room, so I wanted him to meet you guys so he'd get off my ass about it."

Clayton is lying on his bed fanning himself with a magazine. His cheeks are still red. "Katherine, why didn't you tell me you're dating Adonis?"

"He's pretty cute, huh, Clayton?"

"Cute? He's magnificent."

"He's not my boyfriend. He's my best friend."

Pete pipes up, "Why did he say 'take care of my girl' then?"

I shake my head. "I don't know, Pete. He always calls me that; it's like a term of endearment."

Clayton raises his eyebrows and wiggles them. "It certainly is. Listen, I don't know what's going on between the two of you, but you are batshit crazy if you let that one get away."

"Batshit crazy?"

He nods. "Bat. Shit. Crazy."

SUNDAY, SEPTEMBER 4

KATE

I TEXT Maddie and hope she isn't pissed at me anymore. I'm worried about her, and I let her know.

She never replies.

I guess she's still pissed.

I'll give her some more time and try again later.

MONDAY, SEPTEMBER 5

KATE

CLAYTON'S WAITING outside the cafeteria for me at 7:30 pm as planned. I just got off work, and I'm running late as usual. He loops his arm through my elbow as we walk through the door. "Katherine, have I told you lately how much I love you?"

I eye him suspiciously. "No... What's up?"

He lowers his voice to a whisper. "I found a club in Minneapolis that has an under twenty-one night."

I rub my hands together. "Sweet! When are we going?"

He grimaces but tries to look hopeful. "Tonight?"

I shrug. "Okay, what time do we leave?"

He stops and spins me to face him. "Do you mean it?"

"Well, yeah. I told you I'd go with you, didn't I?"

He pulls me into the tightest hug and lifts me slightly off the ground. I honestly didn't think he had the strength. I don't think either one of us breaks one hundred pounds. "Oh Katherine, I really do love you. You're the best."

"Oh, Clay. Hey, do you mind if my friend Shelly comes?"

He claps his hands. "The more, the merrier."

I call Shelly while Clayton and I are eating.

"Hey, *dude*." She sounds sarcastic, but I think she secretly loves using the word. I'll convert her yet.

"You doing anything tonight?"

"No, why?"

"Good. My friend Clayton and I are going dancing, and you're coming with us."

"You want *me* to go dancing?"

"Yup."

"I'm not really in the mood for a pretend rave in Clayton's dorm room."

"No, we're going out, like to a real club."

"Where?"

"A place called Spectacle. It's in Minneapolis."

"Kate, that's a gay club."

"Yeah, I know." It's quiet so long I think she's fallen asleep or set the phone down and walked away. "Shelly?"

"It's a *gay* club." She repeats.

"Yeah?" *And?*

"We're straight, Kate."

"I'm aware."

Silence.

"They don't bar vaginas at the door, Shelly. It'll be fun. Come on. *Please?*"

"I don't know." I can hear it in her voice, she's about to give in.

"Shelly, your inner dancing queen is planning an all-out revolution if you say no. I don't want that kind of drama for you. We're picking you up at nine-thirty."

"Oh hell," I can hear her eyes roll through the phone. But then, with a huff, she gives in. "Okay."

Back at the dorms, I spend more than an hour lying on Clay's bed watching him try on outfits. He's more anxious than I've ever seen him.

"Put the gray pants on again." I need to help him out, or we'll never get out of here. He's worse than Gus.

With the gray pants on, he twirls in a circle.

"Wear those. Your ass looks great."

He smiles and agrees, "I do have a nice backside."

"Damn right you do," I say. I roll off the bed and head toward my room. "Speaking of hot pants, I need to go change, too."

"What are you wearing?" he asks as he pulls a new shirt over his head.

"Oh, I don't know, probably just my black jeans."

He gasps. "Jeans? You're wearing jeans? Don't you have a minidress or something?"

I laugh. "Honey, first of all, I'm going with you to a *gay men's club.* I sort of have the wrong plumbing to garner any attention. Besides, everyone's going to be looking at your hot ass in those pants. And I definitely can't compete with drag queens. They're gorgeous. So, my part in this evening is to go with Shelly as the straight friends, the only women in the place without penises. I'm going to dance my ass off and have the best night Minneapolis has to offer."

"Will you at least wear heels? Oh, and something sparkly on top? Do you have anything with sequins? If not, I can let you borrow something."

I love his enthusiasm. "I've got it covered," I smile as I walk toward my room.

I return a few minutes later in my tight black jeans, black heels, and a low-cut black, sequined tank top. Gus calls this outfit "Johnny Cash chic" because it's all black. Clayton squeals when he sees me. "Oh my stars, your chest looks amazing."

I can't help but laugh as I look down at my cleavage. That's the first time it's garnered a genuine compliment completely devoid of any sexual motive or innuendo. "You can never underestimate the power of a good push-up bra, my friend."

We pick up Shelly, and I speed off toward Minneapolis. By the time we get to Spectacle and find a place to park, it's almost ten o'clock.

Clay pries his fingers from my dashboard and clears his throat.

"Katherine, I'm going to preface this by saying that you know I adore you." He clears his throat again. "But that was the most frightening car ride I've ever experienced."

I look at Shelly in the backseat, where she nods in agreement. Her huge, unblinking, dark eyes are fixed on me, and her breath is shallow. "Kate, I don't scare easily, but that was fucking terrifying. I think I pissed myself."

I shrug at the overexaggeration. "What do you mean?"

"I don't know if the speed limit in California is ninety-five miles an hour, because I realize you guys probably do things a little different there, but it's only sixty-five here, which is about how fast you take fucking corners."

I look from Clay to Shelly and back again. They're both nodding, wide-eyed and pale. I hold up my right hand and close my eyes. "I promise to slow it down a little on the way home."

"And use turn signals," adds Clayton.

"And use turn signals," I promise. And then I throw a question silently to God, *Why didn't you tell me I'm a shitty driver? Is California just full of shitty drivers? I didn't think I was so bad. I've never been in an accident. Anyway, thanks for not letting me kill anyone, I guess. Later.*

The line is long out front. They're checking IDs at the door, and Shelly gets a wristband since she's twenty-two. I get a big black X on the back of my hand. The music inside is loud; the bass is thumping deep in my chest. The lights are flashing, and the dance floor is already packed. I'm itching to get out there.

"Come on, Shelly, let's dance!"

She gives me a look and points to the bar behind us. "Oh no, I need some liquid courage first. There's no way in hell I'm going out there sober. You two go ahead."

Clayton takes my hand, and we walk to the edge of the dance floor and stop there so we can keep an eye on Shelly. The music hums through me. I love this feeling. More people pile in, and before long, we're pressed against each other moving to the rhythm of the music. We both know the song, and we're singing every single word. Clayton looks so happy amongst this sea of beautiful men.

Clayton and I dance our way through a few more songs before I notice a guy right next to us, eyeing Clay from behind. He's handsome: medium height with skin the color of dark chocolate. His head is shaved bald, emphasizing his majestic, chiseled face. He catches my eye and raises his eyebrows toward Clayton, as if he's asking permission. I smile and nod my head. He taps Clayton on the shoulder. Clayton turns away from me and before I know it, I've been abandoned for Mr. Cheekbones. I shrug. That's why we're here. Besides, I've watched Shelly throw back two shots and a beer. It's time to dance.

I maneuver back to the edge of the floor and motion with my pointer finger for her to come join me. She looks a little more relaxed than when we walked in, but she polishes off the last of her beer before she joins me.

"I can't believe I'm doing this," she mutters resentfully.

I smile because even though she's scowling, her features have softened. I feel like I'm about to see a transformation take place. "Shelly, relax. Listen to the music. Feel it. You've got this." I take her hands and hold on as the beat sinks in.

She grips my fingers tightly and tries to mirror what I'm doing. She's stiff and self-conscious, but by the second song, she's relaxed enough to let go of my hands.

"Your inner dancing queen is so happy right now! The revolt's been aborted!" I yell in her ear over the music.

She sticks her tongue out at me, but then she smiles, and it's the sort of happiness that's totaling freeing. I don't know if it's the alcohol or if she just decided she doesn't give a shit.

Just then I feel hands on my waist, taking me by surprise. But they're gentle, and they belong to the person who's now pressed against me from behind. I don't look back, but whoever it is can keep up with every move I make. I love dancing with people who feel the music the same way I do. And this guy definitely does. We dance to two more songs before he yells in my ear, "Damn girl, you can dance! I don't usually dance with women, but I couldn't resist. Thanks." He kisses me on the cheek. I look back and smile. He winks at me before he moves away back through the crowd toward the center of the floor. Damn, he was good-looking. Oh well. You can't win em' all.

Shelly's looking at me with her mouth hanging open. I take her hand and lead her from the floor. "Come on, let's get something to drink. I'm sweaty."

Her mouth's still gaping, but the corners are curled up into a smartass grin. "Holy hell, that was the closest thing I've ever seen to two people having sex fully clothed."

She makes me laugh. "What? We were just dancing."

"That was not dancing. That was sexy as hell. You've got to teach me."

So, I do. And Shelly's a quick learner. An hour later and she has me wondering who it was that said they couldn't dance. Put a little alcohol in Shelly and all her inhibitions fly out the goddamn window.

By one in the morning, Shelly and I are exhausted and decide it's time to get home. It takes us a while to find Clayton because the dance floor is still so packed. We find him dancing with the same guy who lured him away from me earlier, like three hours ago. Clayton's shirt is damp with sweat. I feel awful when I tell him we need to leave, and I feel even worse when Mr. Cheekbones pulls Clayton's adorable little face to his and thoroughly kisses him when Clayton tells him goodbye. But I feel a little better when he writes his phone number on Clayton's hand and kisses him again before Clay takes my hand in his and we walk away.

I wait until we're outside on the sidewalk to give Clay a congratulatory high five and hug. "Dude, that was one hot kiss, my friend. I'm kind of jealous." I'm not jealous, really. I'm happy as hell for Clayton.

Clayton floats down the sidewalk to the car on a wave of pure bliss. "This has been the best night of my entire life." He's glowing.

Shelly nods her head. "I had no idea dancing could be so much fun." And just as quickly her eyes darken and her badass voice returns. "Don't you dare tell anyone I said that, Kate. I have a reputation to uphold."

I swipe my finger across my chest twice. "Cross my heart. What happens at Spectacle, stays at Spectacle." I look to Clayton and point at Shelly. "Did you see my girl out there?"

He shakes his head and closes his eyes. "Sorry, I was a little preoccupied."

"She's the fucking dancing queen."

Clayton smiles the most adorable little smile. "I thought *I* was the dancing queen."

Shelly laughs. She has a great laugh. "The title is all yours, Clayton."

Even though I'm wiped out, this night was entirely worth it.

TUESDAY, SEPTEMBER 6
KATE

ALMOST A WEEK OF UNEVENTFUL, perfectly happy life has gone by when I return home from a late run on the treadmill at the campus fitness center to find the red ribbon tied to my doorknob again.

Clayton is the ever-gracious host once more. After I shower, he insists I borrow a pair of his pajamas to sleep in. And they're not even that big on me.

Now *I* feel like Hugh Hefner.

He also bought me my very own toothbrush and toothpaste just in case this happened again. He presented them to me with a Ziploc bag so I could store them away after use and keep them in his desk.

Clayton's the best.

WEDNESDAY, SEPTEMBER 7

KATE

I'm at Grounds unusually early this morning. I was restless and couldn't stay cooped up inside the dorms any longer, so I decided to go for a short run. Predictably, that run ended at the source of my early morning addiction. There's a chill in the air this morning and I'm a little sweaty after the workout, so I sit on a bench just outside Grounds with my arms wrapped around me. I'm listening to classical on my iPod and reading the local newspaper I found on their front step. It's perched on my lap so I don't have to hold it and I can keep my hands tucked up in my sleeves. Even with a T-shirt and a sweatshirt on, I'm cold. It's 5:45. They open at six o'clock. I've been here since 5:30.

There's a knock on the glass behind me. Keller is motioning toward the front door. When the door opens and the bell thunders, I barely notice—that's progress.

"Morning, Katie." He looks tired. He's unshaven, and his dark hair stands out in every direction, like he's just rolled out of bed. It's a little on the long side, like he's overdue for a haircut. And his eyes are still hooded in sleep, but the color is no less striking under half-drawn lids. Their blue matches the T-shirt he's wearing almost exactly.

Despite everything, or maybe because of it, he looks really, *really* good.

I smile. He remembered my name. "Good morning, Keller." I hand him the newspaper. "Here's your paper. I looked it over. No major scandal in Grant to report this morning, but there's a sale on ground beef at Sam's Meat Palace, if you're interested. Oh, and Our Lady of Eternal Light is having a spaghetti dinner Saturday night from five to seven o'clock to raise money for renovations to the basement gathering room."

His crooked smile emerges and falls into a slight grimace. He shakes his head slightly as if the hint of movement made his head hurt. "That's too much information for five forty-five in the morning, Katie."

"The world doesn't stop because you're sleeping...or hungover."

His smile evens out as he puts on his apron behind the counter. "Touché. Just tired. Up all night studying." He looks at me for a few seconds. I realize that I'm smiling like an idiot. I can't help it. "Are you always this happy in the morning?"

I shrug. "It's a genetic flaw. But I've been up for a few hours. Couldn't sleep." I've been trying to get extra sleep lately, but some nights I just can't get comfortable and sleep evades me. I'm more tired than I ever remember being.

"I guess you'll need that large cup of coffee this morning?"

My arms hug back around me again as a shiver pulses through me. "Yes, please."

He nods to the arm cocoon I've forged. "Cold?"

I'm kind of bouncing in place trying to warm myself at this point. "It's freezing out there."

He raises his eyebrows. "Katie, it's probably fifty degrees out there. You think this is cold? *It's balmy.* Wait until this winter when it's fifty below."

I cover my ears. "Stop right there. I'm going to pretend I didn't hear that."

He points to the earbuds dangling out of the top of my sweatshirt. "What are you listening to?"

I lower my hands. "Mozart."

"Classical? Really? Classical's boring." He tries to frown, but only one side of his mouth turns down. He's mocking me, but it's not unkind.

"Boring, huh?" I'm not offended. Most people my age seem to have the same opinion. Sometimes I feel like a classical ambassador.

"It all sounds the same."

Here we go, an early morning music debate. Well, I'm in. "That's such a poor generalization. That's like saying classic rock sucks because you don't like Led Zeppelin, or that '80s new wave is phenomenal because you love The Cure, even if you've never heard anything else from either genre."

He hands me my coffee, which I gratefully take with both hands.

Resting his elbows on the counter, interlacing his long, slim fingers, he fires back. "First off, no one would say Zeppelin sucks."

I nod in concession. "I agree. That was a bad example." I set my two dollars on the counter.

"And The Cure was mediocre," he continues.

I can't even pretend to contain myself. "Dude?! I'm calling bull-shit on you. That's outright and blatant blasphemy. The Cure is epic, timeless, one of the greatest bands. Ever. Period."

He shakes his head. "No way." He smiles. "The Smiths were better."

I allow myself a smile. "Kudos to Morrissey, but Robert Smith is a...he's a God." It's a declaration.

He holds his hands up in defeat, but he's smiling. He puts my bills in the register and hands me my change.

I put the change in the tip jar. "I guess all I'm saying is that you should give classical a chance. It has a bad reputation. Sure, some of it can be boring, but it can also be beautiful and sexy. Check out Debussy."

"Sexy, huh?" A playful smile emerges. I picture him practicing it in front of a mirror, fully aware of its effect on the opposite sex.

I wink. "You might be surprised." I raise my coffee in salute. "Thanks for the early morning conversation. Have a stellar day, Keller."

He salutes back. "See you around, Katie. And thanks for the tip on the ground beef at Sam's."

"Don't forget the meatloaf dinner at Our Lady of Everlasting Glory," I call back without turning around. Sometimes I test people, just to see if they really listen to me.

"That's Eternal Light." I can hear the smile in his voice. "And it's spaghetti," he adds just before the door shuts behind me.

I smile too, because he *totally* passed.

THURSDAY, SEPTEMBER 8

KATE

It's 3:30 pm and I'm on my way to Minneapolis. I don't have to be there until four o'clock, but due to the fact that the last time I drove this stretch, I had Clay and Shelly praying for their lives, I've decided to leave a little early and drop my speed to a respectable seventy-five. I feel geriatric.

The elementary school I'm looking for is supposed to be only a few blocks from Maddie's apartment building. Sure enough, it doesn't take me long to find it.

Sometime last week, I realized that I had this need that wasn't being met. So I talked to my guidance counselor about volunteer opportunities. I didn't tell him the specifics because I don't need psychoanalysis. Besides, I don't need anyone to tell me what's wrong. I already know. It's simple. I miss Grace.

Anyway, Mr. Guidance Counselor put me in contact with this elementary school in Minneapolis that works closely with Grant. Turns out that there's a fifth-grader, Gabriel, whose regular Grant tutor isn't available for two weeks due to surgery. That's where I fit in. I'm so excited because, to be honest, I have way too much free time on my hands. I'm having no problem keeping up with my classes and work, and I need something more. *Something more* makes me feel good. *Something more* is helping someone else. But I'm also a little selfish because *something more* has the potential to help me in ways they'll never know or understand.

I check in at the school office, and because I already emailed them all my paperwork a few days ago they take me straight to the cafeteria where the after-school program meets. The woman from the office introduces me to the director of the after-school program. Her name is Helen, and she's nice, but she keeps her eyes glued to me while we talk, like a mama bear protecting her cubs. "Gabriel has Down syndrome. He's a sweet, sweet boy—ninety-nine percent of the time. Now and again, he can act out."

"Sounds like most kids. I'm familiar."

"Familiar with children with Down syndrome?" she asks, looking doubtful.

"Yes ma'am, my sister," I say. *More familiar than you'll ever know,* I think.

"Oh, I see. Yes, of course. I expect you'll show him the attention and patience he needs and deserves?"

"That's why I'm here."

She nods curtly. "I will expect a full report after each tutoring session before you leave so that I can pass along the information to his mother. You'll come and get me if there's a behavioral situation?"

"I can do that. Where's Gabriel? I'd like to meet him."

She inhales and exhales. She turns slowly and calls out, "Gabriel."

A dark-haired little head turns at the table nearest us. Helen motions him to her. He rises tentatively and stands next to the table as if waiting for permission.

She smiles brightly. "Gabriel, come here, please. There's someone here who would like to meet you." She talks to him slowly and cautiously like he's a frightened animal.

Gabriel approaches us and looks at the ground. Before Helen can say another word, I lower down on my knees in front of Gabriel. He's taller than I am now. I offer my hand. "I'm Kate, Gabriel. I'd like to be your friend. Will you be my friend?"

He doesn't take my hand, but when he lifts his chin to look at me, he's smiling. His smile is just beautiful.

"Hey, Smiley. Let's go to the library so you can show me what kind of books you have in that super cool backpack." I point to the backpack on the floor next to the table he was sitting at. The backpack is black, and it's covered with a pattern of colorful guitars.

His smile grows, and he runs back to grab the backpack. "Walk, Gabriel," Helen reprimands sternly.

He walks back, still smiling at me. I'm still on my knees, and I whisper to him, "Let's go, Smiley."

He reaches down and takes my hand in his and whispers in my ear, "I'd like to be your friend."

I swallow the golf ball sized lump in my throat and stand. Then I smile because for a few seconds I can't speak. I see Grace in his eyes.

We walk down the hall, and I swing our hands back and forth. We don't speak until we reach the library, where all of our tutoring sessions are scheduled to take place.

"Well, Smiley, this is your school, and I'm kinda new here, so I'm gonna need you to tell me where we should sit."

He scans the room and after serious consideration, he leads me to a small table with two chairs near a window.

"I'm so glad I let you pick because this is perfect. I would've chosen that table over there," I say, pointing to the corner. "And then we would've missed out on this view." There's a small flower bed outside the window that's still in bloom.

He smiles widely. He's proud of himself. I get the feeling he doesn't get compliments very often.

I point to his backpack. "Can you show me what you worked on in math today, Smiley?"

As he unzips the bag, he looks a little puzzled. "Why do you call me Smiley?"

"Because you have just about the most dazzling smile I've ever seen." He really does. It lights up the room.

He's still puzzled, but he can't hide his smile. "But, my name is Gabriel. Everyone calls me Gabriel."

I take his math book from him when he hands it to me and place it on the table. "It's a nickname. It's like a special name that only friends can call you." He likes this idea. I see it in his eyes. "If you don't like Smiley, I can call you Gabriel. Gabriel is a great name."

He thinks about it. "I like Smiley."

"So do I."

"Now you need a nickname."

I nod encouragingly. "I definitely think I need a nickname. What do you want to call me?"

His head tilts back and forth as he thinks and every few seconds his eyes crinkle up. He's focused on my face and looks over every square inch of it before he blurts out, "Spots!"

"Spots?"

He points to my nose. "Yeah, Spots."

It takes a second, but then I realize he's talking about my freckles. "Of course, I have spots on my nose, don't I?"

He nods enthusiastically.

"Well, I think of all the nicknames I've ever had, Spots is my very favorite." My heart is so happy right now.

Smiley is definitely *something more.*

FRIDAY, SEPTEMBER 9

KATE

SHELLY'S BEEN WORKING on me all week. She's on the phone now, and it's deteriorated into Shelly's version of whining, which is still more like telling than asking. "Kate, you have to come. It's the *Back to Grant Bash*. It's a stupid tradition, but everyone goes."

"Shelly, why do I need to come? I'm sure all of your friends will already be there." The truth is, I'm just too tired tonight.

I swear she's pouting. "Because, *dude*, you're more fun." She knows I love the *dude*. She's trying to butter me up—both sides, front and back, top to bottom. It's working. "No shit, Kate, I have more fun going out with you. You make me step outside my comfort zone."

"But you hate that." She does.

"I know, but I also like it."

That small admission makes me feel less tired. "Will there be dancing? Because, if I can get a guarantee out of you that you'll dance with me tonight, then I'm in."

Shelly exhales. It sounds pained. "I'll dance," she says, although it's a whisper through clenched teeth.

"What? You're going to have to speak up. I didn't hear you," I say the last part in a sing-song voice.

"Goddamn you, Kate. Yes, I'll dance. Do you want me to go outside and scream it for the world to hear? Would that make you happy?" There's a smile in there somewhere. It's wedged between the grimace and the menace.

"Um, yeah, actually that would make me the happiest fucking girl in Grant today. Can you throw in a little booty shake while you're yelling? That would make it perfect."

"Don't push it, Sedgwick."

"But I'm not dressing up. I heard it's a costume party, and I don't do costumes."

"Neither do I," she agrees.

Shelly picks me up from the dorm at ten o'clock, and two minutes later we're parked in front of a frat house on campus. It looks like a ghost town.

"What the hell? Where is everyone?" She looks pissed. I know she said it was stupid, but I think she was looking forward to it. She spots someone coming out of the building's side door, and her whole body tenses. She's like a lion ready to pounce. "Stay here. I'm going to find out what happened."

She tracks down her prey and begins questioning the poor guy like she did me the first time we met. I know how intimidating she can be when you don't know her. (And sometimes even when you do know her.) The guy's hunched over like he's protecting his soft, vulnerable underbelly from an attack. Then she pulls her cell phone out of her back pocket and dials someone. There's a brief conversation with lots of hand gestures, and she returns with the scoop. "Cops broke up the party twenty minutes ago. Some drunken idiot dressed up like Superman decided to jump out of a second-story window on a dare. He broke his femur. It was so bad they had to call the ambulance. That's when the cops came. You know the rest." She rolls her eyes, irritated. Shelly doesn't tolerate stupidity. "Dumbass."

I offer my condolences. "Sorry, dude. To tell you the truth, I'm more bummed about not seeing a grown man jump out of a window donning a Superman unitard. I mean, I'm sorry the party was shut down and I'm *really* sorry the dude got hurt, but that must've been hilarious."

"It's ludicrous," she corrects.

"Hilarious. Ludicrous. The difference is so subtle." I'm going to babble on until she cracks a smile. "They play well together, like they're both members of the same humorous constituency, but—"

A smile starts in her eyes. "Shut up, Kate." It giggles its way out.

"Seriously, a twenty-year-old in tights who thinks he can fly? That shit's not funny to you? I know I'm simple and easily amused, but to me, that's good stuff."

She's laughing now and even snorts a little. I've only heard her snort once before when she laughed really, really hard at the club in Minneapolis. It's her summit. Every time I hear her laugh, I feel satisfaction in knowing I can bring that kind of uninhibited happiness to this serious girl. She's let me in, and that feels good.

She hits the steering wheel with the heel of her hand. "Thanks, *dude*. I needed that." She looks resigned. "Now, let's go have a few drinks."

"Okay. But promise me you'll stop before you attempt any super-hero, second-story leaps of faith."

When we pull up in front of Three Petunias, I assume we're going up to her apartment. No problem; I can walk back to the dorms from here. When she gets out and crosses the street, I'm confused. "Where are we going?"

"To see The Boyfriend." It's funny that she calls him that. I don't think I've ever heard his real name. It's always The Boyfriend. "Let's see if he and his roommate got their drunken asses home yet. They were almost there when I talked to him a few minutes ago."

"How far away do they live?" I'm rubbing my arms because I'm only wearing a T-shirt and hoodie, and it's unseasonably chilly tonight. I didn't count on walking very far.

"Just down the street. They rent out the room behind Grounds."

The walk is short. We turn the corner at Grounds and walk around behind the building. There's a gigantic, ancient Suburban parked in the alley. It's pale green and rusty, but the driver's door is red. Next to the car is the door to what I assume must be The Boyfriend's apartment, or "room" as she called it.

She tries the doorknob, but it's locked, so she beats her fist against the door.

A tall redhead with a thick beard swings the door open and then holds onto it, like he couldn't stand without it. He smiles at Shelly—the same sappy smile she wears when she talks about him. But where hers is small and restrained, his is huge and wide open. "Honey, you're home!" I've never seen anyone slur a phrase so enthusiastically.

She kisses him on the cheek as she enters. "When did you two start drinking?"

The slurring resumes. "I don't remember. Three o'clock, maybe? It's the *Back to Grant Bash!*" This guy is one happy drunk. I like that. I can't be around angry drunks. It reminds me of my mother.

He's physically startled when he glances over and sees me waiting on the threshold. I don't want to be rude and barge in or make any sudden movements because he looks like he's seeing double, possibly triple. He's trying extremely hard to concentrate on just one of me.

I raise my hand and wave slowly. "Hey, what's up? You must be The Boyfriend."

He squints like my image is an out-of-focus apparition floating in front of him. "Kate?" He looks slowly to Shelly. "Hun, is this *The* Kate? The one you talk about nonstop? I finally get to meet her in the flesh?"

Shelly rolls her eyes. "Shut up, Duncan. Let the poor girl in, it's freezing out there."

Duncan steps back and with a wide, dramatic, sweeping gesture, welcomes me into his apartment.

I nod. "Thanks, dude."

He giggles, which is priceless because a guy this big and hairy shouldn't giggle. But there's no other way to describe it. "Wait, I know you. Don't I know you? How do I know you?"

Shelly hands me a beer before I can turn it down or even take my hoodie off. "Duncan, you don't know her. How would you know Kate?"

I look at him again, and suddenly he looks familiar, too. I've seen that beard before, but where? And then it hits me. "Grounds. We met at Grounds before school started. Well, we sort of met. We discussed the weather, I think."

He tries to snap his fingers but fails miserably. He doesn't seem to notice. "Yes. *Yes!* I knew it." He points at me. "You're in the club." He turns to Shelly. "Hun, she's in the club."

I smile and nod. "Yeah, I'm in the club."

Shelly shakes her head, but can't help smiling at him like a lovesick puppy. "Duncan, please sit down before you fall down. And no more alcohol. I'm cutting you off."

He shuffles over to the small loveseat and tumbles down next to her.

I look around the room and realize now why Shelly called it a room and not an apartment. Because it *is* a room, just one tiny open space with high ceilings. Everything about it is small, but it's homey and comfortable. There's a small kitchenette along the far brick wall, a small loveseat, and ratty recliner in the middle, and two screens set up on opposite sides of the door I've come through. I'm assuming Duncan's bed is housed behind one and his roommate's behind the other. Virtually no privacy. I can relate, but when I shared a small room with someone, it was my sister and privacy wasn't a priority. There are three other doors, all of which are closed. One must be a bathroom. Another is probably a closet. And the other looks like it might lead to the rear of Grounds.

Duncan reaches over and clumsily pats the recliner next to him. "Come sit down, Kate. We won't bite. Better take a seat while you can before my roommate gets out of the shower. Some chick was trying to put the moves on my boy at the frat house, and when he wasn't into her, she threw a glass of beer on him. What the hell? I mean, who does that? He smelled awful. Had to clean up when we got home." He's a very dramatic storyteller and much chattier than Shelly.

Shelly laughs. "I'm sure he was leading her on. You know what a tease he is when he's drunk."

"Hun, he's my boy. Why do you have to be like that?" He leans toward her, practically falling right on top of her. This guy is drunk out of his mind.

"You know how he is. When he's sober, he doesn't give women the time of day, but when he's drunk, he flirts like hell just to wind them up." She's looking at me now. "He thinks it's fun getting their hopes up and then when he shuts them down, they always get pissed. And he loves it. It's a cruel game. He's such a tease—" Shelly stops mid-sentence because the bathroom door has just opened and she smiles mischievously like she knows she's just baited someone up.

I hear the voice before I see him. "Shel, this door is paper-thin. You think I can't hear you? That happened once. And it was on a dare from your man here. There's no need to exaggerate." He isn't offended. In fact, he sounds like he finds the whole conversation humorous. "Thanks for having my back, Dunc."

Shelly laughs. She's much more relaxed around her boyfriend. I like that.

And then I see him and I freeze and almost lose the grip on the bottle of beer in my hand. Because stepping out of the bathroom, wrapped only in a towel hanging low on his hips, is Keller Banks. The Coffee God. Damn. He's fucking glorious. I need to blink. And breathe. Don't forget to breathe.

Duncan points, ineffectively, in my general direction. "Banks, we have a guest."

"Hey, Keller." That sounded normal despite my heart beating at a ridiculously fast rate.

His relaxed stance stiffens, and his sleepy eyes widen. "Katie? What? How?" he stutters. "What...what are you doing here?" It's not rude; he's just at a loss for words.

Which is kind of flattering, because he doesn't seem like the type of guy who gets tongue-tied, especially around the opposite sex. Not that he's overly confident. It's just that guys this good-looking seem to instinctively know how to talk to women. I may have the upper hand here. "I'm out with Shelly tonight. Party got broken up; I guess Superman's flight was a bust. Literally. We ended up here by default."

Shelly and Keller look at each other and speak at the same time. "How do you know Kate?" "You're friends with Katie?" They both look confused.

I look at Keller first. "I work with Shelly at Three Petunias. Oh, and she's my dance partner when we go clubbing." I can't say it with a straight face, and I'm smiling by the time I look at Shelly, who's rolling her eyes and glaring. It's an impressive combo. "And I know Keller from Grounds. We debate music, and I keep him updated on important town news."

Keller shakes his head slightly. I'm sure it's hard to think through the haze of alcohol in his system. He's clearly not as intoxicated as Duncan, but he's had his share. He puts both hands up, arms outstretched in front of him, like he's trying to tell us to stop and sways back and forth slightly. I almost step forward to make sure he doesn't fall over. "Wait. Sorry. This is just—"

"I think he's freaked out because there's a woman in our apartment," Duncan says to Shelly in the loudest whisper I've ever heard. "When did he bring her home?"

Shelly cuts off the drunken confusion before it goes any further. "Duncan, Keller didn't bring her home. I brought her here. *With me.* Remember?"

Duncan shrugs and finally lays his head in Shelly's lap.

I take the three or four steps it takes to stand next to Keller. He still looks stunned. I offer my hand. "You need some help there?"

His eyes fight to adjust to my sudden closeness. "Katie." It's more a breath than a word. He's searching my eyes. For what? I'd be turned on if it weren't for the fact that he can't see straight. Maybe he is as drunk as Duncan.

I offer my hand again. "Come on, dude."

He slowly raises his hand and hesitates. "Are you really here?"

"Yup. Had a few cocktails tonight, Keller?"

He nods, his mouth slack, but he eventually takes my hand. His grip is gentle, like he has full control of his motor skills. I know he doesn't. Even when starts leaning into me, his grip remains gentle.

"Keep a hand on that towel, chief. We don't need accidental full frontal. Keep your junk under wraps." I mean, *I wouldn't mind*, I think to myself, but...

Duncan laughs from the loveseat. "That's a first, Banks."

I need to get this guy to bed, although the thought stirs something in me, something deep inside. A need. But no, that's selfish. No! No sex.

I want to.

I *really* want to.

But I won't.

I *can't*.

He's a nice guy; I couldn't do that to him. No attachments.

Lust-filled, innocent, one-sided crushes? Yes, please.

I need to get this guy to bed so he can pass out and sleep this off is what I need to do. Together, we start to shuffle toward the screens.

Shelly calls out, "Keller's bed's on the right."

"Thanks," I grunt out, because at this point, he has both of his arms wrapped around my shoulders and it feels like I'm dragging dead weight. God, he's heavy.

A twin bed and a small dresser are the extent of his bedroom furniture behind the screen. There's an acoustic guitar propped up in the corner next to a fixie bicycle. It's cramped.

"You play guitar, Keller?"

"Yeah," is all he can manage.

I'm doomed. Guitar players just do it for me.

I lean forward at the foot of his bed, and he topples like a domino. A domino that's still attached to me.

We're laying chest to chest, his back on the mattress. I'm sure he's already passed out cold and even though I could lie here all night against his warm skin, I know that's wrong on way too many levels. So I close my eyes and allow myself five seconds of heaven. I inhale the fresh, soapy smell of him, minty and clean. I press my hands against his chest where the visible muscles are taut, even though he's relaxed. Mmm...

Five seconds is up. I open my eyes and rest my hands on the bed next to each of his shoulders and push up, trying to extricate myself from the long arms wrapped around me. They don't budge. I'm about to yell for Shelly to come and help me when I hear his dream-like voice low in my ear. "Stay, Katie."

My heart is racing again. I raise my head and look him in the eye. He's so close. And his lips are so pink. And they look so damn soft. He's just about to drift off, so I whisper back, "You need to sleep, Keller. Close your eyes."

His eyelids drop. He's slipping away. "I listened to Debussy. It wasn't boring. It was sexy." And he's gone, lost to alcohol and exhaustion.

I smile, pull myself forward, and kiss him lightly on the forehead because I need to avoid those lips. "Good night, sweetie." This time, when I try to push up and out of his grip, his arms fall away from me. His legs hang off the bed at his knees, but the towel is still in place. I put his pillow under his head and wrap him up like a burrito in his comforter so he doesn't get cold. His baby face looks so innocent when he's sleeping. Something stirs inside me, not the sexual urge I felt earlier, but a different kind of longing. A different kind of attraction. My chest aches when I look at him. Every part of me wants to sit here and just watch him sleep, stroke his hair, run my fingertips over every perfect feature of his face, and just be near him. I've never felt like this before. And instead of freaking me out, it makes me feel calm.

I need to go. Now.

When I return to Shelly, she's still sitting on the loveseat. Duncan is snoring, his head in her lap. "Sorry this night was so lame, Kate. You're never going to come out with me again." She looks bummed.

I smile. "This night wasn't lame. It just didn't turn out like you wanted it to. That's not the same thing. Of course I'll go out with you again." I look at Duncan sleeping. "And The Boyfriend seems really nice."

She smiles sadly. "He is, especially when he's sober. Sorry you had to meet him like this. He's at work or in class almost all the time; the poor guy hardly ever goes out. And even when he does, he rarely drinks." Her eyes dart down to him. "I can count on two fingers how many times I've seen him like this in the year we've dated."

I hear the love for him in her voice. It makes my heart happy when people feel that kind of love. It's rare. People don't take the time to find it. Or they let it go too easily. Or they don't know how precious it is when they have it.

Shelly knows.

I think Duncan knows, too.

After sliding out from under Duncan and arranging him somewhat comfortably on the loveseat, she covers him up with a blanket and kisses him on the cheek.

"Well, *dude*, let's go back to my place and I'll make you some scrambled eggs and then drive you home. I don't want you walking around in the middle of the night by yourself."

She knows how much I love scrambled eggs. We talked about it at work last week. They're one of my very favorite comfort foods. "You have yourself a deal."

As Shelly turns out the lights and reaches for the door, she looks at me with a stern, concerned warning. "Please don't fall for Keller. I saw the way you looked at him. Don't get me wrong, he's a good guy. Probably one of my best friends actually. He's the type of person who wants to know everything about you and the type of person that you don't mind telling everything, too. In fact, you sort of want to talk to him because he's such a great listener and always there for you when you need him." She sighs. "But on the flip side, he's extremely private where his life's concerned. He doesn't let anyone in except Duncan, and maybe Romero. He and Duncan have been friends for years. Duncan lived with him and his family in Chicago before they came here to Grant. He's like a brother to Duncan, and I love him for that, but he's ... mysterious. Personally, I think there are a lot of skeletons in his closet. For instance, he works his ass off, but doesn't spend his money on anything except flying to Chicago every other weekend—"

"What's in Chicago?" I interrupt.

Shelly shrugs. "Only Duncan knows, and he won't tell. I've always assumed it's a girlfriend because he *never* dates. Every time I ask him about it, he brushes me off. He's definitely hiding something. It's Keller's big secret."

"Secrets aren't always bad, Shelly. Everyone has baggage." It feels like a confession. Like I should follow it up with a humble "Amen."

"Yeah, I know. But Keller's is like a goddamn pheromone where the females around here are concerned. He's seemingly unavailable, so what do they do? They line up to have their hearts broken. Because, you know, *they're* going to be the one to lure him out of a long-distance relationship and win his heart. To his credit, he doesn't lead them on. I was only giving him a hard time earlier. If he's not in a relationship, I wouldn't be surprised if he's gay or a virgin. Not that I give a rat's ass about Keller's sex life. He's my friend. And so are you. And I want to keep it that way. So, the moral of this little story is that Keller leaves a trail of unintentional heartbreak and destruction in his wake. Please, *please* don't let him break yours."

"Keller and I are friends, just friends, I'm not looking for anything more." When the words formed in my mind they were true, but as soon as they leave my mouth and are hanging out there between us, something changes. Why do they feel like a lie? It's that damn baby face...and those damn blue eyes...and that damn body...and that damn smile...and that damn voice.

Damn.

Good thing I can't get involved. And good thing I don't do heart-break. So, I repeat it in my mind over and over again: *Keller and I are just friends. Keller and I are just friends.* By the time we get back to Shelly's apartment, I almost believe it.

Almost.

SATURDAY, SEPTEMBER 10

KATE

MY PHONE VIBRATES in my pocket. It's Gus. And it's 6:45 am in California.

"Bonjour, Gustov," I answer. My French accent is overdone and obnoxious.

"Hey, Bright Side. I didn't wake you, did I?" He knows I'm an early riser.

"Nah, it's practically afternoon here. I'm walking to Grounds as we speak to get some coffee. What's got you sounding so chipper this early on a Saturday morning?"

"We got the day off for good behavior. I'm headed home to have lunch with Ma and surf with Mags and Stan this afternoon."

"Sweet. Tell them all I said hi."

"Dude, I wish you were here. This is like the first normal day I've had in a long time, and it doesn't feel right without you." He sounds sentimental. And I know how that feels.

"Yeah, you lucky bastard. I'll have to live vicariously through you today. Keep that in mind while you do everything for both of us."

"I'll take a picture of the sunset if you want, and email it to you?" He always knows what to say.

"I'd like that. Gracie would like that."

"She would." I hear the smile in his voice. "I'm gonna pay Miss Grace a visit before I go to Ma's this morning. I bought some yellow tulips last night. And I'll stop at a gas station and buy a candy bar. The AC's not working in my truck, and I didn't want it to melt before I get there, so I'll wait until I get closer to pick one up."

Damn, he's thoughtful. "A Twix. She likes Twix candy bars."

"Bright Side, I've purchased no fewer than *three thousand* Twix bars for Grace over the years. I know what kind of candy bar she likes."

I smile because it's not an exaggeration. He's probably bought more. "I know."

It's quiet for several seconds.

"I miss her, Gus," I whisper.

"I know, Bright Side."

The silence returns and he lets me live in it.

And then he pulls me out. "Tell me something amazing that happened to you this week that I don't know about yet."

I think for a moment. Gabriel. My voice brightens. "Thursday was my first tutoring session at the elementary school in Minneapolis."

"Yeah, yeah, that's right!" His usual crazy enthusiasm returns, "How'd it go? Did you tutor a boy or girl?"

Which amps up my enthusiasm and I feel better. "It was amazing. He's a fifth-grader. His name's Gabriel, but I call him Smiley. Gus, he has the sweetest smile."

"I bet he does. Is he special needs?" Gus is the best conversationalist because he's one of the few people I know who really listens when you talk to them. You can feel it, even over the phone.

"Down syndrome. He's a little shy."

Gus interrupts with a laugh. "Well, he's found the perfect person to draw him right out of his shell. You are the cure for shyness, aren't you?"

"As a matter of fact, I think I just might be. Smartass."

He laughs. "That's my girl."

"Anyway, the office staff said he has behavioral issues and the after-school program alluded to it, but he was an angel for me. I think so many people treat special needs kids so different from all of the other kids that sometimes it makes them act out. They're kids, all they really want is attention and kindness, you know? That's what every kid wants."

"And that is why you are going to be the best teacher the world has ever seen. You'll revolutionize the profession." He's always so encouraging.

"I loved being with him yesterday."

"And I bet he felt the same way. Did he remind you of Grace? Was that hard?"

"His eyes remind me of Gracie. There's that expectancy and innocence in them, you know. And they crinkle up when he smiles, just like Gracie. It's good, though. Good to be around him."

"I'm glad. You deserve it."

"How's everything going with you, Rock God?"

"Good, it's good. I can see the light at the end of the tunnel. The album drops Tuesday. But I don't want to think about any of that today. Today is about surfing with friends and spending time with Ma."

"It doesn't get any better than that."

"Listen, Bright Side, I'm just stopping for gas and to pick up Grace's Twix bar. Will you be around late tonight? I'll call you on my drive back to L.A. if you don't have a hot date planned." Maybe it's me, but his teasing voice sounds a little sad.

"No dates. I'll be around unless I'm spooning Clayton in his bed because Sugar's brought home another gentleman caller to woo. I'll just be hanging out. Give me a call."

It's quiet for a beat too long, and then he asks, "Do you and Clayton really spoon?"

"Dude, you haven't been replaced. No one spoons like you do." I've spent hundreds of nights at Audrey and Gus's house over the years and I always slept with Gus. Especially in the weeks I lived with them before my move to Minnesota. There wasn't a night that I slept alone. Whether we slept in his room, or the guest room, or on the sofa, we always slept together. And up until the very last night, it was completely platonic, even though I was always wrapped up in him. I don't think I've ever felt as safe as I did in those weeks. I couldn't sleep unless his arms were around me, and because Gus is a big, gentle hulk of a man, he was like a cocoon that sheltered me from the world. I was so thankful we had that time.

I hear the click of his lighter and that first, familiar drag of a cigarette. "Good to know."

"You should quit."

"Yes. I should."

"You mean it?" I ask hopefully.

"Nope. I love you, Bright Side."

"Love you, too, Gus."

"Bye."

"Bye."

The thunderous bell announces my arrival to an empty Grounds. I'm sure Keller won't be working this morning, since he's probably still comatose. But there he is, standing behind the counter with his hands clamped over his ears, his eyes shut, and his face contorted in pain.

His eyes ease open as I reach the counter and the bell fades out.

"Sorry about that," I apologize quietly. "You look like shit, dude." I mean, he still looks good—*really good*—but he's pale, and there are dark circles under his eyes. Only Keller could pull off a sexy hang-over. And then I remind myself, *Keller and I are just friends.*

I catch him off guard, and he snorts out a laugh. "I guess I deserve that."

And with that exchange, I know that everything's good between us. Keller and I *are* just friends. Because this is how friends act. And it's okay. It's great even, because friends are life's gifts. "I don't know if you *deserve* to feel as bad as you must, but you wholeheartedly earned it."

He shakes his head and rubs his eyes with the heels of his hands and moans, "I'm never drinking again."

I nod in agreement. "Until next time?" I smile.

He answers my smile with one of his own. "Damn, it's like you know me."

I arch my eyebrows. "Well, we were in a somewhat intimate and vulnerable position last night. That tends to lend itself to getting to know each other better."

His expression quickly transforms into unmistakable terror. "Shit. I thought I remembered most of what happened. You *were* in my bed." He gestures between the two of us with his finger. "We didn't... You know..." He's biting at the edge of his fingernail.

I shake my head and laugh. "No. We didn't." Not that I didn't think about it. Want it.

"Are you sure? Because now that you say it, I do remember you lying on top of me, and I'm pretty sure I didn't have a shirt on because I remember how cold your hands felt on my chest." He's blushing as he remembers. He's *blushing*. And it's so cute. It seems too unlikely, but maybe he *is* a virgin.

"You'd just finished a shower when Shelly and I got there, that's why you didn't have a shirt on. I helped you to your bed because you were having a little trouble in the standing and walking department. You fell down on your bed and accidentally pulled me down with you. It was completely innocent. You passed out right after you hit the mattress."

His eyes drop to the floor. "Classy," he mutters under his breath. Then his head pops up, and he squints like he immediately regrets the quick movement, but his face smooths out into this pitiful, pleading frown. "Your coffee's on me this morning." He moves to grab a large cup from the stack.

I shake my head. "That's not necessary, Keller. Listen, really, nothing happened. You were a perfect gentleman, a practically naked gentleman, but a gentleman nonetheless."

His cheeks reddened. "I am an ass. I'm sorry."

I have to laugh again because this embarrassed version of Keller just keeps getting cuter. "Dude, you're not an ass. I'm teasing. Don't be sorry." To reassure him, I add, "Seriously."

He opens his mouth and then closes it, perhaps thinking better of what he was about to say. He tilts his head and smiles at me and after a moment's hesitation. "Katie, can we start over? Maybe hang out sometime? As friends?"

Attachment is dangerous, but friendship is necessary. "Sure," I say, and I extend my hand across the counter. "Hi. I'm Kate Sedgwick."

His defeated smile perks up and he shakes my hand. "Keller Banks."

I set two dollars on the counter and scribble my cell number on a napkin on the counter. He swipes up both, putting the napkin in his pocket and the bills in the register.

After depositing my change in the tip jar, I smile at his sleepy face. "Have a great day, Keller. Hope you feel better."

"Already do. Thanks, Katie. Have a good one."

I turn and wink at him. "Always."

SUNDAY, SEPTEMBER 11

KATE

I try to call Maddie.

She doesn't answer.

I leave a message.

She doesn't return the call.

Yup, she's still pissed.

Later, my phone vibrates in my pocket. It's a text from Gus. *Skype at 8:30CST?*

I fire back, *Sounds bueno.*

When Gus's face appears on the screen, it's surrounded by several others and an instantaneous, obviously planned, "Hi, Kate!" erupts through my computer speakers. Except for Gus, who says, "Hi, Bright Side!" It's all four members of Rook, huddled around the screen.

"Wow. Dudes, what's up? It's not my birthday or anything. Why all the fanfare?"

"Bright Side, I present to you Rook's self-titled debut album." Gus holds up a CD case so I can see the cover.

I slump against the back of my chair, suddenly overcome with emotion. I try to speak, but my voice is little more than a whisper.

"Oh. My. God. Gus, it's *real*." Then I nearly scream, "It's real!" as I lean forward toward the screen. "Open it up, I want to see it!"

He does. The CD inside is shiny, and it says Rook in black letters with their trademark crow standing next to it.

A hysterical giggle starts rising in my throat, threatening to close it off. I can't remember the last time I was this happy. "God, I wish I was there, because I would give each one of you the biggest fucking hug. Congratulations!"

"We wanted you to be the first one to see it. And we wanted to say thank you, as a band, for your contributions. You already know 'Missing You' is epic because of your superhuman talent." He winks. "You do epic like no one else."

I brush off the compliment with a wave of my hand. "Don't tease me, Gus. When do I get to hear the songs for myself?"

Gus smiles. "Already overnighted a copy to your dorm room. You should see it tomorrow. Sorry I couldn't get my hands on one earlier. We can't download it electronically yet."

"No problem. Thanks, dude. I look forward to it. You fine gentlemen have made my day."

Gus looks a little apprehensive. "There's one more reason that we all wanted to talk to you tonight. We have a surprise for you." He looks over each shoulder at his bandmates.

I narrow my eyes. "What?" This feels like a surprise I won't be happy about.

Gus cringes and stalls. Then I hear Franco, the drummer, speaking from behind Gus. "Just tell her, dicklick. Jesus."

"Bright Side, promise not to get mad?"

My suspicions have been confirmed. "That depends."

Franco's face appears over Gus's shoulder, rolling his eyes in exasperation. "Kate, did you pack Gus's balls in your purse and take them with you to Minnesota?"

Franco's face is forcefully removed from my laptop screen, and Gus replaces him. "Fuck off, dude."

My heart rate picks up, and I have this sinking feeling in the pit of my stomach. "Tell me."

Gus takes a deep breath. "We want you to hear the final version of 'Killing the Sun.'" He pushes play on the CD player in his hand and holds it near the microphone on his laptop. "It's probably going to sound shitty like this, but you'll get the picture."

"What's with the CD player? You're not going old-school hipster on me, are you? You sure you don't have it on cassette or eight-track?" I love giving him a hard time.

And he loves giving it right back. That's why we've been best friends forever. "Piss off and just listen."

The familiar single guitar plays and builds and Gus's voice joins in soft and scratchy as always. As the first verse comes to a close, drums, bass, and the second guitar join in and with his voice builds to a crescendo that leads into the anthem-like chorus. I love this song. I'm getting goose bumps like I do every time I hear it. But as the chorus begins, I realize it isn't Gus's voice singing the lyrics. *It's mine.* I'm stunned, too stunned to speak. The rest of the song washes over me in some sort of dreamlike state as I hear my voice over and over again.

I shake my head when it's over. "Um, Gus, I sincerely hope this is some sort of a prank, because I should *not* be singing the chorus on 'Killing the Sun.' *That's your job.*"

Gus sheepishly sets the CD player down and takes a step back, pushing Jamie, the bass player, in front of him closest to the screen. "Bright Side, please don't kill me, but this is how the song was meant to sound. I never realized that it could be so much more until I heard you sing it that night in the studio. I shared the recording with the guys, and we all agreed your voice was the missing link."

"Gus, I'm not a singer."

Jamie pipes up. "The hell you're not. I mean, I always knew you could sing, but I think I may be in love with you now, Kate. Will you marry me? We'd have beautiful, talented babies—"

Gus grabs his shirtsleeve, yanks him back, and steps in front of him again. "That's enough, lover boy. Jamie's right, though. You have this amazing, soulful voice." He looks around at his bandmates.

They're all nodding except Franco, who's shaking his head adamantly. "I, personally, think she could've done better." Franco smiles and winks at me from behind Gus. He always teases me, but he's clearly just thrown the comment out to see if Gus is paying attention.

Gus *is* paying attention. "Shut the fuck up, shithead." With that, the focus is back on me. "Bright Side, we wanted to share you with the world."

Then something occurs to me. "Don't you have to get my permission or something?"

He smiles. "We did. Remember the documents you signed when you went into the studio with us?"

I think back. "Yeah, I guess I should have read them, huh?"

"Please don't be mad. We left your name out of the credits for both songs because you were so insistent about it with 'Missing You.' You're listed only as 'a friend' in the credits, just like you wanted, which I still think is really fucked up and just...wrong. But, Bright Side, playing and singing with us, and what that has turned into, it may be the biggest solid you've ever done me. And that's saying a lot because through the years, you've always been there for me. So, from the bottom of my heart, I thank you."

Well, shit, when he puts it like that, I can't be mad. "You're welcome," I huff out in surrender. "And I'm not mad."

Gus claps his hands once. "That's my girl."

I shake my finger at them all in warning. "But you guys owe me. Big time."

I hear Franco's voice float from the background again. "Kate, are you suggesting I repay the favor with sex? Because it's getting *really* embarrassing the way you keep throwing yourself at me like this. Especially in front of the rest of the band."

I laugh. "You wish, Franco. Not *that* sort of owe me. Like a front-row-ticket-and-backstage-pass-to-one-of-your-shows owe me."

Gus laughs. "Bright Side, we'll get you a ticket to every damn show and fly you there if you want."

I smile. "One show will do."

"Well, we've gotta let you go. MFDM is taking us out to dinner to celebrate. Somewhere fancy and he said we can't wear shorts, so we all need to change clothes." He looks straight into the camera. "We wish you were here."

All Gus's bandmates offer their goodbyes.

I wave. "Bye, everyone. Congrats again."

Gus's face is suddenly very close to the screen, and his voice lowers. "I do mean it from the bottom of my heart, thank you. I love you, Bright Side."

"Love you, too, Gus."

"Good night."

"Good night."

MONDAY, SEPTEMBER 12

KATE

THE PACKAGE from Gus was at the front desk for me when I stopped by in between classes at lunchtime. I downloaded the CD into iTunes and my iPod and have been listening to it all afternoon. It gives me goose bumps. It transports me away to a place that's almost perfect. To a place where everything is good and nothing ever goes wrong and there's no bad news. That's where I need to be today, because as hard as I try to not think about it and not let life get me down, sometimes it does. And I don't want it to. Because life is a gift. So, listening to this music today...it's like Gus has thrown me a life preserver. And it feels *so* good.

TUESDAY, SEPTEMBER 13

Kate

I TEXT Gus while I'm walking to Grounds, *Happy Album Release Day!! I'm SOOOOOOOOO proud of you Rock God!! Love you!!*

My phone vibrates in my pocket later that afternoon as I'm walking to Three Petunias for my three-hour shift. It's Gus.

"Holy shit! It's the Rock God!"

He laughs. "Whatever, Bright Side. Am I interrupting anything? You're not at work yet, are you?" It's funny how with everything going on in his crazy life, he has my schedule memorized.

"Nope, just walking there now. I have about ten minutes. What's up?"

"We added some dates to the tour this morning, and I've got some outstanding news." He sounds super stoked, which means I'm super stoked by association. "We're playing the auditorium at Grant the day after your birthday."

I stop walking. I couldn't possibly have heard him right. "Dude... Grant? As in Grant, Minnesota?"

"The same."

"No fucking way!" I'm jumping up and down now. People are staring. I don't care. Rook will be here in a few weeks.

"Yes!" he shouts. I'm pretty sure he's jumping up and down on the other end of the line, too. "Just let me know how many tickets you need. I'll make sure you get VIP passes for you and all your friends."

"Wow, that is...that is...*outstanding*." I count off my friends in my mind: Keller, Shelly, Duncan, Clayton, Pete, and Maddie. Even though Maddie's not talking to me, I'd better include her just in case. And I should probably throw in one more just in case Clayton or Pete have a date. "Eight tickets including me. Is that too many?" Suddenly I feel selfish, and I answer my own question. "That's too many."

He chuckles at my concern. "I'll make it happen. I want to meet these friends of yours. In a way, I feel like I already know them."

"I swear Gus, if you say anything to embarrass me when you meet my friends, I'll kill you."

"God, Minnesota has drained all the fun out of you, hasn't it, dude? You know I can't operate that way."

He's right, he can't. He'll probably mortify me. But I love it because that's one of the ways he shows his love. I lower my voice. "I can't believe I get to see you again, and it's not on my laptop screen. And you get to see where I live and go to school." I'm lost in thought. These are things I didn't think would ever happen.

"I can't wait." He drops his voice. "Bright Side, I have a favor to ask. Um, do you think that, well...that you could play violin with us on 'Missing You' or sing with us on 'Killing the Sun?'"

It crushes me to let him down, but he knows he's pushing his luck. "Dude, I can't."

He lets out his breath like he's been holding it. "I figured. Okay." He sounds disappointed.

"Gus, I just want to go and watch you guys, like old times. You're going to blow everyone away. Besides, I don't want to steal your thunder," I tease. Because no one could ever steal Gus's thunder. When he's on stage, you barely notice the rest of the band. The focus is always on him. Not that he tries. It just is.

He huffs. "Sweetheart, you could steal my thunder any time."

I laugh.

"Well, our time's almost up."

"Yeah, I'm just getting to work. I'd better let you go. Thanks for the news about the concert and congrats again on the album release. I still can't believe it. I'm so happy for you. You know that, right?"

"I know. I love you, Bright Side."

"Love you, too, Gus."

"Bye."

"Bye."

WEDNESDAY, SEPTEMBER 14

KATE

Gus texts, *Skype? Now?*

I just got out of the shower, and I don't have to be at work for half an hour. And Sugar is at class, so I have the room to myself. I text back as I'm powering up my laptop, *Yes and yes.*

When the connection is made, there's an empty chair on my screen, but no Gus. "Hello? Gus, are you there?"

I hear his voice loud and clear. "I'm here, Bright Side. And hello. I need your opinion about something."

"Okay. Where are you?"

"I'm standing behind my laptop so you can't see me. Dude, I want you to be honest, just please don't laugh, 'kay?"

"Sure."

I see Gus's favorite blue and green shorts walk in front of the screen, and then he lowers himself into the chair.

Before I can stop myself, I gasp in shock. "Holy shit, Gustov Hawthorne!" Gus's almost waist-long, straight hair is gone. It now falls just past his shoulders. With all the length cut away, it looks a little wavy, like mine, though his is layered and rock star shaggy.

"I know, right? The label hired a stylist for us. Said we couldn't go on tour looking like a bunch of surf rats. No more board shorts and flip-flops for a while, I guess."

I don't know what to say. He looks like a different person.

He's chewing the hell out of his bottom lip. "Is it that bad, Bright Side? Just tell me. Do I look like a tool?"

I shake my head. "Dude, I don't know how else to say this, other than to just come out and say it. You look fucking hot."

Judging by the shocked look on his face, that's not what he expected to hear. "Really? I thought you liked my hair long."

"I do, but I haven't seen you with your hair this short since we were kids. It looks sexy as hell. You're going to have to fight off the ladies, you know that, right?" He's always had women of all ages throwing themselves at him. This haircut may take it to a whole new, ridiculous level.

"You think?" He looks a little self-conscious.

Definitely, I think to myself.

THURSDAY, SEPTEMBER 15

KATE

As I'm walking to my car after my final tutoring session with Gabriel, I notice a text on my phone. It's from Clay. *SEE ME WHEN YOU GET BACK TO THE DORMS!*

I text back as I walk. *DON'T SHOUT AT ME! See you in 10. :)*

My phone chimes again as I start my car. *DRIVE THE SPEED LIMIT AND I'LL SEE YOU IN 20.*

I laugh because he knows I'm in Minneapolis.

Clay guilted me into taking down my speed, so I split the difference and pull into the lot fifteen minutes later.

Clay flings the door open just as my knuckles make contact to knock.

"Dude, what's the emergency?" I half laugh because he looks frantic, but not in a something-absolutely-awful-has-happened way, just in an I'm-panicked-and-don't-know-what-to-do-about-it way.

He seizes my shoulder and pulls me into his room. The door shuts quickly behind me. Pete is sitting on his bed across the room, engrossed in a book, but he offers his usual, "Hello, Kate."

"S'up, Pete?" I nod in Pete's direction before returning my focus to the manic little man in front of me.

Clay has a tight grip on my shoulders and his eyes are darting back and forth between my eyes, as if he can't decide which one to give his full attention. "Katherine, I need you," he says, his voice deadly serious.

There's only one way to address this level of drama. I look to Pete. "Hey, Pete, remember when I told you that Clay was a hard nut to crack? Well, I think he's finally succumbed to my overtly salacious methods of seduction. Can you give us a few minutes alone? Thirty minutes, tops."

Pete's cheeks burst into a deep blush, but he does actually crack a smile. God, I'm corrupting him.

Clayton shakes me gently and sighs as if he doesn't have time for jokes. "Katherine, this is serious."

I raise my eyebrows. "Shit. Then spill it."

"Katherine, I need you to come to Spectacle with me tonight."

"That's it? I thought this was serious? You don't need to bail someone out of jail? Or need one of my kidneys?" I tease.

He huffs.

I laugh and tone down the sarcasm because I know this means a lot to him. "But it's Thursday, dude. We won't be able to get in. I don't have a fake ID."

He drops his hands from my shoulders and starts biting at his thumbnail. "What if I told you I knew someone, and we could get in?"

"Then, hell yeah!" I eye him suspiciously because there's something he's not telling me. "Who do you know, Clayton?"

He shrugs, but his cheeks glow and give him away.

I walk over and sit on his bed and cross my legs. "Okay, Clayton. What is it you're not telling me? Because judging by the color of your face, *he* is pretty damn significant."

He stomps his foot. "How did you know?"

"Dude, you're blushing like a whore in church. It has to be a boy."

Pete chuckles from the corner.

"Okay, okay, remember that spicy little number that I danced with the night we went to Spectacle?"

"How could I forget Mr. Cheekbones? Or that steamy kiss?"

He rolls his eyes. "Well, his name is Morris, and I finally worked up the courage to call him the other night—"

"*Right on,* Clayton." I interject.

The blush intensifies and he clears his throat. "Morris manages Spectacle, and he called me earlier today and wants me to meet him there tonight."

I look to Pete, who's dutifully trying to focus on his book and stay out of the conversation. "You hear that, Pete? Our little boy's all grown up. But I don't know if I'm ready for him to start dating. What about you? Have you had the talk with him yet, you know, about the birds and bees and STDs? We might need the mandatory condom on a cucumber demo. You up for it?"

Pete shakes his head slightly, and a smile cracks through again. Clayton stomps his foot again. It's so cute when he does that. "Katherine, I need you to come with me."

I rise from the bed and hug Clayton. I can't tease him anymore. "I'm with you, dude." I kiss him on the cheek. "I. Am. With. You. What time?"

"Can we leave at eight o'clock? We need to get there before they open so that Morris can get us in."

I release him and reach for the door. "Your wish is my command."

Clayton is at my room at 7:45 pm, all but trying to drag me out the door. He knows I'm habitually late. I called Shelly, but she has plans with The Boyfriend tonight, so it looks like I'm on my own.

As promised, Morris is waiting for us at the back door of the club. God, if this doesn't feel extra shady. Well, I guess that's because it *is* illegal, but when I would go to the club with Gus at home, they always seemed to usher me in through the front door. I feel like I should know some special knock or handshake or code word to get in through the back.

Morris is all chiseled cheekbones just as I remembered, and on top of that, he's from Manchester, England, so he has this fantastic accent.

It's polite, proper, and so charming. I could listen to him all night: the way he doesn't pronounce the first or last letter of certain words, or the way he leaves entire syllables out of other words as if they aren't important enough to bother with. And you find yourself agreeing and thinking, why do we bother with the "r" at the end of "better"? It sounds so sexy without it. At least with his accent it does. No wonder Clayton's all aflutter. After talking with Morris for a few minutes, because Clayton seems to be speechless in his presence, I find him to be a proper gentleman—enchanting accent aside—which eases my mind. Somewhat. Still, my primary reason for tagging along tonight is to make sure that Morris doesn't take advantage of my innocent Clayton.

Just to make sure, I send Clayton away to the bar to grab us a couple of Cokes. As soon as he's out of earshot, I turn to Morris. "Morris, dude, I'm gonna cut to the chase. You seem really nice and I think I like you, so don't take this the wrong way." I look him straight in the eyes. "Don't fuck Clayton over. He's special, and he's sweet, and he really likes you. I know this is all just getting started between the two of you, but don't get him all jacked up over you if you don't intend to pursue something with him. Clayton's never had a boyfriend; keep that in mind. His heart's been tucked away for eighteen years, so when he takes it out of his pocket and offers to share it with you, don't treat it like some shiny new toy that will only be forgotten when you're done playing with it. And don't take more than your share, unless you're willing to trade your own for it. Just don't fuck with him for the sake of a one-night stand, okay?"

Morris raises his eyebrows. "Blimey, Kate, you're to the point, aren't ya?"

I raise my eyebrows in return. I'm waiting for his response and he knows it.

"I fancy Clayton. I want to get to know him better." ("Better" with a soft "r" is indeed better.) "Despite the fact that I probably look like a right wanker bringing him here tonight, I've only good intentions. I've been thinkin' of him every minute since we met. I thought..." he pauses and looks embarrassed. "I thought he would never call. And then, he did."

I smile. Morris seems genuinely excited about Clayton. But I have one more question. "How old are you?"

"I'm twenty-one."

"And you manage a club?" I narrow my eyes. My friend's heart is still on the line.

"My uncle owns it. He lives in London and asked me to help him out since I just finished up with university. I've only been at it a month now. S'a long story. Don't even have a proper flat yet." Morris lowers his voice to a whisper. "He's comin'. I won't hurt him. You've my word."

"Thank you."

He nods.

Because Morris is technically working, Clayton spends most of his time dancing with me. On the occasion that Morris breaks free for a song or two and steals him away, I find that there's no shortage of available dance partners. And can they *dance*.

Clayton and I stay until close. I bask in Clayton's bliss during the entire drive back to our dorm. He's so high on love, or lust, that he doesn't even complain about my driving.

We return to the familiar red ribbon on my door. Clayton, as always, is accommodating.

"Dude, I feel kinda funny sleeping with you now that you're spoken for."

"Katherine, hush. You're always welcome in my bed. Now, good night," he says, still with a special glimmer in his eyes.

"Good night."

FRIDAY, SEPTEMBER 16

KATE

I HEAR the text alert from my pocket just as I step through the door into Three Petunias. I'm not working today, but Shelly asked me to stop by; she burned a CD for me and wants me to check it out.

I retrieve my phone from my pocket while I wait for her to wrap up a phone call. The text is from Maddie. *Can I borrow $500? Rent's due tomorrow.*

The fact that I've been thrown for a loop by the text must show on my face because as soon as Shelly hangs up the phone, she asks, "What's wrong, Kate?"

I shake my head. "Nothing. I just got a text from my aunt. I haven't heard from her in a while."

"Is this the aunt who lives in Minneapolis?"

"Yeah, she was pissed at me. I've been trying to get in touch with her for a couple of weeks now."

"Is she still mad?"

I shrug. "Don't know. She says she needs money."

Shelly looks shocked. "And she's asking you? How old is she?"

I'm still running the text over in my head. "Twenty-seven." "You're not going to give it to her, are you?"

I exhale as I come to my conclusion. "Probably. She's dealing with some pretty messed up stuff right now. She says she needs it. She wouldn't ask if she wasn't desperate, right?"

Shelly's looking at me. In her face, I see Audrey's—Gus's mom—motherly and concerned. "I don't know, Kate. You work hard for your money. You need it, too."

I point to the computer on the counter. "Can I use the computer real quick?"

"Sure," she answers, still looking motherly.

I look up the address for Rosenstein & Barclay, the law firm Maddie works for, and jot it down on a piece of paper along with general directions to get there. I have some free time this afternoon, and she said her rent's due tomorrow, so I'll take her the money now. Why is she paying her rent in the middle of the month, anyway?

The building Maddie works in is right smack in the middle of downtown Minneapolis, so after I find an open meter and plunk in a few coins, I enter and take the elevator to the third floor. The elevator opens to Rosenstein & Barclay's foyer. The floors are stone and buffed to a high sheen. There are fresh flowers on the table outside the floor-to-ceiling glass doors that mark the entrance to Maddie's employer. I feel underdressed in my flip-flops, jeans, and *Virginia is for lovers* T-shirt. I'm suddenly regretting not calling first. I mean, lawyers are super busy, right? She's probably in some important meeting, or maybe she's in court. Who knows? Now I feel like an idiot. After I take a deep breath, I pull open one of the giant doors, and a chime sounds announcing my arrival. Jesus, it's the bell's evil cousin.

A woman looks up from the other side of the reception desk just inside the door. She's polite, and she addresses me directly, "Good afternoon." She's dressed in a trim, tailored black suit and looks too professional to be sitting behind this desk.

I clear my throat. "Good afternoon. I'm sorry to bother you, but I'm looking for Maddie Spiegelman. Is she available?"

The woman smiles. "Sure. She should be back any minute." The woman holds her hand up to shield her mouth from the rest of the room and lowers her voice. "She just ran to the restroom. I'm covering the phones for her until she gets back."

Okay, I'm confused. "Covering for her? You mean Maddie's the receptionist?"

The woman nods but looks confused by my question.

"I'm sorry, Maddie's my aunt. I just... I just didn't realize what her position here was."

She nods. "Well, here she is now."

I turn, and Maddie's face drops when she sees me. Her voice is low and malicious as she nears. "Kate, *what are you doing here?*" she hisses.

I hold up the check I've already written out from my emergency stash. "Your text sounded urgent. I wanted to make sure you could get it to the bank today since your rent's due tomorrow."

"You could have called, Kate. A little courtesy, please," she chastises.

"Sorry, dude. If you don't need the money anymore, it's no sweat off my—"

She interrupts me and rips the check from my hand. "No, I'll take the check. I had a lot of unforeseen expenses come up this month. Stuff you wouldn't understand."

I can't help but roll my eyes at her. "Seriously?" *Try me,* I want to say. *Been-there-done-that* is my middle name.

She doesn't reply.

I'm a little irritated, but I'm also worried about her. "Why haven't you responded to any of my texts? I mean, how have you been?"

She inhales deeply and lowers her voice. "I'm fine. There's nothing to talk about."

I lower my voice to match hers. "Why'd you lie to me about your job?" I'm not being mean; I'm just asking a question. A question she should be adult enough to answer.

Or not. She just looks at me like I've insulted her. "You need to leave now. I have work to do. Something you probably wouldn't know anything about, being Janice Sedgwick's daughter. I bet you had it rough living on the beach with all of Mommy's money."

I blink through the shock of her words for several seconds. "Wow. Okay. So that's how it is..." I trail off, dumbfounded, my cheeks hot with anger. I turn toward the door and by now adrenaline is coursing full throttle through my veins as I push the door open. As I cross the threshold, I turn and lock eyes with her. "I'm really glad you can make your rent this month, Maddie. *You're welcome.*" I let the door slam behind me.

SATURDAY, SEPTEMBER 17

KATE

A TEXT FROM MADDIE, *U need to call b4 u come. It's rude.*

Maddie's got one helluva way with apologies. I respond, *Sure.* Because I need to bite my tongue. This is not worth fighting over.

I don't expect a response, and I'm ready for this to be over, but it comes anyway, *Can we talk?*

Of course, I've already softened to her because I can't hold a grudge. Or maybe I'm just a sucker. Either way, I forgive easily. *Call me*, I text back.

Maddie calls immediately and pours her superficial heart out. And because it's her superficial heart, we don't touch on the real issue —her bulimia. We talk about money instead. Which, let's face it: if all the money in the world dried up and blew away, she'd live. If the bulimia doesn't go away, it will kill her. But she's not ready to talk about it yet, so I don't push it. At least for the moment we're communicating.

She says she lied about her job because she didn't think I'd be impressed if I knew she was a receptionist and not a lawyer. Like I care. She could be a garbage collector, and I wouldn't be any less impressed than if she *were* a lawyer. People get way too hung up on labels and titles. Then she tells me she's in way over her head with credit cards and debt, and that her roommate moved out unexpectedly in July, and she hasn't been able to find someone new to take over the other half of the lease. She's two months behind on her rent, and they'd started threatening her with eviction. That's why she called me. She didn't know what else to do. I do feel sorry for her, but it always astounds me how people get used to a certain lifestyle and decide anything less is unacceptable. I went from growing up in a beachfront home to living in a garage with my sister. And you know what? I liked the garage better. I guess Maddie couldn't do a garage. I reveal some of this to Maddie but spare the details, the grief. It's always been a struggle, and that's all she needs to know. I'm not looking for pity, but sometimes if people feel like they can empathize with you, it's kind of like giving advice without actually *giving* advice. Backward I know, but no one likes to be told what to do. They like to figure it out for themselves. As the reverse psychology session is wrapping up, I remember my conversation with Morris last night and have an idea. "Would you be opposed to having a male roommate?"

Her voice lights up. "No, especially if he's attractive and single."

"Attractive yes, single not so much."

"All the good ones are taken."

"Also, he's gay. Does that make you feel any better about him being taken?"

"Um, not really." She laughs, and for the first time since I've known her, I feel like I'm talking to the real Maddie. She sounds sincere and exhausted like her life is just too much and for a moment, she's not worrying about what other people think.

"Sorry. But his cheekbones are exquisite. I wouldn't mind looking at him every day."

"I'll take your word for it." She laughs again, and it sounds good on her.

"I'll get ahold of him today and have him call you. His name's Morris."

"Okay."

"Cool. I hope it works out."

I text Clay for Morris's number, and then call him.

An hour later, Maddie and Morris met, talked, and by 5:30 pm, Morris had packed up his hotel room and moved into Maddie's second bedroom.

I love it when a plan comes together.

SUNDAY, SEPTEMBER 18

KATE

"Um, Sugar, is there something I can help you with?"

My roommate is rifling through my closet when I walk into our open dorm room. I've surprised her, and she jumps at the sound of my voice. It's guilty surprise, and reminds me of when I'd catch Gracie sneaking cookies before dinner. I guess she didn't hear me come in or expect me back so soon.

"No... No, I, um, I couldn't find one of my shirts, and I thought maybe...maybe it got mixed in with your shit on the floor, and you accidentally put it in your closet."

She's lying. Her cheeks are the guiltiest shade of red—a dead give-away. I don't like it, but I'm not going to call her on it, because while she was ineloquently justifying whatever she was doing, all I heard was Gracie's voice in my head saying, "I wasn't going to *eat* them, Kate." I walk past her and hang my bag on the back of my desk chair. I notice two of my shirts on her bed. I sure as hell didn't leave them there. I pretend not to notice. "What's your shirt look like, dude? Maybe I can help you find it."

She licks her lips as her eyes flit to her bed and my shirts. She knows she's been caught, but she lashes out at me anyway. "Never mind. It's probably in the laundry," she snaps.

God, I wonder if she realizes what a terrible liar she is?

As I walk toward the door, I offer, "If you say so. Nature calls, I need to run down the hall." I point to my shirts on her bed as I reach for the doorknob. "And Sugar, if you want to borrow one of my shirts, all you have to do is ask. They're like my kids, though; I'm protective, and I like to know where they are at all times." I don't look back before letting the door shut behind me.

I bump into Peter, who's just walking out of his room across the hall. "Hey, Pete, sorry."

"Hi, Kate. No problem, I didn't see you either."

"Where are you headed, mon frère?"

"Cafeteria. I was waiting for Clayton, but he just texted and said that he's having dinner with Morris in Minneapolis tonight."

That makes me happy. Clayton has talked to Morris every day since we went to Spectacle, and they've gone out every night. Clayton's on cloud nine. "Righteous. Well, I realize I'm no Clayton, Pete, but if you don't mind waiting for two seconds while I use the little girls' room, I'll join for the entrée du jour."

Peter smiles that nervous smile that tells me: (a) He's relieved he doesn't have to go to the cafeteria alone, and (b) He's relieved to not have to ask someone to come with him, so he's not alone. "I don't mind. I'll wait outside."

I run down the hall. "I'll be out in two minutes."

Dining is routine, but Pete and I are becoming accustomed to eating without Clayton. I miss Clay, but I don't mind time alone with Pete either.

At first, I had to carry the conversation with Pete because he's quiet and shy. And I didn't mind because he's kind and funny, and I liked being around him. But then I discovered Pete has this insatiable thirst for national and world news, political and otherwise. And though we sometimes differ on our views, because he leans slightly right and I lean slightly left, we're both open-minded enough to listen to the other person's opinions. Not many people are like that, I treasure open-mindedness. To me, Pete's intellect is a gift. I have to be honest: I was a little insulted at how shocked he was that I could hang with him in debates involving foreign policy or the economic crisis in Europe, but I'm kind of used to people assuming I'm just a dumb blonde. And I admit that I sometimes perpetuate that assessment, because it's just easier and kind of funny. If you're important to people, they take the time to figure out you're not—a dumb blonde that is. Pete's taken the time.

We're talking about the current situation in the Congo when I notice Pete's eyes keep drifting just over my left shoulder. I turn around and pretend I'm looking for something in my hoodie pocket that's hanging on the back of my chair. The cafeteria is almost empty except for one girl sitting by herself in the corner behind me. I see her in here every day. She always sits by herself, and she's always reading, totally immersed. She's small and has mousy brown hair that's always pulled back in a messy bun. She wears glasses that are perched on the end of her nose, the same way old people wear reading glasses, but hers aren't reading glasses. They're big and round. As usual, she's completely wrapped up in her book. The entire building could crumble around her, and I doubt she would notice. I admire intense concentration like that. Reading is an escape from the outside world. Everyone needs a little of that to keep their sanity.

I turn around and go back to eating my peas, sorting out the carrots and pushing them aside because they're repulsive. Cooked carrots taste like baby food mixed with dirt. Only in this cafeteria have I ever seen peas and carrots served together. What a disappointing combination. I always thought they just made that up in *Forrest Gump*—"like peas and carrots"—but I guess not. I liked Forrest and Jenny together and now, sorting my carrots from my peas, I'm left wondering if maybe they weren't right for each other after all. Forrest and Jenny were more like peas and butter or peas and salt, anything but carrots. I gesture over my shoulder with my fork. "Hey, Pete, you know that girl over there?"

Awareness flames in his cheeks and he shakes his head slightly.

I smile inwardly because I'm pretty sure he was checking her out. "She always sits alone; maybe we should invite her to come sit with us sometime."

The blush deepens, but other than that there's no movement. He doesn't speak.

I lean across the table and whisper, "She's pretty cute, Pete. She's got the unassuming, sexy librarian thing going on."

He smiles slightly and gives himself away, but averts his eyes away from mine and stares into his mound of mashed potatoes so intently that I swear he expects them to speak to him.

I lower my voice in hopes that I won't embarrass him further. "Dude, you should ask her out."

He looks terrified and shakes his head again.

I sigh, but keep my voice low. "Pete, you've been checking her out the whole time we've been sitting here. Don't tell me you're not interested."

"I wouldn't know what to say," he says, exhaling. He seems help-less, or maybe hopeless, or maybe a little bit of both.

I extend my hand across the table in introduction. "How about, 'Hi. I'm Peter Longstreet. Do you mind if I sit down?' Conversation would naturally progress from there."

"What if it didn't? What if she ignored me, or...or...or told me to get lost?" Yeah, that's sheer panic I hear in his voice.

I smile. "I don't think people even use the phrase 'get lost' anymore. I'm pretty sure you're safe."

He cracks a smile. "You know what I mean."

I reach across the table and put my hand on top of his to stop his fingers from tapping his spoon against the tabletop. "Pete, dude, you're an amazing guy. She looks like a perfectly nice girl. What have you got to lose? You should go talk to her. Listen, I'm all finished up here anyway, and I've got a paper to get started on, so I'm gonna head back to the dorms."

"You shouldn't walk alone," he says after me. He and Clayton are always worried about me walking around campus after dark by myself. They bought me two cans of pepper spray: one for my keychain and one to keep in my bag.

I smile and release his hand from mine. "I'll be fine. When I leave, give yourself a few minutes to summon some courage and promise me you'll stop by and talk to her on your way out, okay?"

He looks like he might pass out or puke, but he nods and looks resolved in a terrified new way. "Okay."

I slip on my hoodie and grab my dishes. "You're the man, Pete. That's your new mantra. I. Am. The. Man." I wink. "Good luck."

He exhales. "Thanks, Kate."

I drop off my dirty dishes, say, "Hola," to Hector, and on my way out, I notice that Pete's on his way to drop his tray of dishes as well. I know I have about forty-five seconds to make my move, so I make a beeline toward Pete's girl's table. The cute librarian doesn't look up from her book, even though I'm standing less than a foot from her. I'm invading her space, and I feel bad about that, but I don't have time to waste. I clear my throat. Nothing. So I kneel down and start speaking. "Excuse me," I say. Her eyes dart to me. "Hi, my name is Kate. I'm sorry to interrupt, but in about thirty seconds my friend, Peter, is going to stop by to talk to you. He's really nervous about it, but please know that he's a nice guy, a really nice guy. Please hear him out." She frowns, but nods. "Thanks." I exit quickly without looking back.

PETE KNOCKS ON MY DOOR ABOUT FIFTEEN MINUTES AFTER I return from dinner. His smile is so big that I notice for the first time he has dimples in both cheeks. He immediately starts rambling. *Rambling!* He's usually reserved and calculated even when he's being funny, so this is something. "Her name's Evelyn. She's a freshman, American History major. She likes reading the classics, but enjoys biographies and science fiction as well." He looks so pleased with himself.

I glance at my watch. "That's one helluva report."

His smile hasn't faltered, not even a millimeter. "She's easy to talk to."

I slap him on the shoulder. "Excellent. See. She loves you already. Did you get her number?"

His smile slips a little. "I thought it would be too forward to ask her the first time I talked to her. Would it have been too forward?"

I shake my head. "No. If you're feelin' it and she's into you, it wouldn't have been too forward." His innocence kills me.

His eyes flash away from mine, and his lips tighten in frustration. He's upset with himself. "Darn it."

"No worries. You'll have something to talk about next time you see her."

The two-dimpled smile returns. "I'm meeting her at the cafeteria at seven o'clock tomorrow. We're going to eat dinner together."

I clap my hands. "Hot damn, Pete, that's practically a date."

"Thanks, Kate." His eyes go to the floor and then back up to meet mine again. "You know, for the encouragement. I would have spent the rest of the semester just looking at her if it weren't for you."

I don't expect to be thanked for everything, or really for anything. But I never take a thank you for granted, especially when it's one as heartfelt as this one. "That would've been creepy." I wink. "So, you're welcome."

He nods and turns to unlock his door.

"Pete?"

He turns. "Yes?"

"I meant what I said earlier. You're an amazing guy. And Evelyn's a lucky girl." I smile. "Good night."

He smiles shyly. "Good night."

I feel like I've just seen happiness and confidence bloom in my friend for the first time. What a great combination.

MONDAY, SEPTEMBER 19

KATE

"What's shakin', bacon?"

"Hey, Gus. Not much. What about you, mon ami?" It's good to finally hear his voice. We've been communicating through texts the past few days because he's been in nonstop meetings. It's not the same. I like to hear his voice. It tethers me to reality, to the real me.

"More of the same. I can't wait to just get out on the fucking road."

Gus isn't really the type of person who can appreciate every part of a process. He's always been kind of coddled by his mom, and his life has been pretty easy. Not that he doesn't work his ass off. Life's just been easy. He'd rather skip what he doesn't like, even if it's important in the long run, to get to what he actually enjoys. I guess we're all that way. It's not being selfish, it's human nature. Sometimes we need reminding that it's all important—the good and the bad. So, I say, "I know, dude, but preparation's the key, right?"

He exhales, and it sounds less like Gus than I can remember hearing in a long time. "It's just that the preparation and marketing seem like it should be someone else's job, you know? I mean, that's what the record company and our agent and manager are getting paid shitloads of money to do, right, preparation and marketing?" He's getting really worked up. "It's our job to play the music; we shouldn't have to worry about anything else. It's like trying to herd fucking cats, Bright Side. Everything's constantly changing. And so much of it is complete bullshit. We had to spend an hour today listening to some dude coach us on fucking interviews. What to say, what not to say. Here's a novel idea, be honest and talk about the fucking music when someone asks a question."

"Whoa, Gus. Slow down. They're just trying to help protect your image. Are you somewhere you can smoke?" Gus's anxiety level has been increasing incrementally every day during the past month. I don't like to see him stressed out like this. I love his bandmates, but I know he's bearing the brunt of what's going on by himself, because, well, they don't. Or won't.

"Yes," he snaps.

"Maybe—"

I'm interrupted by the click of a lighter and that deep first drag. "I'm one step ahead of you and don't fucking say it, Bright Side."

I know I shouldn't because he's in a really shitty mood, but I also know it's not because of me, so I don't take it personally. "But you should, you know...quit."

"Don't." His reply is clipped and final. I sit and wait for him to finish his cigarette and then the apology comes. "Sorry. I didn't mean to take it out on you."

"I have a question for you. How would you have felt if MFDM came into the studio with his own songs and told you were going to record them instead of Rook's?"

"I would've told him to fuck off."

"Fair, because they need you, obviously, to be involved in the process of recording the music, because it's *your* music."

"Damn right."

"But it was still collaborative, right? MFDM was pretty involved, right?"

"Yeah."

"Okay, so the next step is preparing you for the release of *Rook's* album and touring to support *Rook's* album."

"Yeah. Where are you going with this?" He sounds both impatient and curious at the same time.

"Well, you sort of have to trust that they *are* the experts regarding the album release and tour, but that doesn't excuse you from doing your part. If you don't step up and take ownership of every step of this process, it's gonna come back to bite you in the ass. And you're not going to have anyone to blame but yourself. CYA, dude. Cover your ass."

He huffs, and I know he grudgingly agrees with me. "But it sucks. The meetings are mindless babble. I sit there and after five minutes of listening to them, I wonder when they turned into the goddamn Charlie Brown adults. It's all 'Wah, wah, wah.' And I'm so fucking tired of having my picture taken. What's with all the photo shoots?"

I add some humor. "Maybe you're just so damn good-looking they can't help themselves." Time to bring Gus back to reality. "Listen, Gus, I'm on your side, you know that. *But, seriously, dude?* You're doing something right now that people would sell their souls to do. You just recorded an album of your music. Gustov Hawthorne's music. And it's honestly the best album I've heard in a really long time. You released said album, and you set out on a *goddamn nation-wide tour*. You get to live the life of a rock star every day for at least the next three months. All they're asking in return is that you play an active role in promoting the band, album, and tour to make it as successful as possible. Gus, do I have to remind you that this is *your* band, *your* album, *your* tour? You don't have to sacrifice yourself or lose who you are in the process, but it's in your best interest to partici-pate in *every* aspect. Don't bitch about it; just do it. It's kind of your job."

He sighs, and I know I've gotten through to him. "You're right. I know. I'm whining like a fucking baby."

I smile. "The good stuff is coming, I promise. Before you know it, you'll be playing in a different city every night and your biggest worry will be trying to decide whether you want to hook up with the sexy brunette in the front row who flashed you her tits or the blonde identical twins who show up backstage after the show. Maybe both." The idea itself makes my stomach turn, but I know I'm speaking Gus's language: women.

Gus snorts. "All right, enough about me and my whining ass. How was dinner tonight?"

I try out my exaggerated British accent. "It was lovely, darling. Cheesy mashed potatoes, green beans, and lettuce salad. I dined in the company of Clayton, Peter, and his girlfriend, Evelyn."

"Wait, Pete? Leather Chaps Pete has a girlfriend? When did this happen? Where have I been?" Gus follows my life like a soap opera. It's funny how interested he is in all these people, especially with everything that's going on in his life. Maybe it's *because* of everything that's going on in his life. It's an escape. Like reality TV.

I drop the accent because it's too much work. "Last night. Pete spotted her across an empty cafeteria, and it was love at first sight. I'm proud of him. The dude's never had a girlfriend before. He was scared shitless, but he talked to her anyway, and they hit it off. They already made plans to eat dinner together and then study in the library every night this week. It's cute as hell how awkward they are around each other. They're both trying so hard. I feel like it's restored my faith in humanity."

"Faith in humanity has never been lost on you, Bright Side. But good for him. What's she like?" He's genuinely interested.

"A lot like him, actually—."

He interrupts me. "She's into S&M and wears leather chaps, too?"

I giggle. "No." And then I laugh harder. "No. Eww. I don't... want...that visual."

He's laughing, too. After a few moments, he says, "So, what about you, Bright Side?"

"I'm not into S&M or leather chaps." I deadpan. "My ass is too flat, it wouldn't fill out the chaps. It would just be disappointing."

He laughs, but it's forced. "I'm not even going to comment on the chaps." He adds under his breath, "But there's *nothing* wrong with your ass. *Nothing at all.*"

Back to his original question. "So, what about me?"

"Well, Clayton's got a boyfriend, and now Peter's got a girlfriend, so I was wondering if you...you know...if you've met anyone?" He sounds nervous, which is rare for Gus, at least with me. He knows he can ask me anything.

"I don't want a boyfriend, Gus. You know that."

"God, how can the most positive person I know not believe in love? You're such a contradiction. I'm sure you have guys hitting on you all the time, just like you did at home."

I clear my throat. "Actually, no. No one's asked me out since I've been here."

There's his nervous laugh, and then he says, "You know it's not because they don't want to, it's because you're fucking intimidating, you little shit. It takes balls to even flirt with you, let alone ask you out. You scare the hell out of guys, because they already know before they ask that you'll turn them down. They know they don't stand a chance."

"The only guy that's even flirted a little bit with me is Keller, the guy who works at the coffee shop I go to. But it was just innocent flirting."

"Are you attracted to him?" His voice sounds tentative.

"I don't know, yeah, I mean he's good-looking, for sure. But, I'm not looking for a hook-up right now."

"But if you were?" He's really pushing this.

"I'm not. Besides, he may be in a long-distance relationship, so I don't even know why we're talking about it. I'm not getting in the middle of that. We're just friends." That's final.

He sighs. He's not satisfied with my answer, I guess. We sit in silence. "Listen, dude, I'd better get to my homework. But, Gus?"

"Yeah?"

"I know everything that's going on in your life, between the album and the tour and everything else...that, you know, that it's not all fun and some of it *is* bullshit, but that's life, dude. Sometimes it sucks. But you know what?"

"What?"

"Gus, it *always* gets better." In my heart, I still believe this, but I have to keep reminding myself. It's hard when feelings and attitudes that were once second nature are now something I have to put effort into.

It's quiet for several seconds, and then, "You live up to your name every day, you know that, Bright Side?" The smile's faint, but it's there in his voice.

"I try, dude. I try." Every day, every hour, every minute, I try. "Do epic," I remind him.

"Do epic," he repeats. Repetition is the key. Someday he'll believe it. "I miss you."

"I miss you, too. Every day."

"I love you, Bright Side."

"Love you, too, Gus."

"Good night."

"Good night."

TUESDAY, SEPTEMBER 20

KATE

I'm driving to Minneapolis to pick up an order of vases as a favor to Shelly. She's stressing because her supplier messed up, and she needs to have three vase arrangements done for an early morning delivery tomorrow.

The drive is nice: clear roads, clear sky. I have the college radio station playing.

Just as I'm pulling up in front of my destination, a new song comes on. I hear the first three notes, and my heart stops. It's "Killing the Sun!" Rook's "Killing the Sun" is on the radio! Oh. My. God. It's real. Gus's song is on the fucking radio! And it sounds so much better than it does on my iPod because I know hundreds of other people are hearing it right now with me.

I tear into my bag searching for my cell. I need to call Gus. I need to share this moment with him. This only happens for the first time once. The first time I hear *his* song on the radio.

He picks up on the second ring. "Bright Side—"

I interrupt. "Gus, shut up and listen." I turn the radio up and put my phone against the speaker on the dash. At this point, the song has reached the first chorus and it's my voice is filling the car. I put the phone back to my ear and I'm yelling because I can't contain myself. "Dude, your song's playing on the radio in my fucking car!"

"Okay." He sounds confused. "You listening to the CD? Are you drunk? Why are you yelling?" He doesn't get it.

"Dude, it's not the CD! The college radio station is playing your song! It's on the radio!"

"What?"

I turn down the radio so I don't have to shout over it. "Gus, I'm sitting in my car in Minneapolis fucking Minnesota listening to 93.7 on the FM dial and they're playing Rook."

"No way!" Now he gets it.

"Yes! I had to call and share it with you. This is so rad!"

"No way." He sounds stunned. "It's real, isn't it, Bright Side?"

"Hell yeah, it's real. This is your moment, dude. Your song's on the radio and your tour starts this weekend. You'd better squeeze the life out of every single minute of this."

I hear the lighter click on the other end of the phone and the familiar long inhale that brings his cigarette to life.

"You should quit." I don't wait for his reply. "Oh, and dude, while I'm nagging, I'm only going to say this once, because I feel like I owe it to you as a friend."

"Okay, shoot."

That sounded receptive, so I proceed, "On the tour, three rules: no drugs—don't dumb down this experience, dude; wear a condom *every* time; and don't lose your mind, all right?"

"That's a lot to remember." He's teasing me. "Do you think you could type that up for me and I can tape it up in my bunk on the tour bus as a reminder? Or maybe I could just get it tattooed *on my ass?*"

"Ha, ha."

"I know, Bright Side. No drugs—I'm getting too old for that shit anyway; condoms are a given—they're man's best friend, I never leave home without 'em; but losing my mind..." He pauses. "You may have to remind me again about that one. You've always been my voice of reason."

"Reason is my middle name."

"I thought it was smartass, Bright Side Smartass Sedgwick."

"Compliment accepted. Well, I'd better go. I just wanted to call and let you know you're officially on the radar."

"Thanks, Bright Side."

"Anytime. I love you, Gus."

"Love you, too."

"Bye."

"Bye."

WEDNESDAY, SEPTEMBER 21

KATE

THE KNOCK on my door is unexpected. I just walked in the door from class and I didn't see anyone in the hallway.

When I open the door, it's John, the RA. I like him, but he always seems annoyed to have to do his job. "This FedEx package was delivered for you this morning," he mutters. Damn, he seems really put out. He hasn't been part of the *Grant College Experience*. I've often wondered how, with his total lack of enthusiasm, he got the job. He's a grad student, so maybe he was pumped up in the beginning and has been beat down over the years. My goal before the end of the semester is to make this guy smile.

I take the envelope from him. "Thanks, John. It was really nice of you to bring this to me." I'm piling it on thick because I don't think he gets any attention. And everyone needs attention. He doesn't have many friends and everyone in the dorms thinks he's a dick. I think he's probably just lonely and a little burned out. He's probably done this job about one year too long.

"I was right in the middle of something important when I had to answer the door."

I nod my head, completely buying into what he's telling me. "Oh, I bet you were, and I appreciate it very much."

"Okay, well, I need to get back."

"Thanks again, John."

He nods curtly and leaves.

I have no idea what's inside this envelope, but I tear it open and dig in. Inside are the eight VIP tickets to the Rook concert in Grant that Gus promised me. This is unbelievable. It's not like I've never seen a Rook concert ticket before, but this is fan-fucking-tastic. The tickets went on sale yesterday and the show is already sold out. I guess Minnesota loves Rook. As well they should.

I text Gus a huge thank you and take the tickets with me so I can hand them all out this afternoon. My friendship with Gus is no secret, but his rock star identity is. Most of my friends know my best friend back home is named Gus. But none of them know that Gus is Gustov Hawthorne, front man of Rook. Because to me, he's still just Gus. Always will be. Rook is amazing and I'm so proud of him, but the best part of Gus...is Gus. The Gus who has always been my best friend, the Gus who I surfed with, the Gus who bought Twix bars for Grace, the Gus who let me cry on his shoulder on the worst day of my life, the Gus who teases me relentlessly, but who also encourages me just as much. Gus.

THERE AREN'T ANY COINCIDENCES. I'VE ALWAYS BELIEVED THAT. So, when I step into the flower shop and hear "Killing the Sun" playing on the radio, I smile.

Shelly is singing along softly. She looks up and points to the radio. "Have you heard this song, Kate? It's my new favorite thing on the planet."

"Oh yeah? The planet?" I ask. Her enthusiasm makes my heart happy.

"They've been playing it all week. Some new group called Rook.

They're sick. I don't know what this guy looks like, but his voice is so damn sexy."

I smile because I can't hold it back and offer, "So, Google them."

She smirks. "Why didn't I think of that, smartass?" She pulls her phone out of her pocket and starts typing. "Holy. *Shit*. He's gorgeous, Kate. His name's Gustov Hawthorne. Take a look." She turns the screen toward me.

I laugh because I could look at my phone and see the same face. But he looks different in the photo on her phone because his hair is shorter. This photo is from one of the numerous promo shoots they did last month, after the band had their makeover with the stylist. I shrug. "He's all right if you're into the tall, overly built, super blond, good-looking thing."

"All right? *All right*? Kate, anyone with a pulse would drop their panties for this guy."

I grimace. I have. "I thought you were into gingers? Gingers who cultivate spectacular hair farms?" Duncan's beard seems to be getting bushier by the day.

"I am. I mean, I love The Boyfriend with all my heart. He's real. This guy isn't. He's fantasy material. *And* he can sing and play guitar." She's staring at the screen again. "Shit," she whispers.

I reach in my back pocket and pull out two Rook tickets and toss them on the counter in front of her. "You should really see him in the flesh. No panty dropping when *Gustov* takes the stage, though. Duncan will be there, and that would just be awkward. The other ticket's for him."

Her jaw drops, and she looks from me, to the tickets, back to me. "How in the hell did you get these? I heard this morning the show is sold out." She looks more closely, then holds the tickets up to show me. "Kate, these are VIP."

"Let's just say some friends owed me. Big time. We're all going." By this time, Shelly has me wrapped up in a full-blown bear hug and it's hard for me to speak. But I do have a giant grin on my face.

. . .

At dinner, I give Clayton and Pete each two tickets so they can bring Morris and Evelyn. Clayton's heard me play Rook before, and though it's not the type of music he's into, he likes them. Pete's never heard of them, but he graciously accepts.

I take a detour and stop by Keller's place on my way home from the cafeteria. No one's home. I already had the ticket in an envelope just in case this happened. I write a note on it: *Keller—Hope you can make it. Kate*

I slide it through the mail slot in the door.

A text comes in a few hours later from Keller: *Thanks for the ticket! Can't wait!*

SUNDAY, SEPTEMBER 25

KATE

MY CELL WAKES me from a near-comatose slumber. I pull my hand out from under my pillow and reach across my desk for my phone, knocking off a book in the process. Even through all this I don't open my eyes, so when I press the button to answer and put the phone to my ear, I don't know who I'm about to talk to. "Hello," or something close to it comes out. I think.

"Shit, I'm sorry, Bright Side. You're sleeping, aren't you?"

I blink a few times and lie, "No...no. Hey, Gus."

"Dude, I'm sorry. Call me back later. When you're really awake, 'kay?" It's concerned Gus.

I yawn and look at the clock—it's 8:30 am. It's been a long time since I've slept in this late. "No, really, it's okay. I need to get up."

Gus sounds hesitant. "I just wanted to call, you know, to tell you about the show last night."

My eyes fly open, and I'm suddenly much more awake. Yesterday, I helped Shelly all day with flowers for two weddings. I was wiped out by the time I got home, and I totally forgot about Rook's show. What a shitty friend I am. "Damn, Gus, I'm sorry I didn't call or text you last night. I went to bed early. How'd it go? Did the hometown crowd show you some love?" Their first show was in San Diego.

"The show was great. The crowd was sick! I wish you could've been there."

I smile because he sounds so excited. I love it when he's this excited about something. "I wish I could've been there, too." I look at the clock again and do some sleepy math in my head. "Dude, it's like six-thirty in California. Have you slept at all?"

"No. I can't. I'm still too amped."

"Refresh my memory. When do you play next, and where?"

"L.A. tonight and Phoenix on Tuesday."

"God, do you realize how wild this is that we're sitting here having this conversation? You're on tour!" I shout. I peek at Sugar's bed and am glad to see she's not in it and that I haven't woken her.

"I know. It's insane, right?"

"You're my hero, Rock God."

"Whatever."

I hear someone yelling Gus's name and then Gus's voice becomes muffled. "I'll be there in a minute."

"I'm keeping you from something," I say.

"It's nothing. MFDM got us a suite downtown after the show as some sort of present or whatever, so everyone's still partying inside. I'm outside on the balcony."

"Get back to your celebration, dude, you deserve it. And good luck tonight. This is the beginning of something big. I can feel it."

"We'll see. Thanks, Bright Side. Have a super duper Sunday."

I haven't heard "super duper" in forever, and it makes me smile. "Always. You, too. I love you, Gus."

"Love you, too."

"Bye."

"Bye."

FRIDAY, OCTOBER 7

KATE

I FOUND a five-dollar bill in the pocket of my jeans during European History this afternoon. I took that as a sign that I must treat myself to a cup of coffee for the ride to Minneapolis to see Gabriel. His school called me yesterday afternoon after his tutor didn't show and asked if I could fill in again and meet with him today after school. If my week were a rainbow, he'd be the pot of gold at the end of it. Gabriel is cooperative, and inquisitive, and happy, and sweet, and stubborn all at once. I love that because he's real. He says what's on his mind, and he doesn't hold back. Life would be so much easier if everyone were that way.

As luck would have it, the parking spot at the curb in front of Grounds is open.

The bell thunders and I ignore it. I'm on a mission.

I expect to see Romero behind the counter, but it's Keller instead.

He's smiling that crooked smile of his. That means he's in the mood to flirt. I'm beginning to figure him out. "Heard I was here and couldn't stay away?"

I roll my eyes. "Don't flatter yourself. I'm not stalking you." I pull the crumpled bill from my pocket and let it drop on the counter.

"Found a fiver in my pocket today. I took it as a sign from the coffee gods."

He picks up the bill and looks at it front and back. It's soft and faded—clearly it's been through the wash once or twice. "This thing's pitiful, Katie." He looks at it again and hands it back to me. "I can't accept it."

"What?" I look at the bill in his hand. What did he just say? I have my heart set on this coffee. I *need* this coffee. "Are you denying me, Keller Banks?"

He pours a large coffee, sets it on the counter, and slides it across to me. "Not you, just your money. This one's on me." He pulls two ones out of his pocket, puts them in the cash register, takes the change, and puts it in the tip jar.

I raise my eyebrows and nod toward the tip jar. "Really?"

He smiles. "What? I'm covering for Rome for like twenty minutes. These are his tips this afternoon, not mine. I'd feel guilty if I didn't tip the guy. I mean I have a reputation for being a cheapskate, but I wouldn't stoop that low."

I'm sure he's telling me the truth, so I raise my cup. "Thanks, dude. I owe you one."

"Don't worry about it. Though, I don't know how you drink all that at three thirty in the afternoon. I'd be up all night. Or are you going out? Planning on not sleeping?"

"Caffeine and I are like this." I cross my fingers. "I don't sleep much anyway, but now that you mention it, I do have a big night ahead of me." Lately my sleep cycles have alternated between weeks of insomnia and weeks of coma-like slumber. This week, insomnia is my new best friend. My body doesn't like me much. I'm trying to make peace with it, but it's been hard. In the past, I only slept four or five hours a night, and I was fine the next day. Now, if I'm lucky enough to get three or four hours, I wake up feeling like I need ten or fifteen more. But that's life, I guess.

He looks skeptical. "A big night, huh? I never see you out."

"I'm not much of a partier. Between work and school, I don't have a lot of free time. I guess I *study* at night instead of going out." I widen my eyes and the sarcasm sets in. "*Crazy, huh?*"

He laughs. "I get it. I don't go out much myself. So, what are you doing tonight?"

"I'm tutoring an adorable ten-year-old at four o'clock in Minneapolis." I glance at my watch. "Which I'll be late for if I don't get going."

He smiles. "Lucky kid."

I meet his smile. "No, lucky me. You don't know this kid."

He nods. "And then what? What are you doing after?"

I moan. "I have to write a paper for Literature on *A Tale of Two Cities* that's due Monday. I'm only on chapter four now. I'm not really feelin' it. It's gonna be a *long* night."

He narrows his eyes. "You've never read *A Tale of Two Cities?*"

And I suddenly feel self-conscious. "No."

He pushes away from the counter and runs his hands through his messy hair. "I don't believe it. What high school graduate hasn't read *A Tale of Two Cities?*"

I raise my hand sheepishly. "Uh, this one."

He rests his elbows on the counter and lowers his voice. "It's one of my favorites. I've read it at least ten times. I can help you tomorrow if you want."

Wow, that's surprising. Not that I didn't think the guy was smart. I mean, there's this stillness about him. He's a quiet observer. Those kind of people are always intelligent. But I didn't realize the guy was into classic literature. God, I'm doomed. Keller is already sexy as hell, but this pushes him over the top. I love smart guys. "I thought you went to Chicago on the weekends?"

"I can only swing it twice a month. I'm here this weekend."

"Okay, sure," I say, my mind racing. "Can we meet here tomorrow at eight o'clock? Or is that too early?" I bite my lip, hoping I'm not pushing my luck.

His head drops. "Ah, Katie, you're killing me."

Now I feel like a moron. What college student gets up that early on a Saturday unless it's to work, or they're suffering from insomnia like me? He obviously isn't working if he's offered to help me. "Sorry, dude, you know what, never mind. It's super nice of you, but—"

He interrupts me. "You didn't let me finish." He's still crouched over the counter resting on his elbows, and when he lifts his chin slightly, he's looking at me through these incredibly long, black eyelashes. Seeing those gorgeous blue eyes, my heart almost stops. "For you, I'll do it. Don't be late, though." He shakes his finger at me in warning. "I know you." He glances at the clock on the wall. It's 3:45 pm. "Speaking of which, I've heard you drive like a bat out of hell, but you'd better get going."

I lost track of time. Again. If I don't get going right now, I'll be late. "Shit." I make a beeline for the door and call back over my shoulder, "See you tomorrow. And the coffee will be on me." I raise my cup. "Thanks again, dude. Have a fantastic evening."

The smile is back, and he salutes. "You're welcome. You have a fantastic evening yourself, Katie."

SATURDAY, OCTOBER 8

KATE

THE BELL ANNOUNCES my arrival at ten minutes after eight. Keller's shaking his head, disappointed with my tardiness. But he's also wearing a smile, so he can't be too annoyed.

I drop my bag next to the loveseat he's lounging in. It's the best seat in the house—directly in front of the fireplace. I walk over and warm my hands in front of it while I catch my breath and apologize, "Sorry, dude, I woke up like ten minutes ago in the library and ran all the way here."

"Why are you sleeping in the library?"

"Sometimes my room is *unavailable*...but that's a story for another time. I went there to read last night and must've fallen asleep. Last time I looked at the clock, it was around five o'clock this morning." I can finally feel my fingers again. I really need to get some gloves. I look to the counter and Romero while I unzip my sweatshirt. "Morning, Romero. How goes it?"

Romero's smile is warm and friendly. "Good morning, Kate. I am well. And you?"

I smile through the sleepy fog in my head. "I can't complain." I look down at Keller as I toss my sweatshirt over the arm of the loveseat. "I need coffee." I point at him. "You? Large? Black?"

He glances at the end table next to him. "Breakfast is served." There are two large cups of coffee and two Danishes.

"Is one of those cherry?" I'm practically drooling at the sight of them. I missed dinner last night.

"One cherry, one apple, I didn't know what you like."

"Keller Banks, I think I love you right now." God, I might even mean that a little...which is kind of scary. But I'm so hungry and tired that I don't care.

He smiles as he hands me the cherry Danish and a coffee. "That's the best compliment I've had all morning. Rome usually holds off until after lunch to declare his love."

I notice then that Romero is standing behind me clearing two cups from a table and wiping it clean. "Don't listen to this silly boy, Kate."

Keller throws his hands up in mock frustration. "Come on, Rome. Would it be too much to ask for a kind word in front of Katie?"

Romero shakes his head. "Aye, niño." And then looks to me. "Keller is like a son to me. He's a good man, Kate."

I smile at his sincerity.

Keller glances back. "Now that's more like it, Rome. Impressive. I owe you and Dan dinner for that."

Romero slaps Keller on the shoulder. "You make your chicken fettuccine alfredo, amigo, and you have a deal."

"You're on. You name the day."

I like watching them together. It's sweet.

I'm just finishing the last bite of my Danish when Keller's attention turns back to me and he rubs his hands together. "Okay, *A Tale of Two Cities*. Did you finish it?"

"Nope. Almost though." I feel the need to apologize because he's here to help and I feel like I'm under the scrutiny of one of my professors. "Sorry."

He brushes it aside. "It's okay. We'll get through this. Just promise me you'll finish it." Again with the look of authority.

"I will. I don't like the guilt associated with an unfinished book. I mean, if you start a book and a couple of chapters in you decide you just aren't into it, that's one thing, but once you reach the halfway point, there's no turning back. You're obligated." He's staring at me, so I shake my head. "It's stupid, I know."

He shakes his head almost imperceptibly. "No. It's not. I even finish books I don't like from the first page." He means it. He's in scholar mode, and it's adorable.

I need to break the spell he's casting over me, so I drag my bag over and pull my laptop out. "So, my paper needs to focus on one character from the book. The lesson behind the assignment is to teach us to write *persuasively*. It's a two-part thing: good cop, bad cop. The first half sells the reader on the character; the second condemns him for exactly the same reasons. A devil's advocate type of thing. It's all about spin."

I like that he doesn't seem rushed, that he listens to me and doesn't look past me. He's present. It's like this every time I talk to him. It's rare that people do that. He drags his fingers across the few days of dark growth on his chin. "Mmm, interesting. A lot of possibilities. Which character are you going to write about?"

"Who would you choose?" This seems like a perfect opportunity to see a side of him I don't know. Bookworm Keller is even sexier than everyday Keller. And everyday Keller is way, way sexy.

He raises his eyebrows. "This is *your* assignment, you tell me first and then I'll tell you." Again with the turn-it-around-back-on-you-and-don't- give-anything-away answer.

"Sydney Carton."

"Why?" His voice is low, gentle, and prompting. It makes me feel like I'm on to something good. It's like he's pulling the information out of me without even trying.

"Because I thought he was an ass."

He laughs. "Fair enough."

"What? He was."

"I'm not arguing. And?" He's prompting again.

"And I kind of liked him for it. He was full of flaws. But, he was the most human of them all, you know? People are fucked up, so he was believable to me. I also dug him, because he was smart as hell. I've never thought of lawyers as sexy, but now I think I may have been missing out. I'm kinda crushing on him."

He smirks at my last comments. "Ironic."

"What?"

The devilish smirk still in place, he shakes his head. "Nothing. Do you think you can effectively present both sides of Sydney?"

I shrug. "Sure. I've always been pretty good at accepting the whole of someone, the good with the bad. I see it all but try not to let it cloud my judgment. People are complicated. Life is complicated."

"You can say that again." For a moment, he gets a faraway look in his eyes, but it fades as quickly as it appeared. "It's important that you finish the book before you write your paper. I don't want to give anything away, but you may look at him differently in the end."

I'm sitting sideways on the small loveseat now, one leg bent and resting on the seat cushion. My shin is touching the side of his thigh. "I will." I nudge his knee with my foot. "So, what about you, Professor Banks? Which character would you choose?"

"Sydney, as well. He's fascinating, probably for all the wrong reasons." He raises his eyebrows. "As bad as that may sound. What he does at the end of the book has always intrigued me. To think what drove him to do it. It must have been intense."

My eyebrows rise. "You've piqued my interest, dude."

"You may be sorry," he says, as if in warning.

"So, I have to ask. Are you an English major? I mean, you obviously love literature."

A smile emerges that teeters between sad and mischievous. "I do love it...but I'm pre-law."

I cover my eyes with my hand, regretting the lawyers are sexy comment earlier. I wish I'd kept my lust crush on Sydney Carton to myself.

He laughs and saves me an explanation by shifting the subject back to me. "What's your major?"

I uncover my eyes, thankful for the reprieve. "Special education."

He nods. "Nice. Though you may have to tone down the language when you get a teaching gig."

Despite my best efforts, I blush. "I know. Bad habit. That's what I get for hanging around guys my entire life."

A sudden voice from behind us makes me jump. "Keller B., what's up?"

Keller shifts his attention to a guy standing behind the loveseat. They both lift their chins the way guys do when saying "hi" is just too much work. "Not much, man." Without missing a beat, Keller swivels back around to face me. "Jeremiah, this is Kate."

Jeremiah raises a hand in a lazy wave. "'S'up, Kate?" I smile as I give him quick once-over. Jeremiah is the first person I've seen in Minnesota that makes me homesick for California simply by the look of him. I could pass this guy on a street corner in L.A. and think nothing of it, but here he sticks out like a sore thumb. His black, razor-cut hair is obviously dyed, with long bangs hanging over his dark brown eyes. His lip and nose are pierced and his ears are gauged out. He's wearing a black wool Civil War era coat, and I can see tattoos creeping up his neck and out the top of his collar. His knuckles are each adorned with a tattooed letter, though I can't read what they say. His holey black jeans are tucked into his knee-high, black, lace-up combat boots.

"Hey, Jeremiah." I point at him. "The coat's killer, dude."

The corner of his mouth twitches toward a smile like the compliment surprises him. "Thanks." His eyes shift back to Keller. "Hey, man, you going to the Reign show in Milwaukee tonight?"

"Nah, Duncan's got the Green Machine tonight, and it's too far away anyway." The disappointment on his face is evident.

Jeremiah nods slowly. "Yeah, me neither. No money." He taps the armrest with his fingertips. "Well, I better get going. Later, bro." He throws me a lazy salute. "Nice to meet you, Kate."

I nod once. "You too, Jeremiah. Take it easy."

When Keller faces me again, the disappointment is still registered on his face. I feel like I'm looking at a kid who didn't get anything for Christmas. "What's the Green Machine?"

"My Suburban. Dunc and I share it."

"Ah. So, who's playing in Milwaukee?"

He shrugs. "Reign to Envy. They're my favorite band."

I search through my mental musical catalog and come up with at least two songs I know. And they're good. If the Deftones and The 69 Eyes had a love child, it would sound like Reign to Envy. They're rock, pretty hard, and a little dark, but not so much so that they don't get some radio play. They're still kind of underground but rising fast. They'll be big soon. "Yeah, I know a few songs. They're good."

"Yeah."

"We should go," I offer. "I'll drive if you pay for the gas and tickets. I only have five bucks, but I promise I'll pay you back when I get paid Friday." Now that the idea's in my head, I don't know what I'll do if he says no. I need a concert fix.

He brushes me off. "Katie, Milwaukee's six hours away."

"And? It's only nine o'clock in the morning, Keller. We can leave at two and be there by eight."

Keller's waging a serious internal battle. I can see it in his eyes. "I can't. I have too much going on and I need to study. I have a test Monday morning."

"Yeah? And I have a paper due on a book I haven't finished yet. I swear I'll have you home by breakfast tomorrow."

This shouldn't be as difficult as he's making it. He stops biting his thumbnail and runs his hands through his messy hair holding it back off his forehead. "This is crazy." He's about to crack, I can feel it. He looks me dead in the eye, and I can almost see the tug of war going on in his head. "Are you always this impulsive?" I get the feeling Keller's life is pretty structured and scheduled. He doesn't do anything on the spur of the moment.

"You've gotta seize the moment, dude. Have you ever seen them live?"

He's biting his thumbnail again, and it's the first time I notice his nails are practically bitten down to nothing. They look like mine. "No."

That decides it. I close my laptop and put it in my bag. "Then this is something you need to do. I won't take no for an answer." I stand and put my sweatshirt on. "You'll just regret it later." I sling my bag over my shoulder. "No one should do regret." I grab my coffee before gently bumping my knee against his as I walk by. "Thanks for breakfast and for the assistance. You're my hero, Keller Banks. Now, go study. I'll pick you up at your place at two o'clock."

OF COURSE I DON'T MAKE IT TO KELLER'S UNTIL 2:15. HE'S waiting outside, his messenger bag slung across his torso. Damn, he looks good. It's Keller's typical look: black Converse; slim-fitting, dark jeans; black thermal, long-sleeved T-shirt; and black hoodie. Simple, but not slacker. He always looks put together but understated. He's not trying to draw attention to himself, which ironically seems to draw even more. It must be a curse being that good-looking.

When he gets in the car, I notice that he's wearing black-rimmed glasses that I've never seen on him before. He tells me that he wears them at night when he takes his contacts out. They make his blue eyes that much more intense and vivid. And framed like that, you can't help but stare at them. Brainy Keller is killing me. I haven't been this attracted to someone in a long, *long* time.

Keller's looking over the dashboard of my car. "This is a nice car, Katie. It's a turbo, too. Nice. I bet it's fast." He looks legitimately impressed.

"It can keep up with me, that's all that matters." I tease.

An unconvincing frown emerges as he buckles his seat belt. "Shel told me, and I quote, 'Kate Sedgwick is the worst fucking driver on Earth.' Should I be scared?"

"You'll be fine. Have some faith." I wink. "Besides, I have a lot going on the next few months, I can't die tonight. Where would the fun be in that?"

We merge on the highway, and I drive at my normal speed. My driving doesn't seem to bother him at all. And he's not faking it. I'd know if he was. When he's nervous, he bites his fingernails. I know because it's my tell, too.

"How long have you had this car? Do you like it?" He's genuinely interested in talking cars.

"I love it. I've only had it a few months. I used to have a minivan."

Keller guffaws. "A minivan?"

I smile and narrow my eyes threateningly. "Hey, dude, don't dog on the minivan. I loved Old Blue. She was my first car. We went everywhere in her. She was kind of a necessity. Long story."

He raises his hands in surrender. "Okay."

"Anyway, as soon as I got accepted to Grant this past summer, my friend had doubts about Old Blue's skills in the snow. She was rear-wheel-drive, you know. So, I sold her and bought his aunt's old car. It's all-wheel drive, so it should be good when we get a big snow, right?"

Keller shakes his head. "When did you get so soft, Katie? I thought you were a strong, independent woman. You're scared of snow?"

I widened my eyes for effect. "Dude, I'm not *soft*, I'm from Southern California. I was raised in captivity; I've never seen snow in the wild."

He laughs and pats my arm for reassurance. "Winters aren't so bad. It's just snow. Piece 'a cake. When the first big one comes, I'll teach you."

The conversation turns quiet, and Keller reaches into his bag to crack some law textbook that's thicker than the Bible. He pores over it the entire way. The only time he looks up is when I'm staring in the rearview mirror, and he asks me what I'm looking at.

"The sunset," I answer. "It's showtime."

He cranes his neck to look out the back window and the light bounces off the lenses of his glasses.

It's worth it. It's orange down low near the horizon and pink on top, like the sky's blushing as it forces out the sun.

When the horizon darkens, Keller turns back to his book, and I give the road my full attention. I don't tell him, but I'm happy he shared it with me.

Thanks to open highways and excessively pushing the speed limit, we break the Milwaukee city limit at 7:45.

THE SHOW WAS OUT OF CONTROL! IT TURNS OUT I'D HEARD A LOT of their songs before, but didn't know it was the same band. The front man had incredible energy. He ran from one end of the stage to the other all night and ventured out into the crowd on the floor a few times. It reminded me of Gus. Gus is a phenomenal front man.

Keller and I didn't drink, but that didn't stop us from jumping and singing along to every song. The crowd fed off the band's energy, the atmosphere was buzzing. Keller and I had to hold onto each other's arms or hands the entire time to avoid being split up by the ever-moving crowd. By the final song, we'd been swept up and found ourselves right up against the stage. The singer strapped a guitar on and played it like he was trying the beat the thing into submission. As the song ended, he bent down, grinned at me, and handed me his pick. *Me.*

I wait until we're outside, and as we walk back to my car, I give it to Keller. "Don't say I never gave you anything," I say, my voice sounding distant through my ringing ears. After all, they're his favorite band. And he plays guitar, not me.

Keller's still looking at the pick in his hand when he drops into the passenger seat of my car. My ears are ringing so fucking bad I wonder if I'll be able to hear over the constant din for the remainder of the night, or the week, or maybe forever.

He looks at me with the brightest eyes and a smile that would put an excited five-year-old to shame. "Thanks, Katie. For going. For making *me* go. That's the best show I've ever seen. I haven't had that much fun," he pauses and shrugs, "ever." I suspected Keller doesn't let loose often. I guess I was right.

"It was fun. I think I've been converted into a Reign to Envy fan. Thanks, dude." I back out of the parking space and glance at the clock on the dashboard. It's just after midnight.

"I never would've come on a whim like this. I admire your spontaneity, Katie. I can't do it."

I elbow him in the arm. "I hate to tell you this, but you just did. I would've missed out on some of the best moments of my life if I weren't spontaneous. Honestly, I try not to think about the future too much. I'm a huge fan of the present."

"I'm always looking toward the future," he says, suddenly serious. "I can't afford not to. The future is all I have."

"Sometimes the future is overrated." And scary.

"Not for me."

"I'm not saying you shouldn't pursue dreams and goals. Just don't forsake the present for the unknowns of the future. A lot of happiness is bypassed, overlooked, postponed to a time years from now that may never come. Don't bide your time and miss out on this moment for a tomorrow with no guarantee."

By now we're on the highway headed back home. Silence comes, and we enjoy it for a few minutes. Keller rests his head against the headrest and looks at me through heavy-lidded, happy eyes and just stares. I feel it. "Where did you come from?"

I shrug. "San Diego."

He shakes his head, because that's not a question I was really supposed to answer. It was rhetorical. I get that.

"Do you miss it?"

I stop and think. "Not really. I mean I miss my best friend, Gus, but he's traveling right now, so he's not even there. And I miss the beach sometimes. Surfing."

"You surf?"

"Sure." Why does this seem to surprise people?

"That's legit, Katie. You're hardcore SoCal."

I roll my eyes. "Whatever, dude."

"So, is Gus your boyfriend?"

"Nah, we've been best friends our whole lives."

"You've been friends with a guy your entire life?" He says it like it's something that never happens.

"Sure. What's so weird about that?"

He smiles, and the devil shines through. "Don't take this the wrong way, but if I had a best friend that looked like you, I'd have a hard time keeping it friendly. Is he gay?"

My smile widens at the thought. "Not that it matters, but no, Gus is most definitely not gay."

"And the guy never put the moves on you?"

I laugh at the unexpected question and smile. I don't know if I should answer this question or not.

He crosses his leg and rests his foot across his other knee. "He did, I can see it in your eyes."

Keller and I are friends, and I feel closer to him now after this trip together, so I decide to open up. I don't have anything to hide or be ashamed of. "I don't know who *put the moves* on who first," I say, forming my fingers into air quotes. He laughs at me teasing his word choice. "But it did get a little..." I search for a term that won't sound too slutty, "*carried away* the last night I was in San Diego."

The question comes quickly. "You're not together now? Like, you don't consider him your boyfriend?"

I shake my head. "No."

He shifts in his seat, so he's facing me. "Okay, just so I'm clear on what you're telling me, you had sex with your lifelong best friend the last night you were in San Diego before you came to Grant?"

I cringe. "Yes." I don't know what Keller must think of me now.

"And you're not together, but you're still best friends?" He sounds like he's genuinely trying to figure this out.

"Yes. And it's not some sort of twisted friends-with-benefits situation."

"Friends with benefits isn't a real thing. You know that, right? One person in that type of situation is *always* into the other one, they're just not being honest."

I nod. "You're probably right. In my case, it just happened. It was a one-time thing."

"And that's not weird?"

I glance at him because I wonder if he's looking at me like I have a third eye now. "No. I know it's hard to understand, and maybe it doesn't make sense, but our friendship has endured so much more. I think we could work through just about anything the world has to throw at us and come out closer than we were before." I shrug. "I'm really not a hoe bag who sleeps with every dude she meets, Keller."

He laughs. "I didn't say that."

"I know you didn't, but come on, dude, be honest, you're judging me right now." I'm not being hard on him; I just want to know what he thinks about me.

He thinks about it for a few seconds. "You're right, I am judging you right now, but it's probably not what you think. I don't know the guy, but I hope he realizes how incredibly lucky he is to call you his best friend. And I'm not talking about sleeping with you."

I smile. "I'd say we both know exactly how incredibly lucky we are to have each other."

He nods. "Good. Don't ever sell yourself short, Katie. You're smart, and you're funny, and you're sweet, and you're gorgeous. And the best part is that you do it all without even trying. I hope the lucky guy who wins your heart someday truly deserves it."

"Thanks, Keller."

He yawns. "You're welcome." I catch his smile out of the corner of my eye. "Wake me up in an hour or so and I'll drive. Good night, Katie." He turns and faces the window, and less than a minute later, he's quietly snoring.

I smile for many, many miles. Compliments don't typically sustain me, but sometimes when the right person throws one at you, it goes a long way. I could live off what he's just said for weeks.

SUNDAY, OCTOBER 9

KATE

Gus is on the tour bus headed for a show in upstate New York tonight. He texted me earlier that the bus had a flat tire this morning, so they're behind schedule. It's easier for him to text when he's on the bus, where talking can be difficult and never private. When I finish my lunch, I text him back.

ME: *Are you there yet?*

GUS: *Another 3 hrs*

ME: *That sucks*

GUS: *Yeah*

ME: *Went to see Reign to Envy last night in Milwaukee*

GUS: *How was it?*

ME: *They're no Rook, but I'm a fan now ;)*

GUS: *Heard they put on a good show*

ME: *Yeah*

GUS: *2nd round of US tour in the works. Late spring. Bigger venues*

ME: *Awesome!*

GUS: *After Europe*

ME: *WHAT??!! EUROPE!!*

GUS: *Finalized this morning. Mid-January. I'm still in shock. Wanna come?*

ME: *Ha! Of course, but you'll have to fly solo.*

Mid-January. I don't plan that far ahead anymore.

WEDNESDAY, OCTOBER 12

KATE

IT SNOWED LAST NIGHT! I can't believe it. I thought winter started in December, and it's October! Barely October!

I was intentionally boycotting cold weather and thought I could delay its inevitable arrival by not buying a winter coat. I know that sounds asinine, but it's all a mental game. My snowy nemesis has proven to be a formidable opponent.

I concede defeat by driving to one of the thrift stores in Minneapolis. I white knuckle the drive and keep my speed at a grandma's pace despite the fact that Old Man Winter showed some mercy in leaving the roads merely wet instead of icy or snow-packed. I'm not ready for that yet. I need a baby-step approach to get acclimated to this shit.

My efforts are rewarded when I score an insulated wool coat—blue and green plaid with a furry collar—for five dollars in the boy's section. It fits, it's cute, it's even new. The tags are still on it. And it's so warm.

I can't wait to show Clayton my score, which he'll predictably approve of wholeheartedly. I love that I have someone who appreciates my weird fashion sense.

Thirty minutes before I need to meet Pete and Evelyn at the cafeteria, I get a text from Gus. *Can you talk?*

Sugar is gone, so I reply, *YES!!!*

A few minutes later, I'm looking at Gus's silly grin on my ringing phone. "Konnichiwa," I answer. "How's life on the road today?"

"Well, Jamie kicked my ass at poker all day, and Franco had the beer shits all morning on the bus. So, you know, it's fantastic, Bright Side. *Fantastic.*"

"Is the weather nice?"

"Yeah, we're in Austin. Got here about an hour ago. It's probably eighty degrees."

"Wish I could say the same for here." I sigh. "Get this: it snowed last night. Like real, motherfucking snowflakes." I'm trying to act pissed, but I can't bring myself to it because I'm so happy to be talking to Gus right now. I know I don't have long, so I need to make the most of it.

He laughs. "No way?"

"Yeah, it's October. Isn't snow against the rules or something until at least December?"

"You're asking the wrong dude that question. Is it cold?"

"Yeah, I had to buy a winter coat today. Though for the locals, this is probably still T-shirt weather. I swear Minnesotans have some sort of mutant gene that makes them immune to hot and cold. It's freaky."

He laughs again but then turns serious. "What about boots? Did you buy some boots? You'll need boots." It's funny when he acts parental.

I over-exaggerate a full-body shiver. "Stop. Buying the coat was bad enough. I don't want to give in to the snow boots yet. I need time to work up to that. Maybe next month, or the one after that." The truth is, I'll need to buy the boots new, because used shoes skeeve me out, and I need to save up for them. That will take a while.

"You're right, you'd better pace yourself." He's teasing me.

I tease him right back. "Need I remind you that you're touring the

United States this winter? That includes the northern, frigid states. You're going to need to buy a winter coat, too, you know."

He exhales through gritted teeth. "I know. I'm still in cold-weather denial."

"It's a nice place to visit, denial, but you can't live there forever." Maybe I should take my own advice.

"Bright Side, are you quoting Confucius or JFK? That sounds so familiar." I know without seeing him that he's wearing this dumb, mocking expression that makes me laugh every time.

"Dude, I think it was Yoda, in *The Empire Strikes Back*. It was part of Luke's Jedi training or something."

We both dissolve into laughter. Gus and Grace loved *Star Wars*. We've watched the movies so many times I've lost count.

After we both regain our composure, he says, "Well, Bright Side, they're calling for me. I guess they're ready for soundcheck. Sorry I couldn't talk longer. I just wanted to hear your voice."

"No worries. Don't be a stranger, dude."

"Right back at 'cha."

"I love you, Gus."

"Love you, too."

"Later."

"Later."

THURSDAY, OCTOBER 13

KATE

THERE'S a post-it note stuck on the door of my dorm room when I get back from afternoon class. It reads, *Package at front desk for Kate Sedgwick.* It looks like John's handwriting.

That's strange.

I retrieve the box from the front desk and think there must be some mistake. It's from an online sporting goods company that I've never heard of.

Back in my dorm room, I open the box. Inside, under two sheets of white packing paper, are knee-high, lightweight, insanely warm-looking snow boots.

There's a card inside, too. *Put these to good use. We're glad it's you and not us! Love, Gus and Audrey*

I slip off my shoes to try on my new boots. They fit perfectly. Immediately my feet feel like they've been wrapped in a fur coat. They're so warm. I feel like I've won the lottery. I never would've been able to buy boots like this on my own.

I call them both. I get voicemail for both. I leave over-the-top, gushy thank yous for both, because I am so very thankful, not just for the boots, but for the Hawthornes themselves.

MONDAY, OCTOBER 17

KATE

CLAYTON TEXTS me on my way home from the cafeteria. *Come with me to Spectacle tonight? Pretty please with a cherry on top.*

It's been so long since I've hung out with Clayton. I text back, *OK ;)*

SPECTACLE IS PACKED AS USUAL. MORRIS IS WORKING, SO I GET Clayton to myself most of the night. I've missed him. We sing, dance, and laugh for hours. Before we know it, it's two o'clock: closing time. We wait for Morris to lock up so we can all walk to the parking lot across the street together.

Just as we walk out the back door into the alley, Morris realizes he's left his phone in his office upstairs. "I'll be right out. Wait out front on the sidewalk. I don't want ya waiting here in the alley."

The alley is dark; there's only one dim light bulb over the door. It's kind of creepy. I grab Clayton's hand, and the contact relaxes him. We haven't taken ten steps when I see two guys walking along the sidewalk we're heading for. When they see us and stop, my skin begins to crawl. And when they turn and start walking toward us, my heart leaps into my throat. I'm scared.

After one of them speaks, I know why. "Look at what we have here. A little faggot."

First, I pray. *God, please don't let them hurt us.* And then I scream and turn to run, pulling Clayton behind me.

We don't make it five feet before Clay is tackled from behind by both men.

I'm in full-on panic mode, but I don't freeze up. Instead, I start screaming, "Stop! Get off him, you bastard! Stop!" I jump on one guy's back as he's standing up. I swing my right arm and punch him in the ear, because it seems like the most painful spot within reach. He smells strongly of alcohol and my stomach heaves. He sways under my weight.

After regaining his balance, he manages to pry my hands free from his head and throws me to the ground. "Bitch!" He spits on me.

I land on my side, and the force of hitting the pavement draws all the air out of my lungs. I wheeze trying to pull it in again. My vision is black at the edges; I must have hit my head. The pavement is rough and grates the skin on my cheek. Staccato bursts of pain pierce through my thigh and stomach, and it's all over before I even realize he's been hitting or kicking me. He's turned his attention back to Clayton, who I can vaguely see, crumpled beneath the other man's knees. I fumble in my bag, which is slung across my chest, and when my fingers recognize the pepper spray, I grip it tightly. Before my attacker manages to assault Clayton again, I spray him in the face at close range. He cries out, clutching his fingers to his stinging eyes.

I lunge toward the man sitting on top of Clayton and kick him in the side as hard as I can. "Get the hell off of him, you son of a bitch!" I kick him again and again and again. I can't spray him, or I risk getting Clayton too. At least he's stopped punching. He grabs my foot and pulls me off my feet.

Just then I hear Morris's voice. "Get ya muthafuckin' hands off him." From the ground, I can see Morris unbutton his suit jacket and pull it aside to reveal a handgun in a holster on his hip.

The guy straddling Clayton puts his hands up in surrender and stands slowly. The other guy's already backing away. Even drunk assholes understand self-preservation.

Morris's voice is measured but strained with pure rage. His right hand hovers over the gun. "Get outta my sight or I swear to God I'll blow ya bloody fuckin' heads off."

Both men turn and run for the street without so much as a glance back.

Morris kneels and coaxes Clayton to sit up with his help. His lip is bleeding, and he's holding his ribs. His eyes are shut, and his forehead glistens with sweat. Morris's voice is soft and gentle, "Are ya okay, love?" but his hands are trembling.

Clayton's cheeks are wet with tears. "Um, give me a minute." Clayton takes inventory of his upper body. "Nothing's broken. I'm just sore."

Morris isn't convinced. "We should take ya to the hospital, Clayton."

Clayton sniffles. The tears have stopped. "Sweetie, I've been beaten up so many times, believe me, I'd know if I needed to go to the hospital. This is about a four on the beating scale. It's probably just bruised ribs. I'll be fine in a few days."

I feel physically sick, and my heart is breaking. I figured Clay's had it rough, but I had no idea. "We should call the police. They can't get away with this."

Clayton looks at me like I'm talking gibberish. "Katherine, my boyfriend just threatened someone with a deadly weapon. That's probably not the best idea. Besides, we don't even know who those guys were. I'm a random hate crime. Calling the cops would do nothing but waste my time at this point."

I kneel down on the other side of Clayton and dab the blood off his bottom lip with my shirt.

Clayton grabs my hand. "Katherine, stop. You'll ruin that shirt."

My hand is shaking in his. "Clay, I'm not really worried about the shirt right now." I just watched one of my very favorite people in the world get singled out and beaten for his sexual orientation. People's ignorance and capacity for violence sickens me.

"But that shirt's one of my favorites. It looks great with your skin tone."

I have to roll my eyes because only Clayton would say something like that at a time like this. "Dude, I can get another shirt. You can't get another lip."

Clayton huffs but lets me finish.

Morris's eyes are running wildly over Clayton. He's at a complete loss as to what to do next. "I'm so sorry. I shouldn't have let ya walk out here alone this time 'a night." His dark, wide eyes find mine, and they're way past anxious. "Y'all right, Kate?"

I gesture to the gun on his hip and answer with a question, "Do you always have that on you?"

"Only when I work late. Never thought I'd need it." He's making fists with his hands, looking like he wants to kill someone.

Clayton is visibly shaking. I wrap him delicately in a hug, careful not to hurt him. "Oh, Clay. I'm sorry I couldn't help you."

He pulls back and looks me in the eye. "Katherine, if you hadn't been here, I might not be breathing right now. You're one of the bravest people I've ever met. You scared the daylights out of me jumping on that barbarian's back. And when he threw you down, my heart stopped. Are you hurt? Did you bump your head? Maybe *you* need to go to the hospital."

My back is sore, and my head is throbbing, but I lie. "I'm fine, sweetie." I kiss him on the forehead before I stand and help him up. The hospital is the last place I want to go, especially when doctors start asking questions.

Clayton looks to Morris. "I probably should head home. I have a History test in a few hours."

Morris is back at his side, and his face softens as he strokes Clayton's cheek. "What can I do for ya?" He's quietly pleading. "What can I do?"

Clayton smiles sweetly. "You can kiss me and tell me you love me, and you can walk me to Katherine's car."

He does all three.

When we arrive back at the dorms, I help Clayton to the men's restroom, where I finish cleaning up his face. I check both his eyes and mine for dilation or any other signs of concussion. Nothing. Normal.

Next, I help him to his room. Despite trying to be as quiet as we can, we wake Pete. He looks alarmed when he sees us both. I don't blame him; we're a mess. While I help Clayton change into his pajamas, because his ribs are so sore he can't lift his arms over his head, Pete gets some ice from their mini refrigerator and wraps it in a washcloth. He offers it to me with questioning eyes but doesn't say a word. I tell him to go back to bed and promise to tell him what happened after we get some sleep. Pete nods sadly and returns to his bed. He gets back under the covers but never takes his worried eyes off us. Clayton winces when I gently press the ice pack to his lips and cheek but exhales as the cold provides some relief.

Bending over him, I kiss his forehead. "Good night, Clay." I'm mentally and physically exhausted. I need to get to bed.

Clayton's whisper stops me at the door. "Katherine?"

I whisper back, "Yeah?"

"Thank you. No one's ever stood up for me before."

My heart tightens. "Anytime."

"I love you."

"I love you, too. Now get some rest."

TUESDAY, OCTOBER 18

KATE

WHEN I ARRIVE AT WORK, the bell on the Three Petunias door tinkles lightly, and I'm met by two sets of eyes taking me in with what can only be described as extreme concern. They're laser-focused on the bruise that bloomed down the left side of my face while I slept last night. It doesn't hurt as bad as it did when I woke up this morning, but it looks angry from temple to jawbone. What really hurts is the rest of my body. All of it. If I could put ibuprofen in a drip and mainline it, I would. Though my body did agree to let me sleep for almost four hours, it was unhappy with me on a whole new level when I dragged it out of bed for class. Needless to say, my body and I aren't on speaking terms today. I hope we can be friends again someday.

Clay's face crumples and tears pool in his eyes. "Oh, Katherine, I'm so sorry. Look at your face."

I haven't seen Clay yet today. He was still sleeping when I left for class this morning, and he wasn't in his room when I stopped around noon to check on him. "Clay, how are you doing today?" I don't want to talk about me.

"I feel like I got run over by a steamroller and left on the side of the road to die."

I can relate.

"Well, no offense, but you look like you got run over by a steamroller, sweetie." The cuts on his face aren't as bad as they were last night, but his bottom lip and right cheek are puffy and unnatural shades of red and purple.

He smiles a little. "I just wanted to say thank you again for everything you did last night."

"That's not necessary, Clay."

He kisses me on my good cheek. "It is. You're the first real friend I've ever had, Katherine. And I'm quite certain that when I'm sitting in a rocking chair somewhere as an impeccably dressed elderly gentleman, I'll look back on my fabulously successful life and know without a shadow of a doubt that I could not have been blessed with a better friend than you."

If I open my mouth to let words out, tears will come with them. I don't cry. I nod instead.

Clayton turns and wiggles his fingers at Shelly. "Toodle-loo, dancing queen," he says as he walks away.

Shelly doesn't even have a smartass comeback. She just looks sad. I know by the way Shelly's watching me that Clay told her what happened. Everything. I'd rather no one knew, but at least I don't have to re-hash it.

"Shelly, I'm fine. Can we talk about something else this afternoon?" I smile so she knows I'm not trying to be a bitch. "Let's get to work."

She nods and I know it's killing her not to say anything, but I love her for it. "I need to make a few deliveries this afternoon. Can you handle this place on your own today?"

"Absolutely." As she's walking out the door, I add, "Please don't tell Keller about this," gesturing to my face. "I've been barraged with pity glances all day." I hesitate, then add, "Like you're doing right now." She looks away. "And it makes me uncomfortable. I hate pity. It drains the life out of me." It really does.

She exhales loudly. She sounds more defeated than irritated. After a few beats, she nods agreement and walks out the door.

I settle into my work. I'm slower than usual given the fact that I'm moving at the pace of a ninety-year-old recovering from double hip replacement surgery.

The bell rings; customer alert. My back is to the door, and my hands are temporarily held hostage by the ribbon I'm trying to fashion into a bow around a vase of roses. "I'll be with you in just a sec," I call over my shoulder.

"You didn't come to see me this morning. What gives? Do I need to resort to blackmail or bribery?" It's Keller. What's he doing here?

I keep my back to him as I respond. "Dude, my addiction is strong but can also be sated with free, though considerably less tasty, coffee from the cafeteria. Besides, I was running late." Bow in place, I turn to face him and brace for the shock. "What's up?"

He sucks in a breath. "Christ, Katie, what happened to you?"

I'm thankful the bruises on my stomach and hip, which are yellowing spectacularly, are hidden beneath my clothing and not on full display, or he'd really freak out. "Would you believe me if I told you I fell down a flight of stairs?"

His lips press together so tightly that they become a thin, white line; there's both fear and rage in his eyes. He shakes his head.

"Took up bull riding?"

"Nope."

"Underground fight club?"

"We're getting warmer. Who's the bastard who did this to you?"

Why is it that when a woman has bruises, especially on her face, people assume they were put there through domestic violence? I'm guilty of jumping to the same conclusions myself. It's a societal assumption, unfortunately born out of too frequent reality. "It's not what you think." I let out a huff of exasperation. "There was a disgusting mixture of ignorance, hatred, and alcohol unleashed on my friend, Clayton, very early this morning." I point to my face. "This was a little spillover. I'm fine, Keller."

The fear and anger have vanished from his eyes and protectiveness floods in. At least it's not pity. "This is *not* fine." I look down and see that his hands are gripping the edge of the counter so tight his knuckles are white.

I reach across the counter and rub my palms over his clenched hands. "Hey, relax. I'm okay. Really."

He shakes his head and pulls off his wool knit hat and his hair sticks up in all directions. I'm distracted. Even hat hair looks good on him. I can't help but smile.

"What are you smiling at?" he asks, head tilted.

My smile widens. "Your hair. You have great hair."

He reaches up and runs his fingers through it, trying unsuccessfully to tame it down. Still, I think his hair is one of the most attractive things about him. He clears his throat and his cheeks flush.

"What can I help you with, Keller?" Now that the whole bruise unveiling is out of the way, I can't deny that I'm happy to see him.

He bites the inside of his cheek like he's not sure how to answer or maybe he's just not done with the previous topic. "You sure you're okay? Because I hurt just standing here looking at that bruise."

I put it to bed. "I'm okay."

He nods, but he still looks torn. He proceeds anyway. "I've been sent on a romantic errand by Rome. He asked me to pick up an orchid for Dan. It's their anniversary, and he wants to take it home to him tonight. He was going to come down here at lunch, but he couldn't get away. Do you have anything like that?"

I come out from behind the counter, and together we pick out a white orchid from the display shelves. After he pays for it, I fashion a thick tube of craft paper around it to help protect it from the cold.

He hesitates at the door. "So," he clears his throat, "you should stop by Grounds tomorrow morning. I'll buy you a cup of coffee. You know, so you don't have to drink that poison from the cafeteria two days in a row."

I laugh. "I try to keep myself on a fairly strict rotation to avoid that. I'll see you tomorrow. But I'm paying. Besides, I still owe you for the Milwaukee trip—"

He interrupts. "No, you don't."

I smile. He doesn't know me. Though he insists on not taking money, I'll find a way to make it up to him. "Pretty soon, I'll be so indebted to you you'll have to take me on as your personal servant to work it off."

"Mmm." His eyes brighten. "There's a lot I could do with that."

I smile. "Not so fast. I'd prefer to stick to a cash deal. I don't have a lot of free time to do your dirty work."

His smile turns playful. "Dirty work? Even better." He winks and opens the door.

I shake my head, but my insides have turned to mush. I know nothing can ever happen between the two of us, but God, I love flirting with this boy.

"I need a haircut. Cut my hair and we'll be even," he offers from the door.

"I don't know how to cut hair. A bad haircut would *definitely* not make us even."

"I trust you."

That makes me so happy to hear. Trust is important to me. "You do?"

"With my life. And my hair. You free Friday night?"

I nod. "Yup."

"Eight o'clock?"

I nod again. "Sounds good."

"Your place or mine?"

I know it's not a date, but you don't know how much I like Keller asking me that question. "Friday nights at casa de Kate and Sugar are unpredictable. So yours."

He smiles. "Excellent. Bye, Katie."

"Bye, Keller."

FRIDAY, OCTOBER 21

KATE

It's 8:12 pm when I knock on Keller's door, and butterflies start fluttering in my stomach. I've never been the stomach-butterfly-fluttering type of girl, so it feels strange. I'm stone sober, but it feels like I've had a few drinks and though my mind's not convinced it's buzzed yet, my body's confessing the indulgence. I think I just fell in love with butterflies.

After Keller opens the door and I step inside, he takes my coat. We don't say anything. It's a little awkward. Not uncomfortable, just awkward. So, I offer, "It's not too late to back out, dude. You sure you still trust me now that you've had a few days to think about it?" This trust thing with him is a big deal for me. There are different degrees of trust, and my general feeling is that most people are good, therefore, I trust most people. Friendship is vital to me and trust is part of that. But on a deeper level, there's *trust*. *Trust* is something I don't toss around lightly. Very few people have ever earned it: Grace, Gus, and Audrey. That's about it. It's something that takes years to build. For some reason, I feel like Keller has already fallen into this *deeper* category. Which is good, but also a little scary because it happened so fast.

He smiles and with it the awkwardness disappears. "Implicitly."

Good. Fucking. Answer. "Okay. Let's get this party started."

His bottom lip is sucked in under his upper lip when he smiles again. His eyes are amused. He wants to say something, but he's thinking better of it. Instead, he grabs a folding chair from the closet and sets it up in the open space behind the loveseat. I'm watching him go through the motions, but I'm not really watching; I'm daydreaming. I'm thinking about what his chest looks like under that shirt. I'm thinking about how warm his skin feels there, and the defined muscle underneath. I'm thinking about what he might look like under those—

"Wet or dry?" He pauses when I don't answer and points to his hair. "Do you want me to wet it?"

Oh. Right. *His hair.* That's why we're here. "Um, wet. I think. Isn't that how the pros do it?" Audrey's always cut my hair. Twice a year in the Hawthorne kitchen, whether I needed it or not. I've never been to a salon.

"Wet, it is. I'll be right back."

Keller disappears to the bathroom and reappears two minutes later wearing only his jeans. Jesus, Mary, and Joseph. He looks fucking beautiful shirtless. My mind floods and I feel like he can see every X-rated thought. And now I'm all fluttery in the stomach again. What the hell is wrong with me?

He sits in the chair, and I try to act casual. "What's it gonna be, Mr. Banks? Trim? Buzzcut? I'm up for anything." *Goddamn, am I ever.*

"I was going to say just a trim, but what do you think? You think I should try something different?"

"Nope. I like what you've got going on." I do. So much.

"Trim it is then."

And now I'm a whole different flavor of nervous because I don't want to screw this up. "Keller, dude, is there some sort of backup plan if I jack this up?"

He laughs and shrugs. "It's only hair, Katie. If you jack it up, *which you won't*, we shave it off."

That didn't help. "Ah, no pressure."

He's completely at ease. "None at all."

Once I start cutting, every other thought, the nervous and the naughty, seems to fall away like pieces of hair. He really does have spectacular hair. It's dark brown, almost black and there's a slight wave to it that adds volume more than curl. It's thick, there's a ton of it, but the strands are baby fine and so soft and shiny. He wears it a little on the long side. It falls just below his ears on the sides and touches his collar in the back. And it's always on the defiant side, which in my opinion, is best. I don't like it when guys try too hard with their hair. Naturally disheveled is sexy.

An hour later, I finish up. The conversation has been minimal. I've been focused on not turning Keller's locks into a debacle, and he's allowed me that focus by keeping quiet. After taking a look in the bathroom mirror, he returns to me, sweeping up the hair on the floor. I smile at him because I didn't screw it up.

"Well, you're certainly not fast, but you are thorough. Good job."

I laugh. "Thorough's my middle name. Or maybe I just wanted you to feel like you got your money's worth."

"Every penny. Thanks, Katie. You want something to drink? I've got a few beers in the fridge. You earned it."

I want to stay, but my conscience is nagging the hell out of me. He has a girlfriend. I'm sure of it. I shouldn't be here alone with him, especially with the dirty thoughts that have started running on a loop through my mind again. "No, thanks. I probably better head back to the dorms."

He glances at the ground and a look of disappointment flashes across his face before he looks back up at me and smiles. "Did you drive or walk?"

"I drove. It's fucking freezing out there."

He laughs. "Freezing." He's teasing me. He grabs his hoodie off the loveseat and slips it on. "I'll walk you outside."

We're standing next to the driver's door of my car, and I can't help but smile inside because I've never had a guy walk me to my car before. Again, my mind knows this isn't a date, but the gesture is chivalrous. I'm usually not into that type of thing, but tonight I guess I am.

"Thanks again, Katie."

"You're welcome. It feels good to be out from under the weight of debt and IOUs."

We both laugh and then the laughter fades to silence. We're just looking at each other now like we don't know what to do next. This could go on all night, so I do what I would do if this were any of my other friends. I open up my arms. "Come here."

He's slow to react, but when he does and his arms wrap around me, I'm overcome. Some people excel in the art of hugging. They somehow manage to hug you with their whole being, not just their arms. Their warmth surrounds every inch of you. It makes you feel cherished and comforted.

Keller has mastered the art of hugging.

The dreamy hug lasts about twice as long as your average hug, but not nearly as long as I'd like it to. When we separate, I feel the cold and instinctively reach for the door handle to get in my car.

"Drive safe, Katie."

"Always. Have a great weekend, dude."

"Chicago in the morning. I'm back early Monday morning." He's smiling.

That is why I behaved myself. Chicago. His other life. His girl-friend. "Have fun. See you Monday."

"Monday," he repeats. "I'll see you Monday."

"Good night, Keller."

He nods. "It was. Good night, Katie."

MONDAY, OCTOBER 24

KATE

CLASSES WERE CANCELED TODAY. The snow was out of control this morning. Everyone's calling it an *unseasonably early storm*.

I'm calling it *Mother Nature on steroids*. And she's uncompromising when she's like this.

Now I understand what all the fuss is about. Luckily, it's letting up now, but early this morning when I strapped my boots on and trudged through the fresh snow to Grounds, that shit was *coming down*. It was worth the trip to spend the morning here drinking coffee and reading, though.

The bell thunders and I ignore it in favor of the book perched in my lap. I've got the good spot on the loveseat in front of the fire, and nothing can distract me from my blissful morning.

Except maybe the low, rumbling voice next to my ear. "Is this seat taken?"

I turn my head slightly to the left and Keller's face is right there. Like an-inch-from-my-face right there. He's crouched over the back of the loveseat, chin resting on folded arms. His face is clean-shaven. It's been awhile since I've seen him like this. He looks so much younger with his baby face revealed. "Hey. Of course not. Sit." I move my bag to the floor to make room.

He drops in next to me after removing his coat, hat, and gloves. "Damn, you'd think we live in Minnesota with all the snow outside."

I roll my eyes. "Don't remind me."

He laughs and elbows my arm gently while he takes a wax paper-wrapped sandwich out of a brown paper sack. "Ah, it's not so bad. Look at it. It's beautiful out there." He sounds so sincere that I hold back a second eye roll and take a look out the big picture window behind us.

It's overcast and looks almost like early evening even though it's only late morning. Snowflakes are falling sporadically again. The streets are deserted. And since I'm inside in front of a fire, dry and warm, it *is* beautiful. "How'd you get a flight out of Chicago this morning," I ask, gesturing outside, "with all this *beauty?*"

"I caught an early flight last night before the snow started. They said it was going to be bad. I guess they were right for once." He elbows me again. "You want half my sandwich, Katie? It's turkey."

"No, thanks." I always try to avoid the "No, I'm a vegetarian" answer because it freaks some people out. I don't know why, but sometimes people look at you like you just told them something unfathomable. They get all uncomfortable. So, I only offer an explanation if it's forced.

He insists and is still trying to hand it to me. "No, really, this thing is gigantic. I feel rude eating in front of you. Take half."

I've just been forced. "Don't feel bad, dude, I'm a vegetarian. And I'm not really hungry anyway; I had a muffin a little while ago."

He blinks a few times. "So... Is it okay if I eat this in front of you? I mean, does it gross you out? Because I can wait or...or go sit over there." He nods his head sideways to indicate a seat across the room.

I look at him for a few seconds too long before I answer because the offer was so considerate. "No. Go ahead and eat. Thanks for asking, though. That was... That was nice."

He smiles and takes a bite, mayo and mustard squishing out of the sandwich onto the corners of his mouth. He talks between bites. "Why vegetarianism? Health reasons, religious reasons, animal rights reasons?"

I shrug. "I don't know. I've just never liked the idea of an animal being born, raised, and killed just so I would have something to eat. There are a lot of other options out there for sustenance."

His eyebrows rise as though he's never thought of it that way. He nods. "Fair enough." After he finishes his sandwich, he crumples up the paper wrap and deposits it in the paper bag and claps his hands. "We should go out driving this afternoon. There's a good eighteen inches on the ground now."

I glance back over my shoulder and judging by the snow on the car parked across the street, he's right. This is as good a time as any to learn how to drive in snow. "Sure, how about one o'clock? I have to work at three today."

"Sounds good."

I shift the book I was reading from my lap to the coffee table in front of us, so I can unzip my bag on the floor. "I'll pick you up at your place?"

He nods distractedly as he picks up my book. "Is this any good?" He asks in reference to the book.

"You've never read it?" I'm shocked.

He shakes his head. "No, I've always wanted to."

I think back to his reaction when I told him I'd never read *A Tale of Two Cities* and throw it back at him. "What high school graduate hasn't read *To Kill a Mockingbird?*"

His grin widens. "I deserve that."

"Yeah, you do. I read it every year or so. It's one of those books that even though you like it, it manages to get better each time, and you find yourself falling in love with it all over again."

He smiles, and I know he can relate, having shared with me that he's read *A Tale of Two Cities* several times.

"Besides, one of the characters is a hero of mine. You know that saying, 'What would Jesus do?'"

He nods.

"Well, my version is, 'What would Atticus do?' He's got his shit together. He always knows what to do." I stand up, slipping my arms into my wool coat and pulling my gloves from the pockets. I sling my bag over my shoulder and salute Keller. "See you at one o'clock."

He salutes back. "One o'clock. I'd drive you to the dorms, but Dunc's got the Green Machine."

"No worries. It's a goddamn winter wonderland out there." I widen my eyes for effect. "I can't wait to get out in it."

He laughs at my sarcasm.

My gloved hand on the door handle, I hear Keller call out, "Katie, you forgot your book."

I smile because I left it intentionally. "It's yours. Someone else should get to love it." It's my favorite book. I feel good knowing I'm leaving it with someone who will appreciate it.

"But you haven't finished reading it." He's holding up the book pointing to the bookmark.

I tap my temple. "I already know how it ends. You don't." I wink and smile, but the honesty and simplicity of the words hit me. He doesn't know. He doesn't know my story. And that's how it needs to stay, because I've always preferred happy endings. "You should meet Atticus Finch. He's a badass lawyer."

I PULL UP TO KELLER'S DOOR AT 1:15 PM AND BEFORE I CAN honk, he's out the door as if he's been listening or watching for me. He's shaking his head.

"Christ, woman, are you ever on time?" He's teasing, but I know it's one of his pet peeves.

"No. Another bad habit. Chronic at this point, incurable." I shrug, because it's who I am. And in the grand scheme, there are worse things than tardiness. "On top of that, I had all this *beauty* to contend with. It slowed me down."

He grins. "Well, you made it. That's a good start."

Keller was born to be a winter driving instructor. His patience is saint-like. He talks me through the deserted, plowed, but icy streets to the auditorium parking lot. I'm glad no one's out because I feel like rolling manslaughter waiting to happen. At least when I mess up, no one's in harm's way. Keller never raises his voice above its usual low, practiced, calm, soothing level. It's the voice that guides me safely over icy roads reminding me to loosen the white-knuckle grip on the steering wheel, and to slow down, and to tap my brakes, and not to hold my breath. It relaxes me. It's a steady, constant comfort. I've grown to love comfort.

FRIDAY, OCTOBER 28

KATE

"Happy Birthday to you. Happy Birthday to you. Happy Birthday, dear Bright Side! Happy Birthday to you!"

You haven't lived until you've heard Gustov Hawthorne sing you "Happy Birthday" over the phone. He does it every year, at full volume, every note over-the-top enthusiasm. "Damn, this is quite a wake-up call, Gus."

"Shit. Did I wake you, Bright Side? It's six o'clock there, right? I thought you'd be up." His sentences are running into each other.

"It's okay, dude, I'm up." I've been up since 4:45 am and have already gone for a run on the treadmill at the campus exercise facility across the street from the dorms. Just running a mile is a struggle these days. But I'm up, showered, and walking down Main toward Grounds for my morning coffee.

"Oh, good." He sounds relieved and, now that he's slowed down to normal Gus-paced speech, a little drunk.

"Dude, you sound wasted. Where are you?"

"Um," he says sleepily, then raises his voice, "Hey Robbie, where are we again, dude?" I hear Robbie's answer and then Gus echoes, "Indianapolis. We're in Indianapolis, Bright Side."

He's shitfaced. I can't remember the last time I've heard Gus this drunk. There's a lot of background noise, so I'm pretty sure he's not on the tour bus. "How was the show last night?"

"Fucking sick!" That was way too excited, even for Gus.

"Sweet." Time to bring him back down to Earth. "Question. Gus, I know you're in Indianapolis right now, but *where* in Indianapolis?"

He pauses a few seconds, and I picture him looking around for clues to help him with the answer. "Don't know. Looks like a hotel room. The whole band's here!" He pauses and then shouts, "What's up, Robbie?!" as if he's just noticed him for the first time all night and doesn't remember talking to him twenty seconds ago.

"Gus, dude, thanks for the birthday wishes. I'm gonna let you go now. Do me a favor and find someone sober who can tell you where you are. I'm pretty sure you guys play in Chicago tonight." I've been trying to keep an eye on his schedule. It helps me feel connected to him since we don't get to talk every day anymore. "You're probably supposed to be on the road right now."

I hear the realization sink in. "Shit," he says into the phone, before yelling, "Shit, you guys," toward the rest of the room. "We play Chicago tonight. We need to get out of here."

"Good man, Gus. You'll be fine. Go down to the front desk and ask them to call you a taxi to take you guys back to the venue you played at last night. And call your tour manager; he's probably going apeshit."

"Right. Thanks." He sounds marginally more sober now.

"I love you, Gus."

"Love you, too, Bright Side. Happy birthday."

"Thanks. Bye."

"Bye."

I'm weird about my birthday. I don't tell people about it because I've never really enjoyed celebrating it. My mother was the type that loved to shower Grace and me with gifts on our birthdays when we were very young. We didn't get her time, so we got stuff. It was a substitute that even a five-year-old can see through. As we got older and she became more unstable, she stopped. No more gifts. And still no time. It was part of her decline.

At least I know the "Happy Birthdays" are out of the way when I hang up with Gus because no one here knows. Or at least I don't think anyone knows until I get a text from Shelly around six thirty that night. I'm at the library.

SHELLY: *Happy Birthday!*

ME: *Thanks? How'd you know??*

SHELLY: *Driver's license. Employee file.*

ME: *Breach of confidentiality?*

SHELLY: *Maybe. Pizza. 7:00. Pick you up at the dorms.*

ME: *OK*

You can't argue with Shelly, so I run back to the dorms and am just changing out of my sweats and into some jeans and a clean shirt when I get a text. It's 6:45 pm.

SHELLY: *What's your room#?*

ME: *2 1 0*

Less than a minute later, there's a knock on my door. I open it up to find Shelly wearing a deep purple peacoat. Her nose and cheeks are pink from the chill.

I glance at my watch. "What the hell? I still have fifteen or twenty minutes."

She smiles and walks inside, then throws herself down on my bed. "I know. Keller's driving. He's always early. Like you're always late. He's neurotic about it. Sorry."

I pull the band out of my ponytail and brush my fingers through my hair. "Keller's coming?"

She's looking at the photos on my desk. "Yeah, I told him this morning it was your birthday. It was his idea. You know, for birthday dinner."

"I'm getting more mileage out of this birthday than all nineteen before it."

She points to the photos. "So, what's the story with these people, Kate?"

I'm pretty private. I don't talk about family or Gus to anyone. Only Clay and Pete know about Gus, and that was out of necessity. And Sugar knows names, but beyond that, she couldn't give a shit. "That's my sister, Grace, and my best friend, Gus."

She runs her finger across Grace's face, it's loving. "I didn't know you had a sister."

"The best." That's where it ends. I'm thankful when she moves on to Gus's photo.

She picks it up and holds it in both hands. "*Damn*, Kate, he's fucking delicious."

"That's a pretty big declaration given that half of his face is hidden behind his hair." I'm grateful she didn't recognize him as Gustov Hawthorne. He looks a lot different with long hair.

She looks at me with those big, wide, dark eyes. "But he is, isn't he? I mean, in person, the guy has to be blindingly good-looking?"

"He's pretty easy on the eyes, yeah."

She shakes her head and sets the frame back on my desk. "Damn," is all she can say.

I grab my wool coat and hat, and we're out the door at 6:55. This may be a personal best—five minutes early.

Shelly opens the back door of the Green Machine that's parked at the curb in front of the dorms. "We rock-paper-scissored earlier. Boys got front seat, so we're stuck in the back. My deepest apologies."

"No problem," I answer until I notice that there is one small problem with the backseat.

There isn't one. No backseat, just three beanbag chairs.

"Jesus Christ, Keller. Beanbags?"

Beanbags.

Keller smiles. "Hey, birthday girl. Sorry about the lack of traditional seating."

"Oh, hell." I climb in and plop down in one of the beanbags.

Shelly jokingly introduces Duncan to me. Duncan apologizes for our first meeting the night of the Back to Grant Bash when we exchanged a few words and he promptly passed out drunk. "Not my finest moment," he says.

The beanbags are actually pretty comfortable, and by the time we pull into Red Lion Road's parking lot, I've been converted. "Why don't all cars have beanbags?" I ask Shelly.

Duncan turns around and agrees, "Right?"

Shelly rolls her eyes. "You mean aside from the fact that certain death is guaranteed upon impact? Gee, I don't know, Kate."

I nod and smile. "Yeah, aside from that morbid little detail. I'll stew on that on the ride home. Thanks for ruining my Shangri-La moment, Shelly." We hop out and walk toward the restaurant together.

Shelly slides into the booth next to Duncan, which leaves Keller to slide in next to me. The booth is small. I try to allow a few inches between us, but our elbows are brushing.

Keller nudges me, his voice quiet. "I should've asked first, but you like pizza, right?"

I nod. "Sure."

Shelly looks at all of us. "Two large pepperoni?"

"One pepperoni, one cheese. Katie's vegetarian," Keller says knowingly.

Shelly's forehead wrinkles. "You're a vegetarian?"

I nod.

She looks unconvinced, like Keller and I are trying to pull one over on her. "Really?"

Keller answers for me. "Really, Shel," he says, and tosses a ten dollar bill on the table. It's funny how proud of himself he is to know this about me.

Shelly and Duncan each toss a ten on the table and Shelly says, "Huh, you learn something new every day."

I dig through my pocket and lay a five and five ones on the table. Keller picks it up and hands it back to me. "Your money's no good here, birthday girl."

I pick it up and look at it front and back. "Why do you always have a problem with my money? It hasn't been through the washer or anything. If you don't let me start paying for stuff soon, I'm going to start feeling like a freeloader."

He curls my fingers around the bills with his hand. "This is your birthday dinner. You're not paying. We are. Besides, I bartend here a few nights a week, so I get a discount on the pizza."

"You work two jobs?" I know he's always busy, but I didn't realize he worked two jobs.

He shrugs. "Have to. The tips are great."

Duncan smirks. "The tips are great because sober women like Keller...but drunk women *love* him."

"I'm a good bartender," Keller defends. It's cute how serious he is.

Duncan looks at me and smiles. "Kate, Keller thinks he makes good tips because of his skills behind the bar." He looks at Keller sincerely. "You *are* a damn good bartender."

Keller nods. "Thank you."

Duncan butts in. "What my boy fails to recognize is that half the women in here on any given Tuesday or Thursday night are here for one reason. And that reason is to check out Keller Banks. It's pretty funny, actually."

Sometimes I feel like I go to Grounds just to look at him. He's gorgeous. I can relate.

As if on cue, a cute redhead walks by and smiles at Keller. "Hi, Keller," she says flirtatiously.

He raises his hand. It's a half-wave to acknowledge her. It's polite but slightly confused.

"You know her?" It's Duncan. He's smirking again.

Keller shakes his head. "No idea."

Duncan laughs good-naturedly. "See. Oblivious. It's not your bartending, man."

Keller's blushing, and it's Shelly that saves him. She leans forward over the table and motions between the two of us. "I hate to rewind this conversation, but you mean to tell me that Keller Banks, the tight-wad, bought something for you? With his own money?"

I shrug as Keller slides out of the booth, money in hand, to go place our order at the bar.

Shelly's smile widens as he walks away. "Interesting."

Twenty minutes later, a pitcher of beer and a pepperoni pizza are delivered to our table, followed by a cheese pizza with twenty blazing candles. Shelly, Keller, and Duncan immediately break into a pretty good rendition of "Happy Birthday." I don't like being the center of attention, but it feels good to know I have such thoughtful friends.

SATURDAY, OCTOBER 29

KATE

COFFEE. I definitely need coffee. I was out with Keller, Shelly, and Duncan late last night. I didn't drink, but I had trouble sleeping. I'm going to need a big dose of caffeine to jump-start my day. Rook's concert is tonight, and they'll be here early afternoon. I need to wake up.

There are a few people in line when I get to Grounds. Romero salutes and smiles at me as he takes money from a man in a suit. Keller's behind the bar with his back to me. I don't think he's noticed me yet when he takes an order from the brunette at the front of the line. She flirts. He doesn't. I laugh quietly to myself. God, I never really noticed it before, but Duncan was right; girls try *so* hard with him. He catches my eye and winks. It's subtle. If I hadn't been staring at him, I wouldn't have noticed. I wasn't the only one who noticed it seems. Someone else is staring. The brunette tosses her hair over her shoulder and scowls at me. And for one moment I feel a primal urge rise within me, a need to claim him somehow. I fight the overwhelming need to leap over the counter and kiss him senseless. But then I remember he isn't mine. The urge passes, and I'm left wondering what the hell just happened.

Finally, it's my turn. Keller pats Romero on the arm. "Can you get Katie's coffee, Rome? Large. Black. I'll be right back." He runs toward the door to his apartment. "And I'll pay for it, don't take her money," he calls back as he opens the door. He's back before Romero has the lid on and waves me to the other end of the counter, then walks around from behind it. He hands me a small envelope. *Happy Birthday Katie* is written on it. It's messy, boy handwriting. Maybe he should be a doctor instead of a lawyer. "Happy birthday, Katie," Keller says, smiling.

"Keller. What is this, birthday week? This isn't necessary. You took me out for dinner last night, remember?"

He shrugs. "That was from all of us." He smiles sweetly. "This is from me."

I open it. It's a twenty-dollar gift card to Grounds. "Thanks. It's perfect." Thinking back to our conversation a few weeks ago at the flower shop, I add, "Is this blackmail or bribery?"

"Neither. It's insurance."

"Insurance?"

"Yeah. That's twelve cups of coffee. Twelve trips to Grounds. Twelve chances to see you." He's wearing this cute, boyish smile. He's clean-shaven again, giving him an irresistibly youthful look.

I hug him, kiss him on the cheek, and whisper in his ear before he lets me go, "Insurance sounds a lot like bribery." Then I pull away so I can look him in the eyes. "You don't need to bribe me, you know? I like hanging out with you. Thank you."

I expect his crooked smile, but his expression is still sweet and sincere. "You're welcome. I like hanging out with you, too, Katie." He gestures to the counter behind him. "Listen, I'd better get back to work, but I'll see you tonight. Can't wait for the concert."

"Rook's gonna kill it tonight." I wink as I walk backward away from him and toward the door. "Prepare yourself appropriately."

He laughs as he salutes. "Will do."

Gus texts a little after two o'clock: *I'm here! We're at the venue*

Me: *Be there in 10 minutes*

I grab my bag from my bed, and I'm on a flat-out run for my car. I'm checking my pockets for my car keys as I run down the steps to the parking lot when I see him leaning against the driver's door of my car. I run faster, and the huge grin on his face is infectious. He scoops me up in a hug and spins around, my feet flying high above the ground. I love Gus's hugs. He's so big; I get lost in his arms.

He sets me down and takes my face in his hands. "I can't believe it's really you, Bright Side. Skype is such a half-ass substitute for the real thing."

I agree. I smile and touch his hair. "You look good."

He shakes his head and then nods toward the building behind me. "So, this is your dorm?"

I nod.

"Then, by all means, give me the tour. I need to meet these characters you call friends. I don't have to be back for soundcheck until five o'clock."

We stop by Clay and Pete's room first. Clayton's in Minneapolis with Morris, but Pete's here. He's polite but timid at first until he and Gus talk for a few minutes, at which point he loosens up. Well, as much as Pete *can* loosen up, anyway. I tell Pete that Gus is in town for the show (and leave out that he *is* the show). Gus asks him where he's from, what his major is, and how he likes Minnesota. I think Pete's a little surprised by all the questions and by the fact that Gus is actually listening to his answers with interest. When I tell Gus we'd better let Pete go, Gus's eyes fall on a framed photo of Pete and Evelyn on the desk next to him and a wicked gleam flashes in his eyes. I don't like it. I've seen it before too many times. He's up to no good.

He picks up the frame. "This your girl, Pete?"

"Yes, her name's Evelyn," he confirms with a dimpled smile.

Gus sets the frame back down. "Cute couple. Tell me, does she like cowboys, Pete?"

"Cowboys?" His eyebrows pinch together at the odd question.

"Chaps, maybe?" Gus pushes.

Oh shit, he's going *there.*

Pete shrugs. "I don't know." He's confused.

Gus leans in like he's sharing top-secret information, but he never lowers his voice, "Dude, a word of advice, chicks dig chaps. A little role-playing livens up the bedroom." He raises an eyebrow and smiles like he's just done Pete a favor passing this along. "Just sayin'."

Pete's face flushes a bright red.

As I physically push Gus out of the room, I mouth, "I'm sorry," to Pete.

Gus calls back loudly over his shoulder, "Food for thought, dude. Food for thought."

Pete's shy smile emerges. "Thanks."

I punch Gus's shoulder as soon as we're safely behind the closed door of my dorm room. "I can't believe you just did that."

"What?" he says innocently. Then he bursts out laughing. "I just did the guy a favor. You saw his face when we left. He's considering it, dude. Evelyn will thank me for it, Bright Side. She'll fucking thank me."

I shake my head. Maybe he's right.

Sugar isn't here, so we can hang out and relax. Gus looks over every inch of the small room with the level of curiosity I've only seen in very small children, cats, and Gustov Hawthorne. He's not nosy or intrusive but wants to know all the details...intimately. Whether it's a place, an object, or a woman, they command the kind of attention most people aren't capable of or don't take the time to give.

I walk him around campus and show him where all my classes are. He asks tons of questions about each one. If it were anyone else, I would think I was boring them, but not Gus. He's interested in every-thing in my life as much or more than he is in his own. The road goes both ways. It always has. It's one of the reasons we've been best friends so long.

Our time is drawing to a close, so we walk back to my car. "You want some coffee before we head to the auditorium?"

"Is this the infamous Grounds I always hear about?"

I nod.

"Hell yes. I was so excited to see you today that I didn't sleep much last night. I could use some coffee."

I smile. "Me, too."

The bell thunders on cue as Gus pushes the door open to Grounds. He startles and glares up at it while he holds the door open for me to enter. He ducks down and whispers in my ear, "What the fuck's with the bell?"

I laugh and agree. "Right?"

I do a double-take when I turn my attention toward the counter. It's not Keller or Romero. I've never seen this man. He looks to be in his mid-forties, and he's very handsome. He's tall and looks professional, even distinguished. His dark hair is graying at the temples, and his dark, serious eyes seem out of place here. His greeting is friendly as he smiles at us. "Welcome to Grounds."

And then it hits me. This must be Dan, Romero's partner. "Dan?"

He tentatively answers, "Yes."

I extend my hand as an introduction. "I've heard a lot about you. My name's Kate."

His eyes light up as if he's made an association. "Keller's Katie?"

Gus looks at me as if there's something he's missing and I'm looking equally as confused at Dan. "Um, I'm Keller's friend, yeah."

Dan shakes my hand two or three beats past what would be considered normal. "It's so nice to finally meet you. I've heard a lot about you, too."

I introduce Gus, and I can't help but notice Dan's a little cold to him.

I order my usual large, black coffee and Gus orders the same, and then predictably proceeds to add about a half cup of sugar to it after it's handed to him. It makes my teeth hurt every time I watch him do it.

Gus faces me in the car as we're buckling our seat belts. "Bright Side, are you seeing someone?"

"No. Keller and I are just friends."

"Does he know that? Because that dude acted like a father meeting his daughter-in-law to be. It was kinda weird."

I tag along with Gus to Grant's auditorium. After hugs from the other three members of Rook, I sit in on soundcheck. I'm speechless. Playing every night for the past month has been good for them. They sound flawless. When we were all in San Diego, I used to hang out at their band rehearsals a lot. They were always working on new material and refining their sound, but that didn't stop them from messing around with covers. And I always got to sing the covers, because it was like karaoke with a live band. So it makes me happy when Gus asks, "You up for one song, Bright Side?"

I look around at the band, and they're all smiling at me. It feels like just another rehearsal despite the expanse of the empty auditorium we're standing in. With the band, it feels intimate and safe. I can't hide my smile. "What are you playing?"

Franco's twirling his drumstick between his fingers. I don't even think he realizes he does it—it's an idle habit. "I vote for 'Sex.'"

"The act or the song?" I tease.

He rubs his chin like he's thinking about it. "Can I say both?"

Gus is adjusting the microphone down for me while I climb up on stage with them. "No, you can't. And we're not playing 'Sex,'" he says.

"Why not?" I ask. "That's a great song. You like The 1975."

Gus smiles and shakes his head before he looks back over his shoulder at Franco. "Because, Bright Side, think about it. Franco's got ulterior motives. You singing that song would be—"

Franco's nodding and grinning ear to ear when he interrupts. "Girl on girl."

Gus shakes his head. "She isn't singing with us just to fuel your fantasies, dickhead."

Franco laughs good-naturedly. He shrugs. "I had to try."

Gus is switching out his guitar. "Let's do 'Panic Switch.'"

He knows I love that song. The whole band does. Like all Silversun Pickups' best songs, this one is controlled chaos. If you dissect the song and listen to the drums, bass, guitar, and vocals all separately, it sounds like four completely different songs. Put them together and it's genius. "Hell yes, I'm in."

After Gus messes with his effects pedals, he kicks off the song and just like that, it's on. It feels good to let loose and sing again. Plus, everyone's into it. I sing and dance around the stage like it's just the five of us in Gus's basement. They sound so good.

I text Keller, Shelly, Clayton, and Pete when we're done to let them know I'll meet them at the show before I squeeze the band into my car and take them to Minneapolis for dinner before the show. The options in Grant are limited. The show starts at nine o'clock, so we have plenty of time to eat, drink (I'm the driver, so I stick with water) and catch up on lost time. Things haven't changed a bit. Jamie is still the sweet one; Franco is still the flirtatious, sarcastic one; and Robbie is still the quiet one. Friendship with them, especially Franco, has always come easily. It's natural and comfortable. We respect and support each other.

I take a minute during our drive back to Grant to have them weigh in on a topic of contention. "Guys, I have a question for you. Am I a bad driver?"

Gus's neck snaps to look directly at me from the passenger seat. There's shock in his eyes. But before he can open his mouth, it's Franco's voice I hear from behind me. "Define bad."

"I don't know, dude. Dangerous. Do you feel like your life is in peril with me behind the wheel?"

It's Gus's turn. "There's nothing wrong with your driving. Who told you that? I taught you how to drive, remember?"

I wave my finger in the air as I dismiss him. "And that is exactly why you're biased. Zip it, you don't get to answer the question." I glance in my rearview mirror at my three backseat passengers. "Guys?"

Jamie's grinning back at me. "Why are you asking?"

I glance at the road quickly before I lock eyes with him in the mirror again. "Someone may have voiced a fairly strong level of concern after riding with me."

Robbie laughs next to Jamie and says, "What Kate's trying to say is that she scared the hell out of a passenger."

I smile a guilty smile. "Or two."

Gus starts in, "That's bullsh—," but I cut him off by raising my finger in the air between us again. He slumps back against his seat.

Franco bumps the back of my seat with his knee hard enough that I feel it. "Don't sweat it, Kate. They're pussies. You're a fast, aggressive driver. Nothing wrong with that. Next topic please."

I can see Gus smiling out of the corner of my eye. The validation in that smile alone makes me feel better.

KELLER

I can't lie. I was disappointed when I received the text from Katie saying she'd meet us at the show tonight. We never discussed it, but I'd assumed that we would all hang out before the show and then ride over together. And now I've lost that time with her. I look forward to every minute I get to spend with her. Every minute of every day wouldn't be enough.

But I was crushed when I went to Grounds to grab a cup of coffee around six o'clock, and Dan told me that Katie was here earlier. *And* that she was here with some guy. He couldn't remember his name but said he was tall and muscular with blond hair. The description didn't ring any bells. I pressed him, and he said, "I'm sorry." Good news never starts with "I'm sorry." He said they looked very comfortable with each other. That he had his arm around her when they walked out of Grounds, and he kissed her on the forehead before they got in the car. *Shit.* Why didn't I just tell her how I felt about her? Now she's with someone else. Or maybe she's been with him all along. I knew I shouldn't have opened up my heart to her. She's going to break me in two. I've known it since the moment I laid eyes on her. She'd never hurt anyone intentionally, but it's inevitable...it will happen. It's my own damn fault. Still, this feeling sucks. And I know it's irrational, but I'm pissed at her, too. There's no way I'm going to that show tonight.

After I make my nightly call home to Chicago, I go straight for the only bottle of liquor we have in the apartment: tequila. Tequila is a fantastic distraction, and it numbs terrifically. I know because by the time Dunc and Shel come by to pick me up at 8:30 pm, the bottle's empty and I'm willingly on my way to the concert I swore a few hours ago I would avoid at all costs.

Shel's been texting Katie the whole time we've been standing in line to get in the auditorium. She relays to Dunc and I that Katie was having dinner with some old friends that are in town for the show. Yeah, I know she was out with a *friend*. That's why I'm so fucking wasted right now.

By the time I stagger into the place, the band's taking the stage, and the crowd's going ballistic. After Shel spends some time shouting into her phone to try and locate Katie in the mob, we push our way through hundreds of other college kids to find Katie and a couple of friends of hers. I've met Clayton once before when he came into Grounds with Katie, but I don't recognize anyone else. None of them are tall and blond like Dan described. I exhale the breath I've been holding because at least she's not with *him*. I don't want to look at her, but I can't help myself. She's just as beautiful as every other time I've seen her. Her hair is down and messy like it always is. Messy like she's just crawled out of bed...after having sex. *Shit.* She has on one of her homemade T-shirts that would look ridiculous on anyone else but looks perfect on her. It hugs her body in all the right places. This one says *I heart San Diego*. I don't think I've ever seen it before. She's smiling at me like she's happy to see me. God, how I wish that were true.

Her small hands grip my bicep, and though I'm numb to the physical sensation of most everything else, the contact isn't lost on me. Her hands are cold like they always are, but my skin warms to her touch.

"I'm so glad you're here!" she yells in my ear over the music.

I can't help myself. "Where's your *friend?*" My words are slurred and angry. They don't sound like my own.

She pulls back to look at me, stunned. "Are you drunk?"

"Thoroughly," I say. "Dan said you were at Grounds this afternoon with a *friend*." I wrap the word in air quotes and regret it immediately. Why am I being such a dick? It's not like we're together.

She wraps friend in air quotes when she responds, "My friend *is* here. You guys will meet him after the show." She looks hurt and turns her attention back to the stage. After some shuffling, she ends up sandwiched with Shel on one side and Clayton on the other. I make sure I'm always directly behind her. She never stands still, so it's like aiming for a moving target.

The music is just sound, noise in my ears, for the first several songs. I let it fill me. It numbs like the tequila I'm currently drowning in. I'm not even looking at the stage. I feel like a fucking sicko, but I can't take my eyes off Katie. Her back is to me, only inches away, and the way she moves to the music has me stretching my usual fantasies to extreme levels. Visions of ripping her clothes off and taking her ten different ways right here in front of everyone fill my head.

The songs are running together, but soon the haze lifts a little, and the cacophony turns into words and guitars and drums. My anger begins to burn off with the alcohol. Maybe it's the indecent thoughts I've been having about her, or maybe it's just the fact that it's Katie and I don't think anyone could ever really be mad at her, or maybe it's just that I'm standing so damn close to her that I realize I shouldn't take my time with her for granted.

The next song is a slow ballad. The rest of the band has left the stage, and the singer has switched out his electric guitar for an acoustic one. I have to admit that this guy is talented. The song is sad, and even though my drunken mind can't make out every word, I know it's about losing someone you care for. It's obvious the song is personal; his voice is stripped down and wounded. It feeds some deep longing in me, and I can't help reaching for physical contact. I rest my hands on Katie's hips, and when she doesn't object, I splay my fingers and slowly slide them across her stomach. The tips of my thumbs brush the underside of her breasts and my pinkies drag along the waistband of her jeans. Her T-shirt is thin; I can feel what she looks like underneath. She leans back into me and lets me hold her. Her palms smooth over my forearms and fire tears a path across my skin.

I must be losing my fucking mind. Everything was simple before I met her. I did everything I was supposed to, when I was supposed to, how I was supposed to. And now? Now I have my arms wrapped around her. And she has a boyfriend. And she's gorgeous. I can't stop obsessing about her and I'm two seconds away from doing something really foolish.

One second...

I can't stop.

I rest my chin gently on top of her head and let my cheek skim down her waves. I inhale deeply. She smells *so* good. Her body stills, but her arms don't release mine. I take that as permission. I burrow just beneath her ear and run the tip of my nose shamelessly up and down her neck. My heart is pounding and I know she feels it. One of her hands drops and wraps itself around the back of my upper thigh just below my ass. Her head drops slightly to one side allowing me better access. I press my body into her. She presses back. The advanced, physical state of my arousal should be embarrassing in this crowd of people, but I'm too drunk and turned on to care. Besides, we're packed in here like sardines and everyone's focused on the stage. No one else will notice. My lips press against her neck. It's warm and soft and dewy. I could devour her. I release her from my lips and just as the tip of my tongue makes contact, the hottest moment of my life comes to an abrupt end.

The song is over, and the crowd erupts into deafening applause, which puts everyone in motion. We're torn from the moment by simple physics, a chain reaction of movement, one body against the next.

Dunc elbows me, and when I catch his eye, he raises his eyebrows and smiles. The bastard sees everything.

Katie looks back at me. The corner of her bottom lip is captured between her teeth. Her darkened eyes search mine before they settle on my mouth. My heart stutters.

Shel, who's been pounding beers all night and is as drunk as I am, proves to be my buzzkill. She's jumping up and down like a teenager on crack, hugging Katie and slurring something about how much she loves that song and how hot the singer is.

The nail in the coffin comes when the rest of the band takes the stage again, and the singer takes off his sweat-soaked T-shirt while he's swapping out his guitar. Every female in the building screams, except Katie, who's shaking her head and smiling. The heightened energy in the crowd seems to be carrying her further from me.

The singer takes the microphone from the stand and motions for the crowd to quiet down. They do. I have to give the douchebag props; he's owned the crowd all night. He's got them eating out of his hand. "We have one last song for you tonight. Unfortunately, when we perform this song live, it sounds nothing like the version on the album because you're stuck with my shitty voice singing every word." Laughter rumbles through the crowd, and he raises his hands to hush them again. "You see, we have this very talented friend who has the voice of a goddamn angel. She's the one that makes this song so special, but as you can see," he gestures back to his bandmates, "she's not in the band." The crowd is in a frenzy because they know the song he's talking about. So do I. It's "Killing the Sun." They've been playing the hell out of it on the college station, and it's a good song, but he's right; the woman's voice is what makes it. It's the kind of voice you feel in your bones. It's sexy; vulnerable and confident at the same time.

After another pause to quiet the crowd, he continues. "Well, I have some good news for you, Grant." He looks back at the drummer, and though he's not talking into the mic, the words are picked up for all of us to hear, "Dude, she's gonna be so fucking pissed at me." And back to the audience, "She's in the building, and I'm really hoping she'll come up and sing with us tonight." The crowd cheers, whistles, stomps.

We're about thirty feet from the stage, and I can't help but notice he's staring in our general direction.

"Come on, Bright Side, don't make me beg." He drops to his knees and clasps his hands in front of his broad, bare, muscled chest. The guy looks like Thor from the movies. "Please... Please..." He motions to the crowd to join in his pleas. They do. Everyone in the building is begging now, me included, because with a voice like that, I want to see what this woman looks like.

He shakes his head and laughs. "Okay, you asked for it. You can come up here on your own or I'm coming out to get you. It's your choice." He crosses his massive arms over his chest and pauses a few seconds. "I warned you." Without hesitation, he drops the microphone and jumps down off the stage, climbs over the railing holding back the masses, and makes his way through the crowd. Of course, every woman wants to touch him, so his progress is slow, but when he finally stops, he's standing in front of Clayton, who looks like he's about to pass out. That's when I notice that Katie is crouched down behind Clayton, as if trying to hide. He reaches around Clayton and taps Katie on the shoulder. When she looks up, he's crooking his finger at her.

She shakes her head. "Not gonna happen, dude," she says.

"Come on, Bright Side. I really don't wanna make a scene."

She straightens and squares off against him. "It's a little fucking late for that, don't you think?"

He looks around. Every eye in the place is on him. He shrugs. "Probably." The words are no sooner out of his mouth than he's reached around Clayton and thrown her over his shoulder like she weighs nothing. Her body goes limp as she concedes defeat.

What.

The.

Hell?

I look around, and everyone in Katie's group of friends is

confused. At least I'm not the only one. She sings? How did this never come up? She's on the fucking radio! Why didn't she tell us?

By now, he's lifting her up on the stage and climbing up behind her. The bass player walks up and puts his arm around her while the singer adjusts his microphone down to her level. When he's done, she approaches and looks out at the crowd. The mic picks up what she thinks is a private conversation. "*Oh. Shit.* Would you look at all these people?"

The drummer calls out, "Don't fuck this up, Kate."

She flips him off without turning around to face him. He laughs. She has attitude—I love that about her.

The singer slings his guitar strap across him and takes his place at a microphone a few feet from her. He's grinning at her like he's enjoying the hell out of this. She scowls back, but there's a smile playing at the corners of her mouth. "I'm gonna fucking kill you. You know that, right?"

The audience laughs and cheers, waiting to see what happens. As the singer strums the first chords of the song, he says, "Just wait until after the song, Bright Side, then I'm all yours."

Maybe it's all the alcohol in my system, but what follows is like a surrealistic dream. As the music builds, Katie looks so small, yet so powerful up there. Every time she opens her mouth, her eyes flutter closed, and she brings forth this unbelievably massive wave of sound that washes over me. It's the sonic equivalent of great sex. The song is about living and loving in an infinite moment. Treating this night as if it's your last and you can make it last forever. You can chase away the morning, the end, by killing the sun. It's an anthem. The crowd is jumping, moshing, singing. The energy in this place is insane. Thousands of people are living through the song, through its words.

And each and every one of them is in love with Katie. She's given herself over to them. She's lost in it. After she sings her last verse, she backs away from the microphone stand, trying to take the attention away from herself I'm sure. She kind of bounces in place to the beat. She's watching the rest of the band with an open-mouthed smile, like she doesn't want to miss a second of what's happening around her. That's one of the best things about Katie; she never takes anything for granted. She appreciates it all.

The drummer and bass player join in to sing the last few lines of the song with the lead singer. The harmony is right on, and Katie's smile widens as she watches them.

The moment the song is lost to silence, the singer's shouting into the microphone, "Let's hear it for my girl!" He runs over, shifting his guitar to his back and lifts her into a hug, swinging her around. She holds on tight. She's laughing. It feels wrong to watch them—too personal—too private. But I can't look anywhere else.

My heart sinks again. Of course, *this* is the guy she was at Grounds with. A fucking rock star. How am I supposed to compete with that? The anger and hurt creep back in again. I hate it, but I'm jealous as hell.

The band shouts out words of thanks and leaves the stage, and when the masses are satisfied that there will be no encore, they begin to disperse. Katie is standing on the floor in front of the stage, but behind the barricade, waiting for us. Two big security guards are standing in front of her and won't let the crowd near her.

Now that we can all hear each other, introductions are made back and forth between the friends Katie has gathered. I'm polite but so pissed I can't remember their names two seconds after I hear them. After everyone agrees Katie stole the show and that they had no idea she had this secret identity, we head over as a group to congratulate her. Well, the rest of group congratulates her. I'm pissed, and horny, and drunk, and completely in awe; it's a bad combination. I can't look at her.

We all show our VIP tickets and are cleared through security to follow her backstage. She has no idea where she's going, but Shel is hell-bent on meeting the guy I would love to punch in the goddamn face.

We run into the drummer. His head is shaved bald, and his arms are covered in tattoos. The guy would look threatening if he wasn't constantly smiling. He hugs Katie. "Kate, you sounded like shit. Thanks for ruining the whole fucking show."

She smiles devilishly. "And your beats sucked ass, dude. Clearly this playing every night thing isn't working for you."

He laughs. "I miss having you around, girl." He plants a kiss on top of her head before he releases her.

She introduces us to him. His name's Frank or Fred, I don't know. I'm too drunk and pissed to care.

He gestures to a door down the hall when she asks where the rest of the band is. The door leads outside behind the auditorium. There's a tour bus parked with its engine running. The douchebag is leaning up against a wall smoking a cigarette. When he sees Katie, his fucking face lights up like it's Christmas. He drops the cigarette, steps on it, and walks our way.

What happens next is a blur of emotion, alcohol, and disregard. In no particular order:

Introductions. He's her best friend, Gus. The guy she's known her whole life. The guy she told me she fucking slept with before she moved here. I really hate him now.

Photos and autographs for the others.

Shel projectile vomits next to the bus.

Clayton and his boyfriend and the other guy and girl leave.

Gus wraps his arms around Katie. (It should be *me* with my arms around her.)

He tells her how amazing she was tonight. (It should be *me*.)

He tells her how proud he is of her. (It should be *me*.)

He tells her how much he misses her. (*I* miss her, and she's standing five feet from me.)

The driver opens the door of the bus and hollers, "Gustov, train's leaving in two minutes."

She's wearing a sad smile. She doesn't want *him* to leave. Seeing that smile is killing me.

He squeezes her tight and kisses her forehead. "Thanks, Bright Side. I'll talk to you tomorrow. I love you."

When she answers, "I love you, too, Gus," I come undone.

"Why didn't you tell me you were with him?" My voice sounds strangled and desperate. Is this really me?

"What?" She's confused. "Gus and I aren't together."

He releases her.

I step toward her. "You are such a terrible liar," I say, too loudly.

She's jerked from sight, and I'm suddenly chin-to-chest with *him*. "No one fucking talks to her like that." It's a threat if I've ever heard one.

I *want* him to punch me. Put me out of my misery. So, I narrow my eyes and taunt, "I wasn't talking to you, *bro*." I can be such a prick when I'm drunk.

His patience with me is wearing thin; I can feel it. "You don't know me. Don't fucking *bro* me."

And there's my in. "*Blow me.*"

My shirt is now balled up in *his* fist. "What the fuck did you just say?"

Before I can answer, someone's restraining me from behind. It's not until I hear Dunc's loud, steady voice in my ear, "That's enough, Banks," that I make the correlation between the vise-like hold on my biceps and the fact that I'm being backed away from this disaster my mouth started. My T-shirt splits down the center when I'm yanked free of Gus's grasp. All the while Dunc continues trying to talk some sense into me. "Chill out, man. You're done here."

Katie's in front of me again. "He's my best friend, Keller. What's the problem?" She's not mad, but she looks hurt.

I cough out a crazed laugh. "What's the problem?" I lower my voice so only she can hear me. "The problem is I don't *fuck* my best friends." Her face drops. I have her attention, and I know I should shut up, but my mouth keeps spewing, "Kinda blurs the lines, doesn't it?" Dunc's dragging me away, and I'm not fighting him anymore. I point at *him*. "You win, bro." My voice sounds choked. I repeat myself. "You win." The anger rises in me again as I admit defeat. "She's all yours."

The next thing I know, I'm in the Green Machine. Shel's passed out on a beanbag in the back. Dunc reams me out the entire drive home. I'm in no mood to hear it.

That's about all I remember before I pass out in my bed, but not before puking all over it.

SUNDAY, OCTOBER 30

KELLER

IF THERE'S an award for *World's Biggest Asshole,* last night I won it hands down. I feel like shit.

After Dunc wakes up, we grab a couple of cups of coffee from Grounds and sit down in the privacy of our apartment for a heart-to-heart.

"Keller, man, what was that last night? I mean, I know you've got a thing for Kate, but that was so out of line. That wasn't you. I've never seen you like that." He's not scolding so much as he's just talking.

"I know," I say, looking straight into my coffee cup.

"Have you talked to her this morning?"

I shake my head, which causes a sharp pain to crash through my skull. The thought of it terrifies me. I owe her an apology, but I can't talk to her yet. I'm not mad at her. I'm mad as hell at *me.* I don't want her to feel my anger again, even if it's not directed at her.

"She was here last night, you know?"

This is news to me. "What? Katie came here?"

"Yeah, she showed up about thirty minutes after we got home."

Great. I was passed out in a pool of my own vomit. That speaks volumes.

"She was worried about you."

"She was worried about *me*?"

He nods. "We talked for a long time. She cares about you, Keller. She hated seeing you so upset."

I drop my throbbing head in my hands. "I treated her like shit, Dunc. *I* treated *her* like shit, and *she* doesn't want *me* to be upset." I laugh at how ass-backwards the whole screwed-up situation is.

"I know you sabotage any potential relationship because of what happened with Lily, but it's been almost four years. I loved her too, man, but it's time."

I grind the heels of my hands into my burning eyes. Hearing her name today doesn't make me ache like it used to. "What about Stella?"

He raises his eyebrows like he doesn't have an answer for me. "Listen, Banks, it's your life, but Kate is a really good person. She's been so good for Shelly—you've seen the change in her since she's been hanging around Kate. Shelly's crazy about her, which means I'm crazy about her. But after talking to her last night, I can honestly say Kate's probably one of the most caring and genuine people I've ever met. She's the real deal, man. I asked a lot of questions, and she answered every one. She didn't have to do that ... but she did. She and Gus have a very close relationship, but I believe her when she says they're just *friends*. She's known the guy her entire life—"

"She also slept with him," I interrupt.

He raises his eyebrows again. "And you've never done anything without thinking through the consequences first, Banks?"

"Yeah, but—"

He cuts me off. "*But what, man?* You didn't even know her when it happened. Don't judge. It's not fair."

He's too damn good at seeing both sides. "You're right," I exhale. My head's still throbbing, but I raise my chin to look him in the eye. "I really like her, Dunc. It scares me how much I like her. She makes me want to say screw it all and re-write my future." My future's been mapped out for me my entire life. Even when I screw up, it only takes a minor detour before jumping back on track. My parents always make sure of it.

He smiles, stands, and claps me on the back. "I could've told you all that two months ago. You should've asked me; I could've saved you a lot of trouble."

"Should I call her?" I ask since he seems to be better at this than I am.

"An apology is in order. Get some rest today and call her tomorrow when your head's on straight again."

MONDAY, OCTOBER 31

KATE

I WAKE with a splitting headache at five o'clock, but I don't have the energy to even get out of bed to hunt down some ibuprofen. The pain sticks with me through all my morning classes, just like I knew it would, like I *want* it to. Today's a day I've been dreading since September turned into October. It's Grace's birthday.

This is the first day I've been in Minnesota that I've been homesick for San Diego. The kind of sick that makes my stomach turn and my head hurt so bad I can't see straight. And the only thing that will make it better, manageable, is talking to Gus. He's on his way to Denver to play tonight.

Because my class load is stacked on Mondays, Wednesdays, and Fridays, I don't even have ten free minutes between 7:30 am and 2:00 pm. So, when I'm out of the lecture hall at 2:01, I'm dialing Gus.

"Bright Side, you okay?" This is not the standard Gus greeting.

I try for cheerful. I haven't had to fake cheerful in a long time. "I've been worse." Barely.

"Rough day, huh?"

So much for faking it. This is Gus. "Yeah."

"Yeah." It's acknowledgment, and agreement, and acceptance in one small word.

My chest is tightening and the back of my throat itches and swells. I know as soon as I open my mouth to speak, I'm going to cry. And I pride myself in not crying. I've only cried once in my life that I can remember. It felt so awful, like my entire being was coming apart in a million pieces and would never fit together again. I never want to feel that again.

Gus allows me my silence and then he starts in with a story. God, I love this guy. Even over the phone, he knows I just need to listen to his voice right now. "I've been thinking about Grace all morning, and I decided if I could be anywhere in the world today, doing anything, I wish I was in San Diego fishing from the pier with you and Grace. I'll never forget the first time Grace caught a fish. She reeled it in like mad and was totally hyped until she realized that there was a real live *fish* on the end of her hook. The excitement drained, and she was so bummed. She begged me to take it off the hook and throw it back in the water before it died."

Thinking about her like this lightens the load I've been carrying today. "Yeah, but she still wanted to go again the next week."

"And we never baited her hook after that." He doesn't sound so sad anymore. I can hear the smile in his voice. "She could sit there for hours on the edge of her seat and watch her line move with the tide. And every five minutes or so, she was convinced she had a big one on the line, and she would spin that reel like hell until the hook was out of the water. But, she was never discouraged when there was nothing. She was always relieved."

I can picture her like it was yesterday. This is what I needed. "What did she used to tell you on the way home? 'Looks like I'm having a bit of bad fishing luck, Gus.'"

He laughs. "Every time."

"And you'd tell her, 'It's not that you're having bad luck today, Gracie, it's just that the fish are having really good luck. Besides, we don't eat them anyway, and Ma can buy fish at the store if she wants to eat it.'"

"She would always smile wide; you know the one when her eyes were almost scrunched closed."

"And then you'd suck in your cheeks and make fish lips at her, and she'd giggle and giggle and tell you how silly you were."

Gus laughs harder now. "Gracie had the best laugh. She laughed all the time. That's one of the things you two had in common. You both loved to laugh."

"She was so damn happy, Gus. The happiest person I've ever known. Even when life was shit, she didn't care. She always smiled. God, I miss her."

"Me too, Bright Side. Me too."

I USUALLY TRY TO AVOID NEGATIVE TALK BECAUSE IT perpetuates negative thoughts and worse—negative action. It's like the catalyst for misery. A downward spiral ensues. All that aside, by eight o'clock tonight as I'm leaving the cafeteria, I've reached my limit and have to admit...

Today. Really. Sucked.

My day was shit missing Grace, my head is still throbbing, and my stomach still aches. I'm praying the entire walk back to the dorms. *Please God, let Sugar be gone tonight. I need some peace and quiet and a good night's sleep.*

I hear Sugar's voice lilt through the door before I even have it open and realize maybe God's not on call tonight.

The first thing I notice is Sugar sitting on her bed talking on the phone. She throws me one of her best you're-interrupting-me-I-wish-you'd-go-away glares. She was at the concert Saturday night, and I can't help but notice she's taken the bitchiness toward me to an all-time high.

I half-smile and nod in her direction. "S'up, Sugar."

The second thing I notice is the paper I finished and printed earlier today in the library (because I don't have a printer), the same paper that's due at 7:30 tomorrow morning (because my professor is the old-school-doesn't-believe-in-technology/electronic-submission type and demands an actual hard copy), is strewn across the floor and graffitied with dirty snow boot prints.

I immediately look to Sugar's feet. Sure as shit, she's still sporting the incriminating footwear.

This is the point at which I should proceed to the library to reprint my paper and decompress before I confront her, but like I said, I've already submitted to negative talk, and it's been a shitty day, so the conversation begins with, "What the hell?" albeit quietly. I just want to go to bed.

She doesn't even look at me.

I walk to the side of her bed. My blood is boiling, but I keep my voice even. This is the voice I used with my mother when I was angry with her and needed to get a point across, but Grace was in the room, and I didn't want to upset her at the same time. I've had this voice mastered for years. "Sugar, what the hell, dude?" I point to the papers.

She ignores me, continuing to murmur into the phone. I can't believe it. The girl has the balls to destroy my property and now she's fucking ignoring me.

I raise my voice slightly. "Sugar, what happened to my paper?"

She's still ignoring me.

Fuck that.

Now I'm pissed. I'm not a yeller. I've never been a fan of losing control and to me yelling feels like the culmination of losing control. So, I don't yell. Instead, I find it much more effective to lower my voice to a level that's so quiet the other person almost has to strain to hear it. That way you know they're really listening to every word. "Sugar, I swear to God I am not a violent person, but if you don't hang up that fucking phone and tell me what happened here, I am going to take that fucking phone out of your fucking hand and shove it up your fucking ass."

Her eyes widen. "Um, I gotta go. I'll call you back." By the time she hangs up, she looks defiant again. "What?" she snaps.

"Dude?" I point to the floor.

She rolls her eyes. "Oh, that was an accident. I must've knocked them off your desk when I walked by."

I'm shaking my head. "And then what? What? You *accidentally* did the motherfucking Mexican hat dance on them?"

She shrugs. "Sorry." It's the most insincere apology I've ever heard. She may as well have said, "Fuck you."

I snatch up my bag and flash drive off my desk and point my finger at her from the door. "You know what, Sugar? I'd like for us to be friends, but you're making that pretty *fucking* difficult. You've ruined or not returned several of my shirts this year, you eat my food out of the fridge, and you put me out of my room a few nights a week. *That* I've dealt with up to this point." My accusing finger drops its aim from her to the floor. "How dare you destroy my paper. I'm not sure why you're here, but I'm here to get an education, and that's what's important to me." I narrow my eyes and threaten through gritted teeth, "From now on, just keep your hands *off my shit*."

There's fear in her eyes, but she attempts a brave eye roll. It's pathetic. I can smell fear a mile away, and she's scared of me right now. She manages a snotty, "Whatever."

I want to strangle her, but I settle for something completely juvenile, yet effective. "*Fuck. You. Sugar.*" And slam the door behind me.

The walk to the library is cold and snowy. It only takes a few minutes to print out my paper, but I sit in the stacks and read for another hour until I'm cooled down enough to return to my room. I hate getting this angry. I feel even more drained than before. But in truth, I'm not good at holding grudges.

Sugar is gone when I return. Strangely enough, I feel a little guilty that she probably isn't here because of me, but the guilt fades fast when I get a good night's sleep in my own bed.

I guess God was listening after all.

TUESDAY, NOVEMBER 1 - WEDNESDAY, NOVEMBER 2

KATE

I'M GOING through ibuprofen on a regular basis these days. I'm almost down to the bottom of the bottle, so I stop at the grocery across the street from Grounds on my way home from the flower shop.

When I see him, he's so pale and hunched over that I barely recognize him. I pause mid-step, at war with myself. I haven't seen Keller since Saturday night, and this chance encounter is not how I planned to see him next. I'm not a strategist when it comes to interaction. Usually, I just wing it, but I wanted to give him more than a few days to cool off. For two seconds, the selfish, preservationist side of me shouts, *Turn around and make a break for it before he sees you!* But my compassionate side stifles her with a calm counter, *But he looks like death.* Followed by a demand, *Help him.*

Compassion always trumps self-preservation.

"Keller? Hey, you need some help?"

If I startled him, it doesn't show. Turning his head in my direction takes more effort than it should. His eyes are bloodshot and circled in a disturbing shade of eggplant. His hair is damp at the roots and plastered to his head. He looks like he hasn't seen a shower in weeks, but I know it's only been a few days at most. He's sick.

He looks at me blankly. I don't know if speaking would require too much energy, or if he doesn't want to.

I touch his forehead with the back of my hand. He leans into it. It's hot and damp with sweat. Fevers have always scared me. When Gracie got them, I couldn't sleep. I'd sit up in bed next to her. She always wanted me to hold her hand.

I try to mask my fear and whisper, "Keller, why aren't you in bed? You're burning up."

He's beyond exhausted. I'm wondering how he found the strength to walk across the street.

I scan the shelves in front of him. "What do you need, sweetie?"

He shrugs. He's delirious with fever.

I offer my hand and he wraps his arm around my shoulder instead. He feels heavy, helpless. I lead him to a bench at the end of the aisle next to the pharmacist's window, where I sit him down to lean against the wall. I consult with the pharmacist and grab what he recommends, along with my ibuprofen and two cans of chicken noodle soup, one can of tomato soup, and a jug of orange juice.

After I pay, I return for Keller, and we struggle across the street to his apartment. He's unresponsive at the door, so I search his pockets for a key.

He hits his mattress with a disturbing heaviness. After getting medicine in him, the next step is getting him cooled off. I give myself ten seconds to contemplate my options. In the end, I go with what always worked with Grace. He's so out of it that modesty is the last thing I'm worried about, so I don't hesitate stripping him down to his boxers.

Sickness like this makes me anxious. The kind of anxious you wish you could just walk away from, but you can't. *You can't.* Not because you'd feel guilty, but because sometimes people just *need* you.

His bed is a twin, but I manage to squeeze on the mattress next to him. There's no headboard, so I sit back up against the wall. I hold his hand because it makes *me* feel better and stroke the wet hair off his forehead. And I hum quietly to myself. It's a nervous habit, and it keeps me awake. As his skin cools, I relax. Before I know it, I've drifted off.

I AWAKE, AND IT TAKES A FEW SECONDS TO ADJUST TO THE darkness. The clock on Keller's dresser reads 12:17 am. My neck aches. I fell asleep sitting up. His head is now resting on my thighs, and an arm is draped across my legs, effectively trapping me where I sit. I hold my breath and make a plea to the man upstairs, *Please let his fever be gone*, as I gently check his forehead with the lightest touch. His skin is dry and cool. I blow out the air and look at the ceiling. *Thanks, big guy.*

My bladder is screaming. My belly is growling. My body is killing me.

I weigh this against the relief that Keller's fever broke. Keller's sleeping peacefully. Keller's here with me.

I do what I have to do. I rest my head back against the wall and let the physical closeness fill me. Touch is so underrated. The basic human need for contact. Growing up I got daily doses of hugs, hand holding, and forehead kisses from Gracie, Gus, and Audrey. I miss it. So I'm going to greedily take advantage of every moment here with Keller. Though I fight it, sleeps comes for me. Insomnia has been replaced by persistent exhaustion.

A COUGH STARTLES ME AWAKE, AND INSTINCT TAKES OVER before my senses do. "Gracie?" It's funny how worry and concern get the best of sleep every time. I slept with one eye open on Grace for nineteen years. When someone depends on you to chase away bad dreams, or help them to the bathroom in the middle of the night, or hold them so they can sleep, there's a level of alertness that unconsciousness never chases away.

"Katie?" His voice is raspy and confused.

I hold onto the Grace moment a second longer, and then I let it go with a sigh and offer an apology, "Sorry, Keller. Yeah, it's me, Kate."

He rolls off my lap onto his pillow and looks up at me through the darkness. "What are you doing here?"

"I ran into you at the grocery store last night. You were looking for medicine. I'm sure you don't remember. You were pretty out of it. I walked you home. Duncan wasn't here and I was afraid to leave you alone. I hope that's okay." I glance at the clock. It's 3:53 am.

"You didn't have to do that," he says sadly.

"Actually, I kinda did." I smile. "Didn't I ever tell you I'm allergic to guilt? I could've walked away, but then I would've broken out in hives." He doesn't laugh, so I move onto the next important question. "You hungry, Keller? I bought some chicken noodle soup. I can make it if you want?"

"I'm sorry, Katie," it's a whisper. He's not talking about his fever.

I don't make a production out of forgiveness. Some people do. As if forgiveness is some grand, noble gesture that goes hand in hand with condescension. I hate that. Good or bad, I forgive easily and keep it simple because that's how my heart likes it. I brush the hair off Keller's forehead and kiss it. "I know." I slide my legs off the bed and stretch to my feet. "I'm going to make soup."

After a long overdue stop in the bathroom, I pop three ibuprofen and start two pots of soup. Keller joins me after putting on a pair of sweats and a T-shirt. He tries to help, but I insist he sit down in his recliner.

"Who's Gracie?" He's referring to my half-asleep comment when I woke.

"My sister."

His eyes are sleepy, but his lips smile sweetly. "I didn't know you had a sister."

I nod while I stir the soup that's just beginning to boil.

"Older or younger?"

"Older." I pour the soup into two bowls and carry them to the coffee table in front of Keller.

"Is she in San Diego?"

Normally I dodge any questions about my life back home. It's mine, and it's personal, and it's special. Did I mention it's *mine*? But for some reason, I feel like talking about Grace. "It was Grace's twenty-first birthday yesterday. She was my hero. I always looked up to her. She was the most pure-hearted person I've ever known." He's sitting deep in the recliner and even though he looks like he's been through hell and back, his face looks peaceful. He's listening to me intently, like there's nothing more important in the world than this conversation. It makes me want to continue, to share Grace with someone who never knew her. "Have you ever met someone who's content and happy to their core? And when you're around them it's contagious? Like you want to be a better person just so you feel worthy of being in that person's life?"

He smiles and nods, and I know he understands what I'm trying to say. He has a Grace in his life.

I nod once and smile through the feeling that my insides are breaking into a million pieces, each one of them reflecting my grief. "That was Grace."

He's looking at me now like he fears the worst but is afraid to ask, so I spare him and answer the unasked question, "She died this past May from complications of pneumonia and a blood infection. I took her to the ER three times that week before they would admit her. She couldn't breathe. Her skin looked gray. I threw such a fit when they tried to send us home with a prescription for cough medicine during the final visit that they threatened to call security and have me escorted out. In the end, they admitted her." I take a deep breath before I continue. "Her lungs were filled with fluid. She picked up some kind of blood infection the first night she was there. Two days later, she was gone." I shut my eyes to dam the impending tears. My throat is swelling, and I'm trying to remind myself that I don't cry. I feel my lip quivering. The only time I've ever cried was the night Grace died.

I don't open my eyes when Keller pulls me up by my hands to

stand. I don't open my eyes when Keller holds me tightly against his chest. I don't open my eyes as my tears soak into his T-shirt. I don't open my eyes as he softly murmurs, "I'm sorry, Katie," and rubs my lower back with his open palm.

When I feel the weight of the last few months lift a little, I open my eyes. My fingers release the material at the back of his shirt I have balled up in my fists and take a step back, wiping at my eyes with the backs of my hands. I heave out a deep, crippling breath and look up at him. "I'm sorry. You didn't have to do that."

The corner of his mouth turns up, but there's no joy in it. "Actually, I kinda did."

I think back to our conversation earlier. "You allergic to guilt, too?"

He doesn't blink. "No. It kills me to see you feeling sad. It's fundamentally wrong that the universe would allow it. You and sadness... they should never be paired together." He pulls me into another hug. "You said that you don't like to talk about it. Is that why you never mentioned her before?"

My hands find his shirt again. I have to hold on before the world tilts, and I fall right off the side into oblivion. I suck in a breath and shudder. "It hurts." I wait. "She was my world. Do you know what it's like to be blessed with someone so special, to love them so much it hurts, and then have them taken from you forever?"

He rests his chin on the top of my head and squeezes me tighter. "I do."

I sniff. "I'm sorry. I don't mean to complain...but it sucks, doesn't it?"

"It does," he agrees.

"You don't have to answer this if you don't want to, but who was it?"

"My girlfriend. Fiancée, actually. It happened close to four years ago. Her name was Lily." He exhales, but he sounds more relieved than sad to say it out loud.

"You don't talk about her. Does anyone here know?" I keep my cheek pressed against his chest. I don't want to make him nervous or uncomfortable by looking at him. Eye contact can shut down honesty quicker than anything else.

"Dunc and Rome. I keep my life at Grant and my life in Chicago very separate." He shrugs. "And like you said, it hurts. Though not as much as it used to. It's not that I don't miss her...but that I've learned that the living need to be loved, too. And loving someone else doesn't diminish the love I had for her. I'd never felt loved before her. My parents are very..." he pauses, "driven. Very goal-oriented. They didn't give me love...they just...gave me expectations. They expected good behavior, and good manners, and good grades, and expected compliance with every demand, and expected me to go to law school or medical school because my mother is a lawyer and my father is a surgeon. My entire life was expectations, and I met every one of them. Until I met Lily." He takes a deep breath. "She loved me, with no expectations. That was *so* freeing. When I lost her, I lost that freedom. The expectations returned, but with a whole new set of rules."

Now I have to look at him because this is about more than losing someone you love. This is about losing yourself. "Keller, this is your life. You're the one in the driver's seat, dude."

He half-laughs. "Oh no, I'm not driving. I'm the passenger. That's okay, though. Stella's quite the driver."

I smile at the grin emerging on his face. "Stella?" My heart should be breaking because I feel like I'm falling for Keller, but knowing I can't have him (especially after hearing about what happened with Lily) and knowing that there's a woman out there who makes him this happy. *That* makes me happy. To know there's someone who loves Keller and whom he loves back. All the flirting between us, and whatever happened the night of the concert, was all a misunderstanding or misinterpretation on my part. *We* are friends. *Stella* is his fairy tale.

He tilts his head and stares at me like he's trying to decide if he should say something or not. "What are you doing this weekend?"

I shrug. "Probably studying, why?"

"Would you be opposed to studying in Chicago? I want you to meet Stella." He's wearing his crooked smile that I couldn't resist if I tried.

Thinking back to our trip to Milwaukee and all the prompting I had to do to get him to go with me, I tease, "Are you always this impulsive?"

His grin stretches wide, and he shakes his head emphatically. "Never. You're a terrible influence."

I smile at his honesty. "Well, I have to admit that I'm curious. I would love to go to Chicago with you and meet the mysterious Stella."

He hugs me again and it feels different. Friendly. Sure, I think. My feelings for him can be tamped down to friendship. He kisses the top of my head, and it reminds me of Gus. "Thank you, Katie. You're an amazing woman—a terrible influence, but an amazing woman." He rocks me back and forth for a while.

"That may be one of the nicest things anyone's ever said to me." It went straight to my heart. "You're not so bad yourself."

He laughs. "I'm a jackass, but thanks."

I release him with a sigh. "You better get some more rest, jackass. No work or school for you today. You still look like hell."

He shakes his head. "You're full of compliments this morning."

I smile. "Sorry, Keller, I speak the truth. I realize a woman's probably never told you that before, given your good looks. But, dude, you battled a fierce competitor last night, and it *kicked your ass*. You need to eat this soup, take a shower, and get lots of sleep."

He shakes his head and smiles. His eyes look sleepy all of a sudden. "I love it when you talk clinical."

I roll my eyes, but I love it when being around someone is this easy. Like with Gus. After reheating our soup, we eat, and after Keller showers, while I wash the pots and dishes, I get him tucked back in bed. It's five o'clock. I kiss him on the forehead. "God, you smell so much better. The fever sweats had you smelling pretty rank."

He laughs. "Is it just in your nature to be so complimentary? You're crushing my ego."

"Good night, Keller. Call me later and let me know how you're doing, okay?"

He smiles. "Okay, Dr. Sedgwick."

He stops me when my hand's on the door. "Can I ask you something?"

"Shoot."

"Why didn't you tell anyone here that you were a rock star?"

I laugh at the absurdity of the title. "Um, because I'm not. That's Gus's job. Not mine."

"You were unbelievable the other night. *Your voice.* I can't believe no one knew."

I shrug. I've been dodging stares and questions all week around campus by telling people they must have me confused with someone else. "You know how you said you like to keep your life here separate from your life in Chicago?"

He nods.

"Me too." Because it really is that simple.

"Thanks for taking care of me, Katie."

I smile and nod before I duck out the door. The walk back to the dorm feels longer than ever. I have to stop twice and sit down. My body aches. It's exhausted. By the time I make it to the dorms, I drop into bed fully clothed. Sleep holds me captive until after lunchtime. So much for classes today.

KELLER CALLS AT 2:45 PM AS I'M WALKING TO THE FLOWER SHOP for work. He says he's feeling much better and asks for my email address. I have strict instructions to check my email as soon as I get home.

. . .

THERE'S AN EMAIL WAITING FOR ME AFTER DINNER, A confirmation for a flight to Chicago Friday night, returning to Minneapolis Sunday evening. What?! I thought we were driving. He brushes me off when I call to ask about the ticket. I can't afford $527.00 to fly to Chicago for the weekend. He tells me it's a gift for nursing him back to health.

FRIDAY, NOVEMBER 4

KATE

I PICK Keller up at his place at 4:15 pm to head to the airport. He's fighting to bite his tongue; he wanted me here at four o'clock. Our flight is at 6:30, and apparently he's an arrive-at-the-airport-two-hours-before-your- flight kind of guy. This fact does not surprise me. I'm more a run-to-the-gate-and-hop-on-the-plane-two-minutes-before-your-flight-departs kind of girl.

Since we don't need to check bags, we're through security and sitting at the departing gate at 5:15. I could give him a hard time, but I don't. He's anal and timely, and I can appreciate that in him because it's something I can't begin to comprehend, let alone attempt. I should commend him.

We grab a snack because he says we're eating a late dinner with his mother tonight. For some reason that makes me a little nervous, not because she's a lawyer, and probably a wealthy lawyer at that. I can hang with pretty much anyone. I've met them all. And you know what? They're people, just like me. That stuff doesn't impress me. What makes me nervous is the tone of voice Keller used when he talked about his parents the other night. There's fear and resentment there. And that's always uncomfortable. Good thing I make an excellent buffer.

After our snack, I decide I should call Gus to tell him where I'm headed. I've texted him the past few days but haven't told him about my trip to Chicago yet. I don't know how available I'll be this weekend, and I don't want him to think I'm ignoring him. I also don't want to be rude talking in front of Keller, so I ask, "Hey, do you mind if I make a quick phone call?"

"Of course not. Take your time," Keller says.

Gus picks up on the second ring. "Gus's mortuary, you kill em', we chill em'."

I haven't heard that one, and it catches me off guard. I laugh out loud against my will. "Hey, Gus."

"Bright Side, what's happening in the land of ten thousand lakes?"

"I think that's a misnomer because I haven't seen one damn lake in three months. I'm at the airport, dude, headed to Chicago for the weekend. How about you, amigo?"

"Soundcheck in about thirty minutes. Just had what may go down in history as the most un-Chinese, Chinese food I've ever had. It's weird that there was corn, sweet potatoes, and green beans in my egg drop soup, right?"

"Yeah, that's weird. Also, it was probably made with chicken broth. Hope you don't get the meat shits on stage tonight."

Keller's trying to mind his own business, but I can't help but notice he smiled at that last comment. He's supposed to be reading the textbook in his lap.

"I had the waitress swear on her first-born that it was made with vegetable broth."

"Dude, what if she didn't have any kids? Or she was an atheist?"

"Huh, I didn't think of that. I might be screwed. So, what're you going to Chicago for?"

"Keller invited me. He's from Chicago."

"That a good idea?" I can hear the admonition in his voice.

I offer a curt, "Yes," and glance at Keller. He's shifting uncomfortably in his chair.

He huffs. "Listen, I know you're a big girl, but you're my girl, and I worry about you. I know you said he's a good guy and was just wasted last Saturday night, but that doesn't excuse the fact that the dude was totally fucking out of line." His voice is rising.

"Dude, I *am* a big girl. It's fine." Keller taps me on the shoulder and motions with his fingers to hand him the phone. I widen my eyes and shake my head. He sighs and motions again. "It's your funeral," I mutter as I hand him the phone.

Keller clears his throat and puts my phone to his ear. "Gus? Gus, this is Keller."

I hear Gus's voice but can't make out words. He's talking very loud. Gus, despite his physical stature, isn't a violent guy. And it takes a lot for him to verbally spar, but once it's on...*it's on.* He doesn't back down.

"Gus? Gus—" Keller says, trying to get a word in. "Can I say something please? I'll keep it short. *I'm sorry.* I'm sorry I was rude to you. I'm sorry I treated Katie like I did." He's looking at me. "I'm so sorry about that. If I could take it back, I would. I feel like shit about it—"

Gus interrupts him.

"I know I should, and I do. It will never happen again—"

Gus interrupts again.

"You're right. She does deserve better than that—"

More Gus. He's quieter now.

Keller nods his head like Gus can see him. "Yes, I'll take good care of her. We're staying at my parents' house."

More Gus. Then, "Thanks, man. Later, Gus." He hands me the phone.

Why do I feel like I'm fourteen and going out on my first date? I put the phone to my ear. "Dude, or should I say, Dad, the fifth degree? *Really?*"

He huffs; he's irritated but knows he shouldn't be. I can tell.

"Bright Side..." he trails off, but I can hear the click of his lighter and the inhalation of calm.

"You should quit." I can't hide my smile, he'll hear it, and he's on the verge of letting this go. I know it. He can't hold grudges either. We're alike that way.

"You make me crazy sometimes, you know that?" He's smiling. He doesn't want to, but he can't help it.

"I know, dude. Sorry, it's one of the perks of living in my little world of sunshine and rainbows."

He laughs. "You forgot unicorns."

I laugh, too. "I did forget unicorns. Thanks for the reminder. Have an awesome show tonight."

"Thanks, Bright Side. Have a good trip. Call if you need anything. You know where to find me."

"Ditto. Love you, Gus."

"I love you, too."

"Peace."

"Out."

Keller looks at me and shakes his head. "That may have been the strangest conversation I've both overheard and participated in."

I shrug and repeat, "It's one of the perks of living in my little world of sunshine and rainbows."

"And unicorns."

I smile. "Why do I keep forgetting the damn unicorns?"

He looks at me, and the humor drains away. "Gus seems like a good guy."

I nod solemnly. "He is. He's my best friend. And being a good person is number one on my list of best friend criteria. Always has been."

The corner of his mouth rises. "He's a little protective."

I cringe. "Sorry about that. From what I overheard, that was Gus at about a six. You don't want to see him at an eight or nine. My dad's never been around, so I think he tries to fill that role sometimes."

He raises his eyebrows. "*You think?*"

"Sorry."

He puts his hand on my knee. "I really am sorry, Katie."

I look at his hand on my knee and then to his eyes. "I know." And then I take his hand in mine and tug on it as I stand. "Come with me." I need to change the subject.

He stands, and I release his hand. "Where are we going?" he asks.

"To watch the sunset." I haven't seen one for a few days. I'm due. I can see it through the bank of windows on the other side of the concourse.

We watch it in silence, which is the best way. By the time we return to our seats, a quiet calm has settled over both of us.

OUR FLIGHT DEPARTS ON TIME, AND BEFORE I KNOW IT KELLER is waking me because we're on the ground. I hadn't realized I was so tired. I fell asleep with my head on his shoulder, which in hindsight feels a little strange knowing I'm going to meet his girlfriend, Stella, in less than an hour.

The cab drops us off in front of a ritzy high-rise. These aren't your average apartments. These are very expensive, very large apartments. Oprah probably lives here. The doorman greets Keller, "Good evening, Mr. Banks." He responds with an equally formal greeting. It's like an alternate universe here. Everyone we pass looks professional, and in a hurry, and uptight, all power suits and briefcases. Which is fine. But no one smiles. It's sad. There's plenty of life here, but there's no *life*. It's the difference you feel in the pit of your stomach.

We ride the elevator to the thirty-second floor. We're near the top. The elevator goes to forty. "Have your parents always lived here?"

He looks nervous. "Yup. Thirty years. I grew up here."

I want to say, *I'm sorry*, because this is the least kid-friendly environment I've ever been in, but that would be judgmental, and I need to put the brakes on any preconceived notions. I need to go into this weekend totally open-minded. "How was that?"

We step out of the elevator into a foyer with a white marble floor and dark, rich mahogany wood walls. There's a large arrangement of fresh flowers on an ornate, antique table next to the only door. Keller fishes a key out of the pocket of his jeans and looks around before he slips it in the lock. "You're about to find out."

He opens the door and steps in ahead of me. He cranes his head to look around and then gives me the all-clear and motions for me to come in, like we're in a war zone, and the coast is clear. We take our shoes off and set them next to the door. Keller takes my coat and bag, and I follow him through a formal living room and down a hall. He stops in front of a door and peeks in. "Stella, honey, are you in here?" His voice is sweet and soft like I've never heard it. It sounds good on him. He shuts the door. "She must be out with Melanie. Let's put your things in the guest room."

"Okay."

The guest room is opulent. A king-size, four-poster bed dominates the room. It looks like it belongs in a castle. It's dressed in a luxurious, deep burgundy spread. I'm fairly certain the bedding alone costs more than my car. He sets my coat and backpack on a plush, antique sofa across the room from the bed.

"Let's see who's here." He offers his hand. I take it. I know we're friends, and I don't have a problem holding hands with friends, but it feels inappropriate.

His palm is sweaty.

I pull back as we approach the doorway because something feels off. He's nervous, but there's something more there...like fear. He stops, and I wait for him to turn and face me before I speak, because I want to see what's in his eyes. "Dude, are you okay?" His posture is rigid, and his eyes are wide, alert, like he's mentally and physically bracing for something awful.

He nods quickly. "Let's get the worst part over with."

I squeeze his hand and follow him to the other side of the apartment. He knocks on a closed door. I hear someone talking on the other side. He cracks the door and then opens it very slowly. There's a mature, dark-haired woman in a black pencil skirt, red silk blouse, and black patent high heels pacing the floor in front of an enormous, carved rosewood desk. It appears that her phone is on speaker, and she's firing questions at the person on the other end in rapid-fire succession. I can practically see them shrinking away through the phone. She knows she's in charge, that this person is at her mercy, and the look on her face tells me she enjoys it. She wraps up the call with an irritated tap of a button. Her attitude doesn't shift as she notices Keller standing in the room. "Keller."

He nods curtly. "Mother."

"Dinner's at eight o'clock. I assume you'll be dressed appropriately by then?" It's disdain and insult. Like she's talking to a bratty, eight-year-old stranger.

He's wearing dark jeans and a black, long-sleeved, button-down shirt. He looks damn good if you ask me.

He ignores the jab. "Where's Stella?"

"She's at the art museum with Melanie. They probably got stuck in traffic." It's at that moment that she notices me standing behind Keller. "Oh," is all she says.

I've never wanted to shrink and just disappear, but right now, I do. Instead, I take a deep breath and put on my best it's-nice-to-meet-you smile, the same one that I used on all my mother's boyfriends that she wanted me to impress. I step out from behind Keller and extend my hand. "Mrs. Banks, it's nice to meet you. I'm Kate Sedgwick. I go to school with Keller at Grant."

She shakes my hand firmly. It's supposed to be intimidating. I can play this game. "Kate, you say? Funny, Keller's never mentioned you before." That was supposed to hurt me. She's scraping her eyes up and down me, and her nose is scrunched up like I smell bad.

I shrug. "That doesn't surprise me. We've only been friends a few months. Inviting me along on this trip was a last-minute thing. I hope I'm not intruding?" I feel like I need to make some peace for Keller.

She turns and walks back and takes a seat behind her desk and puts on a pair of reading glasses. She's fixated on a paper in front of her when she answers me, "Well, it's a little late if that's the case, don't you think, dear?" "Dear" is clearly an insult. She keeps reading. She's effectively dismissed us.

I take a step forward and raise my voice a notch to get her attention. I'll call her out on her bitchiness all day long. "Is it, Mrs. Banks? Too late? Because I'd be happy to get a hotel room if that's the case."

She's still writing, ignoring me.

"Ma'am, no disrespect, but I'm trying to ask you a question. Can you please look at me?"

She drops her pen and narrows her eyes. "Sleep in the guest room; you're not sleeping with my son under my roof." She promptly picks up the pen and scribbles away.

I blink the disbelief away. "Excuse me—"

Keller is staring at his socks. He's fuming and interrupts without looking at her. "When is Stella supposed to return?"

She waves him off like a fly. He's an annoyance to her. "I don't know. Call Melanie."

He pulls his cell from his pocket at the same time he pulls me by the back of my shirt out into the hall. I shut the door, grateful for the barrier between us and that spiteful, mean woman. As he's scrolling through his contacts, we hear the front door open, followed by a woman's voice, "Give me your coat, sweetie," and a little girl's giggle. Children's laughter is the purest sound on Earth. I could listen to it all day, and it would never get old.

Keller's smile blossoms into something I've never before seen on him. It's radiant and loving and proud. "Stella's home. Come on." He puts his index finger to his lips, asking me to keep quiet as we tiptoe down the hall.

There's an elegant, blonde-haired woman hanging coats in the closet. She looks about Keller's age. So, this is Stella. I can see the appeal; she's stunning. The giggling little girl has long, curly, dark red hair. It falls in a mass of wild ringlets down her back. Her arms are spread out to her sides, and she's spinning around in circles until she gets dizzy and falls down. The giggles are amplified as soon as she hits the deck. I don't know who she is, but I just want to scoop her up and hug her. She's so happy. I could use some of that right now.

The blonde turns around and spots Keller and a smile instantly lights her face. This is Keller's fairy tale. And I'm happy for him, for them. But, for one selfish moment, I wish it was *my* fairy tale.

Then, in an instant, everything I thought I knew changes.

The little girl looks up at the beautiful woman and realizes she's looking at something across the room. Her little face turns until she's looking directly at Keller and the look in her eyes is like fireworks on the Fourth of July. Like there's nothing on the planet more important and wonderful than him. She scrambles to her feet and squeals, "Daddy!" as she runs to him.

Daddy?

He kneels down to meet her and hugs her tight. "Hi, Stella. I've missed you so much, baby girl."

She pulls back and kisses him on the lips. "I've missed you, too, Daddy."

Holy shit! Keller has a daughter! And she's adorable.

And curious. She looks up at me with Keller's blue eyes and waves her tiny hand. "Hi. Who are you?"

I smile at her, wave back, and kneel behind Keller so that I'm face to face with her. "Hi, Stella, I'm Kate. I'm your daddy's friend."

She pulls back and looks at Keller for confirmation. "You have friends, Daddy?"

He laughs and nods. "I do."

"Do you have playdates? Like I do with Abby?"

He laughs again. "Not really."

Her smile fades as she ponders his answer. "That's too bad, 'cause playdates are fun." She squirms out of his arms and walks right up to me. I'm still on my knees. "Want to see my turtle? Her name is Miss Higgins."

I nod. "Absolutely."

She takes my hand and pulls me to the room Keller looked in when we first arrived. Keller trails close behind. After meeting Miss Higgins, I meet Melanie, the stunning blonde. She's Stella's nanny. She's quiet and nice, and it's obvious she adores Stella. I like her immediately.

We endure an uncomfortable dinner with Mrs. Banks. Afterward, Keller, Stella, and I return to Stella's room so she can get ready for bed. I sit in a big, comfy chair while they retreat to the en suite bathroom. Keller leaves the door open. I can see and hear them. Keller gives her a bubble bath and helps her into fuzzy, pink pajamas. He coaches and encourages as she brushes her teeth. She's so proud of herself when he tells her, "Great job, baby girl." She crawls into her queen-size bed and pats either side of her, indicating we're supposed to both take a seat.

"What do you want to read tonight, Miss Stella?" Keller asks before he plants a kiss on top of her curly-haired head.

"Hmm." She's really giving this some thought. She's a deep thinker like her dad. "The pony book. But I want Kate to read it, Daddy. Is that okay?" She's diplomatic and already a peacemaker at three and a half.

"Sure. I want Katie to read it, too." He winks at me over the top of her head.

I read the pony book. Coincidently, it was one of Grace's favorite books, too. I've probably read this book aloud two hundred times. I am the master of horse neighs and hoof clomps, and I can be very dramatic. Stella giggles when I'm done. "You're silly, Kate."

"I know." I tickle her side, and she giggles more. "It's more fun that way."

Soon enough her eyelids are drooping. They look just like Keller's when he's sleepy. She looks at Keller. "Will you play me a song before I go to sleep?"

"Of course." He kisses her forehead, before pushing himself up off the bed. He retrieves an acoustic guitar from a stand in the corner of her room and returns to sit on the edge of the bed. He turns and angles himself so that he can see both of us.

I can't hold back my smile. "You know I've been waiting for this ever since I saw the guitar in your room."

His eyes are downcast as he strums a few strings. He's tuning, but a smile curls up. "Don't get your hopes up. I just play for fun."

I put my arm around Stella; she snuggles into my side, and Keller starts to play. I recognize the song three or four notes in.

So does Stella. She claps her hands. "I love this one, Daddy."

He's good, technically sound, and he seems comfortable with the guitar in his hands. With practice, he could be great. It's just one more thing to add to the list of things that make him so damn hard to resist.

When he finishes, I raise my eyebrows.

He raises his in response. "What?" he asks quietly out one side of his mouth, as if he's trying to keep it between us and doesn't want Stella to hear.

"The Cure is *so* mediocre." I'm throwing his words back at him from weeks ago. I narrow my eyes, but I can't stop the smile that's spreading across my face. "Lullaby" has always been one of my favorite songs and he played it beautifully, even without vocals. The guitar was haunting.

He tries to keep a straight face but fails. "I lied. I love The Cure... and yes, Robert Smith is a God. You happy now?"

"Mmm hmm." I am happy now.

"Daddy, can you play one more?" Her hands are clasped together in front of her chest like she's begging or praying. "Pretty please."

He laughs. "I have an idea." His eyes shift to mine. "Let's listen to Katie sing."

Stella tilts her head to look up at me. Her blue eyes are wide with anticipation. I haven't even agreed to it yet, but I'm already trying to think of a song.

I'm quiet, and they're both looking at me expectantly. The same eyes in two different faces. I can't say no to those eyes. No to either set. I motion with my fingers toward Keller, asking for the guitar.

"You want my guitar?"

I nod and motion again.

"You play?" It's disbelief.

"Not well," I mutter as he hands it to me. I wink. "Fake it 'til you make it. Isn't that the saying?"

Stella shifts to Keller's side of the bed, and I slide toward the edge, so I'm sitting next to them. I play a few chords to get comfortable. It's been months since I've held a guitar.

I look at Stella, who's climbed into Keller's lap. She's sitting with her knees bent, arms wrapped around her legs. Keller's holding her like a little pink, fluffy ball in his arms. "Stella, this song is called 'Angels.'"

I play. And I sing. I used to play this song for Gracie, and she loved it.

When I finish, I realize I've had my eyes closed the entire time. I pry one open and peek at my audience of two.

Stella is clapping and cheering in a state halfway between mildly awake and dead asleep. "Yay, Kate. You sing pretty." It's enthusiastic sleep-talking.

Keller looks stunned, but in a way that makes me feel proud. "Yes, she does. I didn't know you played guitar, too."

I shrug as I slide off the edge of the bed and set the guitar back in its stand. "Gus taught me. He got tired of me messing around with his guitar, so when I was thirteen or so, he started teaching me. Nothing formal, but enough that I can stumble my way through a few songs."

He shakes his head. "That wasn't stumbling," he says, there's admiration in his eyes. "It was beautiful."

I nod to acknowledge the compliment. "The xx does it so much better, but thanks. You're not so bad yourself."

Stella interrupts, "Daddy, can we have a playdate with Kate tomorrow?" before sleep takes her.

He hugs her. "That sounds like a great idea."

She hugs both of us twice before crawling under the covers. Keller turns on her night light before turning out the light. "Good night, baby girl. I love you."

"I love you, too, Daddy."

As soon as the door clicks behind him, his voice breaks through the darkness of the hallway. "Thank you, Katie." He pulls me into a hug. When he exhales, I feel any tension in him disappear. "You were amazing. You had no idea what you were walking into tonight. I know I blindsided you with Stella, and I'm sorry. I thought you'd freak out if I told you. I should've known better. You never missed a beat. She loves you."

"I'm not gonna lie, I was in shock. But that passed as soon as she looked up at me and said hi. What a smart, funny, adorable little gift you've been blessed with. It took me all of two seconds to fall in love with her. Do you think she'd fit in my backpack? I might take her home with me."

His shoulders bounce up and down with quiet laughter. "She'd probably like that."

I pat him on the back and release him. "I need to get to bed, dude. I have a playdate tomorrow, and I need to get rested up for it."

He laughs again and walks me to the guest room.

"Thank you for sharing her with me, Keller."

"Good night, Katie." He kisses me on the cheek. "Thank you for letting me share you with her."

SUNDAY, NOVEMBER 6

KELLER

SATURDAY AND SUNDAY FLY BY, and once again, I'm forced to say goodbye to Stella long before I want to. Our weekend was typical, we walked around the city, played at the park, ate hot dogs from the cart on the corner, but with Katie there, it was like I was seeing it all in color instead of black and white. The fun was amplified into pure joy. Stella had the time of her life. She laughed almost as much as Katie did, which is saying something; Katie laughs more than anyone I've ever known. She's refined the art of enjoyment and living in the moment. I've never seen anything like it. It's breathtaking. I'm not that way. I try, but I'm too focused on the future, on Stella's future. I lost myself this weekend, and it felt great. I watched the two of them together, and it was hard to not imagine the three of us as a family. Just the thought of it gave me peace I've never known. If there's one person in this world I would like to inspire my daughter, it's Katie.

We even spent time with my father this morning. He's usually working the ER when I'm home on weekends. I don't see him much anymore.

Stella is wrapped around me like a monkey. She's crying like she does every time I leave. It breaks my heart. I rock her back and forth slowly and try to soothe away her sadness. It kills me. I'm stroking her wild, red curls, the ones she got from her mother. "Shh, baby girl. I'll be back soon."

She sniffs and whispers in my ear, "I know, but I miss you when you're not here."

I whisper back, "I miss you, too, Stella. So, so much. But I'll call or talk to you on the computer every morning and every night until I see you next time, okay?"

She nods her tiny head and wipes her wet eyes on my shoulder. "I want to say bye to Kate." She squirms, indicating she's ready to be set down.

My beautiful little daughter walks slowly to my beautiful friend and extends her hands up over her head, asking to be picked up. Katie doesn't hesitate. Stella wraps her arms and legs around her, rests her head on Katie's shoulder, and snuggles in. Not much in this world seems right, but what I'm watching now does. Katie holds her tightly but with a gentleness that's calming. It's what I feel when she hugs me, too, and I imagine that peace seeping into Stella now. Katie kisses Stella's forehead. "I'm so happy I got to meet you, Stella."

Stella's head rises to look Katie in the eye. "Can you come back again with Daddy so we can have another playdate?"

Katie looks at me, and for a second, gut-wrenching devastation flashes across her face, but it's followed so quickly by a smile that I wonder if I only imagined it. She looks at Stella and whispers, "I would love to see you again, Stella." Katie kisses her on the forehead again before she sets her down. "You take good care of Miss Higgins."

Stella smiles. "I will."

After two more rounds of kisses and hugs and "I love you," Katie and I exit the building and climb into a waiting cab. The ride to the airport is quiet. I hate this part of being a father to Stella. The goodbyes.

It's not until we're on the plane that I feel like talking. Katie is perceptive and has given me the past two hours of silence to live in my head and not in the real world. She's been holding my hand the entire time. It's the smallest gesture, but she'll never know how truly comforting it's been. I speak without looking at her, "You know something? I've never seen my father laugh."

There's no disbelief or prompting me to explain further. No questions. She just lets me talk.

"He's never played a children's game either, probably not even when he was a child. And *you* got him to play Go Fish with us, just by asking. You teased him that you were glad we weren't playing Operation because he'd kick our butts...and he *laughed*. He doesn't laugh." I finally look at her and her expression is blank but open. I shake my head and repeat, "He doesn't laugh."

She smiles sheepishly. "It *was* funny. He's a surgeon, after all."

I can't hold back a smile. "I know. I got the joke. But what happened this weekend...everything that happened this weekend... was surreal. My daughter is completely head-over-heels in love with you. My mother addressed you *by your name*. She only started calling Dunc 'Duncan' last year, and I've known him for six years. He lived with us *in their home* for a full year, and she wouldn't talk to him. My father told you to 'Come back anytime, *dude*.'"

She laughs. "It's funny when Shelly says dude, but your dad may have one-upped her." She playfully frowns. "Sorry, I may have been a bad influence with all the trash-talking during Go Fish. I got the feeling he enjoyed it, though, or I wouldn't have done it."

I shake my head. "I thought I was fairly good at reading people, but you take that to a different level. You are simply...enchanting. People can't resist you."

She scoffs and changes the subject. She's good at diverting attention away from herself. "Lily was Stella's mother?"

I nod.

"And Lily was Duncan's sister." It's not a question.

"She was. How'd you figure that out?"

She shrugs like it's obvious. "The hair."

I laugh. "I guess the red hair is kind of a giveaway. Stella takes after her mom. That's a good thing."

Katie smiles. "I'm sure Lily was pretty, but Stella looks a lot like you, too. Same eyes, same smile," she winks at me, "and that's definitely a good thing."

"She does have my eyes. Lily's were brown like Dunc's." Now's as good a time as any to tell the story, I think. "I worked at a pizza place my junior and senior years in high school because I just wanted some normalcy. I wanted to earn my own money, buy my own car. My parents weren't happy about it, but they didn't fight me on it. I met Dunc there, and through Dunc, Lily. Dunc and Lily had their own apartment. Their mom was a drug addict, and they never knew their father, so they'd been on their own for a few years. Dunc is two years older than I am, and Lily was three years older. She was going to nursing school when we met. She was quiet, reserved, and smart. What she saw in a kid like me, I'll never know.

We'd been dating for almost a year when she found out she was pregnant. I was a senior in high school and so confused. I knew I loved her, but my future had always been mapped out for me. I was too squeamish with blood to be a doctor like my father, so I was set on a course to become a lawyer like my mother. A baby didn't fit into my parents' plans for me. They were furious. They wanted her to have an abortion. We refused, and I asked her to marry me. I loved her, and it seemed like the next logical step."

Katie smiles and nods. I take that as encouragement to continue and take a deep breath. "The baby was due right around my graduation and when Lily was scheduled to finish up her nursing program. We planned to marry that summer and move to Grant, where I already had a scholarship in the fall, thanks in part to my grades and in part to my mother being an alum with a very generous pocketbook. Plans all changed when Lily died giving birth."

Katie's lips part slightly; the sincere reaction of a compassionate person. She's the best kind of listener.

This story is one I've never even begun to share with anyone, let alone one that I've finished. But now that it's out there hanging between us, I want to. "They said the complications were very rare.

'One-in-a-million,' they said. But they were *my* one in a million. Losing Lily was devastating, but I was also scared to death by the prospect of being a single father at eighteen. I had no idea what to do with a baby. My parents hired a nanny immediately, because in their home, that's how a child is raised. It's how I was raised. I did my best, but I don't know what I would've done without Melanie to help me. I skipped my first semester at Grant, so I could be there for Stella. Again, my parents were furious because I was delaying their plans. Don't get me wrong, they love Stella. But *I* was a huge disappointment. They convinced me to go away to school, and Dunc came with me. He's always wanted to go to college and get into politics. My parents said the best place for Stella was with them and the nanny so I could focus on my classes and eventually have a career where I could support and care for Stella on my own."

She blinks those gorgeous jade eyes at me and asks simply, "What did you think was best for Stella?"

This is the question that haunts me to this very day. "I didn't know. I *don't* know."

"Keller, why doesn't anyone in Grant know about Stella?"

I rake my hands through my hair. "God, you must think I'm awful."

She shakes her head. "No, I don't." She means it. "I wouldn't be sitting here next to you if I did. I'm allergic to awful people."

I laugh because she always knows how to add humor when it's needed. "I guess there are lots of reasons I don't tell people. She's mine, and a part of me wants to keep her close and not have to share her with more people than I already do. A part of me fears people would judge me for having her so young, for not being the father I should be, for being away from her. I love her so much, Katie. I just want what's best for her. That's all I've ever wanted."

She squeezes my hand tighter. "Keller, you are an unbelievably patient, attentive, engaged, loving parent. Why do think Stella looks at you like she does? Like the sun rises and sets with you? Why do you think she's so sad when you have to leave? You are her world. She loves you."

My throat tightens up with her words. What she's just described is all I want.

She senses I'm getting emotional and begins to trace circles on the back of my hand with her thumb. "Keller, dude, you only get one life to live. Imagine for a moment that you were free of all the expectations in your life. What would you do? How would you live your life with no one watching? What would your future look like?"

I don't hesitate with my answer, "Stella would be with me in Grant. I'd change my major to English. And in a few years, I'd be teaching high school English in a town where Stella could grow up safe and happy." There are tears in my eyes. I should be embarrassed because I was always taught that boys don't cry. Men don't cry. With Katie, I'm free.

She takes my chin in her hand and turns it until I'm looking her in the eyes. She stares at me unblinking for several seconds. She has my attention. "Do. It." It's a command. "Nothing, and I mean nothing, should stand in the way of that, because that is exactly the way your life should be, Keller. That little girl should be with her daddy every day, and you were absolutely born to be a teacher."

She hasn't released me. She's waiting for a response. I close my eyes because I can't look her in the eyes when I say it. "It's not that easy."

"Look at me," she commands again. There's no anger, but the desperation in her voice is unnerving. She cares. She cares about me and what I want. I forgot what that feels like. No one's treated me like this since Lily, and even Lily never pushed me this far. "Please," she says.

I do.

"Raising Stella on your own will be the hardest thing you've ever done. Knowing that another human being depends on you to get her through life? That's hard, and it's tiring, and it's worrisome, and it's scary, but you know what? It's also fun, and rewarding, and fulfilling in a way that nothing else in this world is." She's emphatic. This is too real for her. She drops her hand to her lap.

"You took care of your sister, didn't you?" I guess.

She nods. I wait until she's ready to talk because I know her sister is a topic that's hard for her to open up about. "Grace had Down syndrome. Mentally she never progressed much past where Stella is right now. My mother had issues of her own that made parenting... difficult. So, it was always my job to take care of Gracie. I bathed her, I dressed her, I fed her, I read to her, I played with her, I took her to school. When she was sixteen, and I was fifteen, she was in an accident that left her without the use of her legs. She was confined to a wheelchair after that—"

I interrupt, remembering something she told me weeks ago. "That's why you had the minivan."

She nods and smiles that I remembered. "Yeah, Old Blue was chair accessible." She takes a deep breath and continues. "When I was eighteen, a few weeks before my high school graduation, my mother passed away."

My heart is breaking because this poor girl's life has been so difficult. "I'm sorry," is all I can think to say.

"Yeah." She looks contemplative. "Life was always difficult for Janice Sedgwick. I like to think she's in a better place now. That she's finally happy." She nods. "So, it's okay."

"Where did you live after your mom died? You said your dad wasn't around."

"The months that followed her death were like an avalanche of shit. After the dust settled, I sold everything and Gracie and I rented a place from my mother's old gardener. It was nothing fancy, but it was ours. Grace loved it there. It was the best time of my life. We lived there until she died."

I sit back in my seat and just look at her. You know how you think you know someone? By simply being around them you somehow think you have them figured out? That you know what kind of a person they are deep down? You could literally knock me over with a feather after what I've just heard. The woman sitting next to me on this airplane is the most incredible person I've ever met. "How'd you do it all those years?"

"How could I not? She was my sister and I loved her. Good or bad, I was all she had."

That's exactly the kind of thing she would say. "Who took care of you?"

She smiles, and it shines in her eyes. "Gus. He's always been my best friend. He was my next-door neighbor. His mom, Audrey, is awesome, too. She was like a mom to Gracie and me. She still is."

"He loves you. I thought the guy was going to castrate me over the phone Friday night. It was brutal. I've never known anyone with a relationship like you have with Gus. Two people that close, but who aren't together. It's still hard for me to wrap my brain around."

She shrugs. "Don't try too hard. We're a little weird. Gus's mom swears that she had twins, and we were separated at birth even though he's a few years older. She took one baby home with her from the hospital, and the other moved in next door a few years later."

"I can see that." I'm trying so hard to understand their friendship, but it's so hard not to be jealous of Gus. *I* want the history they have. *I* want to know everything about her. *I* want to be the person she tells everything to. *I* want to take care of her. I want *her*.

When she drops me off at my place, I don't want her to leave. "Thanks for coming with me, Katie."

She unbuckles her seat belt and leans across the small space to hug me. "Thanks for taking me, Keller. I know it took a lot to share that part of your life."

"Not with you it didn't. You give me courage I never knew I had."

She corrects with a whisper. "I didn't do anything. It was there all along, you just had to find it."

I pull back slightly, knowing that I cannot let her leave without doing something I've wanted to do since the first time I saw her. I search her eyes and reach my hand to her cradle her cheek. She's so soft, and she smells so good. Her wavy hair is wild and messy as always, and she looks so damn sexy. She doesn't resist, so I lean in slowly. When my lips touch hers, every thought and every worry leaves my mind. Everything else vanishes except her. She's all I feel, all I smell, all I hear, all I see, and all I taste. Her lips are so soft as they move against mine, with mine, and when they part slightly, and I taste her tongue with mine, I feel a shudder of pleasure run through my body. Her hand slides up my arm to gently clutch my neck. The sensation of her touch coaxes a soft moan from me. It's a sound in the back of my throat that I can't control. Her touch, her taste; it's almost too much. She must feel it too, because she pulls back. When I open my eyes, I notice that hers have turned dark, like her pupils have swallowed the green.

I say, "Come inside with me." At the same time, she says, "I have to go."

Her breaths are deep and erratic. She feels this. She wants this.

"Why are you leaving?"

She looks away. "I have to."

"What happened to the girl who preached living in the present? Because I have to tell you, Katie, I have never been more present than I am this very moment." *Never* been more present...

She has both hands on the wheel now. She's still not looking at me. She swallows and I'm afraid she isn't going to say anything when she whispers, "This is different."

"Why? *Please. Stay.*" I'm begging her.

She blinks a few times. "There are things you don't know about me. I'd only hurt you in the end, and I care too much about you to do that."

I'm lost, confused, frustrated. "What? Look me in the eye and tell me you don't have feelings for me. Because that kiss? That kiss was the most amazing thing I've ever experienced in my entire fucking life. I know you felt it. *You fucking felt it.*"

She looks up at me, and her eyes are glassy. "I did. That's why I need to leave."

I throw my hands up in the air. *"That doesn't make any fucking sense."*

"I know, Keller. I need to go."

I throw the door open, step out, and slam the door before I open the back hatch to grab my bag. I should walk away quietly, but I'm too pissed not to push her on this. "This is bullshit, and you know it. I don't know what's going on with you, but nothing you could possibly say would change the way I feel about you. I haven't opened my heart to anyone in a very long time, and if you told me you weren't interested, fine. It would suck, but I'd walk away, lick my wounds, and go on with my life. But the fact that you aren't even allowing yourself the opportunity to experience whatever *we* might turn into, that pisses me off." I don't know if this is a trust issue or a commitment issue, but I don't like to see her deny herself. And that's exactly what she's doing. "I don't know about you, but this connection we have, this attraction, it doesn't come along every day. It's been years... *years*...since I felt this way. Honestly, I never thought I'd feel it again. Does it scare me? Hell yes. Can I predict the future? Nope. But know this, I would never, ever, in a million years, hurt you. I'd be in it one hundred percent. The ball's in your court, Katie. At some point in your life, you have to trust someone."

I don't wait for a response. I know I won't get one, so I slam the hatch and walk into my apartment without looking back.

TUESDAY, NOVEMBER 8

KATE

THERE'S a note on the door of my Psychology class, something about class being canceled due to my professor having the stomach flu. My first thought is *Hell yes!* Followed quickly by guilt for the mental high five I just enjoyed at the expense of someone else's suffering bowels.

I immediately apologize, *God, I thank you for this small but much-needed blessing. I'm sorry Professor Garrick has the trots, but canceled class means nap time for Kate. I owe you for this one.*

I've never walked across campus and back to the dorms at this time of day. It seems quieter than usual. Relaxing. But as I approach my dorm, I see someone standing next to Clay's car. And it's not Clay. I make a detour so I can get a closer look without being seen.

And as soon as I get the closer look I was after, I immediately regret it. Not because I don't want to be here in this moment, but because assholes really, *really* piss me off.

Clayton is backed up against his driver's door holding his messenger bag tightly in front of his chest. A broad-shouldered guy in a gray hoodie is leaning toward Clay, cocking his head from side to side, standing way too close for this to be a friendly conversation. His fists are balled up, and his posture looks threatening. This isn't good.

I pause for only a split second. There's no way in hell I'm going to let him lay a hand on Clayton, but I also don't want to misread the situation. I start with a loud greeting as I approach slowly from behind. "What's up?" I say, loudly.

The Asshole turns toward my voice. Attention diverted. Clay's shoulders slump a good two inches with relief.

The Asshole gropes me with his eyes. It's fucking creepy. I feel violated. He licks his lips. "What's up?" He grabs his crotch suggestively. "Looking at you, pretty girl, I'd say *my dick* is what's up." He's foul. *And* he just winked at me.

"Was that some sort of a pick-up line?" I ask because I'm genuinely baffled when guys think this sort of thing is attractive.

He winks again.

Yup, I guess it was. I shake my head. "Slow the horse down, cowboy; I'm not sure I caught your name."

He smiles this smarmy-ass smile. "Ben."

"Ben, what?" I fish. Because if he's already done something to Clayton, I want this guy's full name, so I can share it with the proper authorities.

"Ben Thompson." Smarmy smile still in place. "Want to get out of here? Go back to my room?" He glances at his watch. "I've got an hour before class. We can make it quick."

If I could give out an award for *The Least Classy Thing I've Heard All Week*—hell, all year—then this guy would be the big winner. He fucking nailed it. "Dude? Ben Thompson? I've known you for all of thirty seconds, and I've gotta hand it to you, I'm thoroughly repulsed. I think I just threw up in my mouth a little. When I asked what was up, *I wasn't talking to your dick, dickhead*. I was talking to my friend here."

Clayton's eyes are bulging, and he's shaking his head behind *The Asshole*. Maybe I should be scared, but with the week I'm having, I don't feel like I have anything to lose.

His smile makes my skin crawl. "You're mouthy. Mouthy makes me horny, princess."

"Listen, dipshit, this isn't foreplay." I reach over and take Clay's hand in mine. "You're disgusting. Leave us alone."

He's finally getting it. Anger flashes in his eyes. "Fucking cock tease." He's pointing at Clayton now, and it's threatening. "And as for you, you little pansy-ass, we're not done. You'd better watch your back."

I want Clayton to say something, anything, *so badly*, but he keeps his head down and starts walking toward the dorms. And because I'm holding his hand, I'm forced to walk with him. Of course, I can't walk away without the last words, "Fuck off, asshole."

He kicks Clayton's car door before leaving in the opposite direction.

I stop before we reach the dorm doors and turn to face Clayton. There are tears in his eyes. I feel sadness, guilt, and anger boiling up within me. He looks down at the ground, and he's wiping at his cheeks to clear away the tears.

In my softest voice, I prompt, "Hey." Because he looks embarrassed and that's the last thing I want him to feel. "Clay, it's me, Kate."

His chin rises fractionally, and his eyes lift the rest of the way to meet mine. He's trying not to cry, but his chin's quivering.

"Was he threatening you when I walked up?"

He nods.

I don't want to ask the next question, because I'm scared I already know the answer. "Has he threatened you before?"

He nods.

"How long has this been going on, Clay?"

His chin's trembling again. "About a month."

My stomach is in knots. "How often?"

The tears are streaming again. "Every day."

I feel sick. I take pride in being a good friend. Because in life, that's really all that matters, people. And treating them well, being there for them, that's being a good friend.

I. Am. A. Horrible. Friend. How could I not know about this?

I pull him into a hug, and he cries on my shoulder. I rub his back and wish I could bear my sweet friend's burden for him.

I release him, and he sniffles. "Dude, have you told anyone about this?"

He shakes his head.

"You should report him to campus security. Talk to the Dean's office. Talk to John, even. This is unacceptable. You should be able to walk around campus, hell, you should be able to walk around anywhere you damn well please, without being scared."

He sighs, it's defeat if I've ever heard it. "I can't."

"Why not?"

"It never does any good."

That makes me sad. It's basically the same thing he said after the Spectacle incident.

"Do you know how many times I've complained to counselors, teachers, and principals over the years about being bullied or beaten up?"

God, my heart doesn't want to know.

"Too many times, Katherine. And not once did anyone act on it. I was told I was overreacting, or it was a misunderstanding, or even that I was asking for it. Can you believe that? People have looked me in the eye and told me because I was gay, I was *asking* to get picked on. And I've been told that more than once, so apparently it's not an opinion isolated to a single ignorant person."

"You can't let the assholes win, Clay."

He huffs. "It's not a game. It's my life. And I'm tired, Katherine. I just hoped that college would be different. More tolerant—"

I interrupt him. "'Tolerance is bullshit. There's nothing to tolerate. We don't *tolerate* lovely people, *we enjoy their company*. I hate that term."

He sniffs. "Me too." He sniffs again. "What I'm finding out is that college is no different. Different school, same Neanderthals. I'm trying to make it through the semester, because I feel like I'm throwing my parents' money away if I don't." He sighs again. "But I can't come back next semester."

He can't let the assholes win! I walk Clayton inside and leave him inside his dorm room with a Twix bar from my freezer, because eating one always makes me feel better when I'm having a shitty day.

As soon I leave his room, I walk directly to the campus security office. A middle-aged man in a blue jacket greets me, and I get right to the point. "I'd like to file two reports please."

"Two reports?" he questions.

I nod. "That's correct." *The Asshole*, Ben Thompson, will not get away with this.

I proceed to file a complaint on Clayton's behalf with me as an eyewitness, and I make sure to mention that this has been going on daily for a month. Following Clayton's incident, I report sexual harassment for the lewd display he put on for me. Just thinking of the creepy-ass way he looked at me makes me think that he's one of those guys who thinks no means yes, and yes means *hell yes*.

I can't help but think about Keller's mother the whole time I'm in here. I mean, yeah she's abrupt and insulting, but I bet it makes her one helluva a lawyer. I find myself trying to mimic her bluntness. I'm even wearing her strained smile to get my point across—and it works.

I take a few deep breaths just outside the door, because I'm still all worked up. I don't know if what I just did will make any difference, but I have to try.

As the tension begins to ease away, I realize just how much my body hurts today, and I'm more tired than I was earlier. It's not happy about the stress I've piled on. I need a nap ASAP.

THURSDAY, NOVEMBER 10

KATE

I'VE AVOIDED Grounds every day this week because I knew seeing Keller would crush me. I've decided that maybe some distance between us is the best option. After the trip to Chicago and then the kiss, I can no longer deny the feelings I have for him. But the fact that he might feel the same way in return? That worries me for many reasons.

Number one: I am not a selfish person. I never have been, and I don't want to start at this point in my life. Pursuing him would be totally self-serving.

Number two: Guilt. Guilt would be a direct result of number one. And guilt is way too close to regret. I don't want any regrets.

That leads to number three: Trust. Keller called me on it. He was dead on. Trust and my heart are linked. If I trust you, it means I've let you into my heart. And I trust you not to hurt me. The pinnacle of trust, the trust I've never afforded to anyone, is the scariest: true love. It goes back to the whole fairy tale thing. And every time I let myself slip and imagine my own fairy tale, it always involves trusting my heart to Keller. And lately, that feels right and warm and comforting.

Which leads my mind to circle immediately back to number one. *I am not selfish.*

This is the cycle that keeps driving me away from the pursuit of anything more than friendship with Keller. But friendship is the reason I can't cut him out of my life completely. I want his friendship. It makes me feel happy, giddy even. It's like a drug. And I function so much better when I'm on it. That's why I decide to walk to Grounds. I'm also dying for a good cup of coffee. My body may shut down completely without it.

And my body, that's another thing. She's very unhappy with me lately. Just normal functioning has become a struggle. The pain's become so intense that ibuprofen doesn't touch it anymore. It's a pain that's unrelenting and constant. It bears down, like it's compressing me from the inside out. It keeps me awake at night. It's even found a way to physically alter my appearance. I've lost a few pounds. I can tell because my jeans are looser than usual. It also shows in my face. My skin looks pale, and there are dark circles beneath my eyes. I knew it would come to this, so I grudgingly made an appointment for tomorrow afternoon with Dr. Connell. I haven't been in to see him since my first visit in late August. I'm sure he's not happy because he wanted to see me every month. His office calls me every few weeks. I ignore the calls. I know it's immature, but it's my way of dealing with this, and I've been managing pretty well with ibuprofen and extra sleep when I can get it.

When I arrive at Grounds, Keller is behind the counter. His greeting isn't the usual, easy-going, friendly one I'm used to. "Hey," is all I get.

I understand. I totally understand.

I try to smile, but it's hard. I don't fake it very well; at least that's what Gus has always told me. I'm a terrible liar. Withholding information I'm good at, but flat out lying? I'm terrible. "Hey," I respond.

He pours my large coffee and hands it to me in silence. I hand him my birthday gift card as payment. He completes the transaction without a word. He still hasn't looked me in the eye.

There's no one else here, but I whisper anyway. "Listen, I'm sorry. I never wanted to hurt you."

"Too late." His tone is harsh. A beat later he shakes his dropped head. "That was rude. Sorry." It's then that his eyes finally meet mine. The hurt in them disappears with a start and morphs into concern. "What's wrong? Are you sick, Katie?"

Keller hasn't seen me all week, so it's probably more obvious to him than to someone I see every day. "Yeah." Part of me wants to lay it all out on the table. "I've got an appointment with my doctor tomorrow afternoon."

His posture is stiff. He looks like he doesn't know what to do. I could really use a hug right now. But it's not in my nature to ask for comfort or consoling, so I raise my cup in the air. "Have a good Thursday, dude. Tell Stella I said hi to her and Miss Higgins when you talk to her tonight."

He nods. "I will." He looks worried. "Let me know how your appointment goes."

FRIDAY, NOVEMBER 11

KATE

THE APPOINTMENT with Dr. Connell is every bit as depressing and hopeless as I hoped it wouldn't, but knew it would be. Same tests, worse results—more *news*. I can't really call it bad news at this point, it's just *news*. I vowed when this all began that I wouldn't feel sorry for myself, but on the drive from Minneapolis back to Grant, I decide to give myself until midnight to wallow in it.

Wallow like a *motherfucker*.

I now have a prescription for some stronger pain meds, which I stop and get on my way home, but by the time I reach the dorms, I decide that tonight I will medicate with alcohol. I'll drink until I'm numb. Until I can't feel the pain. Until I can't remember what I'm trying to forget. I'll figure out how to cope with this again tomorrow. Tonight I'm going to forget.

Forget like a *motherfucker*.

I turn my cell phone off as I walk down the hall to my dorm room and throw it in my bag. As luck would have it, Sugar is here. My plan for all-out ruination is falling into place. "Hey, dude, how much alcohol do you have in here?" I don't know who buys it for her, but the girl always has alcohol hidden in her closet. I think it's part of the entertainment when her suitors come calling.

She looks a little shocked. We don't talk much, and it's not like me to bust through the door asking questions, making demands, especially something like this. "Umm, I don't know. What're you looking for?"

"Not beer, other than that, I don't care."

I've thrown her off her game, and she's too confused to give me any of her usual attitude. "Okay. Let's see." She rifles through her closet and pulls out a bottle of cheap wine, a fifth of whiskey that's almost empty, and a pint of vodka that's three-quarters full. She seems disturbingly excited to show off her stash. In the world of illegal activity, this is child's play. Still, she's grinning like a crime lord flaunting her illicit business. I file the thought away and vow to address Sugar's inevitable train wreck at a later time. A time when I'm not in the midst of my own fucking derailment. Maybe tomorrow.

I fish through the pocket of my jeans and pull out a twenty. I throw it on the floor and snatch up the vodka. "Thanks." I check my other pocket to make sure I've got my dorm room key, unzip my coat, stuff the bottle inside, zip it up, and walk out the door without another word.

It's time for dinner, but I skip it in favor of the bottle in my coat. It's cold outside, so I head to the closest building that's least likely to be occupied on a Friday night, the library. I know this because I've spent plenty of Friday nights here. The same guy is always working the desk, and he's usually asleep by nine o'clock. I could sit in the stacks drinking all night and never see another soul.

So, that's exactly what I do. I find a little corner in the biography section, plop down on the carpet, and pull out my bottle. I pace myself because I'm shooting for incapacitation, not death. The vodka burns going down. I've never liked the taste of straight alcohol. It's flammable, for God's sake, and it tastes that way. The warmth starts radiating from my belly, and soon enough my ears are hot, and I can't feel my nose or my fingertips. The titles on the spines of the books on the shelf next to me start to blur. I take another glug. The next time I glance at them, the books themselves are barely distinguishable from each other—they're hazy strips of color lined up next to each other. I'm having a little trouble reading the clock on the wall behind me because every time I tilt my head to try to focus, the room starts spinning. I think it says 11:45. My time's almost up. It's almost midnight.

Good thing the bottle is almost empty. I drain the last few drops and stuff it back in my coat. For some reason, I feel like it's time to take a walk. I wander back out into the cold, leaning toward the dorms, but at the last second, my feet decide to stumble on a new course. I take a right toward Main Street.

KELLER

The beating on the door wakes me. I squint at my clock. Without my glasses, it's hard to read. 12:47 am. The beating starts up again. Dunc must've forgotten his key. I thought he was staying at Shel's tonight. I strip the covers back and stretch before I climb out. I'm only in my boxers, and I turn away as the cold air pours in from the open door, shocking my bare skin. "What the hell, Dunc? Hurry up." No one steps inside.

When I look back outside, I realize that it's not Dunc. It's Katie. A Katie I don't recognize. If she looked sick yesterday, it's nothing compared to tonight. She looks pallid and frail. Defeated. She's soaking wet. It's snowing, and I wonder how long she's been outside. Her teeth are chattering, and her lips look blue. She's wearing her plaid wool coat but no hat or gloves. It's not much above zero.

She still hasn't stepped inside. She's waiting on me. I grab the sleeve of her coat and pull her. "Get in here." She stumbles and I catch her by the arm. Her eyes blink too slowly. "Are you drunk?"

"You always have been one of the smartest people I know," she says, her speech slow and deliberate.

I half carry her to the loveseat and make her sit down. I take off her shoes, and when I unzip her coat to take it off, an empty bottle of vodka falls out.

I pick it up. "Did you drink all of this?"

She squints at the bottle in my hands and nods. "Yes. Yes, I did." As small as she is, that would be like me drinking a fifth in a night, which I know from experience is not a good idea.

Her hands and face feel like ice. "How long have you been outside?" Every piece of clothing is soaking wet.

She shrugs pitifully.

All I can think about is getting her warm first and sober second. I take her hand in mine, and when she stands slowly, I walk her to the bathroom. I place her in the shower and pull her shirt over her head. She has bandages wrapped around both arms at her elbows. She said she was going to the doctor today. They must've drawn blood. The thought brings a lump to my throat. Is she in pain? Is everything okay? Seeing this kills me. When I unbutton and unzip her jeans, she doesn't protest. I don't think she even knows what's going on. As I peel the wet denim down her legs, I can't help but think about how many times I've fantasized about this very moment. I also can't help but think about how wrong it feels right now. I'm kneeling in front of her. "Put your hands on my shoulders," I say. I flinch from her cold fingers when she does. After she steps out of the jeans, I turn her so she's facing away from me. I don't want to see her this way. My stomach clenches and I feel like I'm violating her. I close my eyes and unfasten her bra. After slipping her arms out of the straps, I drop it on the floor behind me. Then I pull down her panties. My eyes still squeezed shut tight, I feel around on the wall to turn on the water. I give her a warning, like I would with Stella. "I'm turning on the water, Katie. I want you to stay in here until you warm up, okay?"

"Okay." She sounds so tired.

I gather her wet clothes and put them in the dryer before I put on a T-shirt. I decide to grab a T-shirt and a pair of boxers for her, too. I don't have anything that will fit her, so we'll have to make due until her clothes are dry.

I knock on the door before I enter the bathroom because I feel like a pervert just barging in. Hell, I feel like a pervert knocking first, too. "You doing all right, Katie?"

"Yeah, I'm warm." Her voice echoes from inside the shower.

"Give yourself another minute. You were freezing. I'm going to leave a towel and some clothes here on the floor. Take your time."

Five minutes later, I hear the water shut off. I walk to the closed door and listen in case she falls down or needs me. I hear her bang into the wall a few times, but she sounds like she's doing all right, so I take a seat on my recliner to wait.

When the door opens and she comes out, she still looks drunk, but she doesn't look so miserable anymore. The T-shirt is so long on her that I can't see the boxers underneath, which is unbelievably sexy. Her hair is twisted up in a towel the way only girls know how to do. She's more alert. "Thanks, Keller."

"You hungry?"

She stops to think. It takes longer than it should. "A little. I didn't eat dinner. It was a liquids-only evening."

"Well then, let's get you something more substantial," I say. I reheat the leftover fettuccine alfredo I made earlier tonight. I didn't put chicken in it like I usually do. I guess I was thinking about Katie.

It takes her forever, but she finishes every last bite. I don't mind because it gives me an excuse to look at her mouth. And to think about how it tasted, how soft it was when I kissed her less than a week ago.

The fork clinks against the empty plate when she sets it down, and it brings me back out of my daydream. "That was really good, Keller."

I smile because she sounds almost like herself again. "Thanks. How're you feeling?" She looks better, too. She's removed the towel from her head and her hair is dry but untamed. She looks like Katie again.

"Pretty good right now. My plan seems to have worked. Probably not so good in the morning, though."

I don't share with her that it is morning. It's after 2:30. "Probably not so good in the morning," I agree. "What do you mean your plan worked?"

She shakes her head like she doesn't want to talk about it. The arm bandages are gone. Bruises and angry needle pricks revealed that were hidden underneath before. I point, and she immediately folds her arms across her chest to hide them. "Did you see the doctor today?"

She nods.

"Did they figure out what's wrong?"

She huffs and it's bitter. "They already knew." She stretches her arms out in front of her. They look worse held out for me to see. My stomach hurts again. "This is what they do to make themselves feel better. To feel like they're doing their jobs." The bitter huff again. "It's a game, though, because it doesn't change anything." She draws out the word "anything" like it's three distinct words.

Something is very wrong. I feel like throwing up. "What doesn't change, Katie?"

She looks up at me and smiles, but it's the saddest thing I've ever seen, because it's her most honest, genuine smile paired with hopeless eyes. "The end."

The needle on my anxiety gauge just pegged out. My heart is racing. "What's going on?"

She doesn't answer, and this eerie silence settles between us.

I'm shaking now, I'm so worked up. I'm nervous, and I'm scared, and I'm frustrated. Out of desperation, I yell, "Tell me what in the hell is going on!"

Nothing. She's just sitting there, but she's starting to tremble.

More yelling, "I love you, Katie!" It's a declaration and a promise. It's also clarification, because I don't know what's going through her mind, but she needs to know how much I care about her. How much I love her.

Her bottom lip starts quivering and her eyes fill with tears. "Please don't say that."

I pull my hair because I don't know what else to do with myself. "Dammit, I love you. Why is that such a bad thing? I know you love me, too. *Just let me in.* Say it." My patience is shot.

The tears chase each other down her cheeks, and she sniffs. "I do. I love you." Her voice is quiet and defeated.

This is not the way you want to hear someone tell you they love you. It guts me. I sigh and look at the ceiling before looking back at her and without knowing why I'm yelling again. I can't stop yelling. "Then what's the problem?! You love me! I love you!"

She's reached her limit and erupts back, "*That's* the fucking problem! You love me back! It was never supposed to be this way!"

"Goddammit, Katie," I sigh. "That's not your choice to make. It's mine. I fell in love with you. It would've happened whether you loved me back or not. It's impossible not to love you. You're the most incredible woman I've ever met in my life. Why can't I love you? *Why?*"

She stands, throws her arms in the air, and screams like I've never heard anyone scream before. It's painful and lonely. It's fear and rage. It's exasperation. "Because *I'm dying, that's why!* I have cancer!" She drops back into the loveseat like the words drained her of all energy. "I'm dying," she says, her words turning to sobs.

I feel like someone just stabbed me in the heart. The pain I felt when Lily died was the worst I've ever experienced in my life. Until this moment. It feels like someone is twisting the knife only to pull it out and plunge it back in again. Over and over. My heart just broke for the second time in my life. I can't move. I can't speak. I can't breathe.

Eventually, she wipes the tears from her face with her forearm. I'm moments away from panic when the shift happens. I realize that she's staring at me. And when Katie holds you in a stare...she *holds* you. You *feel* it. It's physical, like you're pinned in place, unable to move, unable to breathe. She stands, walks over, and stops when her knees come to rest against mine. I'm at her mercy and despite what just happened, there's no place I'd rather be. She looks down at me sitting in front of me with those unfathomable jade eyes and takes a few deep breaths. Her eyes never leave mine. "Keller, if I asked you for a favor, would you do it?"

The way she's looking at me I know, without a doubt in my mind, I will do whatever she asks of me. You want me to jump off a cliff? Okay. Walk out in front of a speeding bus? Sure, why not.

"I want one night with you. Just one. I know it's selfish and so wrong of me to even ask, but—"

My lips are on hers before she finishes her thought. Claiming her before she changes her mind. Without breaking our kiss, I reach down and grab hold of her thighs and lift her until her legs are wrapped around my waist. Then I walk us to my bed. I know I should go slowly, but there's so much adrenaline in my system that I can't. I want this too much.

She's not holding back either. Her kisses are assertive and demanding. When I lay her down, she reaches for the hem of my T-shirt, and I shrug it off. My legs are bent, straddling her waist. I'm hovering over her. She runs her hands across my chest and traces her fingertips down my stomach. I shudder and can't suppress the moan that escapes me. Her hands continue down to the ill-fitting boxers she's wearing. Her fingertips hook the waistband on either side, and she pushes them down over her hips and I help her shimmy them off. Lifting the hem of her shirt, I pull it over her head. My breath catches in my throat as my eyes greedily take in her naked body beneath me. She glows in the light of my bedside lamp. If it's possible for a body to look graceful, even at rest, hers does. She's lithe, and even though she's incredibly thin, the telltale signs of an athletic past remain. Her lean build is complimented by the silkiness of her skin and a softness that is all woman. She's a goddess.

I need to slow down. I mentally coach myself, *Slow down, man. Slow...the fuck...down.*

With Lily, I was reserved in the bedroom. Held back by my insecurities, inexperience, youth, and a partner who was much the same. I'm not complaining. That was a different time.

But this is now. *Right now.* And Katie fills me with a confidence I never knew I had. She strips away my fear. I throw every reservation I've ever had out the window. And I take my time. I explore, kiss, lick, nibble, and touch every inch of her body. I'm categorically thorough, memorizing every detail: the elegant curve of her neck where it sweeps down into the sharp angles of her collarbone, her breasts that are at once petite but also round, soft, and firm—they're perfect. The indention of her belly button that begs to be licked, and the inside of her wrist that feels like silk under my touch. I'm rewarded with moans and gasps in all the right places, as well as some I didn't expect. She's extremely vocal with her need and appreciation. I could get off on the sounds and words coming out of her mouth alone. When my lips find hers again, she rolls us over, and I find myself on the receiving end of exploration. She tugs off my boxers and her hands and mouth pass over my entire body: kissing, sucking, rubbing, touching. I'm panting, calling out her name, begging her not to stop. It's eroticism at its goddamn best. I've fantasized about her, but this is more. *This is so much more.* My every nerve is on fire, thrashing, screaming to be clutched, twisted, ravaged, and wrung out.

When the time comes, and I tell her I don't have a condom, she begs, "Please, Keller. I need this. I need you." Her voice aches. I know this is where I should stop. *I know.* But I don't. *I can't.* I've never wanted anything more in my life than I want to be buried deep inside her. I roll her gently to her back, and her knees fall to the sides. Her eyes are closed, and she's breathing heavily.

"Look at me, Katie." Her eyes flutter open slowly, and they're dark with desire. She doesn't blink. "I want to look into those beautiful eyes while I make love to you."

As I slide slowly inside her, she moans, and her eyes drift shut. *Goddamn...*

"Open your eyes," I coax.

Her eyes find mine again. I kiss her once and pull back so I can see those lust-filled eyes.

We find a rhythm quickly, and the feeling of her skin against mine is all I'm focused on. "You feel so good, babe." I'm breathless.

We rock against each other, and she forces the pace. She never takes her eyes off mine. I will never forget this as long as I live. When she calls out my name and begins to quiver beneath me, I come undone. "Katie. Katie. Katie." I can't stop saying her name.

As our bodies still, I roll to her side suddenly aware of just how small she is. I feel as if I'll crush her.

There's a dreamy look in her eyes. She's utterly and completely satisfied. All of her features and angles softened. I can't even begin to explain how much I love the way she looks right now.

"My God, Keller, that was incredible. That's it. It's official. I'm going to hell."

I smile because I can't help myself. No one can ever take this from me. "I'd follow you there."

"No need to follow. Take your time, I'll wait for you." She entices me with a soft kiss.

I return the kiss and deepen it. She responds. I tell her how much I love her and how beautiful she is between every kiss. Though she's keeping up with me, I know she's tired. Reality is setting in.

She's sick.

I press my lips against hers one last time and make a silent vow to make the most of every second I have left with her and to start living my life the way I want to live it.

I squint at the clock. It's almost five o'clock in the morning. "We should get some sleep. You know I'm not letting you out of this bed today, right?"

She smiles and curls into my side. "I hope not."

SATURDAY, NOVEMBER 12

KELLER

OTHER THAN GOING to the dorms to get her medicine, the grocery store to buy condoms, eating periodically, and my morning and evening phone calls to Stella, we didn't leave my bed the entire day.

It was heaven.

SUNDAY, NOVEMBER 13
KATE

I NEVER THOUGHT BEING with someone would feel this right. But it does. *It does*. It's my fairy tale, and even though it's going to be short and have a terrible ending, it's still *mine*. Telling Keller about my cancer was the hardest thing I've ever had to do, but it was worth it in the end. I never wanted him to carry this burden with me, but I can't deny that it feels a little lighter now that he knows. Now that he's helping me. And believe me, I know how wrong that is.

He's still sleeping, lying on his back. I'm on my side curled around him except my head that rests on the pillow next to his. I'm watching him. He looks totally placid, like he doesn't have a care in the world. But I know that's not true. He worries about everything.

He speaks before he opens his eyes, "Morning, Katie."

"How'd you know I was awake?" I whisper.

"Because your breaths come faster when you're awake than when you're asleep." He rolls his head, so we're nose to nose, opens his eyes, and smiles. "I can feel your chest rise and fall against me."

"Keller, I should probably go back to the dorms today."

He wraps his arms around me. "That's a bad idea. I like you just where you are."

"I can't live here."

He doesn't hesitate. "Why not?"

I don't really have an answer for that. Except that it just seems pushy. And needy.

He narrows his eyes. "Have you always been in the habit of denying yourself what you want, or is this something new that you only do with me?"

I'm taken aback. "What?"

"I think for twenty years you've taken care of everyone else and put their needs ahead of your own. I'm begging you to be honest with yourself right now, Katie. Give in to what you really want." He kisses my forehead and grins. "Remember how well that worked last night?"

I can't help but smile even though he's just called me out. He's right.

"Don't you like being here with me?" he pushes.

"Of course, I do. But, I'm totally intruding."

He strokes my lips before he kisses me. "You're never intruding. I don't know what I would do if you left now."

"But I will have to leave someday. I don't want to make this harder on you than it has to be. I can't be that selfish."

He takes my face in his hands. "Don't worry about me. I get to decide who I fall in love with, remember?"

"I know."

"Katie, I know you don't want to talk about it, but isn't there something that can be done, chemo, or radiation, surgery?"

I shake my head. "Inoperable. Chemo is a treatment option, but it would probably only buy me a few months at most. And chemo sucks, it's not worth it to me to be sick from the cancer and sick from the chemo only to put off the inevitable. It's going to happen regardless. I want to enjoy what time I have left with no puking and a full head of hair."

He looks like he's going to cry. "How long do you have?"

"Dr. Connell says without treatment about three months," I smile, because I can't let it get me down anymore. I have to live in the present, and with the medicine I have now, the pain is manageable.

Tears roll down his cheeks. "There has to be something more they can do. Maybe my father knows an oncologist. Where is it, the cancer?"

I wipe the tears from his cheeks with my thumbs. "Don't cry."

"Where, Katie?" He's persistent.

"Both lungs and my liver."

His face crumples and the tears fall again.

"Please don't cry. I don't want to waste time crying."

"I don't want to lose you, Katie. This shouldn't happen to someone like you. It's not fair."

"I don't want to leave you either, Keller, but that's how my story ends. I feel like the luckiest girl on Earth. I get to spend my last months with you, to love you, and be loved by you. I never thought I'd have that. What a blessing you are."

"How about we never talk about cancer again? I hate it." It's like he reads my mind.

I nod and smile. "Deal."

I already told him not to say anything to anyone. I don't want anyone else to know until I can't hide it anymore.

MONDAY, NOVEMBER 14

KELLER

It's cold today. My breath comes out in a fog, and I follow it down Main toward Three Petunias. I know I shouldn't bother Katie at work, but I picked up an extra shift at Red Lion Road tonight, and I can't wait until I get off work to share the good news with her. My entire body is still humming with the excitement of rebellion and self-fulfillment. It feels *so* good. Is this what it's like to be in control of your destiny? I feel powerful. And not like big-ego, dickhead powerful, but powerful like I've finally got my shit together.

The bell announces my arrival. I never noticed bells until the day I met Katie. The way she scorned them at Grounds was so adorable that I'm reminded of it every time I hear one ring now.

Shel looks up from the arrangement of flowers in front of her. She gives me an evil smirk, and I know I'm in for it. "Hey, *Romeo.*"

I decide ignoring her attempts to embarrass me is the best way to deal with her. "Hey, Shel." The heat in my cheeks betrays me and her grin widens.

Katie turns at the sound of my voice. That reaction? It's addictive. A simple act that makes me so damn happy. I've only been apart from her since early this morning when she left for class, but after this weekend, a few hours feels like an eternity. "Hi, beautiful."

She smiles suggestively. "Hi, handsome. Couldn't stay away, huh?"

I shake my head as I walk behind the counter and wrap my arms around her. I *can't* stay away. Her skin smells like my soap. I love that, knowing she used my soap. In my shower. In my apartment. This morning. And now that I have her in my arms, I can't resist kissing her.

Shel clears her throat. "Keller, I'm trying to run a business here. Keep it in your pants."

I smile, shrug, and bat my eyelashes innocently at her. "What?" I know she's just teasing us. After she got over the initial shock of seeing Katie and me together Saturday night, she gave us her blessing. Followed by a stern warning that she would "cut my fucking balls off" if I hurt Katie in any way.

I swore on my nuts that I wouldn't.

Shel eyes me threateningly and then a husky, but feminine giggle escapes. "I hate to say this because cute shit usually makes me nauseous as all hell, but you two are just too cute. I can't think of any other word to describe it. *You're so fucking cute.*"

Katie pipes up, "Aw, Shelly, I don't want to be cute. Why can't I be badass, like you? You never call me badass, dude. It's kind of warping this delusional self-image I have going on in my mind." She laughs when Shelly rolls her eyes and doesn't answer the taunt.

I kiss the top of Katie's head again. "Oh, you are badass, and cute, and sexy—"

Shel interrupts quickly. "Okay, lover boy, that's enough. You'd better have a good reason for being here other than to feel up my coworker."

I smile at Katie in response. "I do. Can I steal her for a second?"

Shel nods. "Make it quick. And if I hear anything remotely sexual going on, I'm warning you now that I'm coming in. So, don't even think about it."

Katie salutes. "Aye, aye, captain."

"Thanks." I lead Katie into the back room and close the door so we have some privacy.

She smiles up at me, but there's worry in her eyes. "What is it?"

"I met with my advisor today."

Her eyes widen with expectation, and I can tell that she's excited to hear what comes next.

My courage soars. "I changed my major."

Her smile becomes triumphant, and she jumps into my arms. "Oh my God. I'm so proud of you. Keller, you did it. *You're doing it.*" She stops wiggling, drops from my embrace, and looks into my eyes. Her expression suddenly becomes very serious. "Are you okay with it? I mean, this is *huge*."

My nerves are ebbing, and calm is taking over now that I've said the words aloud. It's real. I nod.

"Have you told your parents?"

"No. I will this weekend. I want to tell them in person." I clear my throat. "Can I ask you for a favor?"

She doesn't hesitate. "Of course. Anything." Unconditional support is amazing. It makes me feel like Superman.

"Will you come with me to Chicago this weekend?" I don't know what I'll do if she says no.

She cups my cheek with her tiny hand. "Are you sure that's a good idea?" She's not turning me down. Maybe she wants to make sure I've thought this through.

"Yes. I'll break the news to them by myself, but it would make me feel better knowing you're nearby."

She nods her head. "Okay then, absolutely. I'll go."

Her support makes me feel like I can do anything. Anything. I feel stronger already. "Thanks."

"So, now that the decision's been made, what happens next?"

Now she looks worried again. I place my hands on her shoulders to offer comfort. "Changing majors means tacking on an extra year and a half; luckily I was already heavy on the English classes, so that helped. I dropped out of all my current classes that won't count toward my new degree."

She cringes. "Was that hard? I know it bothers you not to finish something you've committed to."

This girl knows me. She *knows* me. "Yeah, that was probably the only part of this that was hard. I hate leaving anything incomplete. It makes me feel like a failure."

She places her finger over my lips to quiet me. "You're not a failure. You changed plans. Huge difference."

When I smile, she drops her finger. "Thanks."

"What about your scholarship?"

"I don't know yet. My advisor is going to talk to Dr. Watkins, the head of the English department, to see what can be done. I wouldn't be surprised if I lose it. But if I do, there are always student loans, right?"

She nods. "Right." She pauses a moment and then repeats, "You sure you're okay?"

"Honestly, I don't think I've ever been more okay with my life than I am right now."

She's staring at me. I usually hate this kind of intense scrutiny, but when she looks at me like this, I feel alive. Like there's finally someone who sees me, the real me. The good and the bad, and I don't have to hide any of it. I don't have to be ashamed. I don't have to pretend. I can just be me, Keller Banks. She smiles her kindest smile and takes my hands in hers. "Damn. I'm in awe, dude. Seriously. *You are doing it.* You have officially taken back a huge part of your life. How does it feel to be such a badass?"

I shrug. "Pretty badass." My response is casual, but her words were like an adrenaline shot straight to my heart. My chest swells with pride and love.

She laughs, hugs me again, and her lips skim my ear. "You're so sexy when you're badass." It's the low, breathy whisper that drives me wild.

My hands run the line of her spine and come to rest on her hips while my lips paint kisses across her neck and up to her ear. "You have no idea what you're in for later. I hope you had a nap today, because when I get home tonight..."

She teases my earlobe with the tip of her tongue before answering. "Promise?"

"Cross my heart."

TUESDAY, NOVEMBER 15

KATE

I T'S BEEN AWHILE since I've talked to Maddie, and even though I get regular updates via Clayton because he's at Maddie and Morris' apartment a lot, I still want that one-on-one communication. Despite the one seemingly genuine conversation I had with her that led to the Morris roommate situation, it's kind of been downhill since. She put her guard back up.

So, with low expectations, I send a text: *Hey, wanna grab dinner Friday?*

WEDNESDAY, NOVEMBER 16

KATE

MADDIE RESPONDS TO MY TEXT: *Maybe*
Noncommittal. What was I expecting, anyway?

FRIDAY, NOVEMBER 18

KATE

MADDIE JUST TEXTED me back to say she's available for dinner tonight at 7:15. It's 6:37. The text wasn't so much an acceptance of an invitation, as it was yielding to coercion. *I wasn't coercing.* You'd think I was twisting the girl's arm. I'm kind of sorry I asked at this point. I'm especially tired today and I'm trying to stay positive, but I'm cranky. This isn't helping.

I feel guilty exposing Keller to the world of Maddie Spiegelman, but I can't do this alone. "Keller, you know that saying, 'You scratch my back and I'll scratch yours?'"

He looks up from the book he's reading and smiles. It's the crooked smile that I love. "Yes," he says suggestively. Now I feel worse, because at this point he thinks there's something good to come out of this.

"I'm going to Chicago with you tomorrow. Will you go out to dinner with me and my aunt tonight?"

He bookmarks the page and sets the book down. "Sure. Are we meeting her in Minneapolis or is she coming to Grant?" I've told Keller I have an aunt in Minneapolis, but I've intentionally left out every other detail about her. It's kind of an *if you don't have anything nice to say* situation.

"Minneapolis. Can you be ready in fifteen minutes?"

He's already halfway to the bathroom. "Can you grab me a clean pair of jeans and a shirt? I'm going to take a quick shower. Wanna join me?"

A smile melts through me because his flirting is relieving some of the tension my body is tangled up in at the moment. "Yes. But that would take longer than fifteen minutes and then we'd miss dinner entirely."

He shrugs. "My loss."

He's more adorable every day.

We pull up to Maddie's building at exactly 7:15. She said she'd be ready.

When she opens the door and her eyes fall on Keller, she gets a hungry, predatory look in her eyes. Like her mind's seesawing between two options: devour him whole or take her time and savor every bite. Keller notices, too. Shit, the blind guy across the street noticed. He shakes her hand when I make the introduction but never lets go of my hand with the other.

I suggest we go to the diner down the street where Maddie and I had breakfast months ago. It's good and cheap, and most importantly, it's not sushi. When Keller backs me, Maddie doesn't complain, even though I know it's not her type of Friday night hangout. She's dressed like a high-priced escort tonight.

We walk three abreast down the sidewalk, Keller sandwiched in between us. Keller is holding my hand with both of his. Maybe he's fearful Maddie would take a free hand if it's left open and exposed. He's probably right. She's monopolizing the conversation and hasn't addressed me with a single question or comment. Everything's been directed at Keller. I'm beginning to think she forgot I'm even here. I'm tired, so it's kind of a relief to not have to follow an exchange or focus too closely. And it is entertaining because she's trying so hard to impress him.

He's not impressed.

At all.

I owe him one.

I take mental notes during dinner, and it appears that Maddie's life is on the same track it was months ago. I'd hoped that Morris moving in would relieve some of the financial burden and allow her to look deeper, find meaning in other places. It doesn't sound like anything's changed.

Maybe it's because I'm tired, or maybe it's the medication I'm on, or maybe deep down I'm just an unsympathetic bitch, but I can't listen to it anymore. My plan for dinner tonight was to put it all out there, because I honestly don't think I'll see her many more times, and I want some peace in my heart knowing I did what I could to get through to her. "So, Maddie." She starts at the sound of my voice. Yup, she forgot I was here. "I haven't seen you in a while. How's everything working out with your new roommate?" I'll start out with the easy questions.

"Morris is just a sweetheart. I'm *so* lucky I found him." She's talking to Keller again. He's doing the nodding thing that I do when I've listened to her too long or what she's saying is unbelievable. I almost laugh. "Keller, it was the *craziest* thing. Morris had just moved here from London."

"Manchester," I mumble, but she doesn't hear me and talks right over the top of me.

"He didn't know a soul and was looking for a place to live, and even though I was *really* enjoying having my *two* bedroom all to myself, well, I just didn't have the heart to tell him no when the poor guy *practically begged* to move in with me."

Wow. That's a slightly different version than the one I remember. I feel like we're playing the telephone game...and I'm the last person... in a *very* long line.

Keller's not stupid either. He can read between the lines. "That does sound lucky. How'd you meet him?"

She dodges the question because clearly she's supposed to be the savior in this story and this is an inconsequential detail. "I don't remember exactly."

I bark out a laugh because (a) she really doesn't remember, or (b) she's pretending she doesn't remember; either option seems kind of shitty to me. This is the kind of stuff I usually let roll right off my back, but tonight I can't seem to let it go. "You don't remember who introduced you to Morris?"

She pries her eyes from Keller and looks at me like a small child who should be seen and not heard. "It's not important, *Kate.*"

I give her a fake smile. "I guess it's not," and then I cough out a, "you're welcome," under my breath.

Keller chuckles quietly next to me. He heard me. He knows what's going on.

"What's so funny, Keller, dear?" She's purring at him. Actually purring. It's starting to get on my nerves.

He clears his throat. "Nothing. Sorry, I was just thinking about something Katie said earlier."

Her mood sours, but she doesn't want to give up now that there's some back and forth going between the two of them. "So, little Kate here never told me she was dating anyone. How long has she been keeping you under wraps?"

He looks at me and winks before answering. That wink tells me something entertaining is about to happen. "I fell in love with her the first time we met months ago, but we've only recently started dating. I've never met anyone like her, someone I'm so compatible with on every level: emotionally, intellectually, sexually. I'm ruined for all other women at this point."

I almost want to blush because I know he means it, but the look on Maddie's face is priceless. I feel triumphant. Triumph squashes the hell out of embarrassment.

He kisses my cheek signaling that he needs me to let him out of the booth. "I need to use the bathroom before we go, babe. I'm ready to get you home, if you don't mind." Another wink.

God, he knows how to make an exit. And this newfound confidence is a turn-on. Now I'm ready to go home and for reasons other than to escape our dinner company.

I slide out, and he whispers in my ear as he passes. "It's all true."

Maddie's almost drooling watching him walk away, eyes zeroed in on his ass. She has no shame.

I clear my throat to draw her attention away because there's unfinished business here. "Um, Maddie, I wanted to ask: how's everything going? You know, have you gone to the doctor lately?" No more easy questions.

She rolls her eyes. "We're not going to talk about *that* again, are we?"

I nod. "Yup." That's the reason I'm here. I feel like I'm failing her as family if I don't bring it up. "We're going there."

"I told you before, Kate, it's *not* a problem."

I need to make this fast before Keller comes back. I don't want to rush this effort because then it seems contrived, but it's all I have. "Maddie, listen, I'm worried about you. I think about you a lot, and I just want you to be healthy and happy. The lifestyle you're living, the dietary choices you're making...they aren't really optimal, dude." I'm feeling flustered because I'm not explaining this very well. I don't want to shame her or make her feel bad. I'm trying to be considerate but firm.

She doesn't like being put on the spot. "Kate, *I am happy*. And as far as my health goes, I'm having no problems whatsoever. Besides, men find thin women more attractive." She shrugs like it's common knowledge. "It's just a fact of life." She looks me over. "It seems you've figured that out yourself. It looks like you've lost some of that baby fat since I last saw you and now you're dating Mr. Gorgeous Blue Eyes." She whispers as if we're in on this together, being too thin, like my weight loss is a product of manipulation and choice, not terminal disease. "It's no coincidence," she winks, "trust me."

I glance up and Keller's standing behind her. He heard everything and the look on his face is murderous. I shake my head minutely. It's not worth it.

He walks up beside me and pulls twenty dollars out of his pocket and throws it down on the table to cover our portion of the bill and tip. He offers his hand. "I've had about all I can take."

Maddie misses the dig. "Who's up for drinks?"

I'm about to pass when Keller beats me to it. "We need to get home. We have a busy weekend ahead of us, and Katie needs to rest."

I beg him with my eyes not to go there. Please don't tell her I'm sick.

She laughs, and it's the kind of laugh when you think you're sharing a private moment with someone at the expense of the third wheel. "Yes, it looks like Kate could use some rest. Beauty sleep does wonders." She tosses her hair over her shoulder. "Not all of us can get away with looking this good on only a few hours of sleep a night."

Wow. Did she really just say that?

Keller shakes his head. He can't believe it either. "You know one of my favorite things about Katie?"

Again, Maddie looks sad, like she has every other time Keller's said my name aloud tonight, as if by saying my name he's reaffirming that she doesn't stand a chance with him. "No, what?"

He pulls me gently to stand next to him. His hand is trembling. He's pissed. I don't know whether to let him say what he's about to say or pull him out the door. In the end, I decide I want to hear it, because he's testing his courage lately and he needs it this weekend more than ever.

"I love that Katie would never, ever, in a million years, treat anyone as blatantly shitty as you've treated her tonight. It's a shame you're so thoroughly self-absorbed that it renders you incapable of getting to know her, because believe me, if you could, you'd be a better person for it."

I squeeze his hand. I feel bad for Maddie, but it feels good to have someone stick up for me.

He looks down and smiles at me. The smile fades when he looks back to Maddie's stunned expression. "I wish I could say it's been a pleasure, but well, it hasn't. Not even close."

With that, we exit. I don't look back. Somehow, I know this is the last time I will talk to Maddie. There's no way she'll talk to me after tonight.

My heart feels heavy as we walk to the car. So, before we get in, I pull Keller into a hug and squeeze him tight. I need him to hold me.

His body's still shaking, and it's not from the cold. "That is one of the most narcissistic, uncaring, disrespectful people I've ever met—"

I interrupt him with a kiss. "Thank you. I'm not really into the whole being rescued thing, but you make one helluva white knight, Keller Banks."

He wants to smile, but he can't. He strokes my hair and stares into my eyes. It's calming him down, so I let him. "Doesn't she piss you off? Why are you so calm about this? She's toxic."

I shrug. "She's not the most pleasant person to be around, but she's got some issues. I wanted to try to talk to her about it tonight."

"If her issue is anything other than being the world's biggest bitch, I beg to differ."

I have to smile because he sounds like Gus. And it's hard to believe I have two people in my life who are this passionate about protecting me. I shake my head, and my smile slips as Maddie's reality slips in. "She's bulimic, Keller."

He shakes his head. "Not good enough. I mean, I know that sounds insensitive as hell, and okay, to be fair that does suck, but Katie you have *fucking*...you know." He can't say it. "She should be worried about you."

"Life should never be a who's-got-it-shittier competition." I look down. "Besides, I don't want her to know."

He raises my chin with a finger and whispers, "Why not?"

I'm quiet, and I have to swallow back the lump in my throat.

"Is it because she already has problems of her own? You don't want her to worry about you? Because to be honest, it would do that woman some good to worry about someone other than herself for a change."

I shake my head. That's the reason I don't want everyone else to know, but not Maddie. With Maddie it's different. It's a fear I don't want to verbalize. Because verbalizing it makes it real. Why does family have to be so difficult? So painful?

He hugs me into him and rubs circles through the back of my coat. He knows this soothes me. "What is it, babe? What are you scared of?"

"I know it's stupid, but what if she didn't care? My mother wasn't wired to care. I dealt with it. My dad's never cared. He's non-existent. His choice. I've dealt with it. What if my aunt finds out I'm dying, and she doesn't care, Keller? She's the only blood family I have left. I'm not looking for pity or love from her, but I don't think I can deal with another uncaring family member. The whole scenario is just a variation on a fucked up familial psychological game I've played my whole life. I don't need to dredge that up again. It's exhausting. I want it behind me, because it fills my head with shit."

He kisses the top of my head. "Amen to that. I know that game well. My head's been full of shit forever."

I stand on my tiptoes and kiss him, because at least I know we have this in common. "Ah, empathy, sympathy's more intimate cousin. It's kinda nice to know you empathize with me on this shitty subject."

He kisses me before offering, "I'll empathize with you anytime."

His lips feel so good that I close my eyes and kiss him again. "I'd rather just kiss you."

"Even better." He deepens the kiss and before I know it, I'm groping him in a public parking lot. It's taking my mind off Maddie, and that's what I need right now.

When he breaks the kiss, we're both out of breath. I scan the parking lot. It's dark and secluded. I glance at my car. The windows are tinted. So, I proposition him. "Have you ever done it in a car before, handsome?"

He shakes his head, and that damn crooked smile emerges. "There's a first time for everything."

He opens the rear driver's side door, sits, and pulls me in facing him astride his lap. I reach back and pull the door closed by feel because my lips are on his again, and I've no intention of placing my attention anywhere else.

Due to the confined space, it's difficult to unzip our coats, but we manage. I throw out a silent *thank you* to no one in particular (because I feel weird thanking God for foreplay) when I realize I'm wearing a shirt that buttons up the front. Keller's amazingly focused, and in no time, my shirt's opened to reveal my one and only lace bra. It's the only pretty piece of underwear I own.

He's moaning into my mouth, and his voice hums through me, reverberating in every cell from my scalp to my pinky toes. I feel his desire as his hips move seductively against mine. We separate and his eyes fall hungrily on my chest. "God, Katie, you are so beautiful." His hands cup my breasts beneath the lace. They feel full in his hands and when his thumbs gently sweep across my nipples, my back arches, forcing them closer to his talented mouth.

Answering the physical plea, he claims my sensitive flesh. Teeth tug with the perfect amount of pressure that radiates unbelievable, just short of painful, pleasure. There's a fine line between pleasure and pain, and Keller's fucking mastered it. I'm panting. And when his tongue traces an outline and fondles the tip of my nipple, I can't hold back. "That's it, baby, don't stop."

I reach down between us, unbutton and unzip his jeans, and slip my hand inside his boxers. The heft of him in my hand recognizes boldness and twitches. I reward it and stroke the length of him slowly in appreciation and admiration.

He groans loudly, "Oh fuck, Katie." He's becoming increasingly vocal during sex.

Damn. The sound of his voice, the *need* in his voice, could finish me off. I lean down and trace the outline of his ear with the tip of my tongue, and he shivers. "Tell me what you want," I say in a low whisper. He loves it when I talk like this.

"I want you. Every last beautiful inch of you." He takes my mouth with his again. He's maintaining the slow pace. There's this level of control and confidence in him right now that's the sexiest thing I've ever seen.

He's unbuttoning and unzipping my jeans now. His hands slide beneath my panties as he palms my ass and pulls me tightly against him.

I'm nearly breathless with carnal need. "Be more specific, baby. What do you want me to do?"

His hips grind out a tantalizing rhythm as his lips caress my neck. As his tongue trails south, he commands, "I want you out of these jeans. Panties, too."

That was almost forceful. I like it. *A lot.* And suddenly, I can't act fast enough. Fast proves complicated given the small backseat, so I settle for seductive. Keller likes to be seduced.

"Jeans, boxers, down to my knees," comes his second demand.

Again I comply, and when he springs free of the restriction of clothing, I want to take him in my hands. I *really* want to. But I wait.

"Now straddle me."

Gladly. I leave him exposed between us. His length pressed up against my belly.

"Touch me, Katie." His eyes are closed. His head tipped back against the seat.

My fingers wrap delicately but firmly. Touch may be my favorite sense: the friction root to tip, the delicious tingle of my hand brushing along my lower belly and his. It's mind-blowing.

He's watching me now. His gaze is heavy, penetrating. I feel it. And it makes me feel powerful in the most basic, intimate sense, knowing how much he wants me. But that power pales in comparison to the control he's *owning* right now. I need to give this to him, not because it's scary, aggressive control, but because it's *I'm going to ask for exactly what I want* control. And it's hot as hell.

"Are you ready?"

I nod because if I start talking, I'll make demands and I want him to finish what he's started. I'm following his lead.

"*How* ready?"

I whimper as his hand leisurely glides between my legs. It's agonizing. The ache intensifies.

"Goddamn, Katie, I love touching you." I feel his breath at my ear, and his low, sexy voice continues, "You are *so* ready."

I bite my lip and feel the sharp impression of my teeth. He's driving me wild. And when his fingers ease inside, I can't hold back. "*Oh God.*" My hips begin to move with him as the sensations wash over me.

Lust has consumed the light in his eyes. "I love watching you. You're so damn sexy. I want you, babe. I need to hear you say it. Demand it. Talk dirty. Tell me what *you want.*"

Holy shit, did he just ask me to talk dirty to him? With our eyes locked, without blinking, I tell him exactly what I want in the voice that drives him crazy. "I want you inside me, baby, *deep* inside me. I want you to feel the desperation and need that's raging through me right now. I want you to fuck me like you have a goddamn point to prove, and you *never, ever* want me to forget it."

The growl rumbles from deep in his chest. He lifts my hips, and in one quick movement, I'm filled with the whole of him. I gasp.

As we start to move together, I know neither of us will last long. That control from earlier? Yeah, it's lost. For both of us. Words are spilling from my mouth, because at this point it's working independently from my mind. "Harder... Yeah, like that... More..." He's giving me everything my body wants.

When he finds his release, he grunts and exhales. It's an animalistic, primal sound, the single most erotic thing I've ever heard. It sends me flying over the edge with him.

We hold each other as our bodies become still and quiet. My face is buried in the crook of his neck. There's a slight sheen of sweat there despite the cold of the car. He smells manly. Manly is my new favorite scent.

"Katie?"

"Yeah?"

"I love you."

"I love you, too, baby."

"I love it when you call me that. Say it again."

I lean back and look into his eyes, because he needs to see how much I mean it. "I love you, baby."

He smiles. It isn't happy, or sad, or flirtatious. It's affirming. It's contented.

SATURDAY, NOVEMBER 19

KELLER

THE WAY they're looking at me makes me feel small and inconsequential. It's like their disappointment in me has reached an all-time high, and I haven't even opened my mouth yet. The last time I demanded their time like this was when I told them Lily was pregnant. I guess I set a precedent for delivering what they consider to be bad news, and they're expecting nothing short of that now.

I glance at my palm, Katie's handwriting: *You are brave.* She wrote it in sharpie this morning before she took Stella to the park. I repeat the mantra in my head, *You are brave.* I clear my throat. "I've decided to change my major and pursue a new degree."

My mother is on her feet. That quickly. One sentence and she's already objecting like she's in the courtroom. Let the crucifixion begin. "You will do no such thing. You're not throwing away years of schooling."

My father's hand rests on her forearm. He's urging her to take a seat without addressing her directly. He's always been the passive yin to her aggressive yang. Once again, they're sitting across the table from me as a united front. Emotionally distant, even from each other, but united. Some things never change.

My father fills in the silence, "What are your plans, Keller?"

I don't want to see the disappointment, but I look at him anyway. "I want to teach high school English."

My mother is on her feet again, pacing away from the table. Her heels clicking on the hardwood floor is the grating equivalent of fingernails dragging across a chalkboard. "Oh for God's sake, Keller, how are you supposed to even begin to support Stella on a teacher's salary?" She manages to make teacher sound like a four-letter word.

"People do it all the time. The endgame for me isn't to get rich. Stella and I will be fine."

She waves me off in irritation and turns away momentarily before firing back. "This isn't a game, Keller. You have a daughter to provide for. I thought you wanted to study law—"

I cut her off. "*You* wanted me to study law, to follow in your footsteps. It's never been about me, about what *I* want."

She shakes her head. "After everything we've done for you, this is how you repay us?"

Unbelievable. "What about me, Mother? I want a career I love, something I'm passionate about. I want to come home every night from work and feel like I've made a difference in someone's life."

She points an accusatory, manicured finger at me. "You don't think I make a difference, Keller?"

I will never win with this woman. "Jesus, this isn't a competition," I sigh. "Your job's more important than mine, more important than his." I gesture in my father's direction. He's been very quiet. "This is about what makes me happy. Me. *Your son.*"

"You'll lose your scholarship." She seems sure of it, and I wonder how many strings she's pulled in the past to get what I currently have.

I don't blink. I can't show fear anymore. I glance at my palm. *You are brave.* "That's a possibility."

She huffs haughtily. "Possibility? *Possibility?* It's a certainty, Keller."

"I'll apply for student loans."

She barks out a cold laugh, as if a loan is below the Banks family.

My father finally speaks up. "What about Stella, Keller? Have you considered how this decision will affect her future?"

Brave, brave, brave. "I'm moving Stella to Grant to live with me. As soon as finals are over—"

My mother lunges toward the table. "What?! Stella is not leaving this house until you have completed your education."

I answer with a lunge of my own. We're nose to nose across the table. "She's *my* daughter."

"I am not paying for Melanie to move to Grant to care for Stella." She thinks she's got me.

"I'll speak to Melanie and let her know that her services will no longer be required after December nineteenth. I'm planning on picking up Stella and her belongings after finals; that's when Duncan's moving out of our place to live with his girlfriend."

She's seething now. "How would you even begin to know how to take care of a child? Visiting every other weekend is a lot different than twenty-four hours a day, seven days a week."

"I'll figure it out."

My mother looks at my father shaking her head defiantly. "Did you hear that? He'll figure it out." She throws her hands in the air. "Wonderful. He'll figure it out."

My father's looking at me, and for the first time in my life, I see sympathy in his eyes. For a second, I think he's going to take my side. For the first time, he's going to stand up to my mother. But as the silence stretches on, my hope fades.

I can't be in here anymore. I feel trapped, like I can't breathe. I know my mother will see my escape as conceding defeat. She'll take it as a victory.

But not this time. This time, I win.

MONDAY, NOVEMBER 21

KATE

ME: *Dinner. Cafeteria. 7:00. I won't take no for an answer.*

Clayton: *That was not a proper invitation Katherine.*

Me: *Fine. Pleeeeeeeease. I miss you.*

Clayton: *I miss you too. See you at 7:00.*

Clay's waiting for me at our table when I get to the cafeteria. It's 7:07.

I set my tray on the table and hug him before I sit down. "God, it's been a long time since I've seen you." I eye him up and down. "You're looking good, my friend, dapper as ever." He does. His bright pink sweater and green dress pants are adorable, and he looks so much happier than the last time I saw him.

His cheeks blush, and he bats his eyelashes. "Thank you, Katherine." And then he looks concerned. He's staring at me. "Katherine, is everything okay? You look a little pale. And you look like you've lost weight. Don't get me wrong, you're still absolutely stunning, but something seems off."

I'm not here to discuss me, that's for sure, so I sweep it under the rug, "I'm fine. I was a little sick last week. It's nothing you need to worry about."

He doesn't look convinced.

I change the subject. "So, how's everything in Minneapolis? How's Morris?" He's been staying at Morris's every night and commuting to Grant only for classes. This has been going on since I found out about *The Asshole,* Ben Thompson. I try not to think badly of people, but *fuck that guy.*

It's like watching a cartoon character come to life in front of me; there are hearts in his eyes. "Morris is wonderful. I never thought I'd find love, Katherine, but I *love* him. Everything about him." He looks around conspiratorially and leans in to whisper, "I'm moving to Los Angeles with him after New Year's. His uncle's opening up a club there and wants him to manage it since he's done so well with the one here."

"Holy shit, Clay. L.A.? That's a big decision." I'm shocked.

He smiles, and it's the smile of an excited child. "I know. Isn't it exciting?"

I nod, because, yeah, it *is* exciting. "Good for you, dude." I mean it, so I say it again, "Good for you."

He knows I mean it. "Thank you, Katherine."

"I don't want to sound like an overbearing bitch, because I'm not judging either way, but I have to ask. You're leaving because it's the right choice for you and the direction you want your life to take, right? You're not running away from the bad stuff here, are you? Because it would make me sad to know that your friends here lose you because of some douche-y asshole."

He laughs. "No. I think I need to get out of the pool and go swim in the ocean. I've never lived in a big city before."

I get it, so I repeat, "Good for you." And then the nagging side of me kicks in. "Just promise me you won't quit school. Get your degree, dude. The world could do with a well-dressed accountant." I don't know why, but the thought of Clay sitting in an office doing something as mundane as accounting has always struck me as funny. His character is too grand to be contained behind a desk.

He rolls his eyes and raises his right hand as if to show there's sworn honesty in his response, "Yes, *Mother*, I promise not to drop out of school. Besides, who else is going to do your taxes and retirement planning?"

Ouch. That hurt. Right in my heart that hurt. I don't want Clayton to know I probably won't ever need to do taxes again. I force a smile instead.

He rubs his hands together and smiles deviously. "I heard a delicious rumor from Pete," he says, pointing at me, eyes twinkling, "that you and Keller are officially dating." He wiggles his eyebrows. "Any truth to it?" He smiles again. "And don't leave out any of the naughty bits."

I'm stone-faced. "Pete's feeding the rumor mill? I'm gonna have to talk to him."

Clay's eyes are wide, expectant. "Well, Katherine?" He extends his arms over his head and points down at himself dramatically. "I'm dying over here."

I laugh and nod. "There may be a bit of truth to that rumor."

He claps the quick, hummingbird wing clap that he always does when he's excited. "Oh my God, Katherine. I'm so happy for you." Then his hands still and he's whispering again. "Katherine, I know you're not the superficial type and neither am I, okay, who am I kidding, maybe I am, c'est la vie. But that boy is hotter than a tamale."

Clayton cracks me up, but I agree wholeheartedly. "Yes. Yes, he is."

He squeals. "Not that I'm trying to rush things between you, because I know you both need to finish school first, and maybe do some traveling. I *really* think you should see Europe someday, at least France. Oh, and the Greek Isles," he rambles, "but I desperately hope things work out between the two of you because... *Oh. My. God.* You two would have the loveliest children ever genetically created." He's beaming.

His adorable smile softens the blow that comes with the words. I'll never have that. Never. And that sucks.

When we finish up dinner, we promise to stay in touch better than we have these past few weeks. I love Clayton, and I want to make sure he's okay until he leaves and moves on to the next chapter of his life. And I move on to mine.

I hug him at his car, and it's so fucking hard to let him go.

I try not to think about dying, but I can't help it lately. And that makes me sad. I don't want to be sad, because in reality...I have a pretty awesome life.

Today, my life is awesome.

I don't want to think about tomorrow.

Or the day after that.

So I repeat to myself: *Today, my life is awesome.*

THURSDAY, NOVEMBER 24

KATE

SHELLY WAS HERE at Keller's place bright and early this morning, groceries in hand: a turkey, a tofurkey for me, and all the fixings. I didn't realize it before, but she loves to cook.

After the turkey's in the oven and everything else is prepped, Shelly, Duncan, and I head to Grounds for some coffee. It's closed today, so we have it all to ourselves. Perks of knowing the staff. We all crowd around the fire and talk about how Keller is going to deal with the weekend ahead. He's at the airport picking up Stella. Melanie is headed to Seattle to spend the holidays with her family and arranged it so that she had connecting flights in Minneapolis going out and returning so she could fly with Stella both ways. This is such a big step for Keller; Stella's never visited him here before.

Shelly is still in shock about Stella. Duncan told her last night at Keller's urging. I tried to ease the shock. "I never would've believed it, either," I told her. "It's really something you have to see to believe." Stella is like a world unto herself. A world where I'd like to live forever.

Keller texts us twice to tell us there are delays with the flight and that he's running late. Then at ten thirty the door to the apartment swings open, and there she is: sweet, little Stella whose giggles fill the air. Shelly and I are making a pumpkin pie in the kitchen. Stella makes a beeline for Duncan on the loveseat. "Uncle Duncan!" she squeals in delight.

He pulls her into his lap and wraps his arms around her. "How's my favorite Stella?" He tickles her.

Her giggles escalate. "No tickles, Uncle Duncan."

He kisses her cheek and loosens his grip.

"Where's Kate?" she asks. "Daddy said Kate's here."

Duncan indicates my whereabouts with a thumb over his shoulder. "I see how I rate, kid," he good-naturedly mutters.

Stella squeals again when she spots me.

I wave. "Hi, sweetie."

She races toward me, hands raised over her head. I scoop her up and hug her tightly against me. I bury my face in her wild ringlets. She smells clean and pure like the air after a rainstorm. She pulls back so she can look at me. "We have a surprise for you."

"You do?"

Keller's carrying in bags from his Suburban. He sets them down just inside the door and scratches his head. "Yeah, it's the funniest thing, but we ran into somebody at the airport..."

Just then, Gus walks through the door.

Stella claps. "Surprise!"

"Holy sh—" realizing I'm holding Stella, I switch gears. "Oh my God, what are you doing here?"

He's wearing his lazy grin and shrugs. "Would you believe that I was just passing through?"

I set Stella down and run to him. He wraps me up in one of his big Gus hugs that I've missed so much. "No."

He kisses the top of my head and reaches over and playfully nudges Keller's shoulder. "It was his idea."

"You planned this?" I'm still in shock.

The look on Keller's face is bright and loving. He shrugs.

I look back up at Gus. "How?"

He smiles. "Your boy here called me last week from your phone. You were sleeping." He winks at Keller. "We've been talking a lot this past week. I'd be worried if I were you, we've got quite a bromance brewing. And did you know the dude has beanbags in the back of his Suburban? *Beanbags*. That's the coolest thing I've ever seen. I may be in love with him myself, Bright Side."

Stella is wrapped around Keller's leg. "What's a bromance, Daddy?"

Gus starts laughing, releases me, and offers his big hand to Stella. She takes it without hesitation. Kids have always loved Gus. "Tell me some more about this turtle of yours, Stella. I'm curious, what does Miss Higgins eat?" The two of them walk toward the loveseat to finish a conversation they no doubt started on the ride here. I know Gus; he's giving me time to talk to Keller.

I wrap my arms around Keller's neck and whisper in his ear, "Thank you, baby."

"I love it when you call me that." He kisses my neck. "You're welcome. He needs time with you, too."

I look around the room. "This is so perfect." It's then that I notice Shelly is standing in the kitchen and looks like she's going to have a stroke. Her eyes are wide. Shock has taken over every feature on her face. I think our visitors have just become too much for her.

I clear my throat and call out, "Hey, Gus?"

He looks up from his conversation with Stella. She's sitting on the loveseat between him and Duncan. I wish I had a camera handy. "Yeah, Bright Side, what is it? I'm learning some seriously important sh—" he smiles when he catches himself about to curse, "stuff about turtles right now."

Stella giggles at him.

I point to the kitchen. "You remember my friend, Shelly?"

He looks back over his shoulder. "What's up, Shelly? Good to see you again."

Her face is bright red. I've never seen her embarrassed like this.

She raises her hand and sheepishly waves. "Hey, Gus. Good to see you again, too."

He's fully turned in his seat to face her now. "I must say that I've never seen anyone toss a sidewalk pizza with such commitment and precision as you did the last time I saw you. I never got to commend you."

Her face is buried in her hands. "Of course, you would remember that." She's still embarrassed about throwing up in front of everyone.

Gus isn't mean-spirited. He's actually being complimentary. He grins. "No, I'm serious. You go for distance. It was impressive. Ride the lightning, my friend." He reaches over and slaps Duncan on the back. "You're a lucky dude."

Shelly mumbles, "Oh my God, I want to die."

I join her in the kitchen and put my arm around her waist. "He wouldn't tease you if he didn't like you. And as gross as it may sound, he was impressed. He's a boy."

Since Grounds is closed, we go back in and gather around the fireplace while the food is cooking. Gus and Keller are on either side of me on the loveseat. Stella is on Keller's lap, and Shelly is sitting on Duncan's lap in a chair next to us.

Gus, as always, is curious about everyone. He asks lots of questions. Of course everyone else is curious about him too, so he fields almost as many questions as he asks.

"Why do you call Kate 'Bright Side?'" Shelly asks.

He looks at me and then back to her. Then back to me. And back to her. He points at me. "Have you *met* the girl?"

Everyone looks at me, and their smiles are endearing. It makes me feel good.

Gus continues. "She's the poster child for positivity. She's a freaking ray of sunshine. She doesn't just *look* on the bright side...she *lives* there."

"Huh, I always thought I lived in the world of sunshine and rainbows?" I tease.

He shrugs. "Same difference. Sunshine and rainbows is a horrible nickname though."

Everyone laughs.

"Bright Side does have a dark side, though," Gus warns. "Don't get her started on stick figure family stickers on cars, because she loathes them. She gets irate—"

I interrupt, because I really do hate them. "That's because they're stupid. I don't need a pointless representation of your family staring at me while I'm sitting at a stoplight behind you. And I can't help but wonder how truly imperfect your family is if you feel the need to perpetuate it on your window for the world to see. I always suspect they're hiding dysfunction behind the façade. Hypocrites."

Gus laughs like he's just proven his point. "See. And she despises Facebook."

"Facebook is the decline of civilization as we know it. It's creating a distorted view of reality. What happened to preferring the company of flesh and blood? People don't realize how important face-to-face human contact is anymore. It's all about numbers and 'likes' and too much information. Do I care that you had a Diet Coke and a bag of Sun Chips while you watched a rerun of CSI last night? No, I don't fu— I don't care. Give me some substance. The entire sphere of your all-encompassing 'friends' family doesn't need to be privy simultaneously to the mundane details of your life...your sad, internet-centered life. I want to have a conversation with you tailored specifically to us. I don't want it streamed, real time, for the world to share in. Facebook is stifling social development. It's suffocating social skills—"

Gus butts in, laughing, "*Okay*, okay, Bright Side." But he's also nodding. It says, *True that*, or maybe it's, *Amen*. It's agreement. He hates social media just as much as I do.

And for good measure, he says, "And don't ever play cards with her. She cheats."

I gasp at the accusation. "I do not," but I'm giggling by the end of my pathetic defense and everyone knows it's an admission of guilt.

Gus nods, grinning. "She does. Trust me."

After dinner, I go outside with Gus so he can smoke a cigarette and we can watch the sunset. Gus takes my hand in his and smiles. "It's showtime."

It's what Gracie always said. I smile and whisper, "It's showtime."

The sunset is bright orange. Brighter than I've seen it in a long time, almost like it's trying to show off for us. To prove to us that sunsets can be pretty in Minnesota, too.

When we return back inside, we all retreat to Grounds again.

Shelly asks, "Why don't you and Gus sing something for us. I saw his guitar case."

Gus never goes anywhere without his guitar. He's had it for years, and it's seen hundreds of hours of attention and play. It's always by his side.

Gus looks at me. "What do you say, Bright Side?"

Stella claps her hands. "I want to hear Kate sing again."

Keller joins her. "Me too." It makes me smile.

Gus returns with his guitar case in one hand and something else I haven't seen in months in the other.

Shelly looks at the cases and asks him, "You play violin, too?"

He shakes his head and sets them down on the table behind us. "Nope." He looks pointedly at me.

I sigh. "Gus."

"I had Ma ship it to me this week, so I could bring it to you. It should be here with you. You should *play* it." It's a dare.

Everyone's eyes are on me.

"You play the violin?" Keller asks.

Gus shakes his head. "Oh no, she doesn't *play*. She *slays* that instrument. I've never seen anyone as talented as Bright Side. Seriously. She kills it." There's pride in his eyes.

Shelly narrows her eyes at me. "What else are you hiding from us?" And the light bulb goes off. "Oh my God, it's you!" she shrieks.

Keller and Duncan look confused. "It's her, what?" Duncan asks.

She's pointing her finger at me and waving her other hand in the air like some crazed fan. "It's you! It's you playing violin on 'Missing You.'"

Gus smiles. "The one and only."

Keller and Duncan are still confused. "What's 'Missing You?'" Keller asks.

"It's only the most amazing song on the radio right now. It's the acoustic song Gus played at the concert," she answers haughtily, as if they should just know this. The song has gotten a lot of airtime on the college station this past week. It was released as the second single off Rook's album. "You have to play it," she begs.

"What do you say? Just once for old time's sake?" Gus asks, raising his eyebrows.

Stella claps again. "Play, Kate, play!" she cheers.

I can't say no to that.

The violin feels cold in my hands. It's been months since I've played, but when I tuck it under my chin, it becomes part of me, like I haven't missed a day. It's comfortable and grounds me. After I rosin the bow, I pull it softly across the strings. It brings me to life. I nod at Gus. "Ready."

There's concern etched across his face. "You sure?"

"Yup. Maybe Grace is listening?" Everyone's letting us have this private moment.

He smiles. "I'm sure she is." He looks up. "Gracie, this one's for you."

I stand and lean back against the arm of the loveseat. Gus takes a seat directly in front of me on the edge of the coffee table. Everyone else stays where they were. You could hear a pin drop it's so quiet. Even Stella hasn't let out a peep. She's leaning back against Keller's chest, his arms wrapped around her.

There's an unspoken language when Gus and I play together. It's always been that way. We hear and feel music the same way. Communication flows back and forth through the music, one reacting to and feeding off the other. Words are spoken with eyes and subtle nods.

He strums his guitar twice letting me know he's ready. I nod and slowly drop into the melancholy intro. I close my eyes and let it flow through me, the violin a natural extension of me and my emotions.

Gus joins in, his guitar soft and his voice gentle. His voice is reassuring. It always has been. You almost believe that nothing bad could ever happen when you listen to Gus sing. It takes me away. I've always loved that.

As the last few words leave Gus's lips and he strums his last few chords, I'm left to play out the rest alone. As I draw my bow across the strings for the last note, I open my eyes. The expression on Gus's face is proud and reverent. "That's my girl."

I smile.

Stella begins clapping wildly again. "Play again, Kate. Play again."

She's beaming at me when I look into her bright blue eyes. Keller's matching blue eyes are shining a few inches above hers. "You never cease to amaze me, Katie."

God, I love him.

I look to Shelly and Duncan. Shelly's mouth is agape. "What the heck, Kate? Why didn't you tell us you played? You're phenomenal." She's floored.

I shrug. "I don't play anymore. My sister loved to listen to me play..." I trail off. The rest is unspoken. I told Duncan about my sister the night we talked after the concert. I'm sure he told Shelly.

She nods in understanding.

Gus claps his hands. "We can't stop now. Stella wants an encore. What's next, Bright Side?"

Even though the pain in my lower back is building to a deep, intense throb, I have to admit I'm enjoying myself. Even if I never pick up my violin again, I want to play right now. I whisper in his ear.

"Sure. We haven't played that in a long time. You sure you can keep up with me?" he taunts.

I wink. "I'll try. Shelly will know this song."

Gus turns to Shelly. "Bright Side and I went to a music school together growing up. She was two years behind me, but she always kicked my—" he looks to Stella before he continues, "butt—"

Shelly interrupts. "Wait. Don't tell me you guys went to The Academy in San Diego?"

"Yeah," Gus says.

"What's The Academy?" Duncan asks.

"It's only one of the most prestigious private secondary music schools in the country. Virtually impossible to get into, and they only accept the most talented applicants." She shakes her head and looks at me. She's smiling. "How did I not know this about you?"

I shrug.

Gus continues. "So, senior year, one of my final projects was to cover a song that was on the charts at the time, something popular, but we had to put our spin on it. Turn it upside down and make it our own, unrecognizable. I, of course, enlisted the help of my talented friend," he points to me and I roll my eyes, "to help me out. The song was hard-driving rock, and Bright Side, because she's a freaking musical genius, turns it into this slow, melodic ballad with this unworldly violin arrangement."

"Don't let him fool you," I add. "Gus rewrote the whole song for acoustic guitar, I just *added* the violin. It was all his idea."

"Let's play it. They can judge for themselves."

So we do. And it's not until the chorus that I see recognition flare in Shelly's eyes and a grin emerges. She knows the song.

Keller hums along softly in Stella's ear as he rocks her. She's wearing her sleepy Keller eyes. By the song's end, she's out cold.

Shelly's still grinning. "That was astounding. I don't know what else to say. Just. Astounding."

Gus stands and takes an exaggerated bow. "Gracias."

I tip my head. "Thank you, m'lady."

Duncan pats Shelly's leg. "We'd better get going, or your mom will have a conniption. We're already five minutes late."

Shelly sighs. "Yeah, you're right." She frowns. "This is just so much more fun than familial obligations."

Duncan kisses her on the cheek and gently urges her off his lap. "You're right about that. But your parents are expecting us. Let's go."

Shelly drags her feet, and by the time they leave, the pain is almost unbearable. It's been ratcheting up over the past hour, but in the last five minutes, it's reached a new level I've never felt before. It's pain that brings nausea and blurred vision with it. While Keller's putting Stella to bed, I excuse myself from Gus and head to the bathroom to take my pain meds. I sit on the floor while I fumble with the cap on my pill bottle, because I don't feel steady enough to stand. My field of vision is constricting, and when I feel my head meet the tile floor with a blinding crack, everything goes black.

KELLER

I'm starting to worry. Katie's been in the bathroom for ten minutes, and I haven't heard any movement or noise.

Gus throws back the rest of a beer. "Where's the john, dude? Bladder's full."

I point toward the door. "Katie's in it."

Gus knocks quietly on the door. "Bright Side, hurry up, I gotta take a piss. You've been in there a long time. You dropping some friends off at the pool?"

I would laugh if I wasn't worried, but there's no response from the other side of the door. My heart is racing. I don't want to worry Gus unnecessarily, but I can't shake the feeling that something is very wrong. I knock. "Katie, babe, are you okay in there?"

Silence.

I slowly urge the door open, but it meets resistance. I cringe and push on it, squeezing through the opening. "Oh, shit."

Gus is on the other side. "What's wrong? Bright Side?"

Katie is crumpled on the floor against the bathroom door. Her pills are scattered everywhere. There's vomit on the floor, and it's spattered with blood. I pull her up into my lap so Gus can open the door. She's passed out cold, but she's still breathing. "Call 911."

His head appears around the door, and when he sees her, there's nothing short of terror in his eyes. "Holy fuck." His cell is out and he's dialing 911 before I can ask again.

I'm rocking her back and forth now, brushing the hair out of her face. It's matted with a wet, reddish-brown liquid. I start whispering in her ear, and I can't stop, "You're okay, Katie. You have to be okay. This isn't it. Don't leave me. Not today. You can't leave today. I love you. I love you."

Gus brings me out of my trance. "What's your address, dude?" As I tell him, he repeats it into the phone. Returning the phone to his pocket, he grabs a towel off the rack and wets it in the sink and begins to gently wipe Katie's face and hairline. He looks me in the eyes, waiting. He's looking for answers.

I tell him what I know. "Katie has cancer."

All the air rushes out of his lungs, and he falls back against the wall behind him. The tears come in a torrent. "No. No. No." He's trying to deny it away. "This can't be happening again."

"Again?" I ask at the same time there's a knock at the door and Gus struggles to his feet to answer it.

Paramedics charge in, and I grudgingly release Katie to their care. I don't want to let her go because I'm afraid I'll never get her back. I tell them everything I know and give them her medication bottle. They have her hooked up to an IV and loaded in the ambulance in minutes. Gus rides with her.

After I wake Stella and load her in the Green Machine, I drive faster than I've ever driven in my life. The hospital is in Minneapolis. Stella is fast asleep in the seat next to me. I'm not a religious person, and I've never said a prayer in my life, but during the entire drive, I find myself pleading aloud, "Please, dear God, *please* give her more time. Please don't take her yet. I need her here with me. Gus needs her. Stella needs her. Shelly needs her. Clayton needs her. I love her so much. Please, please, *please*."

Stella is sleeping in my arms when we find Gus in the ER admittance room. He's filling out paperwork. I slump down into the chair next to him. "How is she?"

His eyes are red and swollen. "She's stable. They're examining her now. Said they were going to call her doctor, the one that prescribed the medication."

I sigh and hug Stella to me. Her head's resting on my shoulder, and she's limp in my arms, heavy with sleep. I set Katie's bag in the chair next to me and with one hand I search for her wallet. When I find it, I pull out her ID and insurance card and hand them to Gus.

After finishing the paperwork and taking it to the admittance desk, he returns. "There's no news yet. I'm gonna run outside, I need a cigarette. Come and get me if something changes."

I nod. He looks how I feel: hopeless, helpless, and tense.

Gus returns ten minutes later and after what feels like an eternity, the doctor greets us. "Family of Kate Sedgwick?"

Gus jumps to his feet. "Yes."

"Kate is stable. We've moved her to PCU room 313. She'll need to stay with us overnight for observation. The trauma to her head resulted in a mild concussion. We spoke to her oncologist, Dr. Connell, and as I'm sure you're already aware, Kate has recurrent and metastatic ovarian cancer—"

"What?" As I start to question the doctor, Gus holds up his hand gesturing for me to keep quiet. I do. He obviously knows this part of Katie's history. I don't.

The doctor continues, "—which has spread to other organs, her lungs and liver. Kate is in the advanced stages, the equivalent of Stage IV, inoperable and unlikely to respond to treatment. Kate's chosen to forgo any such treatment and has opted for pain and symptom management. She wants to be kept comfortable, and that's what we, and her oncologist, Dr. Connell, are trying to do."

Gus speaks first. "How much time does she have left?"

"Although we cannot predict a precise amount of time, Dr. Connell tells us two months, maybe three. The cancer is aggressive. The progression over the next several weeks will be dramatic."

I watch Gus swallow the lump in his throat, and he nods. "Can we see her now? Room 313?"

The doctor nods. "Yes. I'm sorry."

I follow Gus, because I can't focus on elevators and directions. I have a firm hold on Stella; she's the only thing tethering me to reality. I'd get sucked into the black hole of complete despair if I let go.

Katie looks so small in the big hospital bed. She's still hooked up to the IV, which I assume is distributing some intense pain medication. Her eyes are open, but they look hazy, groggy. A bruise is blossoming beneath the surface of her left cheek, and there are stitches along her cheekbone where she must've hit the bathroom floor. She raises her hand a few inches above the bed in a wave. "Hey, it's my three favorite people." Her voice is hoarse.

Gus tries to smile. "How're you doing, Bright Side?" He sits on the edge of her bed and takes her IV-free hand in his.

"Better now." She smiles.

I sit in the chair on the other side of her bed, Stella still asleep in my arms.

She looks at Stella and frowns. "I'm sorry you had to get her out of bed, Keller."

I rub Stella's back. "Don't worry about it. Stella's a deep sleeper. A freight train could pass through this room, and it wouldn't wake her."

Katie's still frowning, but the corners of her mouth are turned up. "She's so precious, Keller. You're so blessed to have her."

The look on her face is heartbreaking. She'll never have children. She'll never have what I have. It's not fair.

"When did you find out?" Gus is whispering. He doesn't want to upset her, but he has to ask.

"Right before I left to come to Grant."

He looks crushed. "But you said your check-up went okay?"

She nods.

"Why didn't you tell me the truth?" He's trying not to cry.

She squeezes his hand. "Because I needed to come here and you needed to go on tour. If I would've told you, what would've happened?"

He doesn't hesitate. "I would've canceled or postponed the tour to stay with you."

"*Exactly.* You would've put your dreams on hold, or thrown them away, to sit at home waiting for me to die. I want more for you than that. You've worked so hard, Gus. You deserve to be out there performing every night, making people happy with your music. Do you know how happy it makes me to know that you're out there living your dreams?"

He nods. "I know, but you're more important."

She shakes her head. "No, I'm not. Our friendship means more to me than you'll ever know. But life doesn't come with a guarantee, Gus. We had twenty years together. *Twenty years.* That's pretty amazing when you think about it." She smiles and her eyes sparkle. "And that friendship won't die with me, I know that. It will live inside you for the rest of your life. It's like a little piece of me gets to go on with you. And I want it to be one helluva ride. You have so many things to do, and people to meet, and someone out there to fall in love with, to have a family with. It's going to be beautiful. I don't want you to stop living your life just because I'm sick. But I promise to keep bugging you every day I can. Nothing needs to change. I still love you, and you still love me, I know that whether you're sitting here in this room with me or you're a thousand miles away."

The tears are streaming down Gus's cheeks. "Why? Why you? Why now?"

She shakes her head. "I don't know, dude. I guess it's my time. Maybe Gracie misses me as much as I miss her and she put in a request with the big man upstairs." She yawns and looks over at me. "Keller, you want to lay Stella in bed with me? There's room, she might be more comfortable."

Even though I don't want to let her go, Katie scoots over and I place Stella at her side. Stella doesn't wake, but she snuggles into Katie's side for warmth and comfort. Katie smiles. "Thanks. I think I needed that." She kisses Stella's forehead and yawns again and looks at me. "I don't think I can keep my eyes open any longer. This is one hellacious cocktail they've got me hooked up to. Come here and give me a kiss."

I oblige, although I feel like I'm falling apart. How can this radiant woman be fading away before my eyes? "I love you, babe."

"I love you, too, baby." Her eyes shift to Gus, and she motions to him. "You too, come here."

Gus kisses her on the forehead. "Good night, Bright Side. I love you."

She mumbles, "I love you, too," as she drifts off to sleep.

I summon my courage and clap Gus on the back. "Come on, man, I'll buy you a cup of coffee."

We grab two scalding hot coffees from the vending machine on the second floor and return to Katie's room. Katie's free arm is wrapped around Stella, whose head is resting on Katie's shoulder in the crook of her neck. I can't help but smile looking at the two of them. I take a picture of them in my mind, carefully cropping out the IV and machines around them, just two sweet, sleeping faces in the frame, Katie's bruises hidden against the pillow.

Gus is smiling at them as he drops into a chair on the other side of the room. "She would've been the best mom."

I slide the other chair over to sit with him. "Absolutely."

His smile grows. "You should've seen her with her sister, Grace. She was amazing. I don't know how she did it. She took care of her sister every day. Don't get me wrong, Gracie was easy to love. But being someone's full-time caretaker is a lot of work, and Bright Side never once complained. Their mom was never around. Janice preferred the company of men to the company of her children." There's disdain and judgment in every word. "And even when she was around, she didn't take care of them. She had some mental health issues that required medication, but I don't know what was worse, Janice on her meds or off. She also drank...*a lot*. And she was a big fan of coke." Gus pauses, shakes his head, and chuckles sardonically.

"Bright Side's home life was a fucking nightmare. She took care of Gracie because her mom couldn't or wouldn't. They spent a lot of time at our house. Ma and I always considered them family. And after her mom completed suicide—"

I interrupt. "Wait. Katie's mom took her own life?"

"Yeah. She hung herself from a ceiling beam in her bedroom one night. Bright Side found her the next morning."

I rub my eyes with my palms; my head is starting to hurt. "Shit."

"Yeah, it was fucked up. Janice had been hitting the bottle hard for a few months and stopped taking her meds altogether. I guess it was finally too much, and she couldn't take it anymore. As bad as it sounds, I was kinda relieved for Bright Side and Gracie. It was like being let out of prison. They were free."

"She must've been bad."

He shakes his head. "You have no idea. Of course, my mom and I didn't find out about most of it until after Janice died. Bright Side got really drunk one night right after her mom died and told me every-thing...the drugs...the beatings." He sighs and tightens his fist that's resting on his thigh. "There's no way we would've let them stay with her if we'd known. Bright Side never said anything while Janice was alive because she was afraid that social services would come in and split up her and Grace. And she was probably right, because there was some bad shit going down. Bright Side took the brunt of it, espe-cially the physical abuse, to protect Grace. God, I don't even want to think about it. It still makes me sick." He shakes his head. "We never knew." He takes a deep breath and continues, "Bright Side was just getting ready to graduate from high school when her mom died. She had a scholarship to go to Grant and play violin, and she gave it up so she could stay in San Diego and take care of Gracie. A week after the funeral, she went to the doctor for a routine annual exam and found out after a series of tests that she had ovarian cancer, 'a serous carcino-ma,' they called it. The next two months were brutal. They operated on her and removed it all. Then she went through a round of chemo. She and Grace stayed with us, and we took her to all her appointments. You don't know hell until you watch someone go through what she did. She lost her hair, and she was so sick with the chemo. She couldn't eat. She threw up all the time. She lost so much weight they had to hospitalize her just to feed her and get fluids in her. It was awful, but she never complained." He points at Katie. "She's a fucking fighter, that little woman. She had faith she was going to get better, and it was all worth it. And she worried about Grace, of course. But eventually, she did get better. She went back to work, and she rented a place for her and her sister. My mom wanted them to stay with us, but Bright Side said they needed to be on their own." He laughs. "You should've seen their place."

"She said they had an apartment."

He laughs again. "That's a stretch. It was a single-car *garage*. They had a double bed that they shared, some boxes they kept their clothes in, and a card table. That's it. They fucking loved it." He laughs again. "Only Bright Side and Gracie could live in a fucking garage and think they were in paradise."

"Didn't their mom leave them any money?" This just keeps getting worse.

"Hell no, that's another thing we didn't find out until after Gracie died. Apparently Janice had been living off Bright Side and Grace's child support all those years. She never worked. Their old man left when Bright Side was a baby and moved back to England where he was from. I guess he met someone and started a family and forgot about the one he had in California. He never talked to Bright Side or Gracie, but he paid Janice a pretty penny to raise them. Janice just spent it all on herself. The guy's loaded, so paying her off was nothing to him. The money stopped when each of the girls turned eighteen, and Janice started getting deeper and deeper in debt. When Bright Side sold the house and her mom's car, it barely covered the debt Janice had racked up. Bright Side walked away with her van and the clothes on their back. She and Grace lived on what she made working in the mail room with me at my mom's advertising firm. It wasn't enough to get by, but somehow they did."

There's a surprise at every turn with this girl. "I never knew she had it so bad."

He huffs. "That's because it's Bright Side we're talking about. The girl never complains. She hates it when people feel sorry for her. I bet if you woke her up right now and asked her about her cancer, she'd tell you that there's someone out there who's worse off than she is. That's Bright Side."

SUNDAY, NOVEMBER 27

KATE

My phone's vibrating across Keller's dresser. I blink the sleep out of my eyes and glance at the clock. 1:37 am. The ringing stops before I answer it, but once I have it in my hand, it vibrates insistently again. It's Franco.

"Hey, Franco." My tongue feels too big for my mouth, making my voice sound thick. This new pain medication makes waking a slow process. As if consciousness doesn't agree with me. It's powerful shit.

"Kate. Sorry to wake you, but what in the hell is up with your boy?"

I pull myself to a sitting position and say, "What? What's wrong, Franco?" I glance at Keller sleeping beside me.

"Gus. The punk ass shows up yesterday afternoon at the venue fifteen minutes late for soundcheck, wasted out of his fucking mind. Then he disappears afterwards. We find him at a bar down the street and have to practically carry him out to get him back for the show, which in hindsight was a mistake of epic proportions. That show was a full-blown shit-storm. He was so drunk he forgot half the words, he refused to play his guitar, he cursed at the crowd, and he fell down twice. It was fucking *brilliant*." The sarcasm weighs heavy in that last declaration. "Sure, he can perform drunk. He's done it a million times. But this? This was beyond fucked up. He's locked himself in the bus now and won't let anyone in. He won't talk to any of us. His phone goes straight to voicemail. What the hell happened in Minnesota? I've never seen him like this."

Shit. This is bad. I know Gus shuts down when he's upset. The only people he'll talk to when he's like this are his mom and me. It's always been that way. I can't hold back the sigh.

"What is it, Kate? What's wrong? It's bad, isn't it?" The anger in his voice softens.

I whisper, "Yeah, hold on," as I slip out of bed.

Keller stirs in bed next to me. "What's wrong?"

I hold the phone away from my face. "It's okay. I'll be back in a few minutes. I need to take this call." I put on my coat and boots and open the door to step outside as quickly and quietly as I can. It's freezing out here. "Okay, Franco. Sorry, I had to go someplace I could talk."

"It's fine. Sorry to wake you, Kate, but I didn't know what else to do. This isn't Gus. I'm worried."

"Yeah, me too." I take a few deep breaths before I speak. "I'm sick, Franco."

"Oh. Fuck." And then quieter, "Fuck." And then louder, "Please tell me the cancer isn't back?"

"It's back." I feel terrible saying it, like I've somehow let him down giving him the answer he didn't want.

I hear a loud crash like he's kicked or hit something followed by silence.

I continue. "Gus found out Thursday night. We spent the night at the hospital. He dealt with it pretty well until we dropped him off at the airport this morning."

"Yesterday morning," he corrects.

"Right, I guess it is Sunday, isn't it."

"So, what's the prognosis?" He sounds scared.

"Not good."

"Oh, Kate." And now he just sounds sad. "I'm so sorry."

Keller's voice breaks through the darkness. "Katie, it's freezing out here. Come inside and talk. You won't wake Stella. She's asleep on the loveseat."

My boots crunch against the snow as I walk shivering back toward the door.

"Listen, Kate, I gotta go. I may have to bust the goddamn door down on that bus."

I'm whispering when I step inside and Keller wraps his arms around me. "I wish there was something I could do to help you. To help Gus."

Franco laughs, but there's only a hint of amusement behind it. "And there's the Bright Side Gus loves so much. We'll take care of him, Kate. You take care of yourself. Fight the good fight. Do you hear me? Fucking fight this."

I nod even though he can't see me. "Okay," I say, even though there's nothing to fight now.

"Later."

"Bye, Franco."

This is why I didn't want Gus to know. I've just become his downfall.

I text Gus immediately: *Call me. That's an order.*

My phone rings in my hand at 2:25 in the afternoon. I've been holding onto it for over twelve hours waiting for this call. "Hey, Gus. You okay?"

"I feel like Bruce Lee is battling Mike Tyson inside my skull." He sounds like he's on the losing end.

"Who's winning?" I have to try to cheer him up.

He coughs. I think it was supposed to be a chuckle. "Bruce is a fast little fucker, but Mike is fierce. It could go on a while, dude."

"Rough night, huh?" I don't want to chastise or nag. I'm sure he's heard enough of that already.

He sighs. "That's what they tell me. Though I beg to differ. I'd take a night I don't remember over the way I'm feeling right now any day."

"Gus, I'm not gonna get all sanctimonious on you, because that would make me the world's biggest fucking hypocrite, but maybe there's a better way to deal with all of this. Maybe a way that's more conducive to keeping the band afloat and the tour train in motion. You need to be able to function, dude. This is your dream, remember? Don't fuck it up." I can feel sorry for him, but I can't baby him. Coddling doesn't do anyone any good.

I hear the click of a lighter, followed by a long inhale and an equally long exhale. For the first time in my life, I don't have the heart to put in my two cents.

"I know, but this is all so fucked up. I'm sorry, Bright Side. I just don't know how I'm going to get through this. I don't even know how to begin to deal."

He sounds sad; it breaks my heart. "I wish you didn't have to. I'm sorry."

"Stop. *Please* don't apologize. You being sick and me worrying about it is not something you're allowed to be sorry for." Annoyance fades to an aching echo.

We're both quiet for several seconds. "You should write, Gus. Get it all out."

He huffs, and I know he thinks it's a bad idea. "No one wants to hear that kind of anger."

"Who says anyone needs to hear it? Just write the song for you. You can share it with me if you want. We could collaborate. Kind of a last hurrah. What do you say?"

"Is that a challenge?" He's thinking now. I don't hear concession yet, but he's thinking.

I know he never backs down when he's called out, so I bully him a bit. "Yes, it is."

"Aw, damn you, woman. You're evil, you know that?" I can hear his smile through the phone.

The weight's lifting off both of us. "So I've been told."

"Well shit. Nothing to lose, right? Maybe I will. Besides, my liver could use a rest. Just the thought of whiskey makes me want to throw up."

"It will help, I promise. I wrote a lot after Gracie died."

"You never told me that."

"That's because I never told anyone. I just wrote. Most of it's for guitar because I couldn't bear to play my violin. It's probably all shit, but that's not what mattered at the time. At the time, it was cheap therapy. That's what I needed."

"Huh. I'd like to hear it sometime, what you wrote."

"Sure. Someday. Now go get some rest before your show tonight and promise me you'll start writing tomorrow."

"Yes, ma'am." He sounds more like himself now.

"Do epic."

"Do epic," he echoes quietly.

"I love you, Gus."

"I love you, too, Bright Side."

"Bye."

"Bye."

WEDNESDAY, NOVEMBER 30

KATE

Gus and I talk on Skype. He plays me what he's written. The acoustics on the bus aren't great, but it's hard for me to hold back my emotion watching him bare his soul. He was right—it's angry. But it's also beautiful, because I know it's Gus at his most raw. He's not hiding. It's just gritty guitar and unfiltered words. That kind of purity tears me up.

When he finishes, there are tears in his eyes, too. I let him compose himself, before I jokingly say, "I think you might have some rage issues, dude."

He swallows hard. "You think?"

I shake my head. "No. I was stalling. I just needed a minute." I did. I still do. I swallow hard. "That was outstanding. What about adding some violin to soften the violent tendencies?"

He coughs and takes a drink of water from the bottle on the table. "Violin might help take the edge off; you know, tamp down the hysteria."

I don't want to laugh, but he needs the encouragement. "I'm all for tamping down hysteria with strings. Can you record what you've got on your cell and email the video to me? I've got something turning over in my head, but I need to hear it again."

"You got it."

"Right on. I'll touch base with you tomorrow. Keep up with the writing."

"Thanks, Bright Side. For everything. This helps."

"Me too, dude. Love you, Gus."

"Love you, too."

"Bye."

"I'm not saying goodbye anymore. I love you."

Skype disconnects, and his picture disappears.

FRIDAY, DECEMBER 2

KATE

IT'S BEEN a few days since I've been to my dorm room. I need to grab my detergent and do some laundry.

I slip the key into the lock, but it's already unlocked. That's strange.

Dorm room 101/Creeper 101—always keep your door locked.

Sugar's lying on her bed, but she's awake. I decide to offer up a friendly greeting and say, "What's happening, Sugar?" even though I doubt I'll get much in return. Hostile or dismissive responses don't count.

Nothing. She says nothing. Fine. Whatever. It's not like we're best friends. Hell, we really aren't even friends at all, so I move on quickly to the task at hand.

As I'm stuffing clothes from a pile next to my bed into my laundry bag, I hear a sniffle from Sugar's side of the room. I've just been put in the position where I have to make a split-second decision—do I acknowledge that she's crying, or don't I? I want to ignore her, but I can't. I glance back and notice she's huddled up in fetal position and tears are silently streaming down her cheeks onto her pillow. Her face is devoid of any emotion, which is the scariest kind of break-down. It's the mask of shock. The mask your body puts on when what you're going through is too intense, and it would rather shut down than contend with it head-on.

Well shit, it looks like I'm not getting any laundry done this afternoon.

Since we aren't exactly friends, I'm not going to go over the top, but I am concerned. I hate to see people cry. "Sugar, dude, you wanna talk about it?"

No response. She doesn't even blink.

I try again, because I can't walk away now. "Listen, I know I'm the last person you probably want to talk to, but I am a good listener."

She blinks and looks up at me like she's just noticed me for the first time. The tears keep coming.

"What's up, dude?"

She sniffles again, and I hand her a tissue from the box on my desk. After she blows her nose, the expression on her face is some-where between sadness and embarrassment. She sniffles again. "I'm pregnant."

For an instant, I think, *And this surprises you, you nympho?* But the mean thought exits as quickly as it entered because I'm certainly not a saint in this department. Only a virgin could pass judgment. That's certainly not me. "How far along?"

She rubs the tears from her cheeks with the backs of her hands. "I don't know. I missed my period last week. I took three tests yesterday. All positive."

My mind is racing. I can't help but put myself in her shoes. It's like some sort of morbid version of living vicariously. God, what the hell would I do if I were Sugar? So I try to be supportive, again without being fake. "Have you talked to the father?"

She shakes her head and lets out a laugh that's part disgust and part self-loathing. "I'm not even sure who the father is."

"Can you narrow it down? Maybe if you find out how far along you are, it would help."

She rolls her eyes, and they land on the tissue she's shredding into confetti onto the bed in front of her. "You know as well as I do how many different guys have come through here." The tears have started up again. "I'm so fucking stupid, Kate."

I have this sudden urge to comfort her, because everyone messes up. *Everyone.* I sit down on her bed and offer another tissue. "You're not stupid, Sugar. Horny maybe, but not stupid."

She blows her nose loudly and glares at me.

It makes me smile. For the first time, I'm having a real conversation with the real Sugar. "What are you going to do?"

"I can't have a baby," she says without reservation. "I just can't."

My heart hurts. Although I absolutely believe that this is a decision every woman needs to make for herself, my head still has me in Sugar's shoes. I know that, deep down, I would want to keep my baby. I swallow and remind myself that this isn't about me, it's about Sugar. And only Sugar knows what's best for Sugar.

But I still play devil's advocate because it's what I would do for a friend. "Can you live with that decision? One, two, ten years down the road? Can you live with it?"

There's fear in her eyes, but she repeats, "I can't have a baby right now."

I nod. She's thought about it. "Have you been to the health clinic on campus? Maybe they can help."

She shakes her head. "No. I'm... I'm scared."

I can't believe I'm saying this. "Go wash your face and put some clothes on. We're going on a field trip, Sugar."

Sugar takes another pregnancy test at the campus health clinic. It confirms what she already knew. She talks to the PA on duty, with me by her side, and takes the standard pamphlets and cards they provide on pregnancy, adoption, and abortion.

By the time we walk out the door, she's resolute. She has a plan. Still, her hands are shaking so hard she can't dial her cell to make an appointment.

I take the phone out of her hand and finish dialing the number on the business card. When a woman answers on the other end of the line, I proceed. "I need to make an appointment for a friend."

We set up an appointment for next Thursday morning.

THURSDAY, DECEMBER 8

KATE

SUGAR HAD AN ABORTION. I took her to the clinic. It's done. Final.

I made sure she got into our dorm room afterward, and that I got her something to eat and drink. She thanked me, and then I had to leave. I'm not holding this against her. I'm not judging her. I'm really not. But my stomach hurts, and I can't stop thinking about Stella. What if Lily and Keller made the same decision? No Stella. The thought of no Stella makes me want to cry.

I run to my car and start driving. By the time I get to Keller's, I'm still out of breath. I don't know what it's like to have a panic attack, but this must be close. My goddamn heart is going to beat itself free of my body. I feel like I'm losing my shit. It's terrifying. I've never felt like this before. I barge into his apartment and double over, hands on my knees, trying to pull oxygen into my lungs and quiet my mind, but the only thing I can think about is nonexistence. And I can't help going down the road where nonexistence equates to death.

Keller's next to me in an instant. "Katie, what's wrong?"

I look up. "Stella. I need to talk to Stella right now." I'm sucking in ragged breaths. "Can you please call her? Right now?"

He looks confused but pulls his cell out of his pocket and calls immediately. He walks me to sit on his bed while it rings. "Hey, Melanie. Can you put Stella on please?" He pauses, waiting. He smiles at me, but it's strained. His eyebrows are pulled together. I'm scaring him. "Hi, baby girl. How's my Stella?"

I can hear Stella's tiny voice faintly. My heart rate begins to slow down.

"Stella, Katie wants to say hi. I'm going to put her on the phone now so she can talk to you."

My hand's already outstretched desperately awaiting Stella on the other end. "Hi, sweetie."

"Hi, Kate. Whatcha doin'?" She sounds so grown up.

"I was just thinking about you and realized it's been a few days since I talked to you. How's Miss Higgins?" This is good. This is what I need.

"She's good. She ate apples this morning. She *loves* apples." She drags out loves for a good three seconds, and it makes me smile.

"Well, good. I'm glad to hear it. What did you do today?" I can breathe normally now, but I need another minute with her.

"Melanie and I went ice skating, and she read me the pony book, but she doesn't read it good like you do. She doesn't make horse noises. It's kind of boring."

"I'll read it to you next time I see you, okay?" I know I shouldn't make promises I may not be able to keep, but I can't help myself.

"Okay."

"I'm going to put your daddy back on the phone. Have a good night, Stella."

"I will."

After he hangs up, Keller takes my face gently in his hands and looks directly into my eyes. There's still worry in his. "What just happened, babe?"

"I don't know. I kinda freaked out. Sorry. I just... I had to take someone to do something earlier... And it was hard... It made me feel..." I realize that I'm rambling, so I stop. I look at his beautiful face. "I think I just had my first freak-out moment about dying. I'm sorry."

SATURDAY, DECEMBER 10

KATE

Gus and I have been working on his song for the past week and a half, and yesterday we played it for the rest of the band. Gus has decided (and by decided I mean he's hell-bent and nothing will stop him) that he wants to record it.

It's eight o'clock in the morning, and he's already calling for the first of what I'm sure will be many calls today. "Hey, Gus, what's happening in Portland today?"

"Portland's rainy. How's Grant?"

"Haven't been outside yet, but I would say there's a one hundred percent chance of freezing-ass cold."

He laughs. "Hey, I won't keep you long, but I wanted to make sure you're free next weekend?" He says it as a question.

"Sure. I have finals this week. I think my last one is Thursday morning. After that I'm free. What's up, dude?"

"I've been talking to MFDM about recording this song, and he lined us up a recording studio in Minneapolis next weekend."

"What about your shows?"

"Postponed. We're all flying in Friday morning, and we'll have the place until Sunday evening when we fly out."

He's not wasting any time with this. It's a good thing because the pain is getting more intense even on my new meds, and I've noticed that it even hurts to breathe sometimes. My lungs just aren't working like they should be. I don't know how much longer I'll be able to play or sing. "Okay. Are the guys going to be ready?"

Gus is all business. "They'll be ready."

"Yeah. Wow, no pressure, dude."

"Sorry, Bright Side. I know this is a lot to put on you. Are you going to be okay? I mean, how are you feeling?" He's stumbling all over himself because he doesn't want to say the wrong thing.

It's time to reassure him. "I'm fine, Gus. Next weekend will be fine. I can't wait to see you guys."

"I can't wait to see you, too. I'll call you later with all the details."

"Sounds good. Love you, Gus."

"Love you, too, Bright Side."

We hang up after that. I guess I can't say goodbye to him anymore either.

SUNDAY, DECEMBER 11

KELLER

WE'VE BEEN DRINKING coffee all night while we're studying for finals. Katie looks exhausted, but she's a trooper.

"Keller?"

"Yeah, babe?"

"Can we take a break for a few minutes?"

That question brings to mind so many things I'd rather be doing right this moment.

Namely Katie.

I set my book down on the floor next to the loveseat and stand up, offering her my hand.

She looks at it questioningly and raises her eyebrows.

I offer it again. "Dance with me, pretty lady."

The smile I love touches her lips. It's the smile that opens up and pulls you inside. It lulls you into her world. It's my favorite place to be. She takes my hand and stands slowly. "Are you serious?"

I pull my phone out of my pocket and thumb through my music. After selecting "Pictures of You" by The Cure, I turn up the volume, set the phone on the coffee table, and lead her by the hand to the open space behind the loveseat. "I never joke about romance."

Katie glances to the floor before fixing me with those incredible eyes of hers and I know what she's about to say means a lot to her. She has this way of telling half the story with her eyes before she even opens her mouth. "I've never slow danced before."

I wrap my left arm around her back, pulling her to me while taking her right hand in mine and resting them against my chest. "You love to dance. What do you mean you've never slow danced?"

"I've danced with guys," she says, nuzzling her cheek against my chest and kissing the back of my hand, "but never a proper slow dance. This is old school. It's nice."

It is nice. The song is melancholy, emotional, but that's what makes it absolutely perfect. And it's almost eight minutes long. Every slow dance should last at least eight minutes. We sway and melt into each other. I could hold her like this all night long. As the song finishes, she pulls back slightly and looks up at me.

I know that look.

I *love* that look.

It is *so* on.

Her fingers are already curled around the hem of my T-shirt. I lean down and kiss her lips. "Are we still taking a break?"

She nods and pulls at the drawstring on my sweatpants. "Mmm hmm."

I pull my shirt over my head and step out of my pants. I lean down, touching her thigh and running my hand up her bare leg until it disappears beneath her pajama shorts. "What did you have in mind?"

She gasps when my fingers pass under her panties. "You choose. You always—" she pauses and her throat hums. *Damn*, that sound. It makes me want to worship her and ravage her at the same time. Her head drops back, and her eyes flutter closed and she continues, "— have the best ideas."

I smooth her wild hair away from her neck. With her collarbone exposed like that, I have to taste it. It's so good that I continue.

She lets me.

Our blissful connection is gentler and slower than times before, but mutual satisfaction doesn't take long to achieve.

Neither one of us is ready to get back to studying. Katie suggests that we get dressed and visit her dorm.

It's 11:45 pm, but during finals week, everyone pulls all-nighters.

I drive us in her car, because Dunc has the Green Machine down at Shel's.

The dorms are busy. Most of the doors in the hallway are propped open, and there's music drifting out into the hallway from several of them. People are loitering in the hall, shuffling around with mugs of coffee. From the looks of it, a lot of people have hit the wall like we have and are taking a break from studying.

We hit up Clayton and Peters' room first. Clayton's a cool guy. He's friendly and always says the funniest things. He and Katie play off each other well. Peter's serious as a heart attack, but he's nice enough. And Katie really likes him. Better than that, he totally, one hundred percent cares about and respects Katie. For that, I appreciate the guy. He knows a good person when he meets one.

Next, we stop at her room. Her roommate is here. I'm not a big fan of Sugar. To be honest, she's a conceited twat. The few times I've been here with Katie, Sugar's acted like a spoiled brat, like she's too good for Katie. She tries to talk down to her, but because Katie's so feisty, she puts Sugar in her place. She doesn't let people fuck with her. It's unbelievably sexy. Just thinking about Katie, I'm getting ready for round two of our "study break." We need to get out of here. Stat.

"You ready, babe? Because I am." When she catches my eye, I wink.

She smiles at the come on. "Oh, I think I *could be ready* if you just give me another couple of minutes to talk to Sugar."

Goddamn. Now I'm definitely ready.

She's talking quietly to Sugar. I can't quite hear what they're talking about, but Katie's voice sounds concerned. I think it's best if I wait out in the hall and give them some privacy.

I'm walking back down the hall from the drinking fountain when I hear a door close and look behind me. I see Katie walking the other way, heading toward the stairs with Clayton. I'm about to call out her name, when that bastard, Ben Thompson, stumbles out into the hall from a room a few down from Katie's. What the hell is he doing here? He's a junior and lives in a frat house on the other side of campus. I've never liked the prick. He's an arrogant asshole and dumber than a box of rocks. That aside, the real reason I can't stand him is because of something that happened freshman year. We both lived in this very dorm, and a girl who lived across the hall from me, Gina, accused him of rape. She recanted her claims the following day, packed up her stuff, and her parents picked her up and took her away. I know the bastard did it. He should be in jail, but instead, the sicko's still here. Rumor has it Gina's not the only one, there have been others. The guy's a shithead.

He's drunk off his ass, and he's following Katie down the hall. I'm not taking my fucking eyes off her, because I swear I will rip his arm out of its socket if he even thinks of touching her.

Katie stops and turns to face him. He must've said something to her. I can just make out the murderous look on her face.

The next thing I know, Ben grips Clayton's shirt in his hand and shoves him into the wall. "Get out of my way, I'm trying to talk to the cock tease. I'll kick your ass in a minute, faggot."

Clayton raises his voice. "You can't threaten me anymore."

I start to run down the hall, pushing people out of my way.

About six steps away, I hear Katie's voice. "Get away from me, asshole." It's forceful, loud. She doesn't sound scared. Little does she know what this guy is capable of.

Four steps away. I see his hand is on her ass as she's turning to walk away. That's it; the motherfucker is dead now.

Two steps away. I launch myself and tackle him from behind. Katie screams and jumps out of the way. We miss her by inches when I hit the floor on top of Ben. Without even thinking, I start pummeling the guy's face. I hit him again and again. My knuckles turn red with blood, his or mine, I don't know. I don't care. Then someone's pulling me off of him.

Ben starts crawling to his feet. His nose is draining blood down his face and onto the front of his shirt.

"What the hell?" He spits blood at my feet.

I try to lunge at him again but can't break the grip of three guys holding me back. "You fucking piece of shit. Don't you ever touch her again, do you hear me? If I even see you fucking look at her, I swear I will rip your goddamn eyes out of their sockets."

He holds up his hands like he's completely innocent. "Sorry, chief. No harm, no foul." He turns to leave like he didn't just get his ass beat.

He stops to blow a kiss at Katie when he walks by her. *He did not just fucking taunt her right in front of me.*

I'm about to pull away and tear this guy to pieces when Katie grabs Ben by the shoulders and knees him square in the balls. It drops him to the floor. It was so fucking brilliant, I have to laugh.

She leans down to his ear. "Karma is a bitch, dude. I hope your pathetic youth has been worth it, because trust me, for a piece of shit like you, your future is going to be hell. Enjoy it, motherfucker, because you've earned every miserable second."

Jesus, my tiny, one hundred pound girlfriend is the bravest, most badass person I've ever met.

Ben is up and stumbling down the hall again, nuts in hand.

Then Katie's delicate, little hands are on my face, and she's frantically searching my eyes. "Are you hurt?"

I shake my head, and I can't stop smiling at her. I'm damn near giddy, which is absurd given the fact that I just beat the shit out of someone...and I've never laid a hand on anyone before in my life. Maybe it's all the adrenaline.

Or maybe it's just Katie.

She smiles that damn gorgeous smile of hers. "You've got a pretty good right hook. Let's go home so we can get you in the shower and clean you up."

I raise an eyebrow. "We? You helping?"

She tugs on the corner of her bottom lip with her teeth. God, I love it when she does that. She shrugs. "I like to help. What can I say?"

Then someone's tapping me on the shoulder and asking, "Excuse me? Are you okay?"

I turn and the dorm RA, John, is standing before me in pajama bottoms and a Grant T-shirt that looks like it's been washed a million times. He was the RA when I was in this dorm freshman year. I know he doesn't remember me, but by the looks of him, he's as grouchy as ever. I've never seen the guy crack a smile.

He repeats, "Are you okay?"

I nod, despite the pain pulsing through my knuckles.

He jabs his thumb in the air over his shoulder. "Good. Go clean up in the bathroom and then get out of here. I don't want to see you in here again." It's a big show. I forgot how much this guy gets off on upholding authority.

I reach for Katie's hand. "Come on."

John shakes his head. "I need to talk to Kate and Clayton first. Kate will meet you outside."

Katie raises her eyebrows and looks at Clayton, who's been backed up against the wall trying to stay out of the bedlam this whole time, before she agrees, "Okay. I'll meet you out front in a minute, Keller."

After scrubbing the blood off my hands, I'm angry all over again. How dare John kick me out. He didn't say a word to Ben, and I'm pretty sure he saw everything. I throw the front door open and pound my way down the stairs. Katie is standing with Clayton and John on the sidewalk.

I point an accusatory finger at John. "You—"

Katie pushes me back with both hands on my chest. "Whoa. One MMA fight is enough for tonight, tiger."

Then I see something on John's face that I've never seen before: a smile. Well, it's not so much a smile as it is the small misshapen, beginning of a grin. But on him, it's the equivalent of an ear-to-ear, face-splitting smile that shows off every tooth. He's looking down at Katie. She has her back to him. He looks up at me and the smile vanishes. He clears his throat. "I apologize for making a scene in there, but I have a job to do." He looks me in the eye. "As far as I'm concerned, this never happened."

I'm confused, and all the adrenaline in my system isn't helping. "What didn't happen?"

"Exactly. You were never here." He's letting me off the hook.

"You're not reporting this to campus security?"

"No. I've been waiting for any opportunity to get Ben Thompson expelled from Grant. And it seems he decided to verbally and physically assault two of my residents before picking a fight with an unknown person tonight."

"Unknown?" I press.

He shrugs. "It all happened so fast, I didn't get a good look at the guy he was fighting with. Come to think of it, Ben was so drunk the fight probably happened after he left here on his way home."

Katie's nodding. "Strange," she muses.

"Strange," Clayton adds. He's wearing an odd little smile.

"Strange," John agrees. "Besides, the assault on Kate and Clayton alone is enough to get him kicked out. I heard and saw it all. He was vile. I won't even have to bring up the fight. Ben's list of violations is as long as my arm, this will be the final nail in the coffin. And it will be my pleasure. I've been waiting three years to see this guy pay."

I nod. Maybe this guy isn't half bad. "Gina?"

He nods and sadness flashes across his face. "Yeah."

Katie chimes in. "Clayton's agreed to file a report, too." She smiles at Clayton like she's proud of him. "We need to go with John to the campus security office."

I don't hesitate. "I'll drive you guys."

She looks down at my scraped knuckles and the blood on my shirt.

I look down at my shirt. "I'll, uh... I'll wait in the car when we get there."

She smiles. "Good idea."

John's already motioning us toward the parking lot. He's back to his usual curt, bossy self. "Ben Thompson will be gone before the sun comes up. I'd bet my MBA on it."

MONDAY, DECEMBER 12

KATE

JOHN WAS RIGHT. The buzz and gossip around campus this morning was unavoidable. Word has it that Ben Thompson was escorted out of his frat house early this morning before classes started. They even boxed up all of his belongings. I look at this as a victory for Clayton over *The Assholes* of the world.

Karma is a bitch, Ben Thompson.

I only had one final this morning, so I'm heading back to the dorms to check on Sugar again before I go to Keller's. I'm worried about her. The pregnancy and the aftermath are really messing with her head. She seems to genuinely want to make some changes in her life, but she lacks a few key elements to make that happen. Firstly, resolve. Peer pressure is her ultimate downfall. It kills her sense of self. Secondly, being proactive. She's floated through life. Everything's been done for her. The girl doesn't know how to make a plan, let alone act on it. And finally, self-esteem. Girls like Sugar do things for attention. The wrong kind of attention. And that leads to self-loathing. It's a vicious cycle.

Deep down, I don't think she's a bad person. I think she lacks a support system and strong role models. She's got balls, I'll give her that. She's proven it over and over, even if she was being a total bitch half the time. If she could just channel that gutsy approach into changing herself, she'd be a fucking rock star.

So, Sugar and I are friends. It feels weird. But it's a good weird. And I'm weird, what can I say.

THURSDAY, DECEMBER 15

KATE

TODAY WAS the last day of finals, and Keller and I decided to make a big meal for all our friends. We invited Shelly, Duncan, Clay, and Pete to join us. We shared a big dish of vegetable lasagna, a crisp Caesar salad, and salty, buttery garlic bread. The food was excellent, and the conversation was better than the food. When you put six completely different people at a table, entertaining things happen.

Of course, all good things come to an end. At least, that's what they say. And I'm beginning to believe that it's sage advice. After dinner, I dropped the bombshell. I hated it. It made me feel like I was vying for attention or something when all I wanted to do was inform my friends here at Grant. Keller wanted me to tell them weeks ago, but I didn't want them worrying, especially when they all had finals coming up. I tried to stay positive when I delivered the news, but as I watched each of them either implode or explode, I aimed for composure instead. Witnessing people I care about experience sadness as a direct result of...me? It sucks.

Shelly flinched several times; her whole body convulsed like it was trying to reject the news. She just kept shaking her head and biting her bottom lip like she was trying not to cry. As soon as

Duncan pulled her into his arms, she began to sob in loud, angry bursts into his shoulder.

Pete's eyes were so wide I could see the whites all the way around. I don't think he blinked for ten minutes. He didn't speak a word.

And Clayton? His precious little face contorted into absolute anguish as soon as the word cancer was out of my mouth. The transformation was instantaneous, and so were the tears. He kept saying, "This can't happen to you, Katherine. It just can't."

There was a lot of hugging after the shock wore off, which helped me immensely. I hope it helped them too.

I'm mostly just glad it's over so we can all go back to just being friends.

SUNDAY, DECEMBER 18

KELLER

WE'RE at the studio early this morning. I brought Dunc, Shel, and Clayton with me. Katie stayed with Gus last night at his hotel in a suite with the band. I didn't sleep. I couldn't sleep. Every time I shut my eyes and didn't feel her next to me in bed I started to panic. It felt like she was already gone.

I'm tired. She looks tired, too, but then again, she always looks tired these days. Still, her tired eyes are happy. They almost always are. I don't know how she does it. Her eyes are twinkling, and she's as entertaining as ever as she jokes around with the band. They're actually all pretty cool guys. They're all so at ease with each other. They're all professionals, Katie included, but they have fun while they're working. The laughter I've heard over the past two days out of this group is probably more than most people hear in a lifetime. And they all adore Katie. Especially Franco, who taunts her mercilessly. I can't feel too sorry for her, though, because she dishes it right back. That's my Katie. She's so damn feisty.

Tom enters, extra-large coffee in hand, and nods to the group. He's not a morning person, so everyone nods a response, avoiding verbal greetings. The band and Katie call him MFDM. I'm not sure what that's about. I'll have to ask her. After Tom takes his seat next to the sound guy behind the soundboard, he clears his throat. "Everyone better be ready to make history today, because I didn't come all the way to Minneapolis this weekend to be let down now. Yesterday was unbelievable, but you guys," he's looking directly at Gus, "are going to have to really step up today to even compete with what you laid down yesterday. This needs to be tight." Tom likes Gus; he's just setting the tone for the day. This recording needs to be perfect if they're going to finish up today.

Gus clears his throat. "Understood." The larger-than-life rock star looks nervous.

Tom nods curtly and then his face softens slightly. "Then get your ass in there and let's get this done."

"I want Bright Side in the other booth. You need to record us at the same time. There are too many harmonies; I can't get it perfect unless I can hear her." Katie sings backup harmony on almost every line of every verse, and they sing the chorus together.

"I thought we decided everyone was going to be recorded separately and then layered on top of each other when it gets mixed."

Gus shrugs, but I can see his eyebrows lift slightly. He licks his bottom lip. Suddenly the easygoing guy I've seen for two days is gone. He looks like he's going to fall apart, and my guess is it has nothing to do with the recording. This is about Katie, and it's just become too real for him. "I need her," he says quietly.

Tom exhales, but his expression softens. He knows the circumstances surrounding this weekend and he's not going to fight Gus on this. He's going to give him whatever he needs to get through. "Okay." I don't think anyone could deny the guy right now. Not even me.

Tom and the sound guy converse briefly, and a microphone is set up in the booth facing the booth Gus will be in.

The sound booth is quiet, which is a little uncomfortable because there hasn't been a moment of silence for almost forty-eight hours in here. Shel is sitting on Dunc's lap in a big chair in the corner. Clayton, Jamie, and Robbie are sitting on a big sofa behind the soundboard. Franco and I are standing off to the side looking through the glass out at the recording booths.

Katie and Gus are directly on the other side of the glass from us. They're chatting quietly, waiting to take their places in their respective separate booths. Katie looks relaxed and happy, like she's done this a million times. She's trying to put Gus at ease. The guy looks so tense. I can't imagine what's going through his head. I've heard the lyrics. They ran through them a few times Friday night. The song is emotional. It's about the pain and struggle of losing someone, trying and failing to come to grips with it, and in the end just giving up. I know he wrote it from his perspective, but it could just as easily have been written by Katie. It's sad any way you look at it. Not knowing the story behind the song, it could be interpreted on many different levels: a death, a break-up, a loss in general. The lyrics are a no-holds-barred mix of anger and total despair. It's poetic and deep and personal, a three-minute rampage. Getting through this is going to be tough. Katie has taken it in stride. She's owning it because she's not personalizing it. She hates pity, so it's not sad to her. It's almost like she's been given the gift to tell her story. And her story, in her eyes at least, isn't sad. Even if, as the song says, she's giving up, in her bizarrely positive mind, giving up is okay in this case. Dying is okay. It will all be okay.

Tom talks into the microphone. "I think we're ready, you two."

Gus and Katie look at each other. Katie says something and holds out her tiny fist toward him. Gus smiles and bumps knuckles with her.

Everyone in the booth has come to attention, and we all seem to be holding our breath. Jamie and Robbie stand, like sitting is no longer a possibility, and hover behind me. Franco is bouncing on the balls of his feet and saying quietly to himself, "Come on, Gus, you can do this."

Katie and Gus each put on their headphones, adjust them, and take their places behind their microphones. Katie still looks relaxed, but there's a shift in her eyes. She's on her game. Gus's eyes are closed, and he's rolling his head and neck from one side to the other, trying to loosen up.

Sound guy flips a few switches, and we can hear each of them breathing through their microphones. Tom hits a button and calls, "You guys ready?" Katie takes a deep breath and nods. Gus is silent. Tom calls out again, "Gustov, you ready?"

He sighs after a few seconds and clasps his hands behind his neck. His biceps flex with tension. His eyes pinch shut. "I need a fucking cigarette." I don't know if he's talking to himself or Tom.

"This is going to be a long day," Tom mutters under his breath before hitting the button to talk two-way to Gus. "Do you need another minute?"

Katie's already pulled off her headphones and walked into Gus's booth. We can hear their conversation. "Gus, dude, you all right?"

He shakes his head.

"Listen, let's do this. This song is *kickass*. I want to hear you sing it, like *really* sing it. Don't hold anything back. I'm excited, I'm ready. C'mon and do this with me."

His face relaxes a little. "You think it's going to be any good?"

"You think I'd be here if I didn't?" she teases.

He nods. "For me? Yes."

She nods in agreement, and sighs and then a grin emerges. "Yeah, you're probably right. But it *is* going to be amazing. Now come on, *Gustov*, put your big boy pants on and let's fucking do this."

He grins back and shakes his head. He's amused by her bossiness.

She winks and taunts him as she exits, "Seriously, you'd better fucking bring it, 'cause I'm ready."

"She's so fucking hot," says Jamie, who's standing behind me. He's not being crude; he's just stating a fact. "Is anyone else oddly turned on right now?"

The entire room—even Clayton and Shelly—answer in unison, "Yes."

Franco elbows me. "You are one lucky bastard, Keller."

Yes. I. Am.

Katie's got her headphones on again. Tom calls out to them, "Are we okay, now? Gustov, you ready?"

Gus takes another deep breath and looks through the glass at Tom. "Yeah, dude," pulling at the waistband of his jeans, "I've got my big boy pants on now." He glances at Katie and smirks.

She claps her hands and laughs.

Tom looks to Katie and calls out, "Kate, you good?"

She puts two thumbs up dramatically in front of her microphone for Tom to see and adds the goofiest grin and wide eyes. Everyone in the booth bursts out laughing, including Tom. "What the hell have I gotten myself into?" He shakes his head. "Where did this girl come from?" He means it as a compliment. It's been obvious all weekend that Tom respects Katie's talent. He's fallen under her spell, just like everyone else she comes across.

Robbie pipes up, "Outer space. There's not another one like her. The both of them, really."

Franco laughs. "You can say that again."

Sound guy flips a few more switches and music seeps into the room. Katie's pre-recorded violin is low and haunting. The intro is long, which is nice because I could listen to her play forever. Acoustic guitar eventually joins in, followed by drums, bass, and electric guitar.

Katie and Gus's eyes are locked. We're all staring at them like fish in two fishbowls, but I think they've forgotten anyone else exists in this world except the best friend standing ten feet, and two panes of glass, away. They've both let the music coming through their headphones take them over. Gus's chin bounces up and down with every strum of the acoustic guitar. Kate's whole upper body is in motion, but it's slow and in time with the violin. Her right hand moves involuntarily at her side as if her bow is in hand. I glance at Franco beside me, and he's tapping out the drumbeat with his index fingers on his thighs. I don't think any of them are even aware they're playing along.

Tom points to Gus just as he leads into the first line of the song. The first two lines are his alone. His voice is low and hushed. There's an undeniable sadness in his voice. Katie joins in to sing harmony on the remainder of the first verse. It's muted and more of an echo to reinforce the emotion that's coming from Gus.

Gus continues to lead the first round of the chorus. His voice builds in volume, while Katie's adds depth.

Emotion builds in the second verse. Although Katie is still singing harmony, her voice grows louder to equal Gus's. His verges on anguish, hers provides a foundation. It's an odd combination, but it works. You feel the struggle in both of them. It carries over into the second chorus. They're both singing their hearts out, and I know the next verse is Gus's alone. It's where the song climaxes. I don't know how the guy can give any more than he already has.

And then we find out. Gus has closed his eyes at this point. His hands grip the headphones, his back arched slightly with effort. He's in the zone. Katie's entire body is moving to the beat of the drums that drive this section. It's as though the music is running directly through her and she's been taken over. I wish I could lose myself that completely. As Gus's words build to an all-out cry of anguish that borders on a pain-filled scream, her smile is ear-to-ear as she pumps her fists in the air, urging him on. The entire sound booth erupts in unbridled cheering, clapping, and whistling. Everyone is blown away by what they're seeing and hearing.

Katie, eyes closed, joins back in, and her voice matches the intensity of his. She's singing the final chorus alone, while Gus repeatedly cries out lines from the previous verse over the top of her. The energy and intensity in the sound booth is palpable. If I'm this amped up, what are Katie and Gus feeling?

Katie belts out her final line. Gus follows it up with a war cry, "I've given up on life. Or life's given up on me. Either way, I'm done." And then his voice hitches and quiets. "Finish me."

Katie's still bouncing in place, eyes closed, smile wide, fists clenched, chest heaving with effort, riding out the end of the song, which is all instrumental. It's the beginning of the song in reverse. The electric guitar and bass drop out, followed a few measures later by the drums. The acoustic guitar and violin dance intimately in the air around us. Finally, the guitar strums its last chord, and the haunting violin plays itself out.

As the last note ends, Gus and Katie open their eyes. Gus smiles a combination of relief and exhaustion. "I love you, Bright Side," he whispers.

She smiles back. "I love you, too, Gus," she answers just as softly.

That wasn't part of the song, but it was captured on the recording and that fact makes me happy. Hearing another man tell your girlfriend he loves her should bother me, but it doesn't. I want Katie to be surrounded by people who love her.

The room erupts again. Tom throws the tightly rolled papers he was holding up in the air, leans back in his chair, and shakes his head. He looks from Jamie, to Robbie, to Franco, and back. "What in the hell *was that?*" The guy is in shock. "Where did that come from? I've never seen Gustov like that. They nailed it." He's blinking in disbelief.

Franco speaks up. "It's Kate, man. She's his muse. Always has been. You saw what they just did together. No one else brings that out in him. They feed off each other. I've never seen anything else like it. Musically, they're so in tune with each other, it's like they can read each other's minds. But, you're right. What we just witnessed was un-fucking-believable. Even for them." He smiles. "I'm guessing you're not going to have them run through it again?"

Tom clears his throat, shakes his head, and hits the button to address Gus and Katie. "I think we're good. You two wanna come back in here so you can listen to this?"

A few moments later, Gus stands behind Jamie and Robbie and rests his arms around their shoulders like he needs them to stand. Katie stands in front of me and leans back against me. I wrap my arms around her and kiss the top of her head. I can feel her struggling a little with each breath. I whisper in her ear, "You *are* a rock star. I just witnessed it. You were amazing."

She rubs my forearms with her soft, small hands. "Thanks, baby."

I love it when she calls me that.

Gus has finally caught his breath. "Goddammit, Bright Side, I think the big boy pants worked."

Her laughter reverberates through me.

The recording sounds every bit as phenomenal as it did live. I feel goose bumps rise on Katie's arms.

Tom looks at Gus as the final "I love you" fades out. "What do you think? You happy with that?"

Gus looks to Katie for confirmation before he answers. She nods her head. He smiles. "Yeah, we're good."

Tom exhales. "Good, because there's no way I was going to let you even attempt to redo it." He points to the soundboard. "That was brilliant."

Next, Robbie, Jamie, and Franco all crowd around a microphone in one of the recording booths to record all the background harmonies. It takes several attempts, but they wrap up an hour later. This piece of the song is minor, but when it's layered in with every-thing else, it's like the cherry on top.

We all listen to the final rough version when we return from lunch. Franco and Katie take turns telling each other how god-awful they sound. It helps relieve the stress that's torturing Gus. He insists on listening to it five or six times. Tom strikes down every suggestion Gus makes to change it. When Katie agrees it should be left as it is, Gus concedes.

A cab arrives to transport the band and Tom to the airport shortly after. That means that it's time to say goodbye to Katie. They don't know if they'll see her again.

Tom hugs her and tells her how honored he is to have worked with her again.

Jamie cries openly as he hugs her. He can't even speak as he turns away to climb in the cab.

Robbie hugs her delicately, like he's afraid he's going to break her. His eyes are glassy when he tells her, "Hang in there, Kate," before ducking in the cab's backseat next to Jamie.

Franco looks up at the sky and blinks rapidly. "I told myself I wasn't going to do this." The tears trickle down his cheeks. He grabs her by the shoulders and pulls her into a bear hug. "I'm going to miss you so much, Kate. I can't say goodbye. This is so fucking wrong."

She's trying to force a smile, but her lip's starting to tremble. "I'll miss you, too."

He kisses her forehead and squeezes her hand before he walks to the cab.

She stops him before he disappears into the cab, "Franco?"

He turns. "Yeah."

"Sorry about all the shit I've always given you. I hope you know I never meant any of it. You're one of most awesome dudes I've ever known."

He smiles through the tears. "Right back at ya, Kate."

It's heartbreaking to watch.

Gus is standing a few feet away, smoking a cigarette. He takes one last drag and flicks it into the street before turning toward Katie. She takes his huge hands in her small hands. It's funny how well they fit together given the extreme size difference. "You should quit, you know," she tells him.

He nods and it's solemn. "I know. Believe me, I know."

She swings their arms between them. Neither one of them wants to say goodbye, like if one of them speaks, it all has to end. So, they stand in silence and stare at each other. The tears from Gus's eyes start slowly, but when they turn into a steady stream, he abruptly pulls her off the ground into a hug.

His voice is considerably calm despite the tears. "This isn't good-bye. I'll see you after Christmas." Their tour ends a few days before the holidays.

She nods against his shoulder. "It's not goodbye. I'll see you in a few weeks."

He squeezes her tighter and his voices breaks. "Promise?"

Her voice sounds thick and muffled. "I promise, Gus."

He sets her down gently and holds her cheek against his chest and strokes her hair twice before releasing her. She's holding on to the hem of his shirt like she doesn't want him to go. He takes her face in his hands and bends down until he's eye to eye with her. "I love you, Bright Side." He pecks her lightly on the lips.

She whispers, "I love you, too."

He strides toward the cab, swings the front passenger door open, and climbs inside. No goodbye.

Katie blows kisses and waves as the cab pulls away from the curb. Tears are silently streaming when she turns to face me. She's finally let them fall.

When she hugs me, it's like she's falling into me. I rub circles into her back. "You have such great friends, Katie."

"I know. I'm so fucking lucky." She means it.

I kiss the top of her head. "We're the lucky ones."

MONDAY, DECEMBER 19

KELLER

My mother hasn't talked to me in a month. She's still upset with me for changing my major...my whole life, I guess. I know it shouldn't bother me because it's what we do, what we've done my entire life. There's a pattern: I try like hell, but it's never good enough, and she's disappointed, I feel like a failure...repeat, repeat, repeat.

I guess it's bothering me because for the first time in my life, *I'm* proud of myself. I feel focused. I feel confident. I feel brave. And I feel all of these things because of Katie. Being around her these past few months has changed me. I'm a better man because of her.

Why can't my mother see that?

Katie and I drove from Grant to Chicago earlier today. We had dinner with Stella and Melanie here at my parents' house. My father's working the ER tonight and Mother refused to join us.

Dinner was melancholy given that it's probably the last time we'll see Melanie for a long time. She's moving back to Seattle. We promised to stay in touch, but we both know how that goes. Promises are easy. She's going to live with her parents and go to school to finish her degree. I'm happy for her. She's a good person. I don't know what

I would've done without her. She's been Stella's angel for almost four years. I can't thank her enough.

Stella cried when Melanie left. It tore me up. And for a split second, it made me wonder if I was doing the right thing.

It's after eleven o'clock now. Stella's been asleep for a little over two hours and my mother's in her office, where she's been holed up since we arrived this afternoon.

Katie went to sleep in the guest room about an hour ago. This past week has been hectic, and she hasn't slept as much as she needs to. I can tell that she's struggling. She's so strong, the strongest person I've ever known, and she tries to put on a brave face for everyone, but when she's alone, she allows the pain to take over. I've seen it, and it breaks my heart. The reality that I'm going to lose her becomes more real every day.

I don't want to lose her.

I'd take her place if I could. She's the only other person, besides Stella, that I can't honestly say I would die for. I wouldn't even hesitate. I would take a fucking bullet for either of my girls.

I throw the covers back off the bed, because I can't just lie here any longer. I pace around my room chewing on my fingernails. There's nothing left of them. I'm anxious as hell, and my mind is racing. I can't turn it off enough to get some sleep.

I throw a pair of pajama bottoms on over my boxers and walk across the hall to check on Stella. She's fast asleep. She looks so peaceful that it makes my heart swell with love. Katie was right. I am so blessed.

My next stop is Katie's room. She's asleep on her left side. She's been sleeping like this for the past week. She says she's just more comfortable in this position, but I know the real reason. The pain is killing her. It's so intense that she can't lie on her back or stomach anymore.

I fucking hate cancer.

She's in a deep sleep, but I know it won't last. It never does. She's the lightest sleeper I've ever seen. She must wake up a dozen times every night, and her discomfort only makes it worse.

When she stayed at my place, I used to love to watch her sleep. She's so beautiful that sometimes I would lie next to her and just watch her. The rise and fall of her chest. The flutter behind her eyelids as her mind raced through dreams. The absolute tranquility was breathtaking. Sometimes I would daydream, wondering, *What would it be like to get to keep her forever? What would it be like to marry her? What would she look like carrying my child? What would our child look like?*

Last week, I stopped watching her sleep. Her pain has begun to take hold of her in the night. Her body stiffens against it. Her face contorts, fighting it. Sometimes she cries out. The tranquility is gone. And that shatters me.

So I don't watch.

Tonight I can't bring myself to be anywhere else but in this room with her, because I feel like I don't have much time left. I don't want to disturb her, so I sit on the sofa across the room from the bed. The darkness shields her from my eyes, but I can still feel her. I lean my head back and close my eyes, taking it all in. I don't know how long I sit there, an hour or more, before I decide I should go to bed and try and get some rest. When I reach the door, though, I can't. I know I won't be able to breathe if I leave this room. So I walk over to the bed and slowly pull the covers back and slide in beside her. The king-size bed is gigantic compared to the twin we're used to sharing. There are *feet* of space between us.

"You're not going to sleep all the way over there, are you?" Her voice is sleepy and hoarse.

It makes me smile and the anxiety that's been building in my chest the past few hours disappears. "How'd you know I was in here with you?"

She laughs. "You're not as stealthy as you think you are, Keller Banks. You'd make a horrible burglar. Or ninja. Don't change your major again."

I inch my way to her side of the bed and press my entire body against the back of hers and wrap my arms around her. She's warm. I could live in this moment forever. I kiss the back of her head twice. "Good night, Katie."

"Good night."

It's quiet, and I'm almost certain she's drifted back off to sleep.

"Keller?"

"Yeah?"

"Thanks for coming in. I hate sleeping alone." She intertwines her fingers with mine and raises them to her mouth to kiss the back of my hand.

"I love you." I have to get the words out before I get any more choked up than I already am.

"I love you, too, baby... I love you, too, baby." She says it twice, so I don't have to ask her to say it again.

I really do love her. So. Much.

TUESDAY, DECEMBER 20

KELLER

WE'RE ALMOST DONE LOADING Stella's things into Katie's car. (She volunteered her car for the trip because, although she does *love* my beanbags, she didn't think they'd be comfortable for several hours of ass time. Her words, not mine.) We can't take much with us because there's not much room at my place back home, but Stella will have everything she needs.

Katie's helping Stella feed Miss Higgins. They gather her cage and everything else that goes along with caring for a turtle. Jesus, it's like moving a goddamn menagerie instead of a solitary, small turtle. Let's just say Miss Higgins has got it good. She may be the highest maintenance turtle in history.

I'm making a final walk-through of the living room to make sure Stella hasn't left anything behind that I know she'll miss later.

"Keller." My father's voice startles me. He clears his throat. It's the same formal throat-clearing that precedes everything he says to me. "Can I have a word with you before you go?"

I know where this is going, and I'm not in the mood for an argument today. He's going to ask me to come with him to my mother's office because that's where she feels the most powerful. And because he's just the errand boy, he'll clam up when we step through the door, and she'll proceed to tell me everything I'm doing wrong. I'll try to defend myself. She'll raise her voice and try to intimidate me into seeing things her way. I've been through this a million times.

Like I said, I'm not in the mood. "Dad, no offense, but I know *having a word with you* and *Mother talking at me* are the same thing. So, no thanks. Not today."

He clears his throat again. "This isn't about your mother, son. This is about Kate."

Up to this point, I've kept my back to him, but I turn to face him when I hear her name. I can't *not* react to her name. "What about Katie?"

More throat-clearing.

"Just say whatever it is you have to say, Dad."

He looks me hard in the eyes, but there's a softness that he reserves only for Stella. He's a sucker for Stella. "Kate's very sick, isn't she?"

I nod. I haven't told my parents about Katie's illness, but my father's around sick people enough to know one when he sees one. And he's observant.

He releases a breath. "I was afraid of that. What's her diagnosis?"

I'm reduced to one-word answers because I don't want to break down in front of him. "Cancer." I hate that fucking word.

"Is she being treated?" His question is clinical, but the softness in his eyes hasn't changed.

Again, one word is all I can spare. "Terminal."

He nods. "I see. How much time?"

I know what he's asking, but I don't want to answer. I hold up one finger instead.

"One year?" He guesses. He knows he's being optimistic.

I shake my head.

He exhales and nods again. "One month." It's not a question.

We stare at each other for a few moments while it sinks in.

Just then Katie walks in carrying Miss Higgins in her cage. She's all smiles, oblivious to the fact that we're talking about her. "I think Miss Higgins is ready for a road trip, Keller. She just had a big breakfast, and Stella says she's all out of reptilian car sickness medicine, so you're going to have to take it easy on the drive home, dude. Miss Higgins's delicate digestive system is in your hands. You up to the challenge?"

It was funny, but I can't bring myself to laugh.

My father's just looking at her. His eyes are still soft with sadness, but there's another thing; a look of admiration, as a small smile lights his face. He turns to me and shakes my hand. "Take care of them, Keller."

I nod and swallow hard because it's not a loving sendoff, but this is perhaps the first time I feel like my father has addressed me as an equal, as a man. "I will."

He nods in return. "Call if you need anything."

"We'll be fine, Dad, thank you."

We leave without saying goodbye to my mother.

THURSDAY, DECEMBER 22

KATE

I SAID goodbye to Pete earlier today. He was uncomfortable, and that was hard because I hate being the cause of heavy feelings in anyone, especially someone I care about. He's going back home until spring semester picks up again in mid-January.

He told me he'd see me then.

He won't.

We both know that. He just didn't know what else to say. I told him that I'm going to miss him.

We hugged.

Clayton helped me box up the last of my things that I'd left in my dorm room, and he put them in the back of my car for me because I couldn't lift them myself. This is the first time I've actually been embarrassed by my illness. Turning into a big pussy is humiliating.

I'm trying not to get sad about this chapter of my life ending, but that's hard when I know Clayton's leaving soon, too. He's going home to spend a month with his family and then moving to L.A. to be with Morris. I'll miss him. And I know this is hard for him, helping me, but I didn't have the heart to ask Keller to do it. Keller has enough on his plate, and I don't want to add to the stress by checking another thing off my final to-do list. Everything just feels so final now. We've gone so quickly from firsts to lasts in this relationship that it doesn't seem fair to burden him with this.

SUNDAY, DECEMBER 25

KATE

"Merry Christmas, Kate." Audrey's voice has always sounded like an angel's voice to me, even over the phone. As a little kid, I remember going over to Gus and Audrey's house and looking forward to seeing her because she always talked to me. And she was nice when she did it. My mother didn't talk to Grace or me much and when she did, she usually yelled. Audrey never yelled. I always thought that if I ever met an angel, she would sound just like Audrey.

"Merry Christmas, Audrey. Did you and Gus eat cinnamon rolls on the beach this morning?"

"We did." She's smiling, I hear it. Gus got home yesterday. She's missed him while he's been on tour. He always makes her smile.

Cinnamon rolls on the beach is a Hawthorne Christmas morning tradition. Every Christmas morning, before sunrise, Gracie and I would walk next door in our pajamas to Gus and Audrey's house. Gus was always awake because he was too excited to sleep on Christmas Eve. Gus *loves* Christmas. So, we would all wake Audrey up, and she'd put a pan of cinnamon rolls in the oven. When they were done, she'd take us out on the beach in front of their house and spread out a blanket. We'd all sit down and eat, and we weren't allowed to open presents until the pan was empty. We did it every year. Those are my favorite Christmas memories. I remember that Gracie and I were always sad to go home after that. Our mother wasn't one to rise much before noon on any given day, and Christmas was no exception. She was never awake when we got home, and she never made us cinnamon rolls.

"I missed being there with you," I say. "I did bake cinnamon rolls for Keller and Stella this morning, though, and made them eat the whole pan before we opened presents. Slight rule change: we didn't go outside. Ten degrees is kinda hardcore."

She laughs. "Celebrating inside is probably best for Minnesota. I'm glad you could share the tradition with them."

"Me too." I want to share *everything* with them. Little things like this are important.

"Have you talked to Gus yet today? I can get him. He's down in the theater room watching a movie while I make dinner."

"That's okay; I talked to him earlier for a few minutes. I'll catch up with him later tonight. I wanted to talk with you, Audrey."

"Of course, dear, what is it?" Audrey has always composed herself extremely well. She wears her heart on her sleeve like Gus, but she's better at keeping her shit together. I bet that she's trying so hard to sound simply concerned and not scared right now.

"Remember how we talked about me coming home when it gets to be too much?"

"Of course, yes."

"I think it's almost time." I'm trying to fight back tears, because I really don't want to cry. This is reality, and this is just the next step.

She takes a deep breath. "Okay, sweetie. Okay... Yes..." Her mind must be reeling, because this isn't Audrey. Audrey never pauses or stumbles over thoughts or words. She always knows what to say.

A fist is clenching inside my chest because I'm beginning to fear that maybe she doesn't know what to do with me. Maybe I'm asking too much.

But she rebounds. "Sweetie, I'm going to put you in the guest room so you'll have your own bathroom. Email me your doctors' names and contact information. I want it for both your doctor here, as well as the one you've been seeing in Minnesota. I'll set up a conference call with both of them immediately and make sure I have everything I need here at the house to care for you properly. Make sure you include a complete list of any medications you're currently taking. I know you're allergic to penicillin, but if you have any other allergies I don't know about, include those too. Health insurance information would also be helpful. Do you have any other special requirements? Anything else I can put in your room? If so, let me know. I'll make sure everything's ready when you arrive."

Don't know why I doubted her. That's Audrey. She's fucking Wonder Woman. "Thank you, Audrey. I think I'll be there around New Year's if that's all right?"

"Kate, you're one of my children. You know that, sweetie. I wish with all my heart that you were coming back under different circumstances, but you are always welcome in my home. I would move heaven and Earth for you. I love you."

"I love you, too, very much."

"I'm giving you a big hug through the phone now. Can you feel it?" She's always been a hugger.

I can feel it.

I don't have the heart to tell Keller I talked to Audrey. He knows this has been coming. When it does, it will crush him. I'm not looking forward to that. At all. I would tough it out here if I could, but I can't do that to him or Stella. I know the end is going to be ugly and demanding on everyone. I honestly don't want to ask anyone to be there with me through it, but if you can't ask your mom, who can you ask? I've always thought of Audrey as my mom. Janice may have been my mother, but Audrey is my mom. Even still, this is the first day of my entire life that I wish she wasn't. Someone like her shouldn't have to go through this.

WEDNESDAY, DECEMBER 28

KATE

I'm angry today. I wish I wasn't. *Goddammit, I wish I wasn't.* But I am.

I saw Dr. Connell this morning. He looked at my charts, my recent lab results, and then to me. He didn't have his poker face on. I called him on it, because frankly at this stage in the game, I'd like to see just one fucking person who didn't look at me with pity in his eyes.

Keller's trying so damn hard not to, but even he slips sometimes.

So, yeah. I'm angry today.

Really.

Fucking.

Angry.

I've been yelling at God in my head all morning. *Why do I have to be the one who's dying? Why can't it be someone else? Someone I've never met who lives far away?*

I know that sounds awful, but it's how I feel today. And that's why I can't go back to Keller's yet. Keller and Stella don't deserve to see or feel this kind of anger.

I'm leaving Saturday to go back to San Diego. I bought my ticket yesterday and told Keller last night after Stella went to bed. To say he didn't take it well would be an understatement. He broke apart into a million pieces in front of me. He tried so hard not to. Watching him fall apart like that, knowing that I was the one responsible for creating that kind of devastation in the man I love with all my heart... yeah, I hated myself.

So, right now, I'm sitting in my car in the parking garage of some random business in downtown Minneapolis, and I don't know what to do next.

And when I don't know what to do next, I talk to Gus. I shouldn't call him angry, but I'm out of ideas, and if I don't do something in the next five minutes, I'm going to fucking lose it. So, I call him. He answers on the first ring.

"Bright Side, how's it hangin'?"

"I don't want to die," I say defiantly.

"Bright Side, what?" He's confused.

Of course, he's confused. No one starts a conversation like that.

I repeat, "I don't want to fucking die."

"Oh, shit, Bright Side." I hear him take a deep breath, a primer for the conversation that's about to unfold. "Talk to me. What's going on?"

"I'm fucking dying, Gus. I don't want to die. *That's* what's fucking going on." I hit the steering wheel with my palm. "Goddammit!" I scream. I've only ever freaked out on Gus twice in my life, once when I found my mother hanging from the ceiling, and again when Gracie died. Gus doesn't deserve this, but I know he'll deal with it better than anyone else would.

"Calm down, dude. Where are you?"

"I don't know. I'm sitting in my car in a fucking parking garage in the middle of motherfucking Minneapolis, Minnesota." That was hostile.

"Are you by yourself?"

"Yes," I snap.

"You're not supposed to be driving while you're on your pain meds."

I don't want his fatherly tone. "I know that."

"Are you in danger or hurt?"

I burst out laughing, surprised that I can't even laugh without sounding angry. The question is absurd to me, though. *I'm dying.*

"Bright Side, shut up for a second and talk to me. Do I need to call 911? What the fuck is going on?" He sounds scared.

I shake my head like he can see me. "No, no. I'm just... I'm fucking mad, Gus. That's all." And at a loss for words because my mind is jumbled up into this bitter, resentful ball. I don't know what else to say, so I repeat myself. "I'm really fucking mad."

"Well shit, by all means, there's plenty of room at my table for anger." He gets it. That's why I called him, after all. "I've been dishing out heaping servings of fury for the past month. I feel better knowing I'm not the only one in this whole debacle with some rage issues. So, fire away. Fucking give it to me."

I do. An explosive, steady stream of expletives flows out of me. I'm cursing it all, shouting out questions, pounding the steering wheel, and wiping away hot, angry tears. Occasionally Gus joins in, yelling affirmations. Sometimes he waits for a pause on my part and takes his turn, and sometimes he just steamrolls over the top of me.

He's not yelling *at* me, he's yelling *with* me.

After what could be hours, but is more likely minutes, I stop yelling. In my outburst, I've lost all sense of time and place. It takes a couple of minutes for my heart rate to slow down and my head to clear. Eventually, my tears stop, and I'm able to take normal breaths. My throat feels tight, and my head hurts a little, but I'm calm. On the other end of the line, Gus gets quiet, too. Silence falls between us.

I know he's giving me whatever time I need. He'd sit here all day and never say another word if that's what I needed.

My voice is raspy when I decide to break the silence. "Gus?"

"Yeah, Bright Side." He sounds like himself again. Calm.

"Thanks." I feel like a huge weight has been lifted off of me. And now I need to apologize. "Sorry, dude."

He laughs. "No worries. You feel better?"

I can actually smile now. "Yeah, I really do."

"Good, me too. I think we should've done this weeks ago."

"I think I should've done it months ago." I mean it. It felt so good to let it all out.

"Bright Side, you know I love you all happy and adorable in your little world of sunshine and rainbows, but you're kinda hot when you're angry. I dig aggressive chicks. And that was *crazy* aggressive."

He knows I'm going to say it, but I can't help myself. "Whatever." I even roll my eyes.

"I think I'm gonna rename you Demon Seed."

"What? I show you my dark side, and now I have to be the fucking antichrist? I don't like that. Why can't I just be Angry Bitch?"

He laughs hard, and my heart swells because I haven't heard this laugh out of Gus in a month. And I love this laugh.

"Well, dude, since it seems my therapy session has wrapped up, I'd better get going. I need to get home."

"Sure. Drive slowly and text me when you get there, so I know you made it. And no more driving after this trip."

"Yes, sir. I love you, Gus."

"Love you, too, Angry Bitch." His voice is low and dramatic. He pauses, because he knows I'm not going to hang up to that. "I was just trying it out," he says innocently.

"I don't think I like it."

"Me neither," he says matter-of-factly. "Love you, too, Bright Side."

"That's better." I like being Bright Side. I like it a lot.

FRIDAY, DECEMBER 30

KATE

"Gus is flying home with you tomorrow." Keller has his arms folded over his chest. He's expecting me to fight him on this.

He expected right. "Gus is flying *here?*" Normally I'd be happy to see Gus, but the fact that I'm being babysat is irritating as all hell.

He nods.

"When does he get here?" Now I cross my arms too, in an act of defiance. Even Stella doesn't act like this. What's gotten into me?

"His flight gets in about two hours before yours takes off. He'll meet us in the terminal and take you from there since I can't go beyond security." It's straightforward Keller. He wants to get through this quickly. He knows I've been grouchy all day, and this is only going to make it worse.

I know they're only thinking of me, but I hate being treated like an invalid. "I'm not a fucking child, Keller."

He rubs his temples with the heels of his hands. "Babe, I know that." My pissy attitude is testing his patience. "Do you want something to eat? It's dinner time. Are you hungry? I can make something so you can take your medicine." He's trying to change the subject, trying to help me. But I'm still upset.

I deflect and go right back for more. "Whose idea was this?"

"Ours." It's exasperated. He wants to be done with this.

"So, you and Gus orchestrated the rescue together? I don't get a vote? All I need to do is get on a plane, Keller. I think I can do that on my own." I don't *want* to be mean. It's not me at all, but today I can't help it. Thank God Shelly and Duncan came and picked up Stella this morning so she could spend the day and night with them. I don't want her to ever see me acting this way. No one deserves to see me this way. Especially not Keller. The pain and misery of my illness is transforming me into someone I despise.

"Jesus, Katie, what do you want me to do? You're not sick enough to have an escort home, but you're sick enough to leave here? Abandon me for San Diego and Gus?"

The words open a fresh, gaping wound of guilt, so I lash out. "Stop right there and back the fuck up. This isn't a popularity contest." I'm so pissed that my head is starting to throb. I'm not choosing one person over another because I care for him more. I have to choose someone—*someplace*—to bear this burden. Huge difference.

He turns his back to me, puts his hands on his hips, and then turns around to face me again. "In my heart, I know that. I *know* that. But I'm jealous. There, I said it. I'm fucking jealous. That's as honest as I can be."

My normally sympathetic self is gone. *"That's stupid."*

His irritation is short-lived. He's not joining me in my anger. His face drops, and I can tell that he's retreating into sadness. "I can't argue with that. It is stupid. Stupid and immature. I'm working on it. Your relationship with Gus was built over decades. I only got a few months. That makes me jealous. I just...want more. I want more time with you."

This is heartbreaking, but I'm still angry. My heart desperately wants my mouth to shut up, but I fire back, "And you don't think I want that?"

He shakes his head and steps toward me to put his hands on my shoulders.

I take a step back out of his reach.

"Babe, I know you want that, too. I wasn't trying to imply—"

I cut him off, breathing heavily and squinting through the pain. "Fine. You want me to stay here? You want to watch my lungs battle for oxygen turn into an all-out war? You want to watch this shit really amp up as my liver finishes its descent into hell? You want to watch them pump me so fucking full of narcotics to relieve the pain that I can't think straight or speak like a normal person? You want to watch me waste away to nothing and starve to death when I can't eat or drink anymore? It's going to be fucking glorious—" I'm yelling when he interrupts.

His hands are covering his ears, and there are tears in his eyes. "Stop! Just stop. I don't want to fight with you. I want to help you. I want to take away your pain. I want to love you. *That's all I want.*" He gives me a desperate look, like he wants to reach out for me again. Instead, he reaches for his coat hanging over the back of the loveseat, slips it on, and walks toward the door. "I'm going to take a walk. Try to calm down. It isn't good for you to get this worked up. I'll be back in a few minutes."

I can't watch him walk out the door, but I hear it shut quietly behind him. The lump in my throat cannot be swallowed back, and before I know what's happening, I'm sobbing. It's the kind of sob that makes me feel like I'm drowning. There's no sound coming out, and I'm gasping for air. My shoulders are shaking violently, and my head is pounding. Physically, my body is fighting against the havoc brought on by each new sob. My muscles are strained and tight, amplifying the pain. I've never believed you could die from pain alone. Surely there's nothing so intense that it would actually stop your heart from beating.

Now, I'm rethinking everything.

I need my medicine.

I take two steps toward the bathroom before a sudden jolt of pain takes me down. Lying on the floor, it feels like I've all but lost control of my body and my mind. I hear myself scream through the silence as oxygen forces its way into my lungs for what feels like the first time in minutes. My second or third exhalation of pained shrieking is accompanied by bile, and seconds later, I spew the entire contents of my stomach onto the hardwood floor. That was the first food I've been able to stomach in two days. And now it's gone.

I'm still sobbing, but the anger is gone. Now, the only emotion I can focus on is fear. Pain is dominant, but fear is creeping in like a predator ready to attack, coming in for the kill. I can't turn my back on it, or it will take me down. Is this what my life has been reduced to? Lying on the floor in a pool of my own vomit, unable to stop crying, mentally unable to calm down, physically unable to stand up?

The edges of my vision are fading to black. Things are going dark, and this scares me more than ever. My entire body suddenly goes rigid with pain. One last thought crosses my mind. *Now I understand why my mother ended it all.*

Sometimes, when something terrible is happening, I try my damnedest to concentrate on the most inconsequential, unrelated detail readily available to me. A detail that, in the grand scheme of things, has nothing to do with the situation at hand. At this moment, that detail would be the fact that it's fucking disgusting under the loveseat. I'm lying on the floor trying to figure out what just happened, but the only thing I can focus on is that Keller and Duncan have probably never swept under this loveseat.

The next thought that crosses my mind is how much my jaw hurts. My teeth feel like I've been clenching them through a long night's sleep. My eyelids feel crusty and sticky. And it smells like something died, like rotten food and urine. My memory is foggy. This is what it feels like to wake up from a deep sleep.

I repeat that thought. This is what it feels like to wake up.

I just woke up?

I roll to my back, which takes great effort. I look at the ceiling. What the hell just happened? My limbs feel like they're filled with jelly and my joints ache like I've just run a marathon. I try to sit up, but I'm so dizzy that I decide to lay back down on the floor.

Looking down at my clothes, I realize where the god-awful smells are coming from. I've puked all over myself and the floor. Shit. This is one of my favorite shirts. Well, now it's history. Pretty sure recycled spaghetti sauce doesn't come out any better than first-generation spaghetti sauce. I feel wet between my legs, too. Great. Pissing myself hasn't helped matters, either.

"Keller?" My voice is hoarse, and my throat hurts. It doesn't sound like me.

There's no response.

I'm able to push myself to my hands and knees. I crawl to the bathroom, take my medicine, and get myself into the shower. My strength is gone, but I can't take this smell anymore. The water feels good, so I curl up on the tile floor and let it soak into my clothes and hair.

The jumbled memories in my head begin reassembling them-selves. I remember the fight with Keller, the yelling. I remember him leaving. I remember crying, and the pain, and the shaking, and the vomiting. And then I remember nothing. And it all makes perfect sense.

"Katie?" Keller's voice is muffled and far away, but the panic is undeniable. The bathroom door nearly comes unhinged when it's thrown open. "Katie?" He's crying. It's ninety-five percent fear, five percent sadness. When he sees me it shifts, five percent fear, ninety-five percent sadness. "Babe, what happened?" After turning off the water, he's on his knees leaning into the shower cradling my head up and out of the water pooling around me with one hand while he's searching his jeans pocket for his cell phone. "Shit, where's my phone? I need to call an ambulance."

I shake my head. "No, no ambulance." I feel like shit for treating him like I have all day. Whatever horrible feelings I was harboring earlier, they're gone. I look him in the eyes and don't like what I see.

"Pretty sure I had a panic attack, and then I blacked out. I'm not going back to that damn hospital."

His face falls, and he brushes the hair away. Then he climbs into the shower with me, fully clothed, and pulls me into his lap. He's holding me, rocking back and forth.

My cheek rests against his pounding heart. "Baby?"

"Yeah?"

"I'm sorry. About earlier. I'm not mad at you; I've just been in a shitty mood." I gesture to my wet clothes. "Obviously, I do need someone to take care of me."

He tightens his hold on me. "I'm so sorry, Katie. I never should've walked out on you like that. I should've been here." He's beating himself up.

I raise my chin so I can see his face. "This isn't your fault."

"Oh Katie, I'm so sorry. I hate this. I hate that you're sick, and there's nothing I can do to make it better. I just want to make it all go away."

"You make it better every day. You may not be able to heal my body, but you heal my spirit. I think that's why I've been so upset all day. I don't want to leave you." Tears are pooling in my eyes. "I don't. But I have to. I can't be a burden to you, especially with Stella here. The end is going to be awful. I've accepted that. I know that you'd go through it with me if I asked you to, but I can't do that to you. Audrey's already made arrangements to have a hospice nurse come to her house to keep an eye on me. I want you to remember the good times, not the shitty ones. Not the end."

He sits me up, and we look at one another with tears in our eyes. "I'd do anything for you, Katie. I'd walk through hell and back. All you have to do is ask."

It's the hardest thing I'll ever say. "I think I need you to just let me go." I squeeze my eyes shut against the tears.

His face contorts in pain, and he fights back a sob. "We still have tonight, right?"

I smile and nod. "We do."

Keller peels our wet clothes off and wraps me in a towel. After he returns with clean clothes for both of us, he dresses and helps me into sweatpants and a sweatshirt and proceeds to comb the tangles out of my wet hair.

I close my eyes. "You're pretty good at this."

I can't see his face, but I know he's smiling. "Years of practice. I'm a dad, remember?"

I think of him caring for Stella as a child. I think of him guiding her as a teenager, of him being there for her as an adult. All of it makes me happy. Keller has a purpose, a reason to keep going after I leave. That gives me some peace. I need to remind him what a great dad he is. "It's one of my favorite things about you."

He raises an eyebrow at my comment. "Really?"

I nod. "Definitely." I'm exhausted, and my body aches all over from my episode earlier. "Can we finish this conversation in bed?"

Taking my hand, he helps me stand. "There's something we need to do first," he says, and walks me through the door to Grounds. It's closed up for the night, so it's dim and quiet. He stops when we're standing in front of the window. He squeezes my hand. "Let's watch the sunset."

I smile and hold his hand with both of mine as I look out toward the horizon. My grip intensifies as the colors shift into brilliant pinks and blues, and it's only as darkness descends that I realize how hard I'm squeezing.

The look in his eyes is love, plain and simple. "I love how passionate you are about the important things in life. Like sunsets." He smiles. "And people."

I stand on my tiptoes and kiss him on the chin. "Sunsets and people, that's what it's all about. Especially people. Extra passionate if his name's Keller Banks."

He squats and scoops me up into his arms. Before I know it, we're standing next to his bed. He pulls back the covers, props up the pillows, and helps me into bed before sliding in beside me. I rest my head back against the wall and look at him. I want to remember him exactly like this.

"I wish I knew you better, Keller." I do.

He slides his arm behind me and wraps his arms around me, pulling me to him. Resting my cheek against his bare chest, I hear his heart beating, slow and steady. He kisses the top of my head. "Katie, you know me better than anyone else. You may not know all the trivial stuff, but you know *me*. The real me, deep down. You know how I think, what I fear, how I love. No one's ever seen me the way you do. Not even Lily."

I smile. "Can we play a game?"

He laughs. "You wanna play a game?"

"Yeah. What's your favorite color?" I prompt. "I want to know *some* of the trivial stuff."

"Okay. Umm..."

"It's not a hard question, baby," I tease.

He laughs again. "I know. I'm going to say black. What about you?"

I don't hesitate. "Orange. Sunset-over-the-Pacific orange. Your turn."

"Mmm... Okay. What's your favorite food? And you can't say coffee."

"Chocolate ... or tacos."

"Which is it? Only one answer. It's not a hard question, babe." He's having fun with this.

"Fine. Veggie tacos. You?"

"My Nana's homemade lasagna."

"Your mom's mom or your dad's mom?"

"My mother's mother. They were nothing alike. Stella's named after her." He smiles. "She visited every year at Christmas and always made lasagna. She died when I was ten."

"I'm sorry."

"Yeah, she was fun. I miss her. What's your favorite animal?"

"Umm, cats. I always wanted a Siamese. I wanted to name him Mr. Miyagi."

"Mr. Miyagi?"

"Yeah, you know, the old dude in the original *Karate Kid* movie."

He shakes his head. He doesn't understand.

"You've never seen the original *Karate Kid* movie?" I'm shocked. Gracie and I were practically raised on my mother's old collection of '80s movies and a VCR. We could recite *Pretty in Pink* word for word.

"No." It doesn't register. He's not kidding.

"Well, you need to. You're clearly lacking in '80s culture."

He smiles. "Clearly."

"Now that that's cleared up, what's your favorite animal?"

"I feel like I should say turtles, given Stella's preoccupation." I laugh, and he continues. "But probably dolphins. I've always wanted to swim with one."

"Did you play sports in high school?"

"Nah, I was a nerd. I ran or rode my bike a lot just to get out of the house, but that was the extent of it, living in the city like we did. You surfed, though. Anything else?"

"No, music-based schools don't put much emphasis on athletics. Just surfing. And dancing."

It's Keller's turn. "Okay, next question: Young Elvis or old Elvis?"

"That's actually a really good question. Old Elvis."

"Why?" he challenges.

"Because young Elvis was handsome, but old Elvis could sing his ass off. 'Suspicious Minds' was the best song he ever recorded. You haven't lived until you've heard a live recording of it. He killed it. What about you? Young or old?"

"I like old Elvis, but mostly because of the jumpsuits."

"Old Elvis did have great stage-wear," I agree. "Okay. Next: if you could travel anywhere in the world, where would you go?"

"Hmm. I'd like to take Stella to see the pyramids in Egypt someday. That's something I always wanted to see as a kid. They seemed so magical. They still do. So, yeah, Egypt. What about you?"

"I saw a documentary about Ha Long Bay in Vietnam when I was in seventh grade and ever since then, it's been the one place I always thought would be remarkable to see in person. Like pictures somehow didn't do it justice. I needed to see it with my own eyes to believe a place so perfect could actually exist."

He's quiet for a few moments, stroking my hair. It feels good, but the silence has me curious. I roll off his chest onto the pillow next to him. We're lying nose to nose. He looks deep in thought. "What is it?"

He hesitates. "Can we just set aside reality and live in this moment for a few more questions? I don't want to make you sad; I just want to pretend we'll both live forever. That anything's possible."

I smile. "You mean I get to live in a fairy tale world of sunshine and rainbows for a little bit?"

He relaxes and smiles, too. "And unicorns."

"Of course. Unicorns. I always forget."

"In my fairy tale, another year and a half has passed. I'm graduating with my English degree. And I ask you to marry me. What would you say?"

I don't hesitate. "Would you get down on one knee?"

"Absolutely."

My heart is fluttering in my chest as if the question is real. "I would say yes. *Hell yes.*"

His smile grows, and he kisses me on the nose. "You don't know how happy that makes me."

It's my turn. I'm anxious about this one. "Would we have kids? A brother or sister for Stella?"

"We'd have one of each. A boy and a girl. And they'd look just like you."

"That's not fair. I think they should have your hair and eyes. And height. Oh, and your lips, too." I kiss them.

He kisses me back and in between kisses, he asks softly, "You like my lips?"

I moan my approval as I deepen the kiss. "Mmm hmm."

After a minute, I have to break the kiss because I'm getting tired and out of breath. Sex is out of the question at this point. Hell, kissing seems to be too much.

Keller understands and holds my gaze. "Your children would be beautiful, and talented, and smart. But I would teach them to drive."

The sweet conversation and his teasing bring a smile to my face again. "And I would let you. You're an excellent driving instructor. And even though our family would be perfect, I wouldn't let you put those stupid stick figure family stickers on the back window of our car."

He laughs. "Agreed. No stick figure family stickers."

My heart feels lighter. He's given me a wonderful gift. "I love you, baby."

"Mmm. Again."

"I love you, baby."

"I love you, too, babe. Always."

SATURDAY, DECEMBER 31

KATE

Dr. Connell gave me a handicapped placard for my car. I've never used it before today. It's lying on the dashboard because Keller and I both silently agreed not to display it until the last minute. After Keller finds a parking spot close to the terminal, he waits until I open the passenger door to get out before he slips it on the rearview mirror.

I open the door and help Stella out of her child safety seat while Keller gets my rolling suitcase out of the back hatch. He's shipping my violin and the rest of my belongings—which don't amount to much—to Audrey's house on Monday.

I'm looking at the terminal and even though it's fairly close, I wonder how in the hell I'm going to walk all that way. Just looking at it makes me feel winded. He sees the apprehension in my face and turns around, searching the lot for something. "Katie, why don't you get back in the car and I'll see if I can find a wheelchair. I'm sure they have one that we can borrow to get you inside." He looks sad to have to say it; like he's afraid he'll hurt my feelings.

I know I shouldn't hesitate. That I should just let him get the damn wheelchair. But the thought of it seems impossible to accept. I stand in quiet protest. He knows this is hard for me.

He walks over and kneels down in front of Stella. "Hey, big girl, you think you can help me out?"

She nods enthusiastically.

He takes her hand and walks her to my suitcase. "You think you can pull this inside the airport?"

She nods again and takes the handle confidently. She tips it, and the handle almost hits the ground before she recovers and finds the right balance. She looks up and beams at him. "Got it. Ready, Daddy?"

He smiles back. "Almost." Keller turns his back to me and squats to the ground. "Climb on, babe."

I can't help but laugh. "Keller, you're not going to carry me."

He shrugs. "It's not carrying; it's a piggyback ride. There's a difference. Ask Stella."

Stella's giggling. She thinks this is funny.

"What's the difference, Stella?"

The giggling stops, but she's still smiling. "Carrying is for when you're too sleepy to walk. Piggyback rides are for fun."

He smiles. "Well said, Stella. See? Come on, babe."

How can I argue with that kind of logic?

Even with Stella pulling the suitcase and Keller carrying me, we make good time through check-in and arrive at security fifteen minutes early. We sit down on a bench and Keller texts Gus our location.

Far too quickly, Gus is standing in front of me. I love seeing Gus, but the gravity of the situation is hitting me. This is another one of those final steps. I'm not dealing with final steps very well.

"Hey, Bright Side." He's squatting in front of me, kissing me on the forehead.

"Hey, Gus." I'm trying to be strong, but an overpowering sadness is rising within me.

Gus shakes Keller's hand, and Stella crawls up into Gus's lap. "Hi, Gus."

"Well hello, Miss Stella."

She's blinking her big, blue eyes at him. "Is Kate going to live with you and your mommy?"

He swallows and nods. This is hard for him, too. "She is."

"Daddy says she's sick."

Gus can only nod.

"Will you take good care of her?"

He swallows again and locks eyes with Keller. "I promise. We'll take good care of her."

Keller nods. It's thank you.

Gus nods. It's you're welcome.

Gus stands, lifting Stella into his arms. "Let's go get something to drink, Stella. I'm thirsty, what about you?" They walk down the corridor towards a newspaper stand and snack shop.

I'm looking at Keller now, and I don't know what to say. I'm scared and I'm sad, but I know he feels the same way. I want to be strong for him, but the lump in my throat is making it so difficult.

He takes my hand in his, and reaches his other hand into the pocket of his coat and pulls out a sharpie. He uncaps the marker and writes on the palm of my left hand. *You are brave.*

The tears spill over one by one as I mouth, "Thank you."

He takes my face gently in both of his hands. There are tears in his eyes, too. "No, Katie, thank you. For everything. You are the bravest person I have ever known."

After what seems like merely a moment, Gus and Stella are approaching again. Stella has a bottle of juice and Gus is empty-handed. He wasn't thirsty; he was just giving us a minute alone.

Gus glances at his watch. "We'd probably better get going, Bright Side. Security lines are long."

I nod. I look down to see Stella tugging on my coat. "Kate." She's raising her arms up over her head.

I wish I could lift her, but I don't have the strength. Instead, I kneel down and hug her. She's so small and dainty. Her hair smells like lavender today. "Be good for your daddy, Stella."

She's clinging to me. "I will. Will you call us or talk to us on the computer?"

I squeeze tighter. "I will. Every day. I love you."

She pulls back and kisses me on the lips. "I love you, too."

The tears are ready to pour out again when I turn to Keller. He pulls me to his chest and slides his arms under my unzipped coat. His hands slide under my T-shirt at my lower back. He rubs circles slowly over my bare skin. Instantly, I feel a little calmer. I close my eyes and tuck my head into his neck. His lips are at my ear, tickling it beneath my hair. "Call me when you land."

"I will."

He kisses my ear once and whispers, "I love you more than you could possibly imagine."

I pull back and kiss him once. His lips are soft and welcoming. He cups his hand at the nape of my neck and pulls me back in for two more before resting his forehead against mine. "My imagination is endless," I say. There are tears in both our eyes now. His shirt is clenched in both of my hands. God, I don't want to let go.

"Good. So is my love." He smiles, and it's the happiest, saddest smile I've ever seen. You wouldn't think that two distinct emotions could live inside one smile, but they can. He's present. This moment is all that matters.

"Mine too. I love you, baby."

His eyes are closed. "One more time," he whispers.

"I love you, baby," I whisper back.

Stella is standing next to Gus again, tugging on the front of his T-shirt. "Gus you need to give Kate a piggyback ride. Not 'cause she's sleepy. Just for fun."

Gus ruffles Stella's hair. "Well, good thing I'm all about fun, kiddo." He turns and squats. "All aboard, Bright Side."

I climb on and Keller hands Gus my suitcase. "Thanks, man."

Gus waves as he takes a few steps backward down the corridor toward security. "Anytime, dude. Anytime."

When Gus turns, my back is to Keller and Stella, so I turn my head and watch them fade away. The three of us wave at each other until Gus turns the corner, and they're gone.

FRIDAY, JANUARY 13

KATE

I SKYPE with Keller and Stella every morning and every night. And because classes don't start up again for another week for him, we also talk several times on the phone throughout the day when he isn't at work and when I'm not sleeping.

I'm sleeping a lot now. The nurse Audrey hired, Tammy, says that her job is to keep me comfortable. And for me, comfort takes the form of oxycodone. Since I'm fond of not being in excruciating pain, it works out. Being hooked up to oxygen has helped too. Breathing was becoming a real struggle, now it's a breeze. Turns out that my body loves an adequate amount of oxygen. This nasal cannula is my new favorite thing.

Gus was supposed to go back out on the road last week, Europe. He refused to go. Their tour manager is pissed. Gus has started calling him Fucking Hitler. The rest of the band is standing behind Gus, so there's not much that can be done except reschedule the shows. I feel guilty that he's postponing his life, but I'm happy that he's here with me.

He spends every minute of every day and every night in this room with me. He's constant, comforting company. We listen to music, or play cards (yes, I cheat—he lets me), or just talk (there's a lot of reminiscing). And almost every day, Franco, Robbie, or Jamie stops by to visit, too. Sometimes they stay for a few minutes; sometimes they stay for an hour. It just depends on how long I can stay awake.

Tammy even lets Gus take me outside onto the deck for some fresh air once a day. He carries me and rolls the carts of all of my new accessories (IV meds and oxygen) out with us. Walking is impossible for me now. Going to the bathroom is even a thing of the past, which I'm really unhappy about. Catheters suck. And pee bags are just gross.

Audrey got home from work about an hour ago. She's been working from home, but every other day she goes into her office for an hour or two. She has a business to run on top of my mess. I don't know how she does it.

She's knocking on the door now with a coffee cup in hand, just like she does every day at this time. "Hi, sweetie. How're you doing?"

I smile, because I can't do anything else when I look at Audrey these days. I always thought she was an angel, and there's no doubt about it now. "Fabulous."

She returns the smile and kisses me on the forehead. "Glad to hear it," she says, before handing me a mug of vegetable broth. "Dinner is served." She looks at Gus. "Gus, honey, I made you something to eat, too. It's in the kitchen."

Gus pats the side of the bed. "I'll be right back." He doesn't like to eat in front of me since I can't really eat anymore, so he eats in the kitchen by himself. I swear he inhales his food, because he's gone five minutes, tops.

"Take your time, Gus. I need to talk to Kate for a few minutes." Her tone is gentle but firm.

He nods and looks at me, raising his eyebrows. "Dude, I think you're in trouble."

I laugh. The past few weeks have been easy between us again. Gus looks exhausted, and I know he's not sleeping much, but his sense of humor is back. I love that. He's let go of some of the stress.

And as for me, I feel like a calm stillness has settled over me. I'm as comfortable as I can be, and I feel content. Peaceful, even, in a way I never have before. Maybe it's the Xanax that Tammy's added to my IV cocktail. I insisted that I didn't need it (I haven't had any issues with anxiety since the panic attack in Grant last month), and although she acknowledged my feelings, she said it might make me more comfortable. I'm all about comfort these days, so I gave it a try. Drugs or not, I'm good. I'm good.

Audrey sits on the edge of my bed next to me and rubs my forearm just like she did when I was small, and she was trying to soothe me. She smiles. "You're looking better this afternoon. You have some color in your cheeks."

"I feel good today, Audrey. I'm glad it shows. How are *you* doing?"

"I'm well, sweetheart." She kisses me on the forehead again. "Don't you worry about me."

But I do. I worry about all of them. This must be draining them. "What's up? Am I in trouble?"

She laughs. "No. There are a few things I need to discuss with you. I don't think we can put them off any longer. I'm sorry to have to be the one to bring all of this up, but it's my job as a mother to make sure you're taken care of."

"Thank you. So, what do we need to talk about?"

She sets the papers she's holding on the nightstand. "You drink your broth. I'll talk."

"Okay." I do as she says, even though I'm getting really tired of vegetable broth. It's the only thing I can stomach these days.

"You already gave me power of attorney, so I'll make sure all of your financial affairs are attended to. The deductible on your health insurance is very low. Last year's deductible was satisfied, and you paid everything in full. This year's bills will be minimal; after your deductible is met, everything's paid one hundred percent. You have enough in your savings to cover it. What other bills do you have?"

I don't want to share this with Audrey, because I know she's going to be hurt that I didn't come to her months ago with it, but it's my responsibility. "Just Gracie's burial costs. I'm on a monthly payment plan. The balance is around two thousand dollars. I don't know if I'll have enough money left after the medical bills to pay for it."

She blinks as if she's confused. "I thought you said Grace's funeral was paid for. That you had some money leftover from the sale of Janice's home?"

I can't look at her. "I lied."

"Oh Kate, why didn't you say something? I would have been more than happy to cover that."

I'm still looking at the bedspread instead of her. "That's why I couldn't tell you. Gracie was my responsibility. She was my sister. It was my job."

She shakes her head. "Well, don't you worry about that. It will be taken care of." It's final. "What else?"

"Other than my cell phone, nothing. My car insurance is paid through April."

"Okay. That brings us to the next item on my list. Your will." She holds my gaze and tears are filling her eyes. "I'm sorry, Kate. This is hard."

I pat her leg. "It's okay, Audrey. I don't know that a will is necessary, though. I don't really have anything. I gave my car to Keller, though he's still fighting me on it. And I want Gus to have my violin, my laptop, and the music I've written. That about covers it."

She clears her throat. "Not exactly. There's something you don't know about."

I prop myself up in bed, because she has on her concerned, protective mama bear face. "I spoke to your father last month."

"You what?" I intend for it to come out much louder than it does, but I feel like the wind's been knocked out of me.

"Years ago I got his name, address, and phone number from Janice in case I ever needed to contact him on your or Grace's behalf. I've called him only three times: once when Janice died, once when Grace died, and last month when I learned of your illness."

I hear the words coming out of my mouth, but it feels like someone else's voice. "What did he say?"

She tilts her head, and her eyes soften. I bet she's trying to figure out how to tell me he's a heartless bastard. "With Janice, he seemed indifferent. The news was received with silence and a thank you for letting him know. With Grace, he seemed sad. I gave him the funeral details. He sent flowers."

"I never saw them. There wasn't a card with his name on it." I'm shocked.

She shakes her head, apologizing. "He sent them anonymously. It was a large bouquet of carnations."

I laugh humorlessly. "That's fitting, Gracie hated carnations. She called them smelly, old lady flowers. She liked tulips. Yellow tulips."

Audrey's lips tip up into a smile. "I know."

I'm nervous now. The next phone call was about me. "What did he say about me?"

"Kate, you are such a wonderful person. Your father's approval or involvement has never mattered—"

"Just tell me, Audrey."

She sighs. "He said the news was regretful. He said he was sorry he'd never known you. I offered to set up a meeting, to fly him over from England. He refused. I'm sorry, honey."

I don't remember my father, so I've never really missed him. Until now. Now, I feel cheated. I feel pissed off that he chose another family over us. I clench my teeth and mutter, "He's a bastard, isn't he, Audrey?"

"I think that's a good name for him, yes. In fact, I could think of a few others I prefer, but bastard will do." Audrey rarely curses. She's mad.

I'd laugh if I wasn't fuming.

She reaches for an envelope on the nightstand. "He did send you this. I opened it already. I hope you don't mind. I wanted to make sure it wasn't anything that would upset you."

I take the envelope, and my hands are shaking. I've gone from angry to scared in a split second. I part the top of the already opened envelope and peer inside. There's no letter, only a small piece of paper. I pinch it between my thumb and forefinger and slide it out slowly. "A check?"

Audrey nods.

I look at the amount. "Audrey, this is *fifty thousand dollars*." I've never seen this many zeroes.

Audrey nods again.

I toss it aside on the nightstand. "Fuck him, Audrey." I'm pissed again. I try not to use that word in front of Audrey because I know she doesn't like it, but I can't restrain myself. "Fuck him and his money. Send it back. Tell him I don't want it."

She looks stressed but resigned. "Normally, Kate, I would agree with you. I would commend your dignity and pride and tell him to stuff it. But, I think you should accept it."

Maybe she's right. "You take it. I'll sign it over to you. It will help repay you for all you've done for me over the years." This isn't my anger talking. I sincerely mean it, and she knows it.

"Oh Kate, I couldn't accept something like that. Gus and I have never lacked financially. We've both been very fortunate. Maybe you know someone else who might be able to use the money?"

It doesn't take me long to come to a decision. I endorse the check and give Audrey specific instructions, and then I write a short thank-you note to my father.

*T*HOMAS,

Thank you for Grace. I wish you could have known her. She was the sweetest, most innocent human being.

Though your money reeks of guilt, and it's against my better judgment to accept it, know that it will be put to good use.

Lastly, I hope you're good to your wife and children and that you tell them you love them every day. Kids need that. Audrey Hawthorne taught me about the love of a parent to her child. She's a wonderful woman. I've never felt unloved. I hope that puts your mind at ease.

Kate

AFTER THE NOTE AND AFTER AUDREY LEAVES THE ROOM, I decide to talk to God, which makes me feel a little guilty because I've been avoiding him for a long time now. *Hey, Big Man. I meant what I wrote to Thomas. I don't know if it's my place to ask you for this, but whatever. Here goes. Please forgive him. I really do hope that he loves his wife and kids and that they love him. Thank you for blessing me with so many people to love.*

SUNDAY, JANUARY 15

KATE

KELLER'S HAD flowers delivered to me every four or five days since I've been away from him here at Audrey's. Gus always puts them on the nightstand next to my bed so I can look at them and smell them up close. I've always said I don't do hearts and flowers. I've since changed my stance. I'm *so* pro hearts and flowers now.

Yesterday I received a box in the mail from Keller. It was labeled "Katie's Dream Vacation" and inside he had packed a travel DVD about Ha Long Bay, two pairs of cheap sunglasses, two small paper drink umbrellas, and a handwritten note of instructions. Following those instructions, Gus and I wore the sunglasses and watched the DVD. Gus sat beside me on my bed drinking a glass of Jack and Coke while I enjoyed my cup of vegetable broth while pretending that it was a pina colada. We garnished our cocktails with the small paper umbrellas. I don't think I've ever seen anything quite as funny as Gus drinking something with a tiny cocktail umbrella in it. It was perfect. The thought that Keller put into this gift was perfect.

Keller, Stella, and I Skyped tonight like we do every night. He showed me the airline tickets he bought. They cost him a lot of money that I know he doesn't have. He lost the majority of his scholarship, and he has Stella full-time now, so the bills are piling up. He wanted to be here this weekend, but I know I'll only see him one more time, and I feel like I don't want it to happen too soon, or it will be over, and then I won't have anything to look forward to. It will be one more "last time" for me. I want to put off this "last time" as long as I can. So, he and Stella are coming to see me Friday evening instead. They're staying until Sunday afternoon. I can't wait to see them, smell them, touch them. It's been two weeks. Two weeks feels like an eternity. Distance sucks. I miss them. I miss *him*.

MONDAY, JANUARY 16

KATE

HEY, God, it's me, Kate. I feel like we never really talked about what's going on except for my angry rant last month, but I want you to know that I'm not mad, you know, about the whole cancer cluster-fuck. It doesn't change the way I look at my life. I had a good one. I wouldn't have changed a thing. Gracie, Gus, Audrey, Keller, my friends, and my music were a gift from—well, you know, you. I get that, so thank you. Each and every one was a blessing. Speaking of which, I'm also here to ask for a solid. Please keep an eye on everyone I love when I'm gone, especially Keller and Gus. As human beings go, they're my favorites and yes, I'm requesting preferential treatment. Audrey, too. Take that as you will. Thanks in advance. And one more thing. I know I may be overstepping my bounds here, but I figure you're used to that with me by now. Don't think I'm a pussy, but when my time comes, can you take me painlessly, like maybe in my sleep or something? I'm kind of over the whole agony thing, to be honest with you. Plus, I know Gus and Audrey will most likely be with me when it happens, and I'd rather not leave them with a traumatic last impression. Oh, and can you let Gracie know I'm coming? You know, if she doesn't already know. Tell her we'll sing and dance and read stories and eat Twix bars *and watch sunsets. This is probably the last you'll hear from me until I'm standing on your doorstep banging on the door like some obnoxious long-lost relative. I know you're secretly looking forward to hanging out with me. Heaven will be a lot less quiet and a lot more fun once I get there. You have been warned. Don't worry, you'll love it. Okay. Good night.*

TUESDAY, JANUARY 17

KELLER

My cell wakes me. It's ringing in my hand. It's 1:10 am. Gus is calling. I sleep holding the phone for this very reason.

But suddenly I feel paralyzed with fear and grief. I don't want this call. It's too soon. I talked to her just hours ago. Hours ago she told me she loved me and that she would talk to me in the morning. My phone shouldn't be ringing. It's not morning yet.

The ringing dies out.

The ringing starts back up.

The message finally travels from my brain to my fingers, and I answer, but no words come out. I need him to talk.

I hear his breath hitch, and my heart drops into my stomach.

I find my words. "Please don't tell me she's gone."

"No." He's not even trying to contain himself. He's crying openly. "She had a stroke. She can't talk. She can't open her eyes. She can't move the right side of her body. You need to get your ass on a plane and get down here, pronto."

Oh my God.

"We'll be on the first flight."

The earliest flight I can find departs at 6:50 am. With the time change, we arrive in San Diego around 7:30. By the time we get a cab and find the house, it's 8:15.

Gus told us the front door would be unlocked, so Stella and I let ourselves in. The door is heavy and closes with a loud thud behind us. We walk through the foyer and stop in the living room. The house is large and I'm not sure which way I should turn until a tall, blonde, middle-aged woman walks into the room. Her resemblance to Gus is undeniable.

Her eyes are red and swollen. "You must be Keller and Stella. I'm Audrey." Her voice is weary but welcoming.

I offer my hand and feel anxious and awkward because all I want to do is run to Katie. "Hi, Audrey. I'm Keller Banks. This is my daughter, Stella. Thank you so much for what you're doing for Katie."

She grasps my hand in both of hers and squeezes. It's comfort. "Welcome. Let's get you in to see Kate."

I'm not prepared for what I'm about to see. Katie and I communicate through Skype every day. She's been getting thinner and paler, I knew that. I saw her on my computer screen. Seeing her on my laptop and seeing her in person are two entirely different things. She looks emaciated. Her cheekbones are prominent, and her temples are sunken in. Her skin is pale, and there's a yellowish tinge to it. Her tiny hands are splayed over her stomach on top of the bedspread. Her veins are bold and blue under her transparent, papery skin. I take her left hand gently in mine. She feels cool like she always does. I brush my thumb across the back of her hand, then lean down to kiss her on the lips. "Hi, babe. Stella and I came to see you early. Gus said you had a rough night."

There's the slightest hint of movement. Her arm twitches, and then her fingers wrap around mine and squeeze. It's so weak, but it makes my heart melt. I treasure it.

Audrey, Gus, Stella, and I spend the rest of the day gathered around Katie. We take turns talking to her. You would think that talking to someone virtually unresponsive would be difficult, but with Katie, it's not. We know she's listening.

WEDNESDAY, JANUARY 18

KELLER

I'D LIKE to think she's still listening, but I don't know if that's true anymore.

The nurse says that Katie's slipped into a coma. Her body is shutting down. Her organs are failing. She doesn't squeeze my hand anymore when I hold it.

Gathered around her bedside, Audrey and I tell her she can go whenever she's ready. That Grace is waiting for her. That we love her.

Gus says nothing.

THURSDAY, JANUARY 19

KELLER

It's three in the morning. Stella is asleep on the sofa in the living room, and Audrey gently shoos me and Gus out of Katie's room, telling us to get some fresh air while she checks Katie's catheter, which has caused an infection. This is an hourly ritual to keep Katie comfortable. Usually, Gus and I refuse to leave, but I think we've both hit a wall. We need to catch our breath.

The view of the ocean from their deck is unbelievable. The water looks like it goes on forever. What with everything I've been through this past month, I'm beginning to fear that my reality is warped forever. The view is beautiful, but it's a different beauty than if I would've seen it two or three months ago. Two or three months ago, it would have been alive and vibrant, like Katie. My world is slipping back to black, white, and gray. That scares me.

Gus is leaning with his elbows on the railing, smoking a cigarette. His eyes are closed, and his hair is like a yellow bird's nest. I know he's just going through the motions now. He hasn't really slept in weeks. He's dragging. He looks defeated. He doesn't talk much unless it's to Katie or Stella, and Katie hasn't talked back in two days.

"What's your first memory of Katie?"

He doesn't open his eyes or even look at me when he answers, "I've been thinking about that a lot this past week, growing up with Bright Side and Gracie. Almost every memory I have from my childhood involves the two of them. I don't have a first memory because they were always there. I don't remember a time when they weren't. I remember other firsts. The first time Bright Side got stung by a jellyfish, she was four. The first time I heard her play the violin, she was eight. The first time she cussed me out, she was eleven. The first time I realized how beautiful she was, she was sixteen. The bikini was white, by the way."

Hearing these things about her is bittersweet, but I want to hear more. "Is the twenty-year-old Katie much different than the ten-year-old Katie? She seems like an old soul. Like she was born with this amazing wisdom and grace, straight out of the womb."

He laughs but finishes his cigarette and lights another before he speaks. "Bright Side was always different from other kids. Smarter, nicer, funnier," he says. He finally looks at me and smiles, "and mouthier."

"Did her mouth ever get her in trouble?" Talking about her is relaxing me.

He shakes his head. "Does a bear shit in the woods? What do you think? That's the goddamn thing, though; people always back down from her when she stands her ground. And they love and respect her for it, because there's always truth behind it. That tiny little woman can make grown men cower, believe me, I've seen it. Hell, I've cowered." He laughs.

I laugh with him. "So have I."

I'm leaning against the railing now a few feet from him. We're both watching the waves crash against the shore as silence settles between us. He deposits cigarette number two into the ashtray and lights up number three.

"Keller, I'm going to ask you something, and I want you to be honest with me. No bullshit, dude."

He glances at me out of the corner of his eye, and I nod.

"You love her, right? I mean like, you love her with all your heart and soul?"

I nod. "I do. Heart and soul."

He contemplates my answer a second and looks back out at the waves. "Good, 'cause that girl loves you with her entire fucking being. I'd kick your ass if you didn't feel the same." No joke, he means it.

I should keep my mouth shut, because I feel like under any other circumstances what I'm about to say would be inappropriate, but the guy needs to get this out. "You love her, too." It's not a question.

He's focused on waves in the far distance. He takes another drag on his cigarette. "Of course. She's my best friend. Who wouldn't love Bright Side?"

I'm looking at the same waves, because I can't look at him when I press this, "That's not what I'm asking. Heart and soul, you're in love with her?"

His shoulders slump. "You don't want to hear the answer to that one, dude."

"Probably not, but I see the way you look at her. This whole thing is tearing you up on a different level. I feel like I'm looking in a mirror when I look at you."

He huffs and runs his hands through his hair, pulling it back into a ponytail. He wants to let this out, but he's holding back for my sake.

"Gus, you need to talk to someone. Granted I may not be the ideal person, but anything you say right now stays between us."

He finally looks me in the eye. He holds me in a stare before he blinks several times and sighs. "Oh fuck it. Yes, I'm in love with her. I honestly can't remember a time that I wasn't."

It's what I've suspected all along. "Did you ever tell her? I mean, really tell her?"

He turns his back to the water and sits on the railing facing the house. "No."

"Why not?" It's three in the morning. I'm sitting here discussing another man's love for my girlfriend and damn if I don't feel sorry for him. I need some goddamn sleep.

"Because I thought that she always deserved better. I knew she'd find someone someday as amazing as she was. That's all I ever wanted for her." It's one of the sincerest things I've ever heard.

I walk to the other end of the deck. I can't look at him when I say what needs to be said. "I know you slept with her. The night before she came to Grant."

I'm waiting for him to challenge me, to ask how I know something so private. But he doesn't. "Best fucking night of my entire life. Sorry, I know that's really messed up to tell you, but it was."

I turn to face him, and I nod. There's this odd camaraderie thing going on that can only be the result of sleep deprivation and imminent death.

He shakes his head like he's second-guessing opening his mouth again, but he does it anyway. "Keller, dude, you don't have to answer this, but do you ever worry that you'll never be the same when she's gone? Like the rest of your life is just going to be this endless black hole devoid of happiness and love?"

I nod. "I don't like to think about it, but I can't help it sometimes. I've known her such a short time, but she's changed me entirely. I feel like I owe it to her not to waste that, you know? But yeah, it's going to be tough. Every fucking day, man."

He walks over and slaps me on the back. His eyes look tired again. "Let's get back inside. Thanks for listening. We never had this conversation, agreed?"

I nod. "Agreed."

"And thanks for not punching me in the face or ripping my balls off. I'm not sure I could've done the same if I was in your shoes. You're a good dude, Keller. No wonder Bright Side loves you so much."

I have to look him in the eye so he believes what I'm about to tell him. "You're not so bad yourself. She loves you, too, Gus."

He nods and opens the sliding glass door. "I don't like to keep Bright Side waiting. Never have. Let's go."

FRIDAY, JANUARY 20

KELLER

KATIE DIED TODAY.

She went quietly, peacefully. No dramatic exit, which seemed appropriate since she hated to draw attention to herself. She inhaled a breath, then exhaled. That was it. The next breath never came.

It was 1:37 pm. It was sunny outside. The window next to her bed was cracked open so she could smell the salt in the air off the water and feel the breeze on her face.

Gus was sitting on the left side of her bed holding her hand in both of his. I was sitting on her right side holding her other hand. Audrey was sitting in a chair at the foot of the bed with Stella on her lap. She was surrounded by those who loved her most.

When her heart monitor flatlined and beeped, the hospice nurse came in calmly and checked for a pulse. There wasn't one. She nodded her apologies, her sympathies, and then she left us alone.

For Gus, tears came immediately. He squeezed her hand one last time, kissed her on the forehead, told her goodbye and that he loved her, and then he left. We heard the door slam a moment later, and then the sound of his truck's tires squeal on the street as he sped off.

I continued to stroke her hair for a few more minutes, not

wanting to give her up. When Stella climbed down off Audrey's lap and crawled up into Gus's vacated spot and said goodbye to Katie, I couldn't hold back the tears anymore. I slid off the bed and took her face in my hands, closed my eyes, kissed her lips softly one last time, and whispered in her ear, "Thank you for trusting me. Thank you for letting me love you."

I reached across Katie and pulled Stella into my arms, wondering if I was a horrible father for letting her be here to witness this. Stella clung to me. She was calm despite the sadness hanging in the air. I walked to the chair where Audrey sat and put a hand on her shoulder. She covered it with one of hers and squeezed. The squeeze was thank you, and devastation, and solace all at once.

Stella and I walked down to the beach and built a giant sandcastle. It took us hours. We were covered head to toe in sand, and it was dark when we decided it was finished.

Katie would've loved it.

SUNDAY, JANUARY 22

KELLER

THE FUNERAL IS TODAY. It starts in a few minutes. I've been at the church with Audrey the past hour making all the last-minute preparations. Stella's with my father, Dunc, and Shel. They all flew in last night.

The chapel is full as I walk in. It's strange being so intimate with someone, yet looking around, there are very few faces I recognize. I take a seat next to Dunc and Stella climbs from his lap to mine. "Hi, Daddy."

"Hi, baby girl. Have you been good for Uncle Dunc this morning?"

She nods. "We walked on the beach. I found two shells." She reaches into the pocket of her skirt and pulls out two sand dollars. "I brought them for Kate. She likes shells, right, Daddy?"

I nod. "She likes shells. That was very nice, Stella." I kiss her on top of her curly head and breathe in the sweetness that is my little girl.

I zone out for most of the service. I can't tell you if it was long or short. I just couldn't focus. My mind races over images and memories and yet feels completely blank at the same time. It's not until the minister turns the microphone over to Audrey that I snap out of it.

She dabs her eyes with a tissue and sniffs before clearing her throat. "I'm Audrey Hawthorne. Kate lived next door to my son and me for the better part of her life. I've always considered Kate and her sister Grace my daughters. There were so many things I loved about Kate. So many things we're all going to miss about her. We decided that, in lieu of a eulogy, we would write letters to her instead. I'd like to read them now." Audrey takes a breath and unfolds the first letter.

DEAR KATE,

When I think of you, I still picture you as a six-year-old playing on the beach with Gus and Grace. The joy that radiated from you was tangible, physical. Everyone around you felt it.

That joy never faded as you grew up. You were absolutely delightful to be around. I am so proud of the woman you became. You were so strong, so intelligent, so talented, so loyal, so charismatic, and so beautiful.

Gus and I were truly blessed to have you in our lives and to call you family.

I'm hugging you now, can you feel it?

I love you,

Audrey

DEAREST KATHERINE,

I'm absolutely certain I fell in love with you (in the most platonic sense, of course) the first time I laid eyes on you. At first, I thought it was just your extraordinary fashion sense, but then you went out of your way to talk to me, to actually talk to me, and I knew, without a doubt, you were the kindest soul I'd ever met. I was at a very low point in my life when you sat down at my table that day at freshmen orientation and literally graced me with your presence. Your friendship *opened up a world of possibilities I'd never imagined for myself. And your courage has proven to me time and time again that life isn't easy for anyone. We all have to fight to make the most of the life we're given. I'll never forget you. You are quite simply the loveliest person, inside and out, that I will ever encounter. You are my real-life angel.*

All my love,
Clayton

DEAR KATE,

I miss our playdates. I miss your tickles and hugs. I miss your songs. I miss you reading to me. Miss Higgins misses you, too.

Love,
Stella

KATE,

As a band, we'll miss your ungodly talent. Your devotion made all of us better musicians and forced us to up our game whenever you were around. You had more talent in your little finger than we all have combined. We wouldn't be where we are now if it weren't for you. Thank you.

As your friends, we'll miss you. Everything about you: your tenacity, your take-no-prisoners attitude, your encouragement, and your kindness. Most of all, we'll miss your sense of humor. Nobody could make us laugh like you did. Especially if it was at Franco's expense.

We miss you,
Jamie, Robbie, and Franco
P.S. We hope they have a Formula One track in heaven and that God puts you behind the wheel your first day, because you are going to kick everyone's ass. Godspeed Kate.

DEAR KATE,

You taught me that it's okay to step outside my comfort zone and do things that scare me or make me uncomfortable. It's okay to be silly and to make mistakes. It's okay to laugh at everything or to laugh at nothing at all.

You never knew it, but I've battled demons my entire life and because of you, I'm facing them in therapy now. Thank you for walking through my door six months ago, dude. It's one of the best things that ever happened to me. You changed my life.

Love,

Your dance partner

P.S. You are the baddest badass I've ever met.

KATIE,

It's hard to put into words what you mean to me. I admire the way you lived your life. It inspired me. It made me fall in love with you. You challenged me like no one else ever has. You showed me what courage and bravery are. Your sincerity, open-mindedness, endless support, and love made me a better person, a better father, a better partner, a better man.

I miss you so much it hurts.

I'll love you forever, babe.

Keller

BRIGHT SIDE,

I'm not good at this shit and you know it, so I'll keep this short and sweet. I hope you're with Gracie right now, sitting on a cloud sharing a Twix bar. I hope the sun shines every day in heaven, that the waves are always huge, and that the sunsets are spectacular. I hope they serve strong, black coffee morning, noon, and night, and veggie tacos on Tuesdays. And I hope they have a violin made just for you and that you play it every single day.

You told me to do epic. I try. You mastered it. You made every day epic. I'll miss that.

I love you,

Gus

I CAN HEAR SNIFFS AND SOBS IN THE AUDIENCE NOW. AUDREY'S struggling to keep composure, and just when I think she's hit the breaking point, she takes a few deep breaths. "Kate spent her last weeks in my home. She gave me this," she holds up a sealed envelope, "and asked me to read it at the end of her service." Her hands are trembling so badly, I wonder if she'll be able to open it. Very slowly, she tears away the end of the envelope and pulls out a folded piece of paper. Her eyes run over the page, and she covers her mouth with her hand. "I'm sorry. I can't."

I want to get up and read it, to help her, but I know I won't be able to stop the tears that are already flowing or to swallow past the lump in my throat. The minister is standing at Audrey's side now, a hand on her shoulder, gently urging her to hand the letter over so that he can read it aloud when someone speaks from the back of the church. "Wait." He clears his throat as all eyes turn to watch him walk up the aisle. "I'll read it." It's Gus. He disappeared after Katie died and though he texted Audrey a few times, we haven't seen him for two days. He wasn't here earlier, and I was afraid he was going to skip it altogether. He's wearing a suit, but he looks like hell. Sleep hasn't come for him yet.

He puts his arm around Audrey's shoulders and kisses the side of her head before he takes the paper. He swallows several times and begins to read Katie's words:

I SINCERELY WISH WE WERE ALL SOMEWHERE ELSE TODAY. DOING *anything but this, because funerals are a downer, and they suck. But since you've all been nice enough to gather together for me, I'd like to take this opportunity to lay down some ground rules. These rules go into effect this very moment and do not expire until you do.*

Number one: Don't cry for me. I had the most amazing life. It was worth celebrating, if I do say so myself; so when you think of me, smile, laugh, be happy. No crying.

Number two: Live every day as if it's your last. I know that's cliché, and you probably think I read it on a bumper sticker (come to think of it, maybe I did), but it's true. Do it.

Number three: Be spontaneous. Life has too many rules and restrictions and schedules. Change your plans to make room for fun. Be late every once in a while (I'm looking at you, Keller) and enjoy the moment for what it is or for what it can become.

Number four: Don't judge each other. We all have our own shit. Keep your eyes on yours and your nose out of everyone else's unless you're invited in. And when you get the invitation, help, don't judge.

Number five: Dance your ass off (I'm looking at you, Shelly and Clayton).

Number six: Do epic (I'm looking at you, Rook). Music makes the world a more beautiful place. Yours is epic. Continue. Every day. We love you for it.

Number seven: Treat friends like family. Gus and Audrey blessed me with this lesson. Pass it on.

Number eight: Let yourself love. With every fiber of your being.

Number nine: Take time to watch the sunset every once in a while. Bonus points if you do it with someone you care about.

Number ten: Don't cry for me.

Remember, I'm in heaven now, and I'm watching you. Apply the rules. I'll know if you don't.

Don't piss me off.

I want to thank each of you for making my life so much better than it would've been if I'd never met you.

Love you all. Peace out.

Bright Side

· · ·

A SMILE IS PLAYING AT GUS'S MOUTH. "THAT'S MY GIRL." IT quickly fades to sadness. With a nod, he leaves the microphone. He ushers Audrey back down to her seat in the front row and sits beside her.

The minister finishes up with a prayer, and everyone stands to exit. This is the part I've been dreading more than any other. I kiss Stella's cheek. "Baby girl, you go with Papa and Uncle Dunc. I'll meet you outside."

She nods her tiny head, and her curls bounce. "Where are we going?"

Blinking back tears, I answer, "We're all going to take Katie to the cemetery. That way she'll have a special place where everyone can visit her."

"Like Mommy?"

"Yes, just like Mommy."

Dunc takes Stella from me when he sees I'm about to lose it. "Come on, Stella. Let's go outside and chase the pigeons."

I watch Stella, Dunc, and Shel walk past and wait for my father to follow before I stand. He stops in front of me and rests his hand on my shoulder. "I'm sorry, son. No one should know the loss you've endured in your short life."

I nod.

I close my eyes and try to clear my thoughts, but all I see are those jade eyes smiling at me behind my closed lids. I want to sit here forever and look at them.

But I can't.

Gus, Jamie, Robbie, Franco, and Clayton are all waiting on me.

No one says a word as we surround her casket. It's lighter than I'd imagined it would be, which only makes me think about how frail and thin she was at the end. She probably only weighed seventy-five pounds. It was heartbreaking.

The walk to the hearse is short.

The drive to the cemetery is long.

The rest is a blur. I can feel the panic rising.

The minister's still talking when I hand Stella to my father and duck out from under the tent for some fresh air. I notice yellow tulips and a Twix bar lying on Grace's headstone next to Katie's plot.

When I walk around the back of the tent, Gus is standing there smoking a cigarette. He doesn't look at me but slides the pack out of his pocket and points the open end in my direction. "Want one?"

I've never smoked in my life, but I'm not thinking straight, and I'll try anything if it will ease the anxiety strangling me. I slip one out of the pack and take the lighter he hands me. I have no idea what I'm doing, but I light it and inhale with all the nervous energy that's coursing through me. My lungs burn, and I can't hold back the sudden, insistent cough.

"First time?" Gus asks.

I cough again. "It's that obvious, huh?"

"You should quit," he says blandly.

I hand the lit cigarette back over. "Yeah, you're probably right."

One last drag finishes his off. He drops it to the ground and steps on it with his shoe while he starts in on mine.

"*You* should quit," I offer.

"I know. Bright Side always told me the same thing. I feel guilty as hell every time I smoke one now, you know. I fucking can't give it up, though. I've tried." He looks at me then. "Did Ma give you your envelope?"

"Yeah." Audrey gave me an envelope from Katie this morning. She said Katie gave her two CDs in two envelopes; one for me and one for Gus. She did this a few weeks ago and asked Audrey to give them to us today.

"You listened to yours?"

"Not yet. You?" I plan on listening to it tonight after we get back to Minneapolis, after I get Stella to bed. I need quiet and privacy because I know whatever it is, it's going to tear me wide open.

"Not yet." He sounds nervous.

The crowd is filing out of the tent to their cars.

I gesture to the tent. "Come on, let's finish this."

He stares at the ground, and I swear he's checked out completely when he finally blinks a few times and answers, "I can't, dude. I said goodbye two days ago. I gotta get outta here. I can't take this anymore."

"Okay. We'll see you back at the house then. We have to pick up our bags before we head to the airport."

"I won't be there." It's final.

"Where're you going?"

"Don't know. I gotta get away for a while." There's a distant look in his eyes.

I need to let him figure this out on his own. We all need to find our way. I offer my hand, and he shakes it. "Stay in touch, man. I'm here if you need me."

He claps me on the shoulder. "Thanks, dude. You too."

I watch him walk all the way across the cemetery until he disappears in the distance. I have no idea where he's going, especially on foot. His truck's still at the church, and that's miles away.

Katie's death keeps hitting me, like waves crashing against the shoreline. It's at this moment that another wave hits. She's gone. I'll never see her again. I'll never hear her voice again. I'll never touch her again. This realization drops me to my knees, and I begin to sob. I'm sobbing because I want her back. I'm sobbing because I fucking hate cancer. I'm sobbing because life isn't fair.

There's a hand gently pressed against my back, and I sense more than see someone squat down next to me. "Son?"

My father. I want to stop crying, but I can't. I look at him, gasping for air. "I...want...her...back," I say, blubbering. When he doesn't say anything, I continue. "Why Katie?"

I expect a logical explanation, a clinical explanation, but instead, he takes my hands in his and pulls us both to our feet. Then he hugs me.

He *hugs* me.

And he lets me cry.

When the tears cease, he releases me and hands me the handkerchief from his pocket. I dry my face and blow my nose. And without saying a word, he walks me to his rental car and helps me into the backseat where Stella and Dunc are waiting.

Just when you think you know someone, they change. Or you change. Or maybe you both change. *And that changes everything.*

WEDNESDAY, JANUARY 25

KELLER

A LETTER ARRIVED from Audrey today. Seeing her name opens up the fresh wound. I wait until Stella's in bed to open it. As I unfold the stationary, a smaller piece of paper falls out and flutters to the floor. I leave it.

DEAR KELLER,

It was one of Kate's final wishes to leave you this. She shared your situation with me, and I couldn't agree more. I hope, in Kate's memory, this helps you achieve your goals and aspirations.

I enjoyed having you and Stella here with us, though I wish it could have been under different circumstances. Your daughter is delightful. Cherish her. I miss hearing her voice and laughter. The house is quiet without her. My door is always open to the two of you should you ever want to visit. Please tell Stella I said hello.

I hope that time heals your broken heart and leaves you with only the most lovely memories of Kate. She was a beautiful soul.

Love,

Audrey

. . .

I'M CRYING AGAIN. I CRY SO OFTEN NOW THAT SOMETIMES I don't even realize it until the tears are already streaming down my cheeks.

The piece of paper, Katie's wish, is lying on the floor in front of my dresser. Picking it up, I flip it over and see that it's a check folded in half. I open it. There's a sticky note on it with Katie's handwriting:

KELLER,

My father sent me money recently. I gave Audrey some for my funeral. I want you to have what's left. I hope it covers the remaining tuition that your scholarship doesn't. You're going to be a great teacher!

I love you, baby.

Kate

I PEEL BACK THE STICKY NOTE, AND IT'S A GOOD THING I'M standing in front of my bed because my legs give out. The check is for forty thousand dollars. And it's made out to me.

I can't help but think of what Clayton wrote about Katie at the funeral. She really is an angel.

FRIDAY, JANUARY 27

KELLER

WE'VE BEEN HOME for five days now. I'm back to work and classes, and Stella started preschool and her new daycare routine. She settled right in. I knew she would. She's flexible and friendly and curious. She could thrive anywhere.

I've avoided Katie's CD. It's been on my dresser next to a photo of the two of us since we got home and I unpacked it. I've had it in my hands, prepared to tear it open three different times, but I couldn't bring myself to do it.

I'm staring at it again now.

It's staring back.

It's after eleven and I should be asleep, but sleeping without her here with me is difficult. I've been sleeping in my recliner the past few nights.

I pull back the covers on my bed and crawl in. I bury my face in my pillow and inhale. It still smells like her. She's been gone from the apartment for a month now, and I can't bring myself to wash the pillowcase. I still sleep with one of my shirts that she slept in. It still smells like her, too, though it's starting to fade. Sometimes I wonder if it's disappeared completely and it's only my imagination stirring the scent of her. Rolling to my back, I stare at the ceiling. "Katie, I miss you. *So fucking much.* Every second of every day, I think about you. I'm going to listen to your CD now. I know it's going to make me cry, but I'm working on the whole being brave thing. You're still in my head leading that charge, so here goes." My hands are shaking when I reach for the envelope. I run my fingers over my name written in her distinctive script—it's petite, bold, and one-of-a-kind, just like she was.

I slide my finger under the flap and hesitate. Suddenly this envelope in my hand is the scariest damn thing I can imagine. I feel hot, like I might throw up. My breathing is accelerating like I'm in an all-out sprint. I pinch my eyes shut in an attempt to shut everything else out.

"You are brave," I remind myself. I say it several times before I open my eyes again. They're burning and wet with panic. One more time, I'm looking directly at the CD. "You are brave. *I am brave.*"

I tear back the flap and pull out the CD inside. It's unmarked. No label. No indication or clue as to what I'm in for.

I pull my laptop out of its bag next to my bed and power it up. I bring up my folder of photos before I insert the CD because I need to look at her face while I listen to this. I have a few dozen that I took over the past couple of months. Some are of both of us, some of her and Stella, and some of just Katie. Earbuds plugged in and inserted in both ears, I wipe my eyes, open up the CD menu, and push play. Nothing could prepare me for what I'm about to hear. It's her voice. Speaking to me. If I close my eyes, I can pretend she's in the room with me. That's just what I do.

"Hi, Keller. I know you're listening to this after I'm gone and this is probably a little strange, but if it were me, I'd want to hear your voice again. So, here goes, baby.

"I grew up believing it was my job to take care of everyone. My sister needed me. My mother needed me. I grew up believing in love, both giving and receiving. Gracie, Gus, Audrey, my friends...I loved them, and they loved me. They kept me from turning into the bitter, jaded person I could have become. The person I fought against. I grew up believing I had to be strong. I needed to keep my shit in check because people depended on me and I wanted to be there for them.

"Do I regret any of it? Hell no. I don't do regrets. It made me who I am.

"But the day I walked into Grounds and met you, talked to you, flirted with you? Something in me changed. It was one of the best days of my life. Period. Besides being outrageously attracted to you physically, because let's face it, Keller, you're sexy: your eyes, your face, your hair, your ass... Mmm... But there was also something genuine about you that was even more attractive than your good looks. You were friendly, a bit vulnerable, a bit nervous, and very, very real. I knew we had to be friends.

"I fought falling for you. I fought it hard, because I'm Kate Sedgwick. And in addition to being the type of person who doesn't do relationships, I was dying.

"Still, you sucked me in. I fell in love with you a little more each day. I loved your smile. I loved that you read classic literature. I loved that you hated it when I was late. And I loved your patience. I loved the way you listened to me like I was the only person in the world. I loved that you played guitar. I loved that you liked your coffee black (the best way to drink it). I loved that you were not only a daddy, but an amazing daddy. Your dedication to your daughter is the sexiest damn thing, which I know sounds weird, but it is. I loved that you were thoughtful and romantic. I loved that you have this natural instinct for teaching. Anything. I loved that you work your ass off. I loved your persistence and inability to take no for an answer. I loved that you wore your passion on your sleeve and that you couldn't always keep your emotions in check. You called me out on my shit. People don't do that to me. I needed it. And I loved it.

"You gave me my own real-life fairy tale. I trusted you with my heart. I've never done that before, but you made the leap so worthwhile. Your love, the way you made me feel loved deep in my bones?

It was heaven. Physically and emotionally, I felt so...*loved*. When you talked to me? When you looked at me? When you touched me? I felt worshipped. I felt beautiful. I felt cherished. I felt your devotion and your passion. It was overwhelming in the most exciting and satisfying way. I hope you felt it in return.

"Through all of this, you taught me that it's okay not only to depend on another person, but it's okay to let them carry the burden with you, even *for* you. I could let myself cry in front of you. And I don't cry. I could be weak and vulnerable when I needed to be, and you didn't judge me. You could be strong for both of us. I could give my fears a voice. I could talk about my family and my past. You don't know what a relief that was for me. Your support was just...unbelievable.

"I went to Minnesota prepared to strike college off my bucket list. But what I never imagined was that I'd find you. Thank you, Keller Banks.

"Now I need to talk about your future, because it's important to me that you hear this. Finish your degree and teach high school English. You have a gift to share. You'll be just like Sidney Poitier in *To Sir, With Love*. Lucky kids. Find a special place in the world for you and Stella, where she can blossom into the incredible woman I have no doubt she'll become. Encourage her, support her, love her...I know you will. And please, please find someone you can share that huge heart of yours with. Because when you give yourself over to love, baby, it's breathtaking. You love mind, body, and soul. No doubts. No questions. No restraint. Find that kind of love again. And when you do, I hope that she makes you as happy as you've made me. Stella needs brothers and sisters, Keller. Miss Higgins is an awesome turtle, but she's a terrible substitute for a sibling.

"I know that you're sad right now. Grieve, but don't hold onto it. Grief smothers out life. Let it go. Remember me and be happy. You have an incredible life ahead of you. Make the most of every minute. Starting right now.

"You are brave. Repeat it with me: you are brave.

"I love you, baby... I love you, baby."

My heart is aching, and my face is wet with tears. It's then that I realize I'm smiling. Smiling while my broken heart is threatening to split me in two. The smile is one small bit of happiness that never leaves me—it's Katie, through and through. I never knew happiness could feel like this before I met her. My heart had been closed off for a long time, but she broke it wide open when she walked through the door of Grounds that day. It only took moments. Not only was she adorable with her messy hair and intense eyes and that damn home-made T-shirt, but she was confident and funny and kind. She was the most honest person I've ever met. She had life all figured out, and she knew how to treat people, to make them feel special and valued. I gave her everything I had. I let her see the good and bad. I showed her things no one else had ever seen. She forced me to take a hard look at myself and my life. And her love gave me the courage to change it.

I still can't wrap my head around the fact that she's gone. The black hole that Gus and I talked about—I'm fighting it every day. I'm fighting for her...and for me...and for my daughter.

Katie had an unbelievable gift for making the best of any situation, good or bad. It sounds easy, but in any situation short of nirvana, it's difficult. Katie's happiness, her consistent optimism, was work for her. I don't think she'd deny that. It took courage to persevere through every day. The happiness, the thoughtfulness, the humor was part of her, but it was also deliberate, a conscious choice. I can't help but think back to what Gus said months ago. Katie didn't just look on the bright side...she lived there.

He was right.

And that made her the bravest person I've ever known.

You are brave...

LETTER TO THE READER FROM A VERY GRATEFUL WRITER

I wrote *Bright Side* thinking no one would ever read it. I was an unknown indie author with no readers who said "dude" a lot and loved music, coffee, tacos, and badass heroines in books. And I thought there was nothing more badass than a positive attitude and some kindness—Kate evolved out of that. I fell in love with her spirit; it was everything I aspired to be.

When I finished writing this book, my editor asked me, "What do you want people to take away from reading *Bright Side?*"

I responded with, "The last three words. *You are brave.*"

(Because it's true, *you are.*)

And I've discovered, in the most beautifully surreal experience that life/fate/luck has provided me these past several years since *Bright Side* released, just how brave people truly are. I hear from readers on a daily basis from all over the world who share their very personal stories of tragedy and triumph and perseverance and heart with me. I'm unbelievably honored to have the opportunity to be on the receiving end of such heartwarming exchanges and to have developed so many friendships. What a gift, my heart is so full—all because of their willingness to let Kate into their hearts and be affected by her spirit. It's something I never in my wildest dreams imagined I would get to take part in.

Lucky.

I'm so damn lucky.

I do not consider myself to be a great writer. I just like to put real words on paper that means something to me and make me feel— simple love stories about life, or life stories about love, depending on how you look at it. And I'm still an indie author who says "dude" a lot and loves music, coffee, tacos, badass heroines, positive attitudes, and kindness and I thank you from the bottom of my heart for taking the journey and reading *Bright Side*.

I also still want to be Kate when I grow up.

All my love.

And hugs.

Lots and lots of hugs.

Do epic!

Kim

ACKNOWLEDGMENTS

They say it takes a village to raise a child.

It also takes one to write and publish a book.

Love and thanks, from the bottom of my heart, to the *Bright Side* village:

B., Debbie, and Robin—*Bright Side's* first readers. Thank you for your encouragement throughout the entire writing process. I loved the random texts and feedback as we worked through the journey together (i.e.: "You'd better not..." "I feel sick to my stomach." "I bawled my eyes out!!!" "I loved..." "And Clayton!" "More Keller, please." "OMG.") Having an even split from the ladies on Team Keller and Team Gus reassured me I was onto something good with them both. Deb, Keller is all yours. Robin, Gus is all yours. Which leaves Kate for B., which I know wouldn't disappoint him. *At all*.

Tammy Johnson, RN, BSN and Dr. John Okerbloom, MD—*Bright Side's* consultants on all things medical. Thanks to my crazy smart sister who shared her crazy smart friend with me. Two of the nicest people *ever*. Together, with the patience of a couple of saints, they fielded and answered many, many questions. Thanks for helping me bring some realism and compassion to Kate's story. You two are the best!

Kody Templeman—*Bright Side's* music sensei. Thanks for reading through all of the band/touring/technical music-related bits of the story and giving it your stamp of approval. Answering my questions and lending your support meant the world to me, my talented friend. *As a sidenote to anyone reading this, you should check out Kody's bands: *Teenage Bottlerocket* and *The Lillingtons*. I'm serious. Check them out. They're freaking awesome!

Jess Danowski and Inside the Pages of a Book—supporter and believer. You have guided me through the world of indie publishing and promotion with the precision of a Jedi master. I bow down to you. Thanks for believing in me!

Eric Johnson—my link to a younger generation. Due to the fact that it's been...A LONG TIME...since I attended college, I had to lean on my nephew to keep this old lady legit. (You thought I was kidding about putting you in the acknowledgments, didn't you, Eric?) You earned it. Thanks, dude!

Monica Parpal—*Bright Side's* editor extraordinaire. Not only are you amazing at what you do, but you always make me feel like you have as much invested in my projects as I do. Thank you for loving Kate and for all of your feedback that made this book so much better than it would've been without you. You're my hero, Monica!

Christine Estevez—Thank you for proofreading this story and catching all the things that escaped numerous other sets of eyes. And, as always, thank you for your friendship. You're the best!

Murphy Rae—I honestly don't have the words to thank you properly for this cover. You captured Kate and the spirit of this story perfectly. Gah, I just love you, you talented, magical goddess!

Mom and Dad—"World's Greatest Book Pimps." As cheerleaders go, you are the masters. You are my street team, and I couldn't ask for better. Thank you! I love you!

B. and P.—my two favorite people. You are my world. I couldn't do what I do...life pretty much...without you. I love, love, love you!

Musicians around the world—I cannot write without the magic you create. Music inspires me like nothing else. Thank you for sharing your passion with the rest of us.

To me, Kate Sedgwick is the epitome of a very real, very strong woman. I am so lucky to be surrounded by strong women in my own life and each one of them inspired a little piece of Kate. Thank you to Barb Harken, Debbie Clark, Robin Stonehocker, Barb Konecny, Tammy Johnson, Andi Hando, Erika Sosias, and Monica Parpal for being such badass women. I love, admire, and respect each one of you for your intelligence, attitude, confidence, humor, and kindness. You do epic every day.

And lastly, to you, the almighty reader: you humble me. Every. Single. Day. The fact that you spent your precious time reading my book means more to me than you'll ever know. It blows my freaking mind if you want to know the truth. Writing a book and sharing it with someone is the equivalent of giving a speech butt-naked to a crowded room. It's putting it all out there for the world to see. People judge you, good or bad. Thanks for your continued support! It makes me feel less naked.

I'm going to leave you with one last thought, because sometimes life is hard. For all of us.

You are brave...

Now go...*do epic!*

That's an order.

Do it.

Please.

BRIGHT SIDE PLAYLIST

Music inspires. Absolutely and endlessly. These are the songs that brought Kate's journey to life.

"We Might Be Dead By Tomorrow" Soko
"400 Lux" Lorde
"Eula" Barnoness
"Sleeping Witch" Royal Thunder
"Jump Into the Fog" The Wombats
"Bug Eyes" Dredg
"Done With Love" Teenage Bottlerocket
"Waiting All Night" Rudimental featuring Ella Eyre
"Same Love" Macklemore and Ryan Lewis
"Mutilate Me" Teenage Bottlerocket
"Lullaby" The Cure
"Angels" The xx
"My Song 5" Haim
"Sex" The 1975
"Panic Switch" Silversun Pickups
"Sweater Weather" The Neighbourhood
"Nothing Left to Say" Imagine Dragons (This song inspired the studio chapter.)

"Northern Lights" Thirty Seconds to Mars
"Pictures of You" The Cure
"Let Her Go" Passenger
"Everything to Nothing" Manchester Orchestra
"Favor's Keeper" Index Case

CONTINUE THE STORY AND LET THE HEALING BEGIN...

Excerpt from Gus by Kim Holden

Sunday, January 22
  Gus

Every step I take is heavier than the one that came before it. I don't know where I'm going, only that my destination is a mind-numbing amount of alcohol.

As I step from the grass of the cemetery lawn to the concrete sidewalk, I feel a shift inside my chest. The softness of grief hardens to anger again. It's been this way for days now. Grief. Anger. Grief. Anger. Grief... Anger...

I don't want to feel anymore. I'm fucking tired of it.

I've spent the past few trying to drown death in a shabby motel room on the unquestionably shady side of town. There's a liquor store next door that sells Jack and cigarettes. That's all I need.

Speaking of cigarettes, I'm almost out. I'm smoking my last now. At the thought, I hear her voice in my head saying, "You should quit."

I answer, "Don't fucking start with me today, Bright Side."

The woman I just walked past on the sidewalk gave me an exceptionally wide berth, which leads me to believe I said that out loud. I scrub my hand over my face in the hopes that it will erase delirium. It doesn't.

"I need some fucking sleep." Yup, I'm talking to myself again.

Whatever. I need a drink.

There's a bar on the next corner. It looks dark and dingy—perfect.

When I open the door, the stench of stale beer, sweat, and cigarette smoke hits me. I'm home. At least for the next few hours.

As I walk toward the bar, I notice the dozen or so middle-aged patrons are sizing me up. The vibe of the place screams that these people are regulars. This is where they drink away their rent and grocery money on a daily basis. And I'm intruding. I glance down and realize the suit and tie doesn't help. I loosen the knot of my tie and slip it off, stuff it in my pocket, take off my suit coat, and undo the top few buttons of my shirt as I take a seat on a stool at the end of the bar.

The bartender greets me with a nod and slides a cocktail napkin in front of me as I roll up my sleeves.

I reach for my pack of cigarettes while I order. "Jack. Make it a double." It's habit, the pack is empty. I knew that. "And a pack of Camels."

He doesn't card me and points to a vending machine in the corner before he reaches for a highball glass and the bottle of whiskey. I slide from the stool and buy two packs of cigarettes from the vending machine. When I return, my drink's waiting for me.

So is a woman that's probably my mom's age. I bet she was attractive twenty years ago, but the brutality of a hard life and poor choices is etched deep in the creases of her face. I reach around her for my drink. She smells like cheap perfume and even cheaper sex. Before I can escape, she's talking.

I don't want to talk.

"What's a handsome thing like you doin' in a place like this?"

Why not just ask me if I'm up for a fifty-dollar fuck, or a twenty dollar blow job, and skip the chitchat? I don't answer and take a seat three stools away.

She moves one stool closer. "Anything I can help ya with, cutie?"

Her hands are jittery. She's looking for money for her next fix. I wouldn't touch her with a ten-foot pole, but I half want to toss some money at her because I can identify with her need to escape reality right now.

Even though I feel sorry for her, I don't have it in me to conjure any genuine compassion. I drop my head and shake it. Usually I'm not the asshole, but today is different. I tilt my head and look her in the eye. "Can you bring back the dead? I could use some fucking help with that."

I guarantee she's never heard that one before. She's blinking at me, a rapid-fire, fluttering succession of confusion.

I let my eyes fall to the glass of amber liquid I'm swirling in my right hand and answer my own question, "I didn't think so." I tip the glass back and drain it in two gulps. I place it on the bar top upside down and gesture at the bartender for another before I look at her again. "Leave me alone." It's a demand. Her tight smile tells me she's heard that one before, probably too often for her addiction's liking.

Solitude is my companion and we get along famously, until sitting upright on the stool becomes difficult. I don't know how much time has passed, but I know it isn't enough to make a dent in my heartbreak. I'm ten or twelve doubles in when the bartender refuses to serve me anymore. I want to yell and throw a full-on fucking tantrum, but the truth is I'm too tired for the drama. My vision is blurry and my limbs are past the point of numb and have moved into a mechanically uncooperative state. Movement is a struggle. I just need to sleep, so I let the guy call me a cab instead.

The cab takes me back to my motel. The walk up the stairs is slow, labored, and clumsy. I'm not sure I even shut the door behind me before I stagger to the bed and drop face-first onto the filthy bedspread. It smells dank and musty: a disgusting mix of age, grime, and God knows what else. The room is spinning, sucking me into a vortex of dizzy relief, an escape from the here and now. I don't know if sleep comes for me or if my body just makes the unconscious decision to shut down. I'm grateful either way.

Tuesday, January 24
    Gus

Have you ever slept a day away? I mean, like fall asleep and wake to find an entire day has lapsed without you bearing witness to even a minute of it?

It's fucking beautiful...medicinal...sedative. I don't dream. Well, I probably do, but I never recall them upon waking. I've never been more appreciative of this gift than I am this morning. It was more than twenty-four hours of nothing. Like I said...fucking beautiful.

I remember Bright Side's mom, Janice, used to hole up in her bedroom for days at a time and sleep. I always thought it was sad...a wasted opportunity. Now I think I understand. Because the last thing I want to do is get up from this bed, step out of this room, and face whatever life has in store on the other side of that door. I'm not ashamed to admit I'm hiding. I'm *fucking* hiding.

After I take a piss, I look for my suit coat, which I find in an unceremonious heap by the door. For two seconds, I think about how much I hate this goddamn suit. It's less than a year old and I've only worn it twice—both Sedgwick funerals. I'm burning the bastard when I take it off. I fish through the pockets for my cigarettes, lighter, and phone.

I hesitate with a quick glance around the room before lighting up. I usually don't smoke indoors, but the overall degradation of this place practically begs for it.

I power up my phone. I shut it off days ago when I left home because I didn't want to deal with everyone...or anyone. I checked in with Ma about the funeral via text, but that's it. I'm already cringing before I see the number of missed calls, texts, and emails because I know it's going to be too many.

87 missed calls

72 texts

37 emails

"Dude," I say, exhaling exasperation, or denial, or indifference. I can't decide which at the moment, so I toss my phone on the bed and finish my cigarette, followed by another...followed by another. It's fifteen minutes of nothing more than breathing through my addiction. I can't stop thinking about her. Nothing specific, nothing I can visualize or recall. It's just pain and emptiness. Darkness. The light, *the bright light*, is gone. I'm fighting to draw calm out of the cigarette with each deep pull; to dispel the darkness.

The calm doesn't come.

So, I pick up my life—my phone—again, and skim through the missed calls first: my mom; my bandmates: Franco, Robbie, and Jamie; our producer, MFDM (the Motherfucking Dream Maker, his real name's Tom, but he loves it when I call him MFDM); and our tour manager, Hitler (not his real name obviously, but it suits him given his tendency toward overall insensitivity. Our next tour's been in suspense. Apparently, in his mind, said tour and the almighty dollar take priority over us dealing with terminal illness and the death of a human being.). The only name I want to see, both on an instinctive and selfish level, isn't here. And it never will be again.

I skip the texts and emails and call my mom instead. She answers on the second ring. "Gus, honey, where are you? Are you okay?"

I hate hearing her worry like this, but knowing my desertion is fueling it makes it worse. "Hey, Ma."

She repeats, "Where are you? Your truck's still at the church."

"Yeah, I know. I've been staying at a motel." My throat feels dry and scratchy as I speak.

"Gus, you should come home." My mom's never been one to tell me what to do. Suggestively guide? Absolutely. But tell me what to do? It rarely happens.

I don't answer.

She sighs, "Honey, I know this is hard—"

I cut her off. "*Hard?* Please tell me you did not just say this is *hard*, Ma, because that's the understatement of the century." She sniffles and I know she's starting to cry, which makes me feel like shit because I know I'm the catalyst. "Sorry, Ma."

"I know." The pain that rises out of those two words reminds me that we're in this together. She misses her, too.

I throw on my suit coat and pick up my lighter and cigarettes and stuff them in my pocket. "I'll be home in a half hour. Love you."

"Love—"

I end the call before I hear her finish.

By the time I settle up my bill at the motel, take a cab to the church to get my truck, and drive home, an hour has passed. It's lunchtime.

When I open the front door, the aroma of garlic and caramelized onions assaults me. Veggie tacos. My stomach growls on cue. I can't remember the last time I ate.

I kiss Ma on the forehead on my way through the kitchen. "I need to get out of this damn suit. I'll be right back."

When I return, we eat in silence. Ma's a lot like Bright Side. Or maybe Bright Side was a lot like Ma. They both understood the power of silence. Some people are threatened by silence and try to avoid it or fill it with needless bullshit. Silence isn't the enemy. It can bring comfort and clarity and validation. It's a reminder of time for what it is...presence. Which sadly doesn't mean as much as it did a week ago.

Eight tacos in and my stomach starts screaming for mercy. "Thanks for taco Tuesday, Ma."

She smiles, but it doesn't begin to reach her eyes. "You're welcome." She looks tired. "By the way, Franco's been by every day to check on you."

It's her way of telling me to call him. "Yeah, I'll call him when I get out of the shower."

Two phone calls down (Franco and fucking Hitler), and I'm ready to throw my phone out the window into the fucking ocean, crawl into bed, pull the covers over my head, and forget everything. We're leaving for Europe Thursday morning to begin the postponed tour. Our self-titled debut album, Rook, has done well in the states since its release late last year, but it's nothing compared to how it's blown up in Europe. Hitler can't wait to get us over there. I know I'm an ungrateful, selfish asshole for not wanting to get back out on tour, but the honest-to-God truth is I don't even know how to function anymore. Bright Side wasn't only my best friend; she was like my other half...the other half of my brain, the other half of my conscience, the other half of my sense of humor, the other half of my creativity, the other half of my heart. How do you go back to doing what you did before, when half of you is gone forever?

ABOUT THE AUTHOR

I love reading, writing, traveling, music, coffee, tacos, tattoos, nice people, my big dude (husband), and my not-so-little dude (son).

I also love making new friends.
Please come and find me in one of these spots.
We'll hang out.
It'll be fun.

https://www.instagram.com/kimholdenauthor

https://www.facebook.com If Facebook is your thing, look for my group, Bright Siders. That's where I hang out the most because it's jam-packed with the nicest people on the planet.

https://www.kimholdenbooks.com

Email: kim@kimholdenbooks.com

Made in the USA
Columbia, SC
28 April 2023

15894841R00254